Previously a truck driver, Matt Gantry suffered a serious road traffic collision at the age of twenty two. He broke numerous bones and at the scene of the accident, was twice injected with adrenaline to restart his heart. His lengthy stay in hospital involved a month in an induced coma and brain surgery. It is his belief that it was this brain surgery that has given him the imagination he now enjoys. Matt has long held an interest in the special forces. He lives in England.

This is his first novel.

The Gamer

Matt Gantry

Facebook: Matt Gantry
Instagram: @mattgantryauthor
goodreads: Matt Gantry
YouTube: Matt Gantry

For my father

For the most devoted dad in the world. A lover of
books who was only able to read the first three
chapters of my own. Thank you for giving me the
best grounding possible for life ahead.

ACKNOWLEDGEMENTS

With special thanks to Verna, Tango and everyone
who helped to make this book possible.

The Gamer

PREFACE

He was asleep, but his eyes darted back and forth. His mind was active. He was experiencing the rapid eye movement stage of his slumber.

In his mind he was running down a corridor, the same as his avatar on-screen had done in his console game SAS: We Dare We Win. He moved with speed, yet smoothly, MP5 sub-machine gun raised to eye level, ready to lay down fire. One shot at a time. Up ahead, still some distance away was a right hand turn in the corridor. There was music playing, the type that violated eardrums. Striding forwards, the music became louder. The noise became deafening. It must be worse for those in its immediate vicinity. Over the noise, he heard a door slam. Just. He sensed somebody was coming his way and they weren't hanging around. He hid in a side room.

Once the shadow of the runner had passed and opening the door, he continued along the corridor. Turning right at the end of the passageway, he headed towards the noise. Towards the hostages. Even though the door was closed, the music was so loud it was becoming unbearable. Readying himself behind the door, he was acutely aware that he had no backup. There was no team behind him. He always worked in a team of four, or eight. That was the base minimum. This time however, he was on his own. On this occasion he didn't have the luxury of any support. A superhuman effort was required if he was to save the hostages and one in particular. He made a quick check of his surroundings. There was no one nearby. He opened the door.

The room was lit more than the corridor. An intentional move by the terrorists. It gave the hostages little chance for rest and ensured they were sleep deprived. Unable to fight back. The room was huge, a vast conference hall. The hotel's biggest. Sitting with their backs against the walls were the hostages. He saw the music video with the noise coming from the speakers, being projected onto a white wall at the front of the room. The terrorists in the room were either looking at that, or facing the hostages. They weren't looking at him. They didn't know he had entered. He saw his prey, four of them, standing in the centre of the room, beating the hostage he'd come to rescue. To him, she was the most important person in the world.

One terrorist from the group in the centre looked up and saw him. Music blaring, the terrorists deafened, Harry pulled the trigger. Then again. Two 9mm rounds thudded into the terrorist's upper body and neck. He died instantly and dropped to the floor. The music covered the sound of gun fire. Nobody heard. Harry moved forward, MP5 aimed at the remaining three terrorists. Pulling the trigger a third and fourth time and fifth and sixth time, two more terrorists dropped. The last terrorist in the group saw what happened and spun around. The trigger was pulled once more. The terrorist didn't get chance to bring his rifle to aim.

Harry was woken from his dream. His past reality. He knew he wouldn't fall asleep again. The curtains were pulled wide and the bedroom window was open. The night was hot and sticky for late summer. He sat up in bed. Aided by the moonlight, he looked around his bedroom. Drum kit in the corner. Posters on the wall. Racing bikes and women in bikinis. Shelves filled with the special forces books he'd read. DVDs and video games sat on another shelf. He zoned in on the TV at the foot of his bed, his PlayStation beneath. He still hadn't completed the last level of SAS: We Dare We Win. He didn't have the faintest bit of interest in it anymore. Harry Fearn had done it for real. He looked at his bedside table and smiled. The silver plated Desert Eagle was sitting next to the lamp. Only he knew where the firing pin was hidden.

Six weeks earlier

CHAPTER ONE

Miss Brewster stood at the front of the class. She looked at her tutor group. It was the final ten minutes, of the last hour and her students were to be going home for the summer break. She had called them back for one last meeting. She wanted to thank them. Miss Brewster had a smile on her face. The fifteen boys and twelve girls had performed well over the last year. However, she was slightly disheartened by a few of the more flippant answers she had received, when she asked the class to write down what they wanted to do when they left compulsory education. The next year was an important one. The young men and women in front of her would be going into the final year of their A-Level studies. Their performance would directly affect their futures.

"It's been a pleasure to teach you this year, you've all worked very hard and I'm sure it will be reflected next year when you take your A-Level exams. However, when we reconvene in September and I ask about your aspirations for your careers, I would like more sensible answers than astronaut, pornstar and blade. That is not to say I don't think you will be able to do, or be suitable for those jobs. I just think it highly unlikely. You'll have to work extremely hard to achieve your desired career. Thank you, class 12C. I'll see you all after the summer break," she said.

The scrape of chairs pushed back and the footfall of teenagers scrabbling to escape school for a whole summer, filled the room. Harry made a beeline for the exit. Miss Brewster called him over before he bolted.

"Special Air Service, really Harry?" asked his form tutor.

"How did you know I wrote blade, Miss?" he asked.

"I've seen the doodles and drawings in the margin of your work book. Winged daggers? Men abseiling off the side of the page? That's all very SAS, Harry," she said.

"How did you link that to a blade though, Miss?" Harry asked.

"Because I know the difference between a blade of grass and the type of blade you're talking about," she said.

"How?" he further enquired.

She smiled and held a glint in her eye.

"I just do," Miss Brewster said.

He didn't think she would really know the answer.

"Go on then Miss, what's a blade?" Harry asked.

"A blade is any soldier that serves in a regiment of the British Army, with a blade, or dagger on the badge," she said. "Basically, the special forces."

"You're good, miss," he said.

"Ok. Now it's your turn, tell me what those special forces regiments are?" she said.

"Easy," Harry said, "the SAS, the SBS and the SRR."

Miss Brewster smiled. She always did when she spoke to Harry. He wasn't a naturally gifted student, more of a studious pupil.

"Correct. Well done, Harry. Have a nice summer," she said.

He dashed for the exit.

"You too," he shouted.

Freedom beckoned from the educational prison where he had spent the last school year.

Miss Brewster smiled again as Harry rushed out of the room to catch up with his friends. He was going to do well in life, whatever he chose.

*

Over five thousand miles away, the boss padded barefoot onto his veranda. He wasn't tall, nor was he short, just an average height. Since taking a supervisory role within his company, then a managerial position, middle age spread had formed around his midriff. The boss carried a steaming mug of coffee, brewed with the finest beans his country had to offer. He rubbed his eyes with the back of his hand. The caffeine in his mug was much needed. He hadn't slept well for a week. There were many things happening right now. All of them played on his mind. Taking a sip he felt a little sharper and looked out at the savannah before him. His vast estate was filled with lush green vegetation and to the south, tropical rainforest. He loved it here, it was so much nicer than the slums in which he had lived until he was twenty five years of age.

The white Japanese sports utility vehicle travelled at speed along the track towards his luxurious home. A dust cloud would have been created had it not rained in the early hours of the morning. The boss's country was experiencing a secondary rainy season. Although it was no longer raining, the ground was still wet, the temperature high and the air humid. The boss's linen shirt would soon start to sticking to his body and his hair would grow damp. He would need to slick it back over his head.

The SUV swung into view. He knew who it would be. The Germans were the experts he needed and so far they had proven their worth. Today was about going over the plan again and again. Making sure there were no holes. Ensuring they were taking everyone and everything they needed. One week from now, although not able to realise it for another two weeks after that, the boss would rule the world.

*

Harry caught up with his friends just outside the school gates. He loosened his neck tie and undid his top button. It was more for symbolism, than comfort. He was sticking two fingers up to the establishment and saying, 'Look at me, I'm rid of you for the summer.' Ridiculous when you think that he, nor his friends were school rebels. They were just normal, everyday middleclass kids. They liked to push the occasional boundary they hoped wouldn't get them into trouble. The boys might wear a pair of trainers, instead of a robust black shoe. The girls, in the summer at least, would wear a skirt that showed off more of their leg than appropriate and higher heels than permissible. As they walked home however, the uniform code was the last thing on their minds. They talked excitedly about what they were doing over the summer holiday.

Thomas was off to France with his family. Laura was going on holiday to Spain with her boyfriend and his family. Darcie was going to be working in the office at her dad's plumbing company and Eloise was taking a trip to Wales, to see her older brother and his wife.

"What about you, Harry?" asked Darcie.

"Well tomorrow, I'm catching a flight to Florida," he said.

"America? Wow, that's amazing. That'll be a brilliant holiday!" she replied.

Harry looked miffed.

"It's not a holiday. My parents are too busy working in the city. I'm being sent to work in the hotel my aunty manages in Fort Lauderdale," he said.

"At least it'll be sunny and the girls will look amazing in their bikinis," said Thomas.

Laura rolled her eyes. Harry chuckled and smiled.

"You wrote pornstar, didn't you?" he asked.

Thomas matched Harry's smile and laughed. They each said their goodbyes and the group broke up to walk to their respective homes.

Laura and Harry only lived a few streets apart and walked the rest of the way home together. Walking alongside him, Laura thought Harry could have been a businessman returning home after a day at work. He exuded maturity. His school blazer and tie could have easily been a suit and tie, his school bag a briefcase. However, she knew he wanted a different life to that.

"Why do you want to join the SAS so much and not work in a high flying career?" she asked.

"It's just what interests me, it gets me. I'd much rather be doing something like that than sitting behind a desk," he said. "I know I'd be really good at it."

"But you're easily the kindest and most intuitive boy I know," she said, "the army doesn't suit you."

Harry smiled.

"Thanks," he said.

"You're not brash and loud like a lot of boys at school, you're considerate, pleasant and gentle. Very helpful too," she added, "you're so smart you could be king if you wanted."

"No royal blood I'm afraid, so that's unlikely," he said.

Harry towered over Laura as they walked side by side. She looked up at him.

"How tall are you now?" she asked.

Harry made a point of looking down and resting his elbow on her head.

Six foot, six foot one probably by the time we get back to school," he said. "How about you, my little friend?"

"Five foot three," she replied, "twat."

Harry laughed and gave Laura a squeeze.

He was a twat, but a giant gentlemanly twat. Laura knew he could do anything if he put his mind to it. Why he wanted to join the army was beyond her.

They reached the turn for her street.

"See you when I get back from America," Harry said.

"Yeah, look after yourself, twat," she told him.

Harry smirked.

He had four more streets to walk before he got home. Although a little skinny, his height was his friend and meant nobody ever hassled him. He knew how to stay safe in a city filled with nearly nine million people. Reading books about the Special Air Service, combined with SAS: We Dare We Win, had taught him well.

He walked on the pavement facing the oncoming traffic and could see the vehicles heading his way. He heard the screech of car tyres. His eyes instantly looked around. It was nothing, but could have been something. Just an idiot driving too fast. Ninety nine percent of the time it was nothing and was always going to be nothing, but nine million people living in London meant that some of them weren't nice. One day he might get into a situation where someone wanted to do him harm.

Harry could see an old man approaching on his side of the street. He looked for his hands, he could see them. The old boy wasn't carrying anything. There weren't any bulges in his clothing either. Nothing unusual about him. Unless he made a sudden move, he didn't present an immediate threat. The old guy passed, giving Harry a nod. He smiled back. It wasn't just the people in plain sight. As Harry walked along the street he passed a shop window. He looked into the shop, but not at what was inside. He was looking at the reflection the window provided. There was someone behind him. Harry recognised the kid from school. It was just someone in the year below. Obviously he didn't present a threat.

The next shop window told Harry the kid had turned off, but now there was a man behind him who was walking quickly. More quickly than he was. Harry increased his pace, crossed the road and looked back to check there wasn't any traffic coming. Looking out for cars also gave him a valid reason to look behind. He was taking the opportunity to check the man out as well. The man tailing him was white, in his mid-forties with blonde hair and dressed in a shirt and jeans. Not a typical gang member and it was unheard of to see gangs in this part of the city. The reflection of next shop window on the other side of the street told Harry the man had crossed the road as well. He was fairly sure he was being followed. Fuck. Maybe this was the one per cent of the time.

Harry didn't want the man knowing where he lived. He should have turned right. Instead he turned left. He walked to the next road junction. No more shop windows to get a reflection from. Just houses. He sensed blondie was still following and turned left again. At the end of the road Harry planned to turn left a third time. Nobody would turn left three times. They would turn left earlier. Then right. Three lefts just made their walk longer. His heart started beating faster. He was going to have to make a pre-emptive strike on blondie. Get in there and make a first move before he knew Harry was onto him.

Twenty feet till he needed to turn left. What if the man had a knife? What if this was a mugging? In his mind he envisaged how he would fight. Ten feet to the corner. His breathing increased. He balled his fingers into fists and clenched. Breathing out he turned left. Harry's eyes were wild and enraged. The man shouted something. Double fuck.

As soon as Harry turned left he stopped dead and stood with his back to the gable end of the house on the corner. He could hear the man shout again and start running. Footsteps getting louder. He would appear on Harry's right as he rounded the corner. Harry made a plan in his head. The footsteps were close now. On the right, a head of blonde hair flashed past him. The man turned and couldn't immediately see him. Blondie had something in his right hand. What was it? A knife? Some other object to harm him with?

Harry pushed forwards and grabbed out at him, holding anything he could. His shirt. Harry gripped tighter.

"What the fuck do you want?" Harry growled.

The man screamed. He was more scared than Harry. Good. Harry pushed the man back. Then dragged him forward. At the same time he brought his knee up towards blondie's groin.

Whatever he was carrying, he waved at Harry.

"Your book, your school book," Blondie squealed.

The upwards directional travel of Harry's knee stopped just in time.

"Fucking what?" Harry said through gritted teeth.

Aggression in his voice.

"Your school book, it fell from your bag, I saw it happen," Blondie said.

He waved a school book in Harry's face.

"Oh God, I'm so sorry," Harry said, "I thought you were following me."

"Forget it, you nutter," Blondie said.

He fought himself free of Harry's grip, dropped the text book on the floor and turned on his heel.

"Get lost," were Blondie's last words.

He ran away from Harry and back down the street as fast as he could.

Harry felt bad. Really bad. That poor man was trying to help him. Harry had been a second away from making him infertile and breaking his nose. Harry turned back and was just about to shout sorry. Except he couldn't even see Blondie anymore. It appeared not everyone in London had bad intentions. Still, Harry's guard would remain up. He didn't know when he would next need it.

When he reached his house, he grabbed a bottle of Pepsi Max from the fridge and ran upstairs to the PlayStation in his bedroom. Tonight was the night he would storm the Iranian Embassy, kill the terrorists and rescue the nineteen hostages. With the PlayStation game SAS: We Dare We Win, complete, he needed pack his suitcase for the next morning.

Five minutes later Harry was readying himself. He was going to do this. He was now equipped to take on the most challenging and final level of the game. He had honed his special forces soldiering skills in the game's previous ninety nine levels. To start, he had chosen which British Army regiment to begin his military career with. Each regiment had its own advantages when you tried for SAS selection. Harry chose to become a member of the 2nd Battalion, the Parachute Regiment. Joining that regiment gave him the best military foundation possible. He then put in plenty of personal fitness training to prepare his character for SAS Selection. He passed on the first attempt. Then came jungle training. His character needed to excel or would get binned, kicked from the SAS and sent back to the Parachute Regiment. When he returned to the UK he passed the final escape and evasion phase and became a fully badged trooper (private), in the Special Air Service.

Having passed selection, he went on operations. Fighting on a battlefield and carrying out top secret missions, to capture high value targets in hostile countries. Wiping out murderous warlords commanding brutal dictatorships in Africa. He was subjected to more training and became a patrol medic, as well as passing the course to become a sniper instructor. He flew in helicopters all over Great Britain and captured homegrown terrorists, neutralising modern day pirates attacking cargo ships in the Gulf of Aden. He conducted hostage rescue missions once a ship had been seized by Somali pirates, stealthily creeping into Asian Palaces to assassinate rogue leaders who threatened world peace, as well as lying in wait for days on end, just to catch a glimpse of the leader of a terrorist cell and gather as much information as possible.

His headset was on. The controller in his hands. Harry was hearing messages from the rest of the team. His SAS trooper avatar was ready to abseil down the Iranian Embassy walls. He was ready to carry out the assault. He was pumped up and ready to go ballistic. Ready to attack with speed, aggression and surprise. Harry heard the command of 'Go. Go. Go,' and stepped off the edge of the roof. He abseiled down the walls of the victorian Town House. Once on a balcony, Harry climbed across to another balcony and pressed the frame charge against a window. He climbed back and ducked down. The charge exploded and he was intent on bursting through the hole created by the explosion. The screen went blank. Looking up he saw his mum standing in his bedroom. She looked angry. Pointing and holding the PlayStation's plug in her other hand. Pulling his head set free, Harry gave him mum a dirty look. The kind of stare only a teenage boy could muster.

"What did you do that for?" he said.

"Less of the attitude, Harry," his mum said. "This is your last night at home before you go to see your aunty in Florida. I'm taking you out for dinner tonight to your favourite restaurant. You know, the one with people dressed up as cartoon characters."

His face recoiled.

"That's not my favourite!" he exclaimed.

"Well, it was when we went for your birthday," his mum replied.

Harry didn't hide his disappointment.

"Yeah, when it was my fifth birthday. That was twelve years ago," he said.

His mum tried to get him back on side.

"Well, we can go somewhere else if you like," she said.

"Is Dad meeting us there?" he asked.

She sat on his bed and put her arm around him.

"I'm afraid your dad's working late tonight, but he'll see you in the morning when we drive you to the airport," she said.

She gave Harry a hug.

Bloody typical. His dad couldn't even be arsed take the night off and spend it with his son, when he wasn't going see him for six weeks. Harry wanted to plug his PlayStation in and storm the Embassy, but his mum wouldn't let him. She pulled his suitcase from the top of his wardrobe and told him he had to choose the clothes he was taking on holiday.

"It's hardly a holiday," he said, "you're packing me off to see Aunty Alison and work in her hotel."

"I thought you liked Alison?" his mum asked.

"I do, Alison's cool, she's one of the reasons I agreed to this whole joke of a holiday," he said.

Secretly, Harry fancied the pants off Aunty Alison. She was in her mid-forties and always dressed nicely. A tight blouse and a skirt that showed off her legs and a nice pair of high heels. She was every young boy's dream. If she had any kids, which she didn't, she would be a bona fide MILF.

"Don't think that we're packing you off, please Harry. Your father and I think you would have a far better time abroad, even if you are working some of the time. Imagine if you were stuck here with no one around. I'm so busy at the lettings agency and your dad is at the security company almost every hour of the day. At least this way you'll get a lot of sun and earn some money. You might even meet a nice young lady. You do understand we love you dearly, don't you, darling?" his mum said.

"Yeah I know. Thanks mum," he answered.

He wasn't sure if he, or his mum meant it.

With no more PlayStation, Harry lay back on his bed with his hands behind his head and dreamt about Aunty Alison.

Alison wasn't his real aunty, she was his uncle's ex-wife. His third ex-wife to be exact. What Harry's mother thought of his uncle had been summed up perfectly in one sentence seven years earlier. The comment had been prior to his impending arrival at their house, with his latest in a string of airheads and floozies. Harry's dad had been given the unenviable task of asking on behalf of his brother.

'I can't stand that philandering bastard of a man and no, he cannot stay in our home with his new woman. We'll probably never meet her again, anyway!' she had shouted.

That new woman was Alison. Regardless of her preconceptions of her brother-in-law and his seemingly endless trail of women, he had a new one every time he was in town, Harry's mum and Alison hit it off instantly.

Alison was an accomplished lady. Having gained a first class degree she had entered the world of hospitality and rapidly worked her way up to managing departments in hotels. Her first appointment as hotel manager had come at just thirty years of age. She was intelligent and articulate. Harry's mum loved her from the get go. Alison had a wonderfully natural way with people. Her effulgent smile could melt hearts and immediately pacified angry hotel guests. It was impossible for anyone to be hostile with this charming and charismatic woman. At Harry's mum's invitation, she and Harry's uncle stayed in their spare room that night. She was Harry's uncle's usual trophy wife material. Petit. Busty. Blonde and gorgeous, but she was definitely in a league of her own when compared to his previous women.

It wasn't only Harry's mum that fell in love with the now forty four year old, Alison. Harry adored the lady that would marry his uncle, a mere six months later. He was more than happy to spend the summer with her.

Fourteen years after her first appointment as a hotel manager, she had been relocated to Florida. She was managing a newly acquired and refurbished, five star hotel for one of the biggest hospitality groups in the world. It was the centre piece of their impressive chain and they had wanted the best in the business to manage it. They hadn't interviewed for the role. They'd head-hunted and cherry picked Alison from a leading competitor.

"Are you ready, Harry?" his mother shouted up the stairs.

Harry was awoken and shouted back, 'Five minutes'. Shit. He must have drifted off to sleep.

Harry and his mum took the London Underground back from the Hard Rock Café, where they had instead eaten dinner. He eyed a passenger in the train carriage with suspicion. He always checked everyone out. It was under his skin. In his blood. SAS: We Dare We Win, just made him better at it. He checked people weren't shifty or nervous. He made sure they didn't have anything hidden under their clothing. They could be carrying a gun, machete, or more likely in today's society, a bomb. A passenger, a male in his thirties of Middle Eastern descent, stopped looking nervous when he was joined by a white woman of similar age. It could be a first date. It was possible they were hiding their relationship because of a religious thing. It was entirely plausible they were having an affair.

"Harry. Harry. Harry, are you coming, or what?" his mother urged.

He snapped out of scanning passengers when she grabbed his arm and pulled him up and off the seat. It was their stop on the underground. Harry fought off his mother's grip on his arm as they climbed the stairs to the station's exit.

As they exited the tube station, the heavens opened. Rain poured down, soaking them through. The July summer's day had quickly turned and London was now drenched in a downpour.

In the hammering rain, Harry's mum ran to the first black London taxi she saw and opened the door. The taxi pulled up outside the family home five minutes later, just as the rain subsided and the sun began to shine through once more. As soon as the front door was opened, Harry bolted through and ran straight upstairs. Not removing his soaked clothes, he plugged in and switched on his PlayStation. He was ready to complete the last level of SAS: We Dare We Win.

His mum barged into his room.

"Harry, what on earth do you think you're doing?" she asked.

"Finishing my game, you wouldn't let me earlier," he said.

"I'm not going to let you now, either. It's half past nine and you still need to pack your case. You're getting up at five o'clock in the morning so that your father and I can take you to the airport. It's time for bed, you need plenty of sleep," she insisted.

"I can sleep when I'm dead," Harry replied.

Aghast, his mother strode over to his PlayStation and started pulling out wires.

"What are you doing?" Harry asked.

"That was a stupid and hurtful thing to say, you're seventeen years old for goodness sake! Do you really think I want my son to be talking about dying? If I could have my way, I wouldn't let you out of this house. London is full of gangs, guns and knives these days. Acid attacks too. Maybe you'll be safer in Fort Lauderdale this summer. Just for the sleeping when you're dead remark, you can have your computer back when you're home from America," his mum said.

She gathered up the remaining cables and took them, along with his PlayStation, out of his bedroom.

Harry slumped back on his bed.

"So unfair," he shouted.

He muttered the less audible word of, 'Bitch,' once she was out of his room.

When his mum returned an hour later, he was fast asleep on his bed and fully clothed, bedroom light still blazing. A packed and zipped up suitcase sat at the foot of his bed. Drawing the curtains and flicking the light switch, she silently mouthed, 'Good night,' and closed his bedroom door.

CHAPTER TWO

Beep. Beep. Beep. Buzzed the monotonous and loud alarm clock. Harry jumped out of bed. Heart pounding, he clumsily fumbled around and switched off the noisy alarm. He was just about to crawl back into bed when there was a knock on the door. He knew it was his dad. The knock actually waited for a reply before entering.

"Yeah," he shouted.

His dad walked into his room.

"We're leaving in half an hour, Harry," his dad said. "Jump in the shower and I'll put your suitcase in the car."

Before he left the room, his dad passed Harry two hundred American Dollars and fifty pounds, Sterling.

"Don't tell Mum, alright?" he said with a wink, "oh and do you fancy a McDonalds for breakfast?"

Harry beamed with delight.

"That's amazing, thanks dad and yes, Maccy D's sounds immense," he said.

"Good lad," his dad said, "now go and jump in the shower."

By 0650 he was in West London at Heathrow Airport. While they waited for the British Airways' check-in desk to open, Harry and his dad tucked into their McMuffins and hash browns. His mum sat opposite drinking a skinny latte. Even though he was stuffing his face with a burger, his mum was brimming with pride. Harry didn't know it, but he was her magnum opus. She would miss him terribly, but on the third week of his summer trip, her and Harry's Dad would make a surprise visit.

At seven in the morning the check-in desk opened and Harry was third in line. Check-in provided an even better surprise than money and a Maccy D's breakfast.

"Thanks mum, thanks dad, that's the best surprise, ever," Harry said.

He wrapped his arms around his mum and she hugged him back. They all said their good byes and Harry shook hands with his dad. His dad was surprised with the strength of Harry's handshake. He knew his son would grow taller than him and now he was certain, he was already stronger.

"Stay safe, son," his dad shouted after him.

Harry walked down to security and his mum shed a tear. He walked with a certain amount of style. Sauntering down to the end of the queue, he was fairly sure he would be the only seventeen year old flying business class. For all their faults, his parents were pretty good at surprises.

Once he had passed through the hand luggage scanners and metal detectors, Harry meandered towards his British Airways' departure gate. He walked through throngs of holiday makers jetting off to all manner of destinations. He looked at each plane and imagined he was clad head to toe in black. Ready to storm a plane as a member of 22 Regiment, the SAS. His vivid imagination ran wild with all of the possibilities of a hostage rescue. Eventually reaching his gate, Harry realised he wouldn't be able to sit there and wait for his plane to depart. His boarding time was three hours away, there would be a shed load of flights leaving the gate before his own.

He walked a little further until he found a different fast food joint. Harry bought some more food and slumped on one of the many untaken seats. The restaurant was empty at that time of the morning. He had the option of sitting out of the way in his airline's business class lounge, but that didn't interest him. Even if he did like the stuff, he doubted the staff in the lounge would let him have his complementary glass of champagne. He was happy where he was. He wanted to people watch. More importantly, watch out for any protuberances in people's coats. Bumps that had somehow got past security and hid a sinister device. Just like he had on the London Underground, he was on the lookout for nervous and shifty passengers. Passengers who were up to no good. People who looked out of place, or had something missing about their appearance. Rather than partaking in a surprise attack on a terrorist held plane, he was now playing an undercover blade, blending in and on the lookout for a group of hijackers. He imagined an undercover operative embedded in a terror cell had passed forward intelligence, regarding an imminent attack on a trans-Atlantic jet.

There was still an hour and a half before his flight departed and Harry was bored. He had polished off his second burger in as many hours, in addition to some spicy cheese bites and a large drink. Harry had an ectomorph's body shape just like his dad. Tall and slender, he could eat anything he wanted. There wouldn't be any inches added to his waistline. He had been people watching for nearly an hour. Nothing was happening. A few flights had departed and that section of the departure lounge was empty, it would only get busier when another flight was ready to leave. Bored out of his brain, he went for a stroll around the duty-free shops.

Aftershaves didn't interest him and he wasn't curious about expensive chocolates. Harry wasn't enthused about bottles of twenty five year aged Scottish Whisky, or cheap cigarettes and especially not silly little statues of London's Tower Bridge. However, he found a gold mine in the paperback section of one shop. Harry loved reading. It had all started four years ago when on a family holiday in the South of France. He had started to read his dad's copy of the legendary Special Air Service story, Bravo Two Zero. He had read the book continuously on the two day drive home and by the time their ferry docked at Dover, Harry was on the last chapter. Since then he had read plenty more books, the vast majority about the SAS. He found a few books on the Special Air Service, most of which he had read and the couple he hadn't, he bought. Carrying his new hoard of special forces literature back to the seating area, he stumbled upon one of his other big loves - first person shooter arcade games.

Dashing back to the duty-free shop to ask for some change, he returned to the games arcade regretting his decision not to wear a belt. The twenty pound coins he had just been given, in return for his dad's last shiny note, pulled down his trousers. Harry was in all kinds of heaven. A whole section of the gaming area had been allocated to shoot 'em ups. He wasn't interested in the zombie games where a player just shot slow moving brain-dead targets. It was the games which required skill and tactics, a steady heartbeat, rhythmic breathing, a level head and deadly accuracy that piqued his interest. Harry dropped three pound coins into the 'X-Ray Target' arcade game and raised the machine's blue semi-automatic rifle. Nestling the weapon snuggly into his shoulder and placing one hand on the forward grip, he shot the start icon.

The first level saw him flying as a gunner in an army attack helicopter. The helicopter flew itself, but he had to control the crosshairs and take out the enemy soldiers on the ground. The machine's speakers blasted out a constant stream of machine gun noises as Harry shot away at soldiers, tanks and buildings. Oil barrels exploded. More soldiers fell to the floor. He strafed the area with a frighteningly high rate of fire. Harry even fired missiles to halt the steady march of men and tanks. Standing straight, he took a deep breath and waited for the start of level two. For only a matter of seconds the machine was silent, but soon the immediate area was once again enveloped in warfare. In the next level of the game he took command of a tank's cannon. He blasted his way through to complete the level in next to no time.

Standing straight again and taking a gulp of his drink, he failed to notice he had gained the attention of two armed police officers. Both were watching him and both had smiles on their faces. While playing level three, Harry stormed an African palace as part of a twenty man team. Running along a corridor, his avatar dropped and carried out a forward roll. He missed the hail of gun fire and gained a vantage point from where he could kill the remaining terrorists and save the hostage aid workers. The next few levels were all much the same, but with different scenarios being played out each time. By the end of level eight and with only two levels to go until Harry had completed the game, he realised time had got the better of him. He heard a tannoy announcement. His flight to Florida finished boarding in five minutes. Wiping his brow, he holstered his weapon and picked up his book filled carrier bag. He was startled.

"You're pretty good at that, laddie," a Scottish voice boomed.

"Thanks," Harry said.

He turned around to see who the voice came from.

Wow! The comment from the unknown voice had been a massive compliment. In front of him stood a man mountain dressed all in blue and holding a carbine.

"We're helping to find a missing three year old boy who's escaped from his parents, you haven't seen any unaccompanied young children around here, have you?" asked the same Scottish Policeman.

The man was huge, easily six foot six or more.

"Don't worry, he's not as vicious as he is ugly," said his smaller and slender, female partner.

Harry's eyes grew wider as he took in the blue clad monster before him. The female police officer needn't have worried. Harry wasn't afraid. He was in awe. Some seventeen year olds have footballers as their idols. Some have pop stars or movie stars, but this was Harry's type of idol. The huge policeman in front of him was carrying a Heckler and Koch G36, as well as a Glock 17 holstered to his belt and a taser. He was everything Harry aspired to be.

"No I haven't, there were a few kids mucking about on that dance machine over there," he said and pointed to the back row of arcade games, "but no small children."

Harry looked them up and down. He was seriously impressed. He had seen photos of the armed police and videos on YouTube, but he had never actually spoken to them.

"So you want to be one of us, one day?" the intimidating Scotsman asked.

"Honestly?" Harry said and then proceeded to answer his own question, "I want to join the British Army and then the SAS."

"Nice plan," the female officer said, "my nephew's in the Parachute Regiment."

"Which battalion?" asked Harry.

"Three Para," she replied.

"Everyone knows two Para are the best," Harry said.

"Well as long as you don't join a Scottish infantry battalion," she said.

"Hey," boomed the voice of the huge Scotsman, "I used to be in a Scottish infantry battalion."

"Only joking, don't get your kilt in a twist," she said to her colleague.

It was only at the last moment Harry heard the tannoy announce that it was the final call for his flight to Miami. The gate was about to close.

"That's my flight, gotta run," he said.

Harry turned and ran to his boarding gate.

"Nice to meet you," he shouted back to the two officers.

The last person to board the plane, Harry was spared the evil glares from the rest of the passengers on his flight. As soon as he stepped into the fuselage, he turned left and walked straight into business class. Settling down in his spacious and very comfortable seat, he buckled up and took out one of the books he bought earlier. He was extremely happy having a spacious seat in business class. He would have been happy with a seat in economy class, as long as his seat wasn't by a door.

He was tall and the extra legroom would have been great. However he knew from playing SAS: We Dare We Win, if the plane was taken over by terrorists, it was those doors that afforded the extra legroom that the SAS would use to gain access. In the console game he had stormed many empty aeroplanes when practising and two when he was on real operations. The passengers sitting next to the doors had been injured on both occasions.

Harry hardly noticed the plane taking off. He was engrossed in a tale about D Squadron, Special Air Service, rescuing some British soldiers who had been taken captive in Sierra Leone. As soon as the plane was up in the sky, airhostesses came around and offered the passengers drinks. Harry was handed a glass of beer, albeit with plenty of lemonade. Perks of business class, he thought. Hitting the recline button on his seat, he drifted off for a snooze.

*

The boss lay in bed with his wife curled up next to him. It was still the early hours of the morning on the other side of the Atlantic. She was fast asleep, but his own sleep had been intermittent and disrupted since he first drifted off. The boss had gone to bed as the dateline ticked over from Friday to Saturday and had lay awake for the first hour of the new day. It was 4am now. He hoped he would get at least another hour's sleep before it was time to get out of bed. There were many things on his mind and that was why he presumed he couldn't sleep.

CHAPTER THREE

Nine hours, two movies, eight chapters of his new book later, the wheels of Harry's gargantuan trans-Atlantic aeroplane touched down at Miami International Airport. As the plane taxied towards the terminal, the pilot announced that it was 1600 hours, Miami time. Harry altered his watch and yawned. He would be thinking of heading to his bedroom if he was back in England and at school, but he wasn't. Tired or not, he couldn't wait to get through the airport to the arrivals hall to see his Aunty Alison.

At seventeen years old, Harry was regarded as an adult, other than being able to vote in an election and buy a pint of beer, in England at least. However, a mistake of some kind had occurred and the airport believed he was fifteen. Therefore, he was classed as a young and unaccompanied traveller. This brought even more perks not even his business class ticket would cover. He was given priority treatment.

The same British Airways hostess who had treated him to a glass of shandy asked him to follow her. She had enjoyed serving Harry. He appeared to be a thoroughly decent young man. In their brief exchanges, she had got the impression he was wise beyond his years. So many of the customers in business class were highfalutin and their extravagant job titles only served to heighten their own self-importance and with it, their inflated egos. Harry was taken to a golf buggy waiting in the terminal. The hostess introduced him to Tyrone who was driving and told him to have a great holiday.

Tyrone was an African-American gentleman in his sixties. Harry opted to sit up front with him, rather than sit on the bench seat at the back. They zipped towards passport control and passed crowds of passengers.

"You ever been to Florida before, son?" Tyrone asked.

"I've never even been to America before," said an excited Harry.

"Who are you coming to see? Must be a pretty wild vacation if you've managed to shake off your folks," he exclaimed.

Suddenly a switch flicked in Harry's mind. This was the first time he'd thought of the trip in this way. A wild vacation. I'll have some of that, he thought. The excitement in Harry's parentless mind was palpable. He didn't have his parents watching over him, or waiting to make sure he got back home before his curfew. There were to be no groundings or ramifications for his actions. As long as he didn't take the piss, he was free to do what he wanted. Even if he was going to be working in the hotel for some of the time. Maybe not quite sex, drugs and rock and roll, but he'd definitely be having fun and hopefully sex. Hotel working or not, Aunty Alison was to be his guardian for the duration of his stay. He was cool with that and replied to Tyrone's question.

"Yeah, it's going to be pretty wild," he said.

Harry slouched back in the chair of the buggy, put his feet on the dashboard and for a second, felt like a king being carried forth by his servants.

Tyrone swatted Harry's leg with the back of his huge paw.

"Feet," he growled.

Before he knew it, the golf buggy arrived at the passport control booths. Saying goodbye, Tyrone pointed Harry to the fast track queue. Unlike his fellow travellers in the normal queues, he waited only fourth in line, not twenty fourth in line. Soon after joining the queue, Harry stepped up to the booth. The officer inside gave Harry's passport and ESTA a quick visual scan and handed back his documents. Harry was told to enjoy his stay in America.

There was a lady from the airport waiting for him on the other side of the passport control booth. They walked together to collect his suitcase from the baggage hall. He wasn't given priority treatment this time, but it wasn't long before his case appeared with all the other cases from his flight. Saying 'shit' after his first missed attempt, Harry managed to grab hold of his case and pull it from the carousel the second time it passed. The wheels of the suitcase hit the shiny tiled floor. The handle was pulled up. Harry and the lady from the airport headed off to arrivals so he could finally start his holiday.

Being from London Harry was used to large numbers of people crammed into small spaces, but the arrivals hall was on another level. The noise was just as loud as a home game of Arsenal Football Club, back at home. It was a few seconds before he saw his aunty, but as soon as he did he realised why he had a crush on her. She was gorgeous and could have passed for a thirty four year old, never mind the forty four year old she was.

Harry walked over to her and when Alison saw him, she smiled. Perfect white teeth and red lips. She wrapped her arms around his torso and pulled him into her, squashing her pronounced chest against his flat stomach. She leant up, pulled him close and kissed him on the cheek.

"It's good to see you, Aunty," Harry said.

He returned the hug.

"You too Harry and just call me Alison, please, I was never your proper aunty and it makes me feel old and frumpy," she said, "I'm sorry I'm still in work clothes, I came to the airport straight from the hotel. Work is really hectic at the moment, we've got a big conference starting on Wednesday."

He wasn't at all bothered about her attire. He was happy to see her. He was even more happy to see her in high heels and little red business skirt and white blouse. He had always been a fan of the sexy secretary look. Alison stood back and took a look at the strapping young man in front of her.

"Oh gosh," she said, as she put a hand over her smile, "it must be two years since I last saw you and look at yourself, you're massive. The last time I saw you, I'm sure you were smaller than me, now you're taller! How are you doing?" she asked.

"I'm really good thanks. I'm six foot now, dad reckons I'll be as tall as him, but I reckon I'll be taller. At least six foot five," he said.

"I love you to bits, you're turning into such a charming and handsome young man," Alison said.

She pulled him into her again. This time with her arms wrapped around his neck and hugging him even tighter than before.

"Do you want me to help with your case?" she asked.

Harry smirked.

"Nah, I'll be alright thanks, I'm not ten anymore," he answered.

"Sorry, I keep thinking of you as that adorable little boy I met when I first came to your house," she said.

Alison gestured by tilting her head for him to follow her.

"Come on then," she said.

Harry followed Alison out of the cool, air conditioned arrivals hall. As she strode off a few feet in front of him, he couldn't help but look at her heels, shapely legs and pert bum. She definitely had an onion ass. It was so perfect, just looking at it made him want to cry. Once she slowed her march to allow him to draw level with her, they small talked in the thirty degree heat as they made their way to her car. Alison wanted to know how everyone was back in England. His family had obviously been the better part of her marriage to his uncle.

"The only reason I agreed to come on this trip was because you were going to be here," he said.

She stopped and smiled and hugged him once more. This time he smelt her perfume. She was a woman to die for.

"Thank you Harry, that's really sweet of you to say," Alison said.

Once they had driven out of the multi storey carpark, Alison lowered the roof of her sporty, orange BMW. They pulled onto the dual carriageway and she put her foot down. The cool air was back with the breeze ruffling past their heads. The fast air racing past them also ruffled Alison's blouse, so much so that Harry was able to steal glances of the red bra holding her pronounced chest in place. He thought he had better stop before she noticed. He reached around and pulled his sunglasses from his hand luggage. Harry knew what James Dean had felt like in his Porsche 550 Spyder, with a model doing the driving. This time he didn't put his feet on the dash.

The drive from the airport to Fort Lauderdale took a little over an hour. When Alison pulled up at her apartment, Harry knew he was right in thinking her pad would be just as stylish as her and her car. The third floor apartment only had two bedrooms, he presumed that was all she needed. The second bedroom was to be his own for the duration of his stay. The room came with a double bed and his own wet room and shower. He slid the bedroom's built-in wardrobe open. Inside hung five crisp white shirts, a pair of black trousers, neck tie and a waistcoat. A pair of shiny black shoes sat at the base of the unit. His uniform, he guessed.

Alison fixed him a glass of cola with ice and they sat out the back of her place on the balcony. Her apartment was on the edge of town. The balcony faced east and the views extended over a golf course. Beyond that, but too far for the eyes to see, was the Atlantic Ocean. They chatted for an hour or more. Harry loved it. She was treating him like an adult, not a kid. Alison was asking questions about his school and the subjects he had taken in the last year. The question of what he wanted to do once he had left school cropped up again. He answered pretty much as he did on the last day of term.

"I want to join the British Army and have a go at SAS selection," he said.

Alison nodded her head, but looked at little dismayed.

"I would have thought you'd have grown out of all those guns and bullets, by now," she said.

"No chance, I really want to do it and it's a better answer than train driver," he said.

While he was laughing at his own joke, Alison had been weighing up his comment.

"Work hard and you'll do it Harry, you can do anything if you put your mind to it," she said.

"Thanks," Harry said.

"Do you want to watch a film and have pizza for dinner?" she asked.

"Sounds good," he said.

Alison chose a horror film. The pizza Harry picked out was ordered from a local pizza parlour. It was the size of a dustbin lid. Alison sat next to him on the couch to watch the film. She reaffirmed her status as cool when she handed him an ice-cold bottle of Budweiser, straight out of the fridge.

Alison turning down the lights to near total darkness made him wonder. He'd seen clips on the internet when young men and older ladies sat together on the sofa. What happened was entirely different to watching a film. He never found out if those internet videos were realistic. His jet lagged eyes closed and he fell asleep halfway through the movie.

When the horror film finished, Alison tousled his head of thick, dark blonde hair. He found enough energy to say good night, walk to his room and hit the sack.

CHAPTER FOUR

Harry's body clock was still out of sync with the new time zone. The next day he woke at five in the morning, but he was up and at em' and felt fresh and invigorated after an early morning shower. The temperature outside was still cool and he threw a hoodie over his t-shirt. Walking through to the kitchen and opening the blinds, he found the sun was still creeping into the sky. An hour later he was sitting on the balcony and saw the sun fully illuminate the eighteen holes. Alison came through in bare feet and a silk dressing gown not long after. She went straight to the percolator and joined him on the patio with a mug of steaming coffee. He managed to look at the early morning golfers on the course, rather than Alison in her skimpy dressing gown, naked underneath, with curves in all the right places.

"I usually have breakfast at a little restaurant next to the beach and then go and relax, sunbathe and read a book. Sound agreeable?" she asked.

"Definitely," he replied.

By eight o'clock they were sitting in a restaurant a mile up the coast, Harry tucking into a ham and cheese omelette, Alison with French toast and maple syrup.

There were more questions about his life over breakfast. Alison was keen to know if he was dating, or had a girlfriend.

Harry felt embarrassed. Alison was cool and he shouldn't feel this way, but she was nearer his mum's age than his.

"I'm not, but I wouldn't say no to a girlfriend," said Harry.

"If I was seventeen again, I'd snap you right up, I'm sure the right girl won't take too long," Alison said.

She gave Harry a warm smile and let him know she had meant every word.

Harry shrugged and tried make out as if girls weren't a big deal in his life, hoping against hope that she knew exactly what he was imagining and that girls were, a very big deal.

Alison paid the bill. They left the car where it was parked and made their way to the beach.

*

The sleeping tablet he had taken an hour before bed, allowed the boss a marginally better night's sleep. Like the previous morning and every other, the boss stepped onto his veranda with a mug of coffee. Taking a sip, he smiled. What caused a bigger smile was the fact he exported more of his product than coffee beans, his country's biggest export. He looked out at his garden and to the mountains behind.

*

Strolling down the beach they found a good spot to sunbathe. Sitting down on his out thrown towel, Harry removed his shirt and gave himself a meagre splash of the factor fifty suntan cream his mum had given him. She didn't want him to burn, but he actually wanted to get a tan this summer. As he quickly rubbed the cream in, he was reminded how unhappy he was with his chest. He felt it was under developed and was looking forward to using the hotel's gym facilities. His chest being un-tanned and pasty certainly didn't help matters. Harry took his new SAS book from his bag and after taking a few photos of the beach for his Facebook, he lay on his front to read. He couldn't concentrate.

Alison laid her towel down and flicked her flip flops from her feet. Harry was pretending to read his book, but out of the corner of his eye he was watching Alison. Her sunglasses placed on her towel, she pulled her white strappy top over her head and dropped it on her day bag. Harry's jaw dropped to the floor. She looked even sexier in a white bikini. Her bust was incredible. Just as pert as her ass and bigger than any he had seen before. He wondered how her bikini top had the strength to contain them. She shuffled her linen trousers over her bum and they fell to the sand. Oh my God. She's perfect. That ass. Those boobs. Harry got a bigger eyeful of ass when she bent over. Her linen trousers joined her top. Alison stood straight. Harry thought he'd died and gone to heaven. Hands behind her, she arched her back before placing her sunglasses back onto her face and lying back on her towel.

After a moment, or four, Harry managed to avert his gaze. It wasn't long before he was fully engaged in tales of SAS heroics and derring-do. He was so engrossed, he didn't even notice Alison sitting up to cover herself suntan lotion. The first thing he knew of it was when she passed him the bottle of lotion.

"Harry, do you think you could rub some lotion into my back, please?" she asked.

"Erm. Yeah, of course," he said.

His mind raced with the possibilities the situation could lead to. He had completely forgotten he was on a public beach with people walking past. Alison lay face down. With one hand she reached around and undid the top half of her bikini. Her back was completely naked. That was maybe the single sexiest thing he had ever seen in real life.

It was amazing. He was surprised she hadn't felt his drool landing on her back. He thought about straddling her and rubbing the lotion in. He'd seen pool boys on internet movies do that, but he didn't dare. He knew he'd mess it up. Instead, he knelt beside her started to rub her back. Alison felt something wasn't quite right. She lifted herself onto her elbows and turned her head towards him.

"Harry, you are using the lotion, aren't you?" Alison asked.

"Err, oh no. Sorry, I err, forgot," he said.

What a complete idiot. He'd fluffed it. He even missed a glance at her side boob when she lifted herself onto her elbows. Harry managed to squirt some of the lotion onto Alison's back and rub it in on his second go. He was touching a woman. A real fully grown one. Semi-naked with proper tits and everything. Fuck, this was amazing. Thank God he'd not gone with the straddling idea. She'd have felt the boner in his shorts.

"Thanks Harry, that was really helpful," Alison said.

Harry went back to his book, disappointed not to be rubbing suntan lotion into Alison's onion ass.

In the early afternoon they packed away their things and took a wander through the sand towards the smell of barbequed food.

As they strolled down to the beach hut café, he was aware Alison was only wearing her bikini and flip flops. He was doubly aware that she had some sand sticking to her upper left thigh and onion ass. Jesus, it made her look even sexier. He was even more aware than that, all the men on the beach were looking at them. Or to be more precise, her. Did the men looking at her think he was with her? Her toyboy? Fuck yes, he hoped. He smiled inwardly and took thorough delight in the moment. He just prayed he didn't get another boner.

They waited for their order to cook. Alison passed him a bottle of beer. A person had to be twenty one to drink in the USA, but Alison was a regular and the worst the staff could do was tell her not to give him anymore. Looking at the magnificent coast line and the miles of golden beaches, Harry turned to look back at the city. Dozens and dozens of hotels sat on the coastline. Busy bars and shops selling towels and swimming shorts filled in the gaps in the skyline. Tourism wasn't a large part of the Fort Lauderdale economy, it was the Fort Lauderdale economy.

Eating lunch had come with its own challenge. Two challenges to be exact. Two huge challenges that jiggled when he told her a joke. She laughed so hard the burger in her hand shook and a splodge of mayo landed on her chest. Alison took a finger and wicked the sauce from her cleavage. Fuck! Instantly, Harry's shorts tightened. She was sat opposite him looking gorgeous. Her big tits trying their hardest to pop out of her bikini top. Beads of sweat were even starting to form in between her mounds. Eating lunch was a pleasurable challenge.

The afternoon was much the same as the morning. Sun bathing, reading and Harry did a lot more watching the girls go by. Sadly for him, there was no sun screen rubbing.

Alison said it was time to pack up their things. She was going to take him on a quick tour of the hotel before he started work there the next day.

The quick tour of the hotel was exactly that. They walked around the hotel at less than a brisk walk, but faster than the stroll down the beach. Alison said hello to all of the hotel employees she saw. She knew them by their first names. Harry was impressed. It must be something for a cleaner, for the general manager to know your name and say hello. He thought it must make them feel pretty good.

Alison played an excellent tour guide. She told Harry various facts and figures about the hotel and its massive function rooms and restaurants. The five hundred bedrooms at the Atlantic Grand meant the hotel could hold over one thousand people per night. All of the twenty four function rooms were named after the most populous states of the USA. The biggest room being the California Great Hall. The room could hold a reception for up to six hundred and thirty people. Next in size were the Texas and Florida rooms.

She walked through the biggest kitchen in the hotel. If the heat wasn't bad enough, the noise was absurd. Hisses of steam at every turn. Ovens running noisily. Pans frying. New pans being thrown on stoves with a metallic clang. The biggest noise however, came from the head chef. A constant stream of expletives, followed by instructions, were directed towards his staff. He must have thought he was God. Harry thought he was a dick. His management style definitely needed improvement. The largest of the three restaurants in the hotel seated two hundred diners at once and could cater for six hundred diners in an evening's service.

As well as the size and grandeur of the hotel, Harry was impressed by the hotel's client list - tobacco companies, international pharmaceutical companies, global fashion houses, worldwide clothing brands, food corporations and major players in the energy drink world. The hotel had hosted conventions for the comic book and gaming industries, as well as huge wedding fairs and bridal shows, awards ceremonies and much more.

Standing on the beach at the end of his tour, he looked out at the vista of the North Atlantic. Looking back at the hotel, the view was equally impressive. A four lane highway ran between the beach and hotel. Beyond that the glass gargantuan of a hotel rose up like a huge block of ice.

The Atlantic Grand was massive. A twenty one floor goliath that was bigger than anything else in Fort Lauderdale. Entirely glass on all four sides, the hotel glimmered in the sun and looked as blue as the ocean it fronted.

He could even consider the hotel industry being one he could get into, if things with the British Army didn't pan out. His mind shifted to Alison and her absurdly good figure. But he thought he would need to find a girl his own age if he was to pop his cherry while in the States.

CHAPTER FIVE

Harry's job at the hotel was that of a conference porter. By day, he would be kept busy serving the hotel's conference clients, welcoming new arrivals, directing them to events and meetings, serving cold drinks, tea and coffee, plus, anything else that was required of him. For the first week however, Alison had chosen for him to join the team of evening conference porters. The work would be full on. Busier than the daytime, but far less customer facing. The evening team changed room seating plans, added or removed digital display equipment, emptied bins in conference rooms, filled coffee stations with fresh cups and made sure everything was spick and span. The work was heavier, but Alison knew Harry could do it.

The day after the beach was Harry's first shift at the hotel. In the duty manager's office he was acquainted with a few of the people he would be working with. His immediate boss was Amanda, the hotel's French conference manager. She was a bit too slender. Emaciated would be too harsh, he settled for vegan. She was average height for a woman and had a bob of dark hair surrounding a hard face. She looked like a someone run ragged with stress. Her career maybe, or her personal life. Who knew? Stress or no stress, Harry thought she had a permanent resting bitch face, with the ability to go from nought bitch in point three of a second. Harry wasn't sure about her. She seemed a bit sharp and no nonsense, too thin and wiry. Maybe it was just her. Maybe it was her French roots. She might be the kind of woman you wanted in the conference game, but Harry knew she'd be pretty crap at heaving tables around.

The next employee Harry met was Antoni Sousa. He didn't even get up from lounging in an office chair. He exuded arrogance, cockiness, not confidence. The one thing Harry always tried to be was confident and to never come across as cocky. Girls hated that. Antoni Sousa appeared to take an instant dislike to Harry. He didn't get up to greet him. Didn't shake his hand. All he was interested in was the game he was playing on his smartphone. Harry was damned if he was going to put his hand forward. He said hello. All Sousa managed was a begrudged half nod, much like an ape at the zoo. He probably didn't like Harry because he could tell without even standing up, Harry was taller. On the other hand, Antoni Sousa had bigger muscles than Harry's non-existent muscular frame. He guessed Sousa was mid-twenties and could have been a model on the pages of a clothing company's website, classic South American good looks with dark hair and dark features. He would stand out in a crowd. Even though Harry was tall, he wouldn't. He blended in. He looked average. If Harry knew anything, it was that the dislike was mutual. The reason he disliked him though, was about to become apparent.

"This young lady," Alison said, "is Kelsi and she'll be teaching you the ropes for your first week."

Kelsi smiled. It completely threw Harry.

"Err, yeah. Er, hi. Hello, I mean," he said.

Her smile had caused him to lose his mind. He knew he'd just come across as a clown. After her smile Harry noticed her hair. Light strawberry blonde, falling halfway down her back. Her eyes had a greenish blue hue to them and screamed youth and vitality. Her smile had full lips. He noticed her tan. She could have been one of the women he'd seen at the beach yesterday. Even though she was wearing a below the knee skirt and blouse a size too big, Harry could tell she was in shape. Developed and feminine, like some of the girls studying A-Level Physical Education at his school in England.

He put his hand forward. Her hand was delicate. He was taller than her. That was always going to be a given. He thought she was five foot four, maybe coming up to five foot five. Then she smiled again. His visual senses were over-powered and he was stunned into silence. He felt as if he couldn't speak. He struggled to reply to her 'Kelsi,' with his own name. He did. Just.

"It's okay Alison, I'll take it from here," she said.

She asked him to follow her. Kelsi's accent sounded like she was from a southern state in America. They made their way out of the office and down a series of corridors.

*

It was late morning when the last of the boss's men arrived at his warehouse. The men he had hired for the job were handsomely paid, it was a risky job and some of them would not make it back to their families. Their wives and children wouldn't see them again, but what other choice did they have? The boss knew the slum they had been recruited from. He used to live there.

After they had showered, the men were issued new clothes and boots. Wearing their dark green boiler suits they looked like an army. Given their individual weapons, they were told to make sure they were clean and in good working order. They already knew how to strip and clean an automatic rifle, the Germans had taught them. Their training had been short, but they didn't need to know much more than basics.

*

Harry was embarrassed. He had been lost for words when she introduced herself. He'd come across as a blundering British idiot.

"Sorry," Harry said, "I should have introduced myself properly. My name is Fearn, Harry Fearn."

In the corridor Kelsi stopped and turned around.

She raised an eyebrow and gave a mocking smile.

"A bit like Bond, James Bond?" she asked.

She giggled and smiled. Harry was almost happy to be lost for words once more. He felt like a prick. A stupid English prick. The mishap with his name made look like a buffoon, but he still smiled. He didn't mean to, she induced his smile. His smile caused her lips to arc. They both laughed. A thunderbolt of something more passed between them.

"I suppose I walked straight into that one, didn't I?" he asked.

"Yes you did, Harry Fearn," Kelsi said, "actually, my full name is Kelsi Millicent Maguire."

Her pace of conversation meant he had to re-say in his head, what she had just said, to even have half a chance of understanding her.

"Where are we going?" Harry asked.

"Down the corridor and then into the elevator and up two floors," Kelsi answered.

She had the conversational speed of a machine gun.

He had hoped the task in hand would somehow appear in her reply. It hadn't. That being said, he liked the matter of fact way in which she spoke.

He was lost in thought as they continued towards the elevator. His eyes followed her fine looking ass down the corridor. She was fit with a capital F. He wondered if all the girls in Fort Lauderdale had onion asses. Then he remembered Amanda. She looked like she needed a good meal. Kelsi stopped at the elevator. Standing next to her, he liked what he saw in the elevator door's reflection.

"So Harry, Alison tells me you're her nephew and you're from London, England," said Kelsi.

"Yeah, she's my mum's sister in law, not even that anymore to be truthful. She divorced my uncle because he's a bit of a knobhead and yeah, I'm from London," he said.

Kelsi smiled. Harry smiled back.

"Where are you from, Fort Lauderdale?" he asked.

"Actually, I'm from Biloxi, in the great state of Mississippi," she said.

She spoke with the confidence and temerity of a woman twice, or three times her age.

"My great, great, great, great granddaddy was an Irishman," she said. "He moved over to the United States in 1850 during the potato famine in Ireland. He sailed to Boston, Massachusetts and settled there. Then his son, my great, great, great granddaddy, moved south to Mississippi."

Kelsi's Southern accent enthralled him. He loved hearing her talk. Accent or no accent, he was quickly learning that once she started, he would have difficulty shutting her up.

"He worked on a farm, as did his son, my great great granddaddy. He was gifted part of the farm, only a small part mind, by the farm owner, after he saved his life during a cattle rustling incident. His son, my great granddaddy fell on hard times during the Great Depression and was forced to sell the farm back to the new land owners to make ends meet," she told him.

The elevator arrived. The doors opened and Harry gestured for Kelsi to enter first.

"Why thank you, young man," she said.

He followed her into the elevator and took a cursory glance at her figure. She turned to face him with that charming smile. All Harry could think of was how good she would look on the beach in a bikini. Her figure was just as good as Alison's. Better in fact. She was his age too. He was dumbstruck. Kelsi tapped some buttons on the elevator's control panel and the doors closed.

"So my great granddaddy sold the farm and moved to Detroit to get work. He became a sheet metal worker in a car factory," Kelsi continued. "That was where his son met my grand momma and they had my mom. My mom met my dad, but he was killed in a bar fight when I was only two months old. My mom and I moved back to Mississippi, to get away from the big city and be nearer our cousins."

"I'm sorry to hear about your dad," said Harry.

"Thank you, I wish it had never happened, but it did and there's nothing I can do to change that," Kelsi said.

The elevator pinged. Harry followed Kelsi onto the new floor and along the next corridor. She stopped off at a store-room full of stationery and bottles of water. She passed Harry a large plastic box and told him to hold it. She filled the box with bottles of water, headed paper and pens emblazoned with the hotel's logo. She didn't mess about. She was fast and efficient. Harry liked that.

"Come along now, Harry," Kelsi said.

They paced the hallways back the way they had come. More importantly than her looks, which were superb, he liked the way she had about her. He liked her stance. The way she moved. He liked her approachable demeanour. Her confidence.

The box and its contents turned out to be for the Wisconsin room. Once Kelsi had placed the bottles in their positions on the tables around the room and Harry had laid a pen on each notepad, the room was complete. Ready for tomorrow's conference.

The entirety of Harry's first shift was much of the same. Some conference rooms required less work than the first, others required a total overhaul.

Now in the last hour of their Monday evening shift, Kelsi and Harry took one of the hotel's four staircases. The main staircase exuded splendour. The wide, rich carpeted steps ran from the lobby on the first floor, up to the second floor. The second flight of that impressive staircase climbed from the second floor up to the third floor. That was all that existed of the main staircase. It only served the first three floors of the hotel where all but one conference room was situated. Two elevators, either side the stairs on the first floor, ran all the way to the rooftop terrace on the twenty first floor, as well as serving the three basement floors, the back office and staff canteen on the first basement floor, the gym and sauna on the second basement floor. Finally the elevators served the linen room, maintenance department and loading bay on the third and final basement floor. This elevator and staircase arrangement was identically replicated at the back of the hotel

The staircase Kelsi and Harry were now climbing was at the front left corner of the hotel. It stretched the entirety of the hotel's twenty one floors and three basement floors. A mirror image of this staircase was situated at the back right corner of the hotel. It wasn't like the main staircase. It wasn't wide, carpeted or constructed from oak. It was a service staircase and constructed from concrete and finished with speckled floor tiles. A plastic coated handrail sat aloft of metal balusters and formed the safety railing for the stair's entirety. The stairs were dual use. Primarily they were as a fire escape. In the event of a fire, the elevators would be automatically shut down and guests and workers would use the fire escape stairs. Guests only knew it was there because the illuminated fire exit signs told them. Secondly, staff would use the stairwell as it was often quicker than waiting for an elevator to become free, especially if they only wanted to travel up or down a couple of floors.

Reaching the fifth floor landing, Kelsi didn't turn left to the steps that led to the sixth floor and didn't turn right through the door that led to the hotel bedrooms. Instead she called the service elevator in front of her. The service elevator was located next to the service staircase and ran up and down all the floors of the hotel. It was used by the cleaning staff, porters, conference porters, maintenance staff and room service waiters. The elevator groaned as it came to rest on their floor. Harry slid the outer concertina door wide, then he pulled the industrial steel door on the elevator car itself. Kelsi entered and Harry followed her into the vertically sliding box. He pulled the doors closed in reverse order. Kelsi hit the button for the twenty first floor.

"Where are we going now?" Harry asked.

"We've done our jobs. There's only half an hour left until the end of shift, why not enjoy it?" said Kelsi.

Harry was none the wiser, but thought he would roll with it.

"What is it, with Antoni?" he asked.

"How do you mean?" asked Kelsi.

"I don't think he likes me," replied Harry.

Kelsi knew the answer and avoided eye contact with Harry.

"He doesn't like any man that talks to me," she said.

"Why?" he asked.

"I used to date him," Kelsi answered.

"Used to?" Harry asked.

"Yeah," she said.

Harry fancied Kelsi. Who wouldn't? She was gorgeous. Smart and sassy. Antoni Sousa was the high school jock who had previously bagged himself the beauty. Harry saw himself as the awkward nerd who would never get a look in.

"Why did you break up? he asked.

"He turned out to be a cheating asshole," she said.

That killed the conversation. He didn't know how to answer. 'Sorry about that,' was all he could manage. They rode the elevator in silence. He heard it groan again as it came to a rest on the twenty first floor. He repeated his routine with the doors and Kelsi stepped from the elevator.

"Wow," Harry exclaimed.

He had just seen the breath taking view.

"Good, isn't it?" Kelsi asked.

Although it was dark, Harry could see all of Fort Lauderdale and the whole of the Atlantic Ocean. The rooftop was multi-purpose. Primarily it was a place for people to sunbathe. It was also a meeting area. Tables and chairs were dotted all around. The third use was a bar, now shut down for the night, Harry bet it did a roaring trade of a daytime.

"The view is amazing, I can see for miles," he said

"The horizon is two point nine miles away, more because you're high up at the top of the hotel. Maybe fifteen miles, could be as far twenty," she answered.

Harry laughed.

"Geeky," he said.

Her brow furrowed.

"I am not," Kelsi flat out stated.

She talked slower. Maybe she had also been nervous about meeting someone new earlier. This time her voice was softer and much more endearing.

"Things like that interest me is all. Guests ask me that question all the time, so I looked it up. They want to know how far they can see. They think that they can see hundreds of miles, you can't even see the Bahamas from up here and they're only a hundred and ninety miles away. They forget about the curvature of the earth," she said.

"How do you know the Bahamas are that far away?" he asked.

"Jeez Louise, do you think I might have looked that up, also?" she sarcastically said.

"Point taken," he said.

Kelsi searched behind the rooftop bar and returned a moment later. She handed him an ice cold bottle of Budweiser and gestured for him to follow her to the south side of the hotel. They looked out on downtown Fort Lauderdale.

"Where did the beers come from?" he asked.

"My friend Kim who works on the rooftop bar," Kelsi said, "she left them for me, just don't tell Alison, okay?"

"Yeah sure, why did she leave them?" Harry said.

"I get her the occasional pack of marker pens from the porter's stores. She has a four year old son, he uses them for colouring. It's a you scratch my back and I'll scratch yours, kind of thing," she answered.

He twisted the bottle's cap and took a swig of the ice cold nectar and smiled. The Atlantic Ocean was to his left. Fort Lauderdale was bathed in light from clubs, bars and shops in front of him and the best bit about America so far was to his right. Even if she did have an ex who wanted to kill him.

Leaning on the railings and looking down on the city, Harry sensed Kelsi was less than happy. He thought it might be because he'd mentioned Antoni.

"What's the matter?" he asked.

"Nothing, I suppose," she said.

"Really?" Harry asked.

He knew she wasn't telling the truth.

"No, it's Antoni. You made me think of him, is all," said Kelsi.

A tear rolled down her cheek.

Harry didn't know what to say, or do. He'd never had a girl start crying in front of him. His mum maybe, but did that really count? He was sure she would construe it the wrong way, but he did it anyway. He shuffled along the railing and closed the gap to no more than an inch. Harry put his arm around her and kissed the top of her head. Letting his lips linger, his nostrils filled with her scent.

He'd fluffed it. She was going to hate him. What an idiot he had been.

She looked up and smiled.

"Thank you," she said.

She pecked Harry on the cheek and went back to leaning on the railing, staring out at nothing. On the inside, Harry's soul was on fire. He smiled an iceberg of a smile. His smile on the inside was much bigger than his lips portrayed. His arm stayed where it was. He felt the need to get to know her a little better.

"If I may be so rude, can I ask the year of your birth?" he said.

Still under his arm, Kelsi turned in to continue the conversation. She didn't speak, just smirked. That made him smile. His smiling made her smile and she chuckled to herself.

"That Harry, was a very gentlemanly and very English way to ask a lady her age. I like it. I'm eighteen," she answered.

Harry had guessed right. She would be in her late teens, but not in her twenties.

"You?" she asked

"I'm seventeen," he said.

"Well Fearn. Harry Fearn. May I just say that are a very mature young man and to my liking," she said.

She looked into his eyes.

"Ditto," said Harry.

She pursed her lips. He thought about what he'd just said.

"Oh God, not ditto. I mean, yes ditto, but not ditto. Ditto with a modification. I mean you come across as a mature young lady, not a young man and definitely to one's liking," he said.

He'd made an arse of himself again.

Her smile was back.

"I'm messing with you, Harry," said Kelsi.

She was smiling even more than before and put a hand on his chest.

Harry smiled and squeezed her a little tighter. He knew what flirting was, he just didn't know he'd been doing it.

All in all, it hadn't been a bad first day.

CHAPTER SIX

At one o'clock in the afternoon the boss's plane took to the air. After they were finished unloading the last truck that brought their supplies to the airfield, his men and their equipment would follow. For now, only the boss and the two Germans travelled towards America. The two Germans were to secure the airfield at which they were landing and eliminate any problems. The pilot was to return home, he was too valuable to lose.

*

Harry took the service staircase to the first basement floor and staff room. Kelsi told him she always entered the hotel via the staff entrance. She would walk down the outside concrete steps on Granada Street and enter by the clocking-in machine on the first basement floor. She would then make her way to the canteen for a cup of coffee before she started her shift. He had beaten her to it.

He passed Antoni Sousa in the corridor. He muttered something under his breath. Harry thought it was probably a hollow threat. He sat at an empty table near the coffee machine. Kelsi came for her coffee a few minutes later. Harry greeted her with a mug of freshly made, steaming coffee and she greeted him with an equally warm smile. Who said chivalry was dead?

Fifteen minutes later they were sitting at a ten seat, round chipboard table in the California Great Hall. There were plenty more bare chipboard tables dotted around the room. The only other feature of any significance was the half constructed stage area at the front. What they saw now was something the general public would never see. An event under construction. This was the back bone of a large event. Everything else, table cloths, cutlery, wine glasses, was just window dressing. The room filled with staff and the space began to look a little less utilitarian. Alison entered the room and climbed the stairs to the half constructed stage and greeted the staff.

They knew the hotel was about to host a large event - they just didn't know what. All had been kept in the dark. The Atlantic Grand had previously held large scale events. Last year a global energy drink company had booked every room in the hotel for a weeklong conference. The hotel then held a large conference for the pharmaceutical industry. On that occasion it was for two weeks. Tomorrow was to be the biggest and most prestigious event since the refurbishment. This event was going to be the icing on the cake. Not a televised and glamorous awards ceremony. Not an event with hordes of fans coming to see their fictional idols. This one was to be even bigger. The weeklong event was a governmental summit. It was current affairs. It was world leaders. It was global. The conference was tackling a serious issue. The stakeholder countries weren't meeting about a topic they had discussed before; climate change and global warming, pollution, or economies. The event the hotel was hosting was just as important, but it was a subject all too often swept under the carpet, hidden and forgotten about, dealt with on an individual basis, not tackled with the full force of many nations united in their goal. Alison told them the governments of the world would be meeting about drugs. That got a big laugh from the younger staff in the room. One voice heckled, 'I know a man that can help them with that'.

"Thank you for your, as always, helpful input, Jay," said Alison.

She gave him a look as she finished speaking. Her face said, 'I like you Jay, but I won't hesitate in firing your ass if you do that again'. Jay shrugged and put his upturned hands forward. He attempted to look innocent, as if someone else had made the remark.

"Don't forget Jayden, just because I didn't see who shouted the remark, doesn't mean I didn't recognise the voice. Maybe if you hadn't taken so many drugs, your brain would still work," retorted Alison.

The room was filled with jeering and raucous laughter. Jay just got owned by the boss.

"The governments in attendance will be meeting primarily about the war on drugs," she said.

Every employee was handed a shiny new name badge. The world would be watching. They had to look pristine. Everything needed to be present and correct. Straight after the meeting, each member of staff was to make their way to the Secret Service outpost in the New Jersey suite. It became clear why they had been asked to bring two forms of identification and one of them photographic. They were to have a current photograph taken. Their thumbprints and retinas scanned. Then they would then be given an identity card. For the last six months with only Alison's knowledge, the Secret Service had checked every employee's past and present. Employees' parents were checked. Their children and step-children were researched. Who did the children come into contact with? Was it anyone of interest? Past wives, husbands, boyfriends and girl-friends had been looked into. Even hobbies and past times were searched. Three employees owned guns. Their firearms licences all checked out. Even so, it didn't stop a bogus search of their houses the by Secret Service posing as firearms certificate enforcement officers. Criminal records had been searched. Two people had convictions for driving whilst under the influence. One had received a five year driving ban on his third DUI conviction. One employee had a solicitation bust on her police record. All of the convictions were long enough ago for the Secret Service not to worry. One of the hotel maintenance staff wasn't in the building. Forty years previously, he had been taught by a high school professor whose brother dated a member of a revolutionary left-wing terrorist group. He was told to take the week off. Not a single person present aroused any kind of suspicion. They were all model citizens.

All the street drains in a two block radius of the hotel had been searched and sealed by the Secret Service. Starting at midnight and for the next week until the conference ended, only the main entrance at the front of the hotel and the delivery bay would be open. All other entrances and exits would be alarmed and covered by closed circuit television cameras. Every employee would need their new identity cards to access the building. They would only be allowed to use the main entrance. Staff would be required to walk through metal detectors and put their bags through an x-ray machine in the lobby. If there was an issue, they would be frisked by security guards. If something didn't check out with their ID, they would be sent home and wouldn't be allowed to enter the building.

The only other means of entrance to the hotel would be the delivery bay. It was to be manned by security personnel twenty four hours a day and was strictly for goods only. No foot traffic was permitted. Any goods entering the bay would be checked against the manifest and the hotel's own delivery schedule. The goods would also be sent through an x-ray machine.

Alison read out a list of countries and their representatives who would be attending.

Being host to the event and having nearly seven million residents between the ages of fifteen and sixty four, who used cocaine, the USA was in attendance. Washington DC was just over a thousand miles away. The man who led the US contingent was their loud and brash, Twitter addicted, outspoken, controversial and often rude and racist, womanising, former US Marine turned successful businessman, turned politician and President of the Unties States (POTUS), Huey Ace. He would be joined by White House Chief of Staff John Robinson, the Administrator and Deputy Administrator of the Drug Enforcement Agency and the Commandant of the Coastguard, Admiral Knowles. There was also sure to be a gaggle of glamour modelesque secretaries following in Huey Ace's wake.

The United Kingdom of Great Britain and Northern Ireland was next. Two point four percent of the population of UK aged between sixteen and fifty nine, used cocaine regularly. The government officials they were sending were Foreign Secretary Charlie Hoveringham, Home Secretary Fiona McKerral, The Minister of State for Immigration, Minister of State for Security and Economic Crime, The Minister of State for Policing, as well as Jacinda Armstrong, the head of the UK's Military Intelligence, Section Five (MI5).

Twenty eight other countries were attending the inaugural world summit, known as the DW30 by the press. The other countries attending Drugs War Thirty made up the top thirty countries whose population were most effected by cocaine. Each of these countries brought at least five ministers from their government, or heads of department from their security services. As well as secretaries, press secretaries, advisors, heads of communications and body men. The hotel would be practically bursting at the seams.

In addition to the countries that comprised the DW30 Summit, another fifteen countries had representatives at the conference. Each looked to make the next drugs war summit, DW45.

The remaining rooms in the hotel were booked out by the press. Television news was there. NBC and CNN from the States. BBC World News and Channel Four from Great Britain. The state owned French broadcasters were present. The SBS media outlet represented six attending countries. The rest of the press contingent included more TV companies, newspapers, radio broadcasters and online publications.

Alison ended the meeting by reminding the staff the conference was going to be hugely important for the company. This wasn't a one off. They wanted to be the go to hotelier for all the coming DW summits around the world. The hotel's performance and their behaviour was to impact directly on the chances of the hotel chain winning the work to hold this type of event in the future. She thanked everyone for attending and the hard work she was sure they would put in over the coming week.

After they had visited the New Jersey meeting room to collect their ID cards, the evening's work was setting up room plans. Harry lost count of the different types of room setups he used. There must have been at least ten different styles. It was a busy shift. The work was heavy and constant. Tables lifted and carried. Round tables rolled all around the hotel. Huge stacks of chairs pushed on purpose built trolleys between one room and the next. Kelsi definitely got the lighter end of the stick. Once Harry had moved the tables and chairs into the room, she dressed the tables with table cloths and pushed the chairs under the table's edge. She also had the less enviable and more tedious task of preparing drinks stations with hundreds of glasses and coffee cups and ensuring they were flawlessly clean.

*

The boss's Gulfstream landed twelve miles north-west of Miami. Opa-Locka West Airport was one hundredth of the size of Miami International. After damage caused by Hurricane Wilma, the site had been derelict since 2005. The boss knew about the runway because some of his first shipments to the states had been through this airport. That had been in the early days. The authorities soon got wise to his importation techniques. Use of the airport ceased. His plane landed on the three thousand foot runway with ease. Most runways at modern commercial airports were over four times longer. The lack of runway length would prove a problem for commercial airliners, but not the cargo plane his men would arrive in. That was exactly why the boss had chosen to buy the third hand Hercules C-130.

The Germans climbed down the Gulfsteam's steps. Weapons in their grasp, they set about securing the airfield. They ensured nobody else was present and the boss's operation wasn't watched. The boss stayed in the plane. He made hot drinks and talked with the pilot until the Germans returned. Once the boss was satisfied, he gave the operation the green light. The Gulfstream turned around and taxied for take-off. The boss walked over to the semi-truck that had been left at the airport by one of his American contacts. The small jet took to the skies. The boss neared the truck and trailer. The keys for the truck had been left where his contact said they would be - driver's side on front tyre.

Right on schedule the Hercules cargo plane came into view. The pilot knew getting the plane to stop in such a short distance was going to be a big ask. Ideally the runway would have been a thousand feet longer and the pilot could have guaranteed the plane would come to a halt. The men in the main cargo hold were instructed to buckle up. Taking into consideration the weight of the behemoth, the temperature and pressure, the pilot slowed his airspeed as much as he dared. Luckily the weight in the hold wasn't anywhere near the total tonnage the plane could carry. The pilot touched down as soon as the runway began. He hit the brakes hard and applied maximum reverse thrust. The boss watched as the plane careered towards the end of the runway. After the strip of tarmac ended there was only swampland and alligators to keep his men company. The plane kept coming. The deceleration appeared to be minimal. Inside the cockpit the pilot gulped and said a prayer. The plane rolled over the red hatching marks at the end of the runway and the boss had visions of the plane taking a dip into the surrounding swamps. The hatchings ran out. So did the tarmac. The front of the plane dipped as it rolled over onto the soft grass. The fuselage was still pushed forward. The double front wheel dug a six foot deep scar into the grass. The plane came to a stop ten feet after the runway ended. The boss gave a sigh of relief.

*

It was midnight by the time Kelsi and Harry reached the roof top. Like the night before, Kelsi ducked behind the closed down bar and picked out two cold bottles of beer. The ice in the bucket normally remained frozen. When she picked the bottles out tonight, only cold water remained.

They took up their position leaning on the railing, this time facing the Atlantic Ocean.

"Big day, tomorrow," said Harry.

"Hopefully tomorrow will be the quietest day of the week ahead," she replied.

"Why?" he asked.

"The reception desk deal with the check-ins," she said. "The reception porters take guests' bags to their rooms. We're just there in support of them. The kitchen cook the guests' dinner. The banqueting staff serve the dinner. The first full day of a new conference is busier. The hotel is new to everyone, they don't know how to get between one conference room and the next so conference organisers are pulling their hair out because delegates are late for meetings. Second day of the conference, everyone knows what should be happening. They want to make alterations and are asking for more. A lot more. Tomorrow will be easier."

Harry raised his bottle to Kelsi. They clinked their beers together.

"To an easy day," he smiled.

"An easier day," she said.

They were silent. Both looking out at the ocean.

"Harry, would you mind putting your arm around me, again?"

CHAPTER SEVEN

Harry knew very little about the gym and lifting weights. He had always cycled for exercise, an art in itself in London where cyclists were likened to criminals by car users. His real passion lay in his racing bike. He and his dad would drive out to the countryside on a weekend, their bikes on a rack at the back of the car. They would ride for miles and miles. Cycling meant he had a developed a good set of muscular thighs, but the rest of his body needed work.

He had watched hours of videos on YouTube to try and become competent with weight lifting, so he wouldn't look a fool in the gym by doing it incorrectly. He had trained his chest on the first day in the hotel gym before work. On the second day he had trained his back. Today he was working on making his arms bigger. He got talking to an English woman in the gym. She was with the DW30 Summit and when he asked what she did, she said she worked for MI5. Harry was impressed. MI5 did all the secret security work for the United Kingdom. James Bond was MI6, he did the international secret security work. She asked why he was in the hotel and was surprised to find he was working there. She asked where he was from and he told her London. They carried on talking between Harry's sets of bicep curls.

He dried off in the locker room after a shower. Harry thought some of her questions about his family were strange. It was almost like she knew his dad. His dad worked for a big security company, but he didn't know a lot else. Maybe their paths had crossed because of his work. If he saw her again, he'd ask her.

*

Only some of the conference guests had checked in by the time Harry started his shift at four in the afternoon. He stood at the front desk and waited to be given his next menial task.

A contractor stood amongst guests checking in at the polished oak reception desk. He wore big heavy work boots, oil stained white t-shirt and hard wearing trousers. The receptionists manning the desk weren't getting the opportunity to speak to him. His exasperation was showing. The man who looked more like a tanned surfer with swept back blonde curly hair, was at the end of his tether and about to blow. Before he did, Harry took the initiative.

"Anything I can help you with, Sir?" Harry asked.

"Please. I just need to get this to Cheryl in the office," he said.

He held up what looked like a form. Harry took hold of the slip of paper.

"What is it?" Harry asked.

"It's a service report for the crusher," the contractor said.

Harry looked at the paper, then at him, then back at the paper. He was even more bemused.

"That big red machine the size of a container in the loading bay, it compacts all the hotels waste. Just think of it as a big trashcan. I just gave the machine its yearly service and it's all working fine. Can you ensure Cheryl gets the service report please, dude?" the contractor asked.

"Not a problem, I'll take it to her now," Harry said.

"Thanks man, you're a life saver," the contractor said.

He picked up his toolbox and walked towards the exit.

"Sorry, what's your name please, Sir?" Harry shouted.

"Mark Baxter, dude, I've signed and printed at the bottom of the form," he said.

Harry didn't have a clue who Cheryl was. All he knew was that she worked in the office and needed the paper that was currently in his hand. He made his way behind reception and into the back office.

"Cheryl?" he asked in a raised voice.

A brown haired woman in her fifties looked up.

"Yes," she said.

Harry walked over and passed her the piece of paper, telling her what the contractor had said.

Cheryl smiled.

"Thanks, sweety, you should talk up more often, I love an English accent," she said.

Harry headed back to the reception desk with a spring in his step and grin on his face. He was immediately handed a Mexican take away menu and told to deliver it to a room on the eighth floor.

Officially, nobody was allowed on the roof of the hotel from the first morning of the DW30, to the end of the summit. However, curiosity had gotten the better of Kelsi and Harry.

Throughout their shift they had seen the Secret Service moving equipment to the top of the hotel. On one occasion they had even shared a service elevator with an agent. They had been told they weren't allowed to share elevators with them, but the special agent asked if the pair wanted to ride with him until they reached their floor. Harry had watched the man in awe. They had been in their civvies earlier, but when Harry had seen the Secret Service Agent later on, he had been suited and booted. He had an earpiece fitted and pistol holstered at his hip. He was even wearing sunglasses and looked like one of the Men in Black. This boy was ready to rock and roll. The Secret Service was an entity Harry knew little about. His curiosity was extra strong.

Their plan was straightforward. When they reached the roof and were questioned, they would simply say they had forgotten the rules. Harry's apprehension grew as he saw the control panel of the elevator displaying the floors, seventeen, eighteen, nineteen, twenty. The car stopped on the twenty first floor. He pulled the internal door. When Harry opened the next door he fully expected one or more armed Secret Service Agents to be staring at him. Agents with hands holstered on their Glock 19 pistols, or even pointed directly at him. Harry pulled the exterior door just enough to see the agents in front of him. Except there was nobody there. Not a single soul on the rooftop.

There would be Secret Service Agents on the roof of any building the POTUS was resident of, for no matter how long his stay. In an undisclosed location more agents would be listening to the communication between local airport air traffic control towers and any aeroplanes in the area. If an aircraft had to be told to divert its course more than three times, the Secret Service listening station would inform the agents on the roof of the President's building of residency. Standing ready with a chain gun and surface to air missile launchers, agents would get ready for a potential attack from the air. They could also observe any person or vehicle below them, trying to gain access to the hotel without permission.

Harry didn't know why there wasn't anybody on the rooftop, especially considering all the Secret Service equipment. It was a very serious setup. Harry wouldn't be touching any of the weaponry. He didn't dare.

"Stop," Harry shouted, "you look with your eyes, not your hands."

Kelsi was about to grab hold of the chain gun.

"It's okay," she said, "I've been to a gun club a few times."

"It' not okay, it might be alarmed and then you'll get us shot, sacked at the very least," he said.

Looping his hands around her waist Harry pulled her away from of the heavy duty weapon. He had ruined her fun, but she could see his point. Kelsi liked having his arms wrapped around her. She turned around to kiss him and she wanted him to kiss her back. The elevator at the other end of the rooftop pinged. That was it. Now they were in trouble.

Jay and Kim stepped from the other service elevator.

"There's nobody here," Kelsi shouted over.

"Time for a smoke then," Jay announced.

"I'll open the bar and get some beers," Kim said.

Everyone smiled. Jay pulled a bar stool up and Kelsi joined him. Harry spotted something on the floor.

"Hey, guys, what's this?" he asked.

Jay pulled a packet of cigarettes from a trouser pocket.

"What is it?" he shouted over.

"Looks like blood to be honest," Harry shouted back.

Kim was convinced she knew the answer.

"Probably red wine, the wind is always blowing wine glasses over," she said.

"Does red wine normally go crusty?" Harry asked.

                                   *

Carrying a tray of cold drinks, conference manager Amanda stepped onto the rooftop terrace. The Secret Service agents had their weapons drawn for when the elevator doors opened.

The older, grey haired agent was closest.

"Stay where you are and state your business," he said.

The concertina outer door of the elevator had only been half pulled open. Antoni Souza stayed out of sight and unseen to the agents. Amanda took one pace forward.

"Stop and state your business, or we'll shoot," he repeated.

She stopped. Tray of drinks in her left hand.

She exaggerated her French accent.

"Apologies Monsieur," Amanda said.

The younger, black haired agent looked at her with suspicion.

"What are you doing up here? You're not authorised to be on the top floor," he added.

"Oui oui," she said, "I was just bringing you some light refreshment."

"That is not acceptable madam," the older agent said. "Thank you for your hospitality, but we cannot accept those gifts. Now kindly step back into the elevator and get off this floor."

"Pas possible, monsieur," she said.

Amanda turned the tray in the direction of the grey haired agent. She shot him in the chest with the silenced pistol she was hiding under the tray. A split second before she fired, Antoni stepped out from behind the elevator door. He fired at the younger agent. Grey hair and black hair, older and younger, both died together. Antoni walked straight over and shot them both in the head. Their equipment could stay where it was. Nobody was going to be using it.

Normally when any close protection officer falls to the floor and is horizontal for more than three seconds, alarm bells start ringing. They carry a sensor that enables this to happen. The sensor is also connected to their pulse and will show when their heart stops beating. Every other officer is notified that one of their colleagues is down, most likely through a hostile act. An automatic tracking device on the principal, the POTUS in this case, automatically kicks into life and their whereabouts are recorded from that moment forwards. Unfortunately for the Secret Service and the POTUS, the boss's team of hackers had managed to remotely break firewall after firewall and defeat the system. They had planted a virus which infected the operating system of all the devices in a chosen locality. Fort Lauderdale. The virus stopped information from the sensor reaching the transmitter. As far as anyone observing the status of any Secret Service Agents at the Atlantic Grand would know, they were still upright and their hearts were still beating.

Years before the DW30 Summit had even been thought of, the boss had formed a team of his own. They compromised South America's best listeners and hackers. The listeners had been poached from

Sistema Brasileiro de Inteligencia. They were offered a very healthy wage and resettlement package to move to Colombia and work for his organisation. To obtain the services of the latter experts, the hackers, a jail break had been necessary. A team of mercenaries had staged the jailbreak which had commanded national press coverage. The team of four was formed. They took up their office packed with all the computers and advanced listening software they would need. They were ready to wreak havoc.

*

Taking a beer from Kim, Harry joined the trio at the bar. Jay joined in the conversation after lighting up and smoking a cigarette. He added his own stories of the shift. All in all nothing had happened, nothing that wouldn't normally happen during a big influx of guests, anyway. A few rooms had requested another hair dryer. One senior political advisor from Chile hadn't been happy with the view from his room and wanted to see the Atlantic Ocean, not the hotel's car park. An ambulance had to be called for an elderly correspondent of The Jerusalem Post and a number of rooms had requested more pillows.

Jay pulled the crumpled packet of cigarettes from his pocket and offered them around. Nobody took one. He inhaled his second cigarette and as the tip glowed red, Jay took more smoking paraphernalia from his pockets. Removing a small dark brick from his pocket, he unwrapped the packet and the pungent smell hit Harry's nose instantly.

"Rather ironic don't you think," said Kelsi, "you're rolling a spliff and downstairs there are a few hundred people, meeting to discuss a war on drugs."

Jay smiled and licked the rolling paper to finish his creation. He offered the spliff around. This time Kim and Kelsi took a few drags. In no time the first spliff had been smoked and Jay was rolling a second. Kim closed the bar down and a new spliff was passed around. It was offered to Harry.

He looked at the spliff.

I'm not sure," he said.

"How come, dude?" asked Jay

"I've never done drugs before, I've never smoked either," he said, "I don't want to smoke because I'm joining the British Army when I finish school next year, I want to be as fit as I can be."

Kelsi put a supporting hand on Harry's knee.

"Don't do it if you don't want, Harry," she said.

Jay started blowing smoke rings.

At the back of Harry's mind was the thought of a wild vacation. Sex, drugs and rock and roll. It was telling him to take a drag. He thought if he did, he might even look cool enough to pop his cherry with Kelsi.

"What are you Harry, a man, or you a pussy?" Jay asked.

It was true what he said, but joining the British Army was over a year away. He'd always wondered what weed was like. Just once wouldn't hurt and Jay had just offered a proper challenge.

"Man, or pussy?" Jay asked again.

"Seriously Harry, don't do it if you don't want," said Kelsi.

"Pass it here," Harry said.

Jay handed him the spliff.

"You smoke that end," Jay said.

He pointed to unlit end. Harry smiled a fake smile at Jay.

"Why thank you," he said.

Taking hold of the spliff, Harry gave Jay the middle finger.

He inhaled. Smoke filled his lungs. He coughed and spluttered. Jay laughed as Harry wafted the smoke from his eyes.

"Stop laughing, Jayden," Kelsi said. She shot Jay an evil glare.

Harry passed the spliff back to Jay. He took another drag and passed it to Kim. The spliff made another loop around. Kim to Kelsi, to Jay and then back to Harry. This time he was more effective when he dragged the smoke down to his lungs. A little spluttering this time, but not as much as before. The spliff made its third and final pass around the group.

Harry was pale and visibly sweating.

"Are you alright, Harry?" asked Jay.

"Is weed always so strong?" he asked.

Jay laughed. Kelsi shot him another glare and turned to Harry. She pulled a sad face and put a hand on Harry's shoulder.

"When was the last time you ate?" she asked.

"About midday, but I had a protein shake just before work," he said.

"This isn't weed, Harry. It's still cannabis, but it's hash. It's what's known as Nepalese Temple Balls. It's a bit stronger buddy," Jay said.

"I wouldn't know, I haven't smoked it before!" Harry said.

The beads of sweat on his forehead were growing.

"Let's get Harry to the Porter's Lodge and he can sleep. We'll get something for the munchies and come back to the Lodge. Okay?" Kelsi said rhetorically.

CHAPTER EIGHT

'Help. Help us. Atlantic Grand. Armed men. Machine guns. South American. Help me. Wild men. Rounding everyone up. Please help. Firing their weapons. Going crazy. Guns. Fort Lauderdale. Send the police. Shooting at the ceiling. Someone's been hit. People are screaming. Shooting people. DW30 Summit. Killing people. Please help us'.

That was all the 911 dispatchers at the control centre were able to hear, before the caller's voice stopped talking. Three 911 calls were received. That was all. A burst of gunfire was heard just before the one female and two male voices each went silent.

The three dispatchers who received the calls were all female. Their ages and experience varied. Ruby Wagner was sixty five years old and had been a call handler for the Fort Lauderdale Police Department for the last thirty five years. She was two months from retirement. Ruby was the most senior of the three women working the night shift. She had just returned from the kitchenette with coffee when all three phone lines lit up. She calmly sat down at her desk and slipped on her headset.

"911. Where is your emergency?" she asked.

She began to type. The time of day was logged automatically. It was 1917.

"Okay, so your emergency is at the Atlantic Grand and what is your emergency?" she asked.

Even if the caller hadn't been able to give the details of the Atlantic Grand, longitude and latitude would have come into play and the dispatchers would know the location of the call. An affidavit for the emergency call was automatically sent to the phone network provider. When the information came back, the owner of the phone would be known. A driver's licence check and criminal history check could be made. More about the caller would be gleaned.

The youngest call dispatcher at only twenty two and the second person to answer an emergency call, was Olivia Krause. Her fingers tapped the keyboard at the speed of lightning. She wasn't able to make the caller answer any of her questions. Keywords were thrown at her. She managed to type them all onto the screen in front of her. By the time the caller's voice stopped talking, she knew the incident that was unfolding was a mere five miles away. She also knew the incident was big. Really big.

The third dispatcher was Helen Maples. She'd been doing the job for the last five years. The call she received sounded hideous. She could hear screaming in the background, running, falling, stumbling. Gun shots. The shouts and shrieks of men and women, screams and crying. The voice on the end of the line became breathless. She could hear the caller panting, faster and faster. They were running. The sound of gunfire lessened. A voice that sounded Mexican, or South American, shouted something. That voice was louder and more audible. Closer this time. 'Please. Come quickly', were the last words Helen heard the caller urge. A burst of gunfire sounded. The last sound she heard before the line went dead was the heavy thud of a body falling down. In her head she could picture the hotel perfectly. She had been there only two weeks earlier with her future daughter in law to visit a wedding fair.

All three of the dispatchers were left shaken by the 911 calls, but they carried on with what they had been trained to do. Looking at the computer screens in front of each of their workstations, they could see what details they had just taken, a map of the area and exactly which officers were in the police zone nearest the Atlantic Grand.

Olivia called officer 474 over the radio. She informed him a possible 10-85 was unfolding at the Atlantic Grand, on the corner of Fort Lauderdale Beach Boulevard and Granada Street. He was told to proceed with caution. Rather than just using numeric code to tell the officer about the incident, she used plain English. If the officer mistook the code for a 10-75, the consequences could be catastrophic. Speed and accuracy were key. She told 474 that an untold number of armed men had taken the hotel and its inhabitants by force and were firing weapons indiscriminately. This may be a terror attack or hostage incident, or both. Probable multiple casualties. Olivia then dispatched two more units. Helen dispatched four units, two from elsewhere in the city and two from headquarters.

Ruby radioed central dispatch. Historically, a police dispatcher would dispatch everything. Nowadays they transferred any large incidents to the central dispatch department of Fort Lauderdale Emergency Services. She stayed on the line with central dispatch to relay any information they required that had come directly from the callers. Central pushed the button to the Fort Lauderdale Fire Department. Three fire trucks left the main station less than two minutes later and hurtled with sirens wailing towards the scene. They were dispatched before paramedics. All fire and rescue workers were trained first responders. They were trained to save a life. More buttons were pressed. More fire tenders were called to the scene. As that conversation with the fire department was ongoing, another dispatcher from Central pressed the button to contact Fort Lauderdale Medical Services. All emergency ambulances not currently on a job were called from locations all over the city to attend the scene. Numerous others would be en route from hospitals as soon as they could leave.

The second thing Ruby did was to call her shift supervisor over and inform her of what was happening. This action was twofold. Firstly, if this was a hostage situation, the incident needed escalating to a much higher paygrade. Secondly, years in the job had told her to cover her ass. All the dispatchers had done their job perfectly. They had mobilised the world.

The shift supervisor called the lieutenant on duty. The lieutenant called the chief of police. The Chief of Police of Fort Lauderdale stopped working on his boat and came in from his backyard. He took his bullet proof vest and FLPD wind breaker from the closet under the stairs and came to work.

On his way to the Atlantic Grand, the chief called the department hostage negotiator from his car phone. In five minutes he would also be en route. Next, he called the media spokeswoman for the FLPD. Her husband answered the phone. He passed his wife the handset, saying, 'Darling, I think you need to go to work'. The next people to have their evening ruined were the Federal Bureau of Investigation.

*

There was a problem with the delivery of the guests first course. Service had halted. The banqueting manager had left the California Great Hall at 1915 to go and see what was causing the delay. Crossing the hallway he entered the main kitchen and immediately had the barrel of an AK47 shoved in his face. He was forced into a storage room to join the other members of his staff that had suffered the same fate. He sat cross legged on the floor with plasticuffs tying his hands together. In the kitchen twenty eight chefs were kneeling on the tiled floor in front of their stoves. Their hands also plasticuffed behind their backs.

Armed men had entered the California Great Hall at 1917. Brandishing weapons, South American men took the room by surprise and began screaming unintelligible orders. Guests struggled to hear them over the sound of gunfire. The feeling of euphoria the room had experienced as the comedian hired for the evening told his last joke, transcended into chaos. The men running between the tables and firing into the ceiling looked hellish. Their skin was darker than that of a Caucasian, but lighter than an African-American. They were Hispanic or South American. Dressed in dark green boiler suits with military style webbing belts around their waists and upper bodies, they swarmed the room. Four men and one woman sitting around the Great Hall tried to resist and fight back. Debris caused by shots fired into the ceiling fell on the people and tables below. Four of the guests who fought their aggressors were beaten to the floor with rifle butts. Three guests had their smartphones in their hands and were calling the police. It took the men with guns slightly longer to search them out, they couldn't be heard over the sound of chaos and violence, sobbing, screaming, crying. Two of them were shot. Their bodies fell limp, hitting the floor awkwardly they lay in unnatural positions. Their voices were silenced. The third smartphone user left the room by way of a small back corridor. A raging man in a green boiler suit and carrying a machine gun ran after him. He was heard shouting a warning. Spanish, the guest nearest the back corridor thought. The warning was followed by just one burst of gunfire.

The fifth guest who fought the antagonists was forced to stand with his back to a wall. He was made to look at the gunman in front of him. As he did he uttered in defiance words of foreboding vengeance in his native Tswana. A small number of guests looked at what was happening. Most looked away. He was summarily executed. The South African Minister for State Security was shot in the head. Blood, skull and brain, spattered against the wall and the surrounding tables. The screaming and crying of men and women reached an insurmountable level. Those hit by the flying remnants of the dead South African Minister were trying to wipe away blood and brain. Others were retching and throwing up. The guests were now scared for their lives. That was exactly what the men with guns wanted. They sent a two part message to the guests. One. You are now in our control. Two. If you try to fight us or to escape, we will end your lives in the most undignified way.

*

Kelsi, Kim and Jay, were making their way to the main kitchen to rustle some snacks to take back to the upper Porter's Lodge.

They heard screams and gun fire. Jay told the others to go and hide. He would try and see what was happening.

They ran along corridors and up the nearest service staircase. The conservative skirts of their uniform impeded their progress. Stopping on the fifth floor, they hitched their skirts up and ran faster. Hearing footsteps pounding the concrete stairwell beneath them, they stopped to look who was chasing them. It was Jay. He was running hard. Taking two, three steps at once. They did the same. Their breathing was frantic. The aim was to reach the Porter's Lodge and lock themselves in. To be hidden and not found. They heard sporadic and cacophonous gunfire emanate from below. Jay shouted up to them.

"Run, keep running and hide, I'm being chased," he shouted. "They're trying to shoot me, they want to kill us."

They heard another wave of gunfire rupture the air. They ran and ran. The girls kept to the outer edge of the stairs. Whoever was chasing them was firing upwards. Bullets zipped past. Some smashed into the railings of the staircase. All the time Jay was getting closer. The gunfire growing louder. Now on the thirteenth floor he had caught up with them. They ran together. Became one to form some kind of bond. A type of desperately put together union, to make a team so they could all survive. The chasers with their guns were three floors below. They weren't gaining or losing distance on them, but at some point they were going to run out of road. The stairwell would stop and they would have nowhere to go.

Reaching the landing of the seventeenth floor Jay turned right through a fire door. The other two followed. He ran straight along the corridor and darted left at a junction, down a less used corridor and towards that floor's linen cupboard. The storage area for all the clean bedsheets, pillow cases and towels.

Holding the door open, Kelsi and Kim darted into the room.

"Hide," urged Jay.

Three sides of the room were filled with floor to ceiling purpose built wooden racking. Kim took the right hand side and the floor level shelf, hiding under bed sheets and pillow cases. Kelsi chose the middle wall facing the door. Once Jay had frantically put linen over Kim, he did the same for Kelsi. Both were completely hidden. Speed was now of the essence. Jay took the bottom shelf on the left, directly over from Kim's hiding place. He covered himself with towels as best he could. He was hidden. All tried to equalise their breathing and become silent. The last thing Jay whispered was, 'turn your phones off'.

Because the hotel had only been refurbished two years previously, the door mechanism that ensured the fire door from the stairwell to the corridor closed softly, was in good working order. The mechanism was still working to ensure the door didn't bang when the two men giving chase reached the seventeenth floor. They knew where Kim, Kelsi and Jay had exited the stairwell.

*

Seconds before the armed assault on the California Great Hall began, Marie and Pablo who had been previously masquerading as Amanda and Antoni, came to the lobby of the hotel. With their silenced pistols they killed the three Unified Event Security guards manning the front door. That was all there was. The staff entrance and all other exterior entrances and exits to the hotel had been previously sealed by the Secret Service.

CHAPTER NINE

Right from her time working as an intern for the Governor of Montana, Claudia Cane had championed women. She believed in equal rights, equal pay and giving women the credit they deserved for their achievements. She had brought them to the fore as she made her own first steps into politics. That strategy had continued as she grew politically and became more prominent within the Republican Party. Trucking in North America was a man's world. Presenting the North American Women in Transport Awards would further her fight to bring women to the fore in industry. It would also help to set herself up as the number one candidate for the presidential elections in three years' time.

The winner of the most prestigious award of the night was making her way to the stage. Caroline Byrne had a smile on her face. Her head was held high as she walked towards the front of the room. This was her moment and she was going to enjoy it. She climbed the steps to the stage. Claudia smiled warmly and held forward the award and a bouquet of flowers. Caroline smiled back. Her smile turned to a look of horror as five suits, two of them with handguns drawn, rapidly walked on stage.

The female suit drew her weapon as well.

"Stay where you are Madam vice-President," she said.

The agent pointed her sidearm at Caroline.

"Stay there, please," she said.

Caroline stopped dead in her tracks. The suits took hold of Claudia Caine. The award was dropped. The flowers crushed and trampled. The vice-President of the United States of

America was bundled across the stage and out of a side door. Claudia's feet barely touched the floor. She was manhandled out of the building by her Secret Service Agents. Rushing her towards the exit, the vice-President was told of the situation in Fort Lauderdale and how until resolved, she was in charge of the country.

*

Having FBI and Secret Service Agents on guard at the Drugs War Thirty would prove incredibly costly. DW30 had done what the United States Government does for many of its large scale diplomatic events. After the building had been thoroughly searched, checked and sealed by the Secret Service, Unified Event Security (UES) had been hired to provide security in the hotel. The Secret Service agents on the roof of the hotel wouldn't see the truck approach, they had already been eliminated.

The UES Security Guard posted to the loading bay heard the loud revving engine and raised the roller shutter door. The delivery wasn't on the manifest, but an hour earlier the conference manager had handed him a printed note. The note gave the details of a semi-truck: colour, manufacturer, model, licence plate. The driver's name was Brian. As the driver inched his truck back to the loading dock, the security guard gestured for the truck to keep reversing. When required, he raised a hand and the truck stopped on the spot. The licence plate checked out. The colour of the truck and trailer fitted with what was on the note. He couldn't see the model and the manufacturer of the truck, but he presumed they also matched. According to the note, the delivery should be six pallets of wine, an easy delivery for the driver. He just had to push his pump truck under the pallets and pull them free of the trailer. The driver climbed from the truck cab and walked round to the steel steps. The paperwork for the load was pulled from the leg pocket of his black cargo trousers as he walked. He was wearing a Kenworth baseball cap. The name Kenworth corresponded with the manufacturer of the truck on the printed note.

"Evening," said the security guard.

"Gute nacht," said the driver.

Along with the load docket, he had pulled a silenced handgun from his leg pocket. Klaus shot the guard twice in the chest. He fell to the floor. Klaus stood over him and shot the guard in the head. He dragged the body to the side and opened the trailer.

The first man who stepped out of the back of the trailer was the boss. His full name was Alejandro Diego Munoz. He was better known as Bothrops Atrox. After him came the younger of the two Germans, Christian. Following them were the fifty eight men from his native Colombia that Bothrops Atrox had recruited for the task.

The first German, the older of the pair, had been the driver of the truck. Klaus didn't even look like a Brian. There were three westerners involved in what was about to take place. Christian and Klaus, both ex-members of the elite German Police unit Grenz-schutzgruppe9 (GSG9) and Marie Thouvenin. When Marie was only twelve years old, her family had emigrated to Colombia from France. The boss had known her since she was fifteen years old. Marie Thouvenin and one of the boss's two sons, Pablo Emiliano Munoz, had gained jobs using aliases in the hotel prior to the conference. Both had worked in the conference department for one year and six months, respectively. His other son, the older of the brothers, Santiago Matias Munoz, was elsewhere. The boss climbed the three basement floors from the loading bay. He met Marie and Pablo as he strode along a corridor. He hugged and shook hands with his son, he hadn't seen him for six months. He hugged and kissed Marie and told her to remove 'Amanda's' name badge. He hadn't seen his favourite mistress for over a year. He wanted to be with her again. Fast. First however, there was work to be done. With fifty four of his men, Pablo, Marie and Christian at his side, the boss headed for the California Great Hall

As they walked the first floor corridors of the hotel, Marie told Alejandro that she had put on a small dinner for the official security services in the hotel. Agents from the Secret Service, Diplomatic Protection Service of Great Britain and personnel from five other countries, were having dinner in the second floor restaurant. Nine of the boss's men, overseen by an ex-Colombian Army Sergeant, headed to the restaurant to silence them.

Klaus had stayed in the loading bay to oversee the unloading of the cargo from the semi-truck. Nothing could be left in the trailer. Everything was needed. Five green suited men were left at the loading dock. They pulled, rolled and dragged everything from the trailer. They unloaded wheeled industrial boxes, containers of weapons and ammunition, hard plastic cases full of reels of electrical cable and cameras. More plastic tough cases crammed full of computer equipment were taken alongside LED flatscreens, sensory equipment and control panels, as well as sheeted pallets of equipment marked with a skull and cross bones. Once the trailer was empty, Klaus dispatched the four men to pre-selected hotel bedrooms. They removed what they needed and disposed of it in the compactor. That was the last time anyone would exit the hotel until it was over. The loading bay shutter door was lowered and locked. Everything was ready for the assault on the Atlantic Grand. The equipment pulled from the trailer was pushed into elevators and brought up to the first floor. The loading bay was left barren. Under Klaus' close eye, the four men the boss left in the loading bay were his explosives team. GSG9 did more than just armed raids. The explosives team heard shooting. The assault had begun.

The gunfire started. The sergeant and his men on the second floor stepped out from the shadows. They took the lives of twenty one of the world's finest close protection officers. Every one of them was hosed down by 7.62mm AK47 rounds. It was sudden and deadly. It was a bloodbath.

*

The despatchers' emergency phone lines lit up again. The media listening on police scanners had heard about the unfolding incident. They called to get a quote from the dispatchers. The dispatchers didn't tell them anything.

From there on in, their shift supervisor called the immediate shots. All local resources were going to be tied up on this incident for many hours, if not days to come. Neighbouring police departments were contacted. Extra units were arranged to come down to Fort Lauderdale and cover patrols. With all their officers tied up at the Atlantic Grand and a street presence not maintained, Fort Lauderdale's less honest citizens may use the crisis for their own gain. Furthermore, media silence was insisted upon.

In a city of one hundred and seventy five thousand people, five hundred and fifteen police officers served Fort Lauderdale. Police Officers on duty were sent to the scene. Off duty officers were called back to the station. Most were at home, but two had driven down to Miami and were about to watch a basketball game. One sergeant was taking her daughter to a Girl Scouts meeting. Two more officers were at their children's football games. Their sons had to be called in off the field to take their pads off early.

The first police officers at the scene had already begun setting up a cordon around the hotel. The area was sealed tight. Police officers stood behind their cars, plastic cones and crime scene tape. More and more pulled up and strengthened the cordon. Officers fanned out and they made a line around the Atlantic Grand. Tank Bolling, the FLPD Swat Team commander arrived in the FLPD Hummer. He was followed by a heavily armoured SWAT Truck. It was a huge vehicle. Ten SWAT officers climbed out of the back door. Two jumped down from the cab. Dressed in dark grey camouflage pants and black t-shirts, overt bullet proof vests and pockets brimming with ammunition, they were ready for action. Tank posted snipers to the tallest buildings surrounding the Atlantic Grand. He ensured another

SWAT team was ready for an immediate assault if the situation worsened. The police helicopter had been scrambled and was overhead. On the roads outside the cordon, ambulances and fire trucks lined the streets. Parked up and waiting. The crews remained in a staged state. Vigilant and ready for action.

*

The raid on the hotel had been a resounding success. Immediately afterwards, paired terrorists were sent to search all of the bedrooms in the hotel. One pair searched the three basement floors. More gun shots were heard. A total of eighty four people were brought down from bedrooms to join the main group of hostages. Two teams of five terrorists were dispatched to set up camera surveillance equipment on the third floor. The cameras overlooked the hotel grounds and adjacent streets. Ten cameras per side, a full panoramic view was attained. These live images were to be displayed on large screens currently being set up in the Indiana Media Suite. The terrorists now had three hundred and sixty degree surveillance. A team of five was also sent to the roof to apply sensors. The sensors would detect anything that came within twenty feet. Nothing could now land on the roof without their knowledge. Klaus's team had finished rigging the loading bay with sensors and explosives. The team split and began fitting all other exterior doors with more of the same. Once that was complete. The hotel would be sealed. No way in. No way out.

*

The affidavits for information on the 911 callers came back after fifteen minutes. One call was made from a network provider in the United States. The caller was Larry Knowles from New Haven, Connecticut, the Commandant of the United States Coastguard. Another was made from a smartphone registered to a Roisin O'Leary, from Kiltealy in County Wexford, the Republic of Ireland, the most senior secretary to the Irish Prime Minister. The third phone call was made by Felix Schleck, a correspondent from the Letzebeurg Privat newspaper who had travelled to the DW30 from Luxembourg.

The Fort Lauderdale Police Department handled its own hostage situations. However this was much bigger than anything they had dealt with before. The building was bigger. There were more hostages. Many of the hostages were high profile and even higher value. It appeared there were more hostage takers. The world would soon be turning on its television sets, scanning the internet and reading the morning papers. If it wasn't before, the world would definitely be watching the DW30 Summit now.

Officer 474 lifted the crime scene tape for FLPD Bomb Squad and their robot. He kept the tape raised. 474 recognised the unmarked car with emergency lights hidden in the grill. It belonged to Chief of Police Chris Schlemmer.

*

Harry was woken by faraway noises. Dull bangs like fire crackers. Clapping and cheering, he thought. The guests at the DW30 Summit must be having one hell of a party. His head was pounding and he felt groggy. Feeling thirsty and terrible, he rolled off the make-shift bed of boxes. He fumbled around in darkness until he found a bottle of water. Unscrewing the cap and hearing a hiss, he knew it was sparkling water. His choice would have been still water. At that moment he didn't care. He just needed fluids. He gulped down half a bottle and slumped back on the boxes to continue his slumber. He made himself a promise. Never do drugs. Ever again.

*

The boss had to deplete the number of hostages. Every hostage would need access to water. Every hostage would need feeding.

If they were fed and watered, every hostage would need to use the toilet, numerous times per day. The boss would have to use a large number of his men for this purpose. It was easier to eradicate the problem than to deal with it.

He had toyed with the idea of executing them, but that would require a lot more ammunition. All he would be left with was a pile of cadavers that would start smelling in the heat. The more serious matter a mass execution created, was the justification of an immediate response from the special forces. He knew they would be arriving soon. His decision was to let some of the hostages go free, but not just anyone. All the hostages were of differing levels of value. Some of them not valuable at all.

A week before he had taken the hotel by force, Marie had emailed him a final list of the hotel workers and guests that would be present on the first evening of the Drugs War Thirty Summit. He had made his own list. In the California Great Hall that was what his son now read from. Keeping hotel staff hostage wasn't going to help his cause. They were valueless. They were the first names that were read out.

Pablo stood in the centre of the Great Hall with a clipboard.

"Some of you are to be released immediately," Pablo shouted, "Joanna Goulder."

A waitress stood up and walked to the centre of the room.

"Tim Suiters," he called.

An older gent walked to the centre and stood behind his colleague.

"Jayden Jones," Pablo requested.

Nobody moved.

"Jayden Jones," he shouted again.

He got the same result and was about to call out for him a third time. A green boiler suit had a word in his ear. Three staff would not come to the centre of the room. They had been shot and killed while trying to evade capture. Harry's name wasn't called, officially he didn't exist in the hotel, he was being paid from the petty cash tin and Pablo's mind was too busy than to subconsciously engage itself with thoughts of the English kid he had only met briefly. If he had have thought of Harry, he would have assumed the little wimp was hiding and crying for his momia.

The line of hotel workers continued to grow until three lines were needed. Adding up to one hundred and eighty staff, the lines included waiters, waitresses, porters, conference porters, chefs, receptionists and backroom office staff. The hotel manager's name wasn't called. The boss had thought for a long time about this. He decided she was a valuable asset. She would know the hotel inside out. The last person to join the line was the well-known comedian, who would no doubt go on to tell of this moment when broadcasting his weekly Saturday night television show. Bothrops was certain the entertainer must be saved. He regularly watched the comedy show.

Next to be called was anybody from the media. Their presence in the hotel was entirely unnecessary and more importantly, unwanted. The media were not fans of the boss. They either called him by his full name, or Barba Amarilla. Never Bothrops Atrox. Felix Schleck, the journalist from Luxembourg didn't have the opportunity join the queue. Thirty two journalists and reporters joined the lines of releasees.

Political advisers, aides and secretaries were the last to be called. Their four lines came to a total of two hundred and fourteen. Even if she hadn't already been slain in the initial violent capture of the hotel, Roisin O'Leary wouldn't have been called upon. She was the senior secretary to the Irish Prime Minster and she read much of what he read. She needed a high level of security clearance.

The hostages were now divided. Those staying sat at the side of the California Great Hall. They were ordered to strip down to their underwear. Once the hostages had removed their clothes, all the garments were piled in one corner of the room. The terrorists didn't want anyone to have any form of communication on their person. Ordered to drop their communication devices in a bin, they complied. The hostages had first-hand experience of what could happen to them if they resisted. The releasees were stood in the centre of the Great Hall. Terrorists pulled black cloth hoods from three wheeled bins. They handed them out. The lucky hostages were told to pull the hoods onto their heads, fully obscure their vision and place their hands on the shoulders of the person in front. They all did as they were told.

Before the front doors to the hotel were fully sealed with explosives and sensors, the hostages to be released were walked from the California Great Hall to the front of the hotel.

"You are now being released. Keep your hoods on and your hands holding the person in front. Walk down the steps. Once you are in the car park, you may remove your hoods. Walk straight forwards. Do not turn around. If anyone turns around and looks at us, your colleague that is about to leave the hotel will be shot in the head," said an unknown voice.

Once the releasees were at the bottom of the steps, they ran. Some of them not bothering to remove their hoods until they were out of the car park and in the middle of the road. Nobody turned. Fifteen minutes after the first hotel worker had been freed, the last political secretary left the building.

*

A white panel truck drove up to the police cordon. The five tonne box truck buzzed it's air horn and flashed it's emergency lights. Members of the public, fire and ambulance personnel moved aside to let it pass. The FLPD Tactical Operations Command vehicle was allowed through the barriers, kitted out with computers, display screens, communication devices, as well as its own meeting room and bathroom, the command unit was a head office on wheels.

After the command vehicle, a hot food truck came in from the south. The truck's owner had been tipped off by a buddy with a radio scanner. A big incident was unfolding at the Atlantic Grand. Parked up on the other side of the street to the no entry cordon, the driver of the food truck began to set up shop. As soon as his interior lights were turned on, his first customers were waiting. The TV fixed to the back wall of the truck sprang to life. The driver's son, dragged to the scene by his father as his mother wasn't at home to look after him and who was no more than five years old, perched himself in front of the screen to see MTV's latest video. Officer 474 and officer 210 ordered coffees. They were in for a long shift. As their coffee was brewing, officer 474 answered the vibrating smartphone in his pocket. It was his girlfriend.

"You guys down at the Atlantic Grand? You need to watch NBC," she said.

"Hey, change the TV channel to NBC, please," 474 said.

The food truck's driver who was now wearing chef whites, took the remote from his son and flicked through the channels. They all watched as the NBC presenter introduced a live link to events unfolding inside the Atlantic Grand. Officer 210 got the message to the command truck. Six people huddled around the television screen to watch the National Broadcasting Company (NBC).

CHAPTER TEN

The NBC presenter cut to a live link.

"These people are my hostages," said the South American on the screen.

He said it carefully. His English was very good, but it wasn't his first language. He said it slowly because he wanted everyone watching to understand that fighting back and trying to make a rescue attempt was futile.

She shook her head.

"I am sorry, but I have not got time for that man," said Teonnie.

Her tall, black and slender, catwalk model like frame watched NBC from a TV set inside the police command truck.

"Bothrops Atrox is a murderer, a Colombian murderer. Call him a drug lord if you want, but he is just a murderer. Do you know how much money that scumbag earns each year from other people's misery?" she asked.

"Quiet," said the chief of police.

She was his personal assistant. Enjoying a week of annual leave, she was out for a drink on the Fort Lauderdale beachfront with the girls. She'd received a phone call from Chief Schlemmer. All it took were the words, 'I'm going to need you,' and she was on her way to help. She hadn't even been home to change. Still dressed in heels and mini skirt, someone who didn't know her would think she had been hired for her looks. It was anything but. Teonnie had worked for Chief Schlemmer for the last four years and was the most effective secretary he'd ever had. He often thought it was her sass and 'you ain't messin' with me' attitude, that made her so damn effective.

Alejandro Diego Munoz, the boss, was better known as Bothrops Atrox, or just 'Bothrops'. He had been nicknamed after one of his country's most deadly snakes. A venomous pit viper found in the tropical lowlands of his Colombia. He enjoyed almost God-like respect from the country's residents. Many of them and their families had prospered from his good fortune. Those in his country who didn't afford him any respect knew him by the snake's Spanish name, 'Barba amarilla'. Simply meaning, yellow beard.

"Take a good look, you will recognise many of my hostages. Cowering behind me is the President of the United States of America, the leader of the free world, Huey Ace. He doesn't look so free now, does he? He is joined by members from thirty governments of the world. In addition to Huey Ace, we have Canadian Prime Minister Jacob Fournier in captivity. So too is British Home Secretary Fiona McKerral and head of the British Military Intelligence Section Five, Jacinda Armstrong. Dutch Prime Minister Tim De Vries, South African President Bokamoso Govender, The Australian head of customs Alfred Anderson and Jamaican Governor General, Mpho Reid," said Bothrops.

The camera panned out. He proudly pointed to the front line of hostages.

"My God. Unbelievable, everyone is there. Every major player in world politics. Mother above, they got everyone," Teonnie said.

"One person has already perished because he chose to fight back. Three more are dead because they were reckless enough to call for help on their mobile telephones. The people behind me are all in their under garments. This is for security reasons, not because we are pandering to some strange sexual fetish. We are very serious. You will do what we ask. If you do not, your leaders will die," he said.

Bothrops Atrox stood back and smiled.

"This message is for the Chief of the Fort Lauderdale Police Department, Mr Schlemmer. I know he is outside, I've seen him in his bullet proof vest. Tell your SWAT Teams to be very careful. We have attached explosives to every door that leads outside. We have placed sensors on the doors, windows and roof. No matter how carefully you try to get around it," said Bothrops, "we will know when a sensor is triggered."

Five men wearing dark green boiler suits and ski masks entered the television picture. They roughly pulled Huey Ace from the front line of hostages. Even though he had served eight years in the United States Marine Corps, he was easily overpowered. The president was forced to kneel. His mouth was taped shut. He tried to resist and pull away. He got a rifle butt to the side of the face and fell to the floor. Instantly his head started bleeding. He lay limp and barely conscious. Female hostages shrieked and began crying. The begging of the hostage takers to stop, began. A burst of automatic rifle fire thundered from somewhere off camera. The pleading stopped as plaster fell from the ceiling. The hostage takers did not stop. Semi-conscious and with blood running down the side of his face, President Ace was pulled back onto his knees. The plastic ties cuffing his hands together were cut. His arms fell forward. Two masked men grabbed them and pulled his arms away from his body. Another terrorist entered the screen carrying what looked like a bullet proof vest. Huey Ace was obscured from view for only a matter of seconds, but that was all it took for the masked men to put him in the vest. His hands were forced behind his back and retied. Those in the room with him looked forlorn and lost. Women cried and sniffed. Men sighed and whimpered. Others tried to remain composed. A suicide vest packed full of explosives had been strapped to the chest of the President. Huey Ace was dragged to the front of the room to the side of Bothrops Atrox. He was passed a list and read aloud the names of fifteen more heads of state, or government members. They were pulled to the front to join Huey Ace as he regained consciousness.

Teonnie scribbled furiously on a piece of paper.

The front of the room had already been cleared. At the back of the room green suited men directed by a more senior figure, cleared tables of cutlery and plates. Table cloths were pulled and table legs folded. Round tables wheeled off screen. The room left bare.

"The sixteen people behind me are now going to be taken to another part of the hotel. Huey Ace will be sat in the centre, the others sitting around him. If the seal on any door, or glass in any door is broken, a remote detonator will be triggered. The suicide vest will be set off. All will perish and you Mr Schlemmer, will be responsible," announced Bothrops.

The screen went blank.

The next person on the NBC broadcast was the presenter back in the studio. Teonnie handed the piece of scribbled paper to her boss. On it were sixteen names.

"Where was his demand?" Teonnie asked.

Al Brody had been making his own notes.

"He didn't make one," he said.

"So what does he want?" said another voice.

Police officers had jammed themselves inside the command truck to see the broadcast.

"My guess is the release of prisoners in his cartel, both in the US and Colombia," said Al.

"You ever had a job as big?" a different voice asked.

"Nothing in eighteen years since I started pounding the pavements," answered Al.

"Enough aimless chatter," said Schlemmer. "We are dealing with Bothrops Atrox, a ruthless and vicious man. Maybe the most ruthless and vicious man on the planet. Unless you are doing something of vital importance to the current situation, you help Al. Until the FBI arrive he is the senior hostage negotiator at the scene. They are not expected to get here until midnight at the earliest. I want everything we know about Alejandro Diego Munoz. How he started off in life. I want parents' names and siblings' names. I want Al to know everything about his wife, his children, his mistresses, even his pets. Al needs to know everything he owns, every politician he has had killed. All of it. I want every hook on him. Anyway Al can get to him, I want to know what it is, no matter how trivial and I want it in thirty minutes. It's going to be a long night folks."

"This is one hell of a big job," said Tank Bolling.

He made his way down the steps from the command truck. Jim was Bolling's real name, but no one used that. Since a young age, he'd been built like a tank.

"Tell me about it, it's bigger than us," Chief Schlemmer replied.

He followed Tank outside and lit a cigarette.

"Above all, I don't want this becoming another Beslan, or a Waco," he urged.

Chief Schlemmer took a drag.

"Externally, we've got everything covered," said Tank. "My guys are in position on top of all the surrounding buildings. Every rooftop with good visibility has a pair of snipers. We have a team staged and ready to go in at the drop of a hat. Now that looks like it'll be impossible. Internally, we can't get anything covered. When the FBI send in their agents, they are going to do the same and get the exact same result. Outside yes. Inside, no. We're just going to be here for crowd control."

"In an ideal situation, we'd be able to get a pair of eyes inside. There's no way of drilling into the walls to feed a camera inside, the walls are all glass, we'd be spotted and the place is too damn big. We'd need a hundred yards of cable once we are on the inside, just to get anywhere near the hostages. We need to get a man in the hotel to reconnoitre for us. See what the score is, see if what Bothrops says is true," said Schlemmer.

*

It was the sound of a fire engine that woke him. The driver blasting the air horn to clear the crowd as he got closer to the scene. People heard fire trucks every day, but they didn't hear numerous other sirens at the same time, especially not pulling up on the street outside their window. That made Harry roll out of his ad hoc bed and pull the curtains wide. He was shocked. What on earth was happening? From the nineteenth floor he could see everything on the southern side of the hotel and at the intersection below him. And a little to the west.

The streets surrounding the hotel had been shut down. Police road blocks stopped people from entering an exclusion zone. Beyond the police barricades were ambulances and fire trucks, lined up and parked. Fire fighters were out of their trucks, standing around and chatting. It was the same story with the ambulances. At the intersection nearest him, a police van was setting up a search light. The block was awash with emergency services.

*

The unscheduled NBC broadcast had also been playing on a screen in the 911 despatch control room. The dispatchers and their supervisor had been stunned as they watched the unfolding horror at the Atlantic Grand.

Olivia Krause took the next urgent call.

"911, where is your emergency?" she asked.

"Hello," said the English voice, "I'm a hotel porter working at the Atlantic Grand. I don't know if it's an emergency here, or next door. I'm a bit concerned, is there a fire?"

Olivia was stunned. The voice didn't sound urged by anything, or under any kind of duress. It was strange given what the other calls had sounded like. She wondered if she had heard the voice correctly.

"Can you please repeat your location, caller?" she asked.

"I'm at the Atlantic Grand, in Fort Lauderdale," Harry said.

"Are you in a safe place, caller?" she asked.

"Erm. Yeah. I think so, but I don't know what I'm keeping safe from," he said.

Harry was unnerved.

"It's very important you stay in your current location. Please hold the line a second," Olivia said.

She raised an arm and waved Ruby to come over to her work station.

"I've got a man on the line, sounds like a young man, who says he's at the Atlantic Grand," she stated.

"Shit," said Ruby. "Put him back on, I'll talk to him."

The call reconnected.

"Hello caller?" Olivia said.

"Yeah," replied Harry.

"I'm going to pass you over to my colleague," she said.

Ruby plugged her headset into a free port on Olivia's computer. They both listened to the same call.

"Hello caller," the new, older voice said, "my colleague says you're at the Atlantic Grand, is that correct?"

"Yes," said Harry.

"Where are you in the hotel?" she asked.

"I'm in the upper Porter's Lodge, on the nineteenth floor," Harry replied.

"Why are you in the hotel, sir?" she asked.

"I'm a conference porter, I'm working here for the summer. The general manager is my aunty. What's happening? Why do you want me to stay where I am?" he asked.

Ruby knew that question would be asked. She knew she would have to tell him the truth. She also knew to do it in a way that kept him calm. The young man on the phone was in mortal danger.

"What's your name, caller?" she asked.

"Fearn. Harry Fearn," the caller said.

"How old are you Harry and where are you from?" Ruby asked.

"I'm seventeen. I'm from England. I live in London. I'm only working here for four weeks this summer. My aunty manages the hotel," he repeated.

"Okay Harry, thank you. Are you still in a safe place?" she asked.

"Yeah. I'm still here in the Porter's Lodge," he answered.

"What is the Porter's Lodge, Harry?" Ruby asked.

"It's a store room, it's where the hotel keeps all the things the conference porters need to supply the conference rooms. Table cloths for the tables in meeting rooms, paper, pens, bottles of water. Things like that," he said.

"Okay. Harry, I don't want you to be alarmed by what I'm about to tell you. If you stay where you are and don't move from that place, I have no reason to believe you will be in any danger," Ruby said.

That was a guess. A pure guess, but an educated one. She had been doing the job many years.

"Erm, okay," the young voice said.

Harry heard something. The distant sound of doors being opened and banging shut.

"The hotel has been raided by armed men. They have taken hostages downstairs. They haven't made any demands yet. The police outside are there to deal with it. They are very experienced and very good at their jobs. The fire trucks and ambulances are only there as a precaution, so please don't worry about that. If you stay where you are, I have no reason to believe you will come to any harm," she told him.

It was the second time she had reiterated her guess. She didn't like guessing.

"O-kay," said Harry, slowly.

The noise of doors banging shut grew closer.

"Is the number you're calling from the number for your smartphone, Harry?" the voice asked.

"Yeah, yeah it is," he quietly said.

"Ok. I want you to put your phone on silent mode and switch off the vibration function. Will you do that for me?" Ruby asked.

He could hear footsteps padding along the carpet.

"Yeah, sure. What's going on downstairs?" he asked.

Hushed urgency in his voice.

"That's what I'm about to find out. Then I'll call you back. Please do what I asked though, it's very important for your safety," she said.

Ruby clicked off the call.

Harry turned to look out of the window again. The situation below him was still the same. More and more blue lights arriving all the time. He turned to look over his shoulder when he heard voices. Voices talking in a foreign language he couldn't understand. Harry looked at his watch and wondered where Kelsi was. What was she doing? Why hadn't they come back with any food? In truth he didn't care about the food, he just wanted to know she was safe. He heard what he thought was Antoni Sousa. He knew he wasn't to be trusted. Now he thought it was his voice talking in a foreign language. There was definitely something wrong. He could hear at least two people outside. Possibly three. Someone in the corridor tried the door handle to the Porter's Lodge. Harry backed away and ducked down. He hid behind a stack of chairs. He heard the locking mechanism on the door try to engage. Someone tried the door twice more. Nothing happened. The door was locked by a master key, not a standard room key. The conference porters were the only members of staff, apart from managers, trusted with an overall master key. They needed access to rooms in the hotel that stored high value equipment. To all intents and purposes the Lodge looked like a bedroom from the outside. Only a 'private' sign on the door marked it as any different. Sousa didn't have the master key. Kelsi had taken it tonight. He said something with urgency in his tone. The footsteps and foreign voices in the corridor moved on.

Harry needed to pee, badly. He held it till he could no longer hear voices or footsteps. Luckily the Porter's Lodge had a bathroom. A full hotel bathroom with a toilet, sink and bath. Just grubbier than normal as it wasn't cleaned anymore. He could have had a bath, he would just have to remove all the junk from the tub. The room was always planned to be a bedroom, it only got downgraded to a store room for the porters after Alison worked out it would be more efficient to lose the smallest upper bedroom and have a storeroom from which the conference porters could service the rooftop terrace meeting area, than to have them lose hours and hours a year, travelling up and down elevators. Harry aimed his pee on the inside of the toilet bowl. Above the water line so it didn't splash. He didn't flush either. He didn't want to generate any noise. Most store cupboards don't have a toilet and running water, this one did and it just became Harry's stronghold.

CHAPTER ELEVEN

The street was alive. The public were amassing at the police cordon. More and more news crews arrived and set up their camera equipment. Police officers told people to 'stay back'. The crowd's noise and the sound of idling engines of police cruisers was suddenly replaced by Richard Wagner's classical composure, Ride of the Valkyries. Tank Bolling reached into a pocket on his bullet proof vest and pulled free his service smartphone.

He put the phone to his ear.

"Go," said Tank.

Police forces throughout the United States were increasingly using smartphones instead of radios, as ways of communication during incidents. This updated style of communication stopped the perpetrators listening into conversations with a radio scanner.

"It's Weldon, sir. We have movement on the nineteenth floor. Somebody just opened the curtains in a bedroom near corner three. I repeat, that's floor nineteen, corner three" Joe Weldon said.

In all major situations, the corners of buildings were numbered. This made it easier for everyone involved to get a grasp of where things happened. From a tactical perspective, it stopped people getting their wires crossed.

Corner one was at the front of the hotel facing the beach and on the right hand side. That was also where the entrance steps to the hotel were located. The numbering of a building ran in a clockwise sequence. Corner two was at the front of the hotel, on the left hand side. Corner three was directly behind corner two at the back of the building. A small alleyway ran along the rear of the hotel and separated the rear glass wall of the Atlantic Grand and a small office complex. Corner four was adjacent to corner three and directly behind corner one. This corner was at the other end of the hotel's car park and just beyond the loading bay.

"What are they doing now?" Tank asked.

"I can't see the individual at present, but he opened the curtains and looked out for a minute. Then he pulled a phone out of his pocket and made a call. The man spoke on the phone for maybe, two minutes. Then he disappeared from view. I saw him again, but walking backwards. The person with the phone then hung up and ducked out of sight," he said.

"Do we know who they are? Can we see any distinguishing features?" Tank asked.

"The individual's male. Probably six foot, maybe more. He filled the floor to ceiling window. Hang on, he's looking out of the window again. He's a white male, late teens or early twenties and wearing what looks like a hotel uniform," said Weldon.

"Who are you paired with, Joe?" Tank asked.

"Kev Canterbury, Sir. He's the one looking through the scope, I've got the binoculars," he answered.

Tank couldn't argue with the information he was getting. They were two of his most experienced men.

"Okay. Keep me informed if anything changes, I'll try and get a handle on this," said Tank.

He ended the call.

Keeping the phone in his hand in case of another call, Tank quickly made his way to the command truck. He called for the chief.

"He's on the phone," said Teonnie.

She came towards the open door and tilted her head for Tank to come inside. Chief Schlemmer saw Tank approaching and with one hand to his ear, motioned for him to sit down with the other. The chief was poring over blue prints of the building. He scribbled down a phone number in the margin of the technical drawing and hung up the call.

"That was a dispatcher, they just had a call from a kid whose aunty manages the hotel. He's up on the nineteenth floor. Safe, but we don't know for how long," Chief Schlemmer said.

"On corner three?" Tank asked.

"Yeah, how did you know?" the chief asked.

"He opened the curtains. One of my sniper teams just called it in," answered Tank.

"It's a big ask of a seventeen year old and it broaches hundreds of moral and professional questions, but we might have just got our eyes on the inside," Chief Schlemmer said.

*

Clutching herself, Alison was worried sick. Harry wasn't in the room and he hadn't left with the other staff. She hadn't seen Kelsi either. Or Kim and Jayden. She wasn't stupid, she knew the three of them used to congregate on the rooftop at the end of their shift. A few bottles of beer going missing were the least of her concerns. It was entirely plausible Harry would have been with them, now they were nowhere to be seen. She blamed herself. How could she let harm come to her staff and her best friend's child? Racking herself with guilt her blood boiled. She scoured for sight of him in the California Great Hall. Two of her staff had turned on her.

They should have never been trusted from the start of their employment. Amanda had an exceptional curriculum vitae and glowing references. She had come across as a perfect employee on paper and during her interview. She would have been a fool not to employ her. Alison couldn't put her finger on it, but there was just something odd about her. She had never seen Antoni's CV. He had been employed by Amanda. He had always seemed pleasant and polite, even if he was a little stand offish. Now they had shown their true colours. She hated the pair of them.

She didn't know where Amanda was, certainly not in the Great Hall. She found Antoni standing by the main entrance to the room. He was talking to more of her captors, giving them orders. Her glare of fire bore holes into the back of his skull. Her opinion of him had changed over recent months. She considered Kelsi a friend as well as an employee. Kelsi had dated Antoni for a while. One night when she and Kelsi were having a drink at a beach front bar, they saw Antoni in the bar next door. He was kissing another woman. Kelsi had been devastated. Alison had to draw on all her professionalism not to march over and fire him right there and then. These past two months she had been waiting for him to do something wrong. Waiting for him to give her reason to show him the door. It was now clear that if she had fired him on that night on the beach front, they might not be in the current situation.

*

Harry answered after only two rings. According to the sniper team he ducked down and squatted next to the window to take the call. The chief had gone outside. Harry said he could see the man he was talking with. Chief Schlemmer was tall. Harry guessed the same height as himself. Slender and dressed in the jeans he had most likely been wearing while he relaxed home. On top he wore a white shirt under a blue bullet proof vest. The chief leant against a parked police car at the intersection of Granada Street and Birch Road. Just west of corner three of the hotel. He perched himself on the hood of the Ford Charger. Chris Schlemmer thought it was important for the young man to know who he was talking to. Important for Harry to see him so they could start to build a bond of trust. 'That's the only way we're going to get through this,' he told him. He was joined by another man. Shorter and stockier, with a bald or shaven head. Unlike Schlemmer, he was dressed in his police uniform, but also wore a bullet proof vest. The vest was emblazoned with

SWAT in big yellow letters.

Chief Schlemmer spoke to Harry about who had taken the inhabitants of the hotel hostage. About what Bothrops had told them on the NBC broadcast. What they had seen with their own eyes and said why the police needed it confirming. The chief then handed the phone to the other man. He introduced himself as Tank Bolling. He said he had been the commander of the FLPD SWAT team for the last five years. Prior to that he had been a police officer and SWAT officer for eleven years. Tank told Harry what his role was at the incident and how he should go about obtaining the information they required. Finally, Tank asked Harry if he had a charger for his smartphone. He didn't. He would have to try and find one in a bedroom.

Tank hung up the call.

"He seems like a clued up kid. Took the words right out of my mouth on a few occasions. Kept referencing a PlayStation game my nephew plays. SAS: We Dare We Win," he said.

Once he was back in the command truck, Chief Schlemmer asked Teonnie to get every scrap of information she could on Harry Fearn of London, England. His family too. He needed to know everything they could find about Harry, to ensure he wasn't part of a terrorist ruse. He said to tell anyone or any agency she spoke to, it was of great importance and the utmost urgency. He also said to use his name and refer to the current situation.

*

Inside the Porter's Lodge, Harry took a deep breath. He knew the police outside needed the information that had been requested, from a tactical standpoint it would be almost essential. He also knew that he was most likely the only person that could obtain the information and he knew he had the skills to get it.

At only seventeen, he could have joined the British Army, but he would have needed a parent's signature. Even if they had signed him into the military, the army wouldn't have put him in a combat situation until he was eighteen. Now he had the Chief of the Fort Lauderdale Police Department asking him to carry out reconnaissance on their behalf. The situation was life and death. Not just for him. For every single one of the hostages. He had been told the staff had been released. Knowing Kelsi was safe made him smile. He also knew Alison hadn't been. She would be in captivity. He had a decent amount of knowledge of this type of situation. For the past few years, he had read and read real life accounts of the SAS. He was thankful for the console game SAS: We Dare We Win. That game had taught him a lot and it was going to come in to practice right now. Amongst how to fight, use weapons and all the tactics the game had ingrained in him, it had taught him how to be invisible. How to be covert, or as Thomas at school would say, it had taught him how to be a sneaky little bastard.

*

Twenty minutes after he had spoken to Harry, Tank came down the steps from the command truck. He could see the amount of activity beyond the cordon was getting out of hand. The crowd was distracting police officers. They had to keep an eye on them and would be stopped from performing other essential tasks. The noise the news crews made and the hordes of general public standing around to update their social media accounts with eye witness news, posed a risk to his officers' safety. If the terrorists inside the hotel had access to social media sources, which he had no reason to believe they didn't, operational security could be compromised. Tank didn't hesitate in ordering the cordon moved back another block. He would use the newly freed up cordon as an inner cordon. Access to the one block cordon would be on a strictly need to enter basis. The only non-emergency service vehicle he allowed to stay within the new cordon was the food truck. It was parked on Birch Road, a few feet from the edge of the inner cordon. It would be safe there. Chief Schlemmer had previously asked for all food and drink given to members of the emergency services, to be charged to an FLPD credit card. He needed his officers to be in tip top condition at all times.

He pulled his smartphone out and called Weldon.

"What's happening?" he asked.

"We can see the male moving around, can't tell what he's doing," Weldon said.

"He's a good guy, an English kid called Harry," said Tank.

"Jesus, a kid?" Weldon asked.

"Yeah. A seventeen year old. Working in the hotel for the summer. His aunty's the manager," Tank answered. "He's just agreed to be our eyes on the inside. He's going to do recon for us."

"Hang on. He's just drawn the curtains and turned off the lights," said Weldon.

"Let's hope he does okay," said Tank.

*

Sat in the Porter's Lodge, Harry thought some more about his next move. His mind went through his plan for the umpteenth time. He didn't know why Kelsi had given him the master key wristband that night, but she had. He was eternally grateful. He exited the Porter's Lodge and closed the door as quietly as he could. The corridor was illuminated. That was normal. He would have expected nothing less. He turned right out of the Porter's Lodge. Slowly and silently he walked towards the front of the hotel. The Porter's Lodge was on what the police were calling corner three. He made his way towards corner two and the service stairwell. There was no way on this earth he was going to risk riding the elevator. Harry stopped at corner two. He couldn't hear any movement, but that didn't mean there wasn't anybody the other side of the fire door. He took a deep breath and delicately inched open the door. The light concentration didn't change. The stairwell just appeared brighter due to the white paint on the walls. Harry stepped into the stairwell and looked all around. No one to be seen. He couldn't hear anything. Stepping closer to the centre of the stairwell and the handrail, he peered upwards and downwards. He got close to the edge of the rail and leant over. No one there. Moving forwards he rolled his feet to minimise any noise.

The floor of the stairs was covered in linoleum floor tiles. It would prove noisier than the carpet of the corridor. His heel touched the floor first. He rolled the rest of his foot slowly until the toe of his shoe was flat. Repeating the motion he was soon midway between floors nineteen and eighteen. Nobody there. He continued to floor eighteen. He stopped open mouthed and wide eyed. He couldn't hear anything.

Harry repeated this process through eight more floors. He heard a door open on a landing below. Similar voices to the ones he had heard outside the Porter's Lodge. The foreign language that he now he knew was Spanish, Colombia's first language. The voices stopped on the landing below. They talked for a minute. The footsteps moved off, getting quieter, moving away from him. If the footsteps had come towards him, he would have had no choice other than to exit through the fire door behind him, open a bedroom using his master key and hide. He waited until the sound of footsteps had disappeared. He continued down the stairs.

He had moved down fifteen floors at corner two without incident. On the fourth floor he could hear movement below. Voices talking as they walked along corridors. He was scared. Scared shitless, but excited. His heart beat faster. He was getting pumped up and ready. Harry waited on the landing until he couldn't hear any voices. The footsteps inside the fire door would be on carpet. They would be harder to hear, but he didn't think there was anyone close by. Covertly moving down the final steps to the landing for floor three, his heart was in his mouth. This fire door, like all the fire doors, was fitted with a strengthened glass panel in the door's top half. He checked again for any sign of footsteps or voices. Nothing in the stairwell. Nothing on the other side of the fire door. He mustered all his courage and peered with one eye into the chequered glass. There was no one there. He stayed like that for what felt like minutes. All the time listening. Nobody came or went. Everything seemed settled and calm. His fingers took hold of the door handle.

*

In the command truck, Chief Schlemmer asked everyone to gather round. Each person had just three minutes to tell him what they had learnt about Bothrops Atrox. Negotiators used hooks. Something that could capture the hostage taker's mind. Anything from their personal life they could use as bargaining power. Something to pull on. An emotional reminder of why they should stop what they were doing. It could be positive, to praise them for a past event in order to encourage them to do good now, like the release of any elderly hostages, pregnant women, or injured or ill hostages.

At that moment in time the police had nothing. Al Brody needed everything. Marker pen in hand Teonnie stood ready to make notes on the whiteboard. Al was sat at the large central table. His pen and writing book in front of him. Another eight police personnel took their places at the table.

Many things were mentioned. First was the extent of Bothrops' drug empire. He supplied ninety per cent of the world's cocaine and that had made him the most wanted man on the planet. Forty five tonnes per day was what authorities estimated he was smuggling out of Colombia. Treble the amount of any other cocaine producing country. He had previously relied on officials who were susceptible to bribery, but for the last two decades his business had grown to insurmountable levels. He now employed a whole department of workers to come up with new ways of smuggling his drugs. Human couriers on commercial airliners, private jets that would make unscheduled stops, cars, trains, trucks, container ships. He was even enlisting bent cruise liner staff. Bothrops owned hundreds of boats. Speedboats to small ships. He even made his own small submarines, currently operating over fifty of them and each one capable of carrying eight million dollars' worth of cocaine per trip. Then there was the large ex-Russian Navy submarine that he bought. It was capable of making deliveries anywhere in the world. The media was rife with the rumour of a tunnel ten miles long. It stretched from well inside the Mexican border and exited so far inside the USA, it had never been detected. Nobody knew the size of the tunnel. Did it even exist?

A decade earlier Bothrops Atrox had bought a company in Europe. A Portuguese aluminium ladder manufacturer. Ladders were exported by the truckload all over Europe. Dozens of trucks per day left the factory. Before transport, these ladders were packed full of white powder. Once filled, the ladders were mechanically shaken at high speed to ensure any gaps and voids were filled. More cocaine would be added. They were then welded shut and the rubber caps replaced. No one would ever suspect a thing. An x-ray machine scanning lorries at a port would never see a problem. Sniffer dogs would never be able detect the drugs. Bothrops thought this method was infallible.

Aluminium welding was an incredibly skilled job. Bothrops found the best coded welders from all around Europe and paid them well. It was a Friday afternoon when the last batch of ladders were sealed. The welder was sloppy. His mind was looking forward to going home and spending the weekend with his family, having a beer in a bar, watching the football. He forgot to seal three of the ladders. When customs officials at the Port of Eindhoven in The Netherlands opened the truck's trailer, they were very interested in the white powder spilling from three of the ladders. That was a good day. A major smuggling method had been uncovered. The information was shared. Every customs department in every country in Europe was notified. More and more lorries were stopped, over the next week and a whole smuggling method was brought to its knees. The Portuguese Authorities carried out armed raids. Major disruption to Bothrops' European distribution network was caused. Workers were arrested. A Europe wide cocaine shortage had been caused, but authorities still couldn't find out how the cocaine got to Europe in the first place. It was thought the product was coming in from Africa, but no matter how much they tried, customs agencies couldn't work out how. Bothrops was always one step ahead.

It was a known fact that his regular smugglers were highly rewarded. An airline pilot was able to buy a new house in the States every week while he was moonlighting for Bothrops Atrox. What had started as a one man enterprise had grown to a company with a bigger turnover than many multinationals. He had more money in the bank than some western countries. Storing his cash was a problem. He was one the biggest launderers of money in the world. The rest of his money was hidden in the vast caves of the Colombian Pacific Plain. The area was one of the rainiest on earth and it was rumoured Bothrops had spent thirteen million US Dollars having a drainage system installed. Just to keep his cash dry. For the last eighteen years he had featured on the Forbes International Rich List. For the last decade he had been the richest man in the world.

In the country of his birth he was treated as a god. Many of the country's poorer inhabitants relied on Bothrops Atrox more than the government. Thanks to him, the country's population had a higher standard of living than Colombia's GDP might suggest. He had built whole towns. Slums had been demolished. He had built hospitals and schools. He even gave Christmas presents to those that couldn't afford any. He loved the poor. Although he didn't control crime in any way, he had outlawed it in many parts of the country. Many cities were peaceful because of his intervention and generosity. There was no reason to steal. Nobody went short and for that, the people of Colombia adored him. At the same time he kept some areas as slums.

He used those barrios to recruit his staff, sicarios, smugglers, or simply informers. Children and youngsters who washed car windscreens at traffic lights, as soon as the car pulled away, they would be on the phone to their handler. There was a new white face in town. A Drugs Enforcement Agency face, maybe?

He was winning and what all the countries and governments that waged the war on drugs didn't realise, was that the war wasn't controlled by weapons and armed men. It was controlled by poverty. Of that, he had a stranglehold.

Bothrops biggest fear was extradition to the United States. He once offered to pay Colombia's national debt of thirty billion dollars in order to ensure freedom from extradition and to ensure he took up the position of President of Colombia.

He was twenty years of age when he married his wife who was just fourteen. They now have three children, two boys in their mid to late twenties and a much younger daughter. His family live on his two thousand acre mountainous retreat. It includes its own zoo and a prison he built for himself and other members of his cartel after the Colombian government caught up with him. The now empty prison was always more of a holiday park. Inside its walls are a spa and swimming pool, bar, nightclub, casino, brothel and go kart track. As well as countless guest bedrooms for visiting friends and associates.

During his twenty year reign as drug kingpin of the world he had been gunned down on six separate occasions. Received ten bullet wounds, seven of them flesh wounds, three serious wounds causing organ failure. He had spent a total of one year in hospital. These shootings were thought to be retaliation for the twenty four judges his Sicarios had murdered, along with nine hundred police officers who had died while trying to bring him to justice, twelve politicians and one Colombian President whose assassination he had organised. That was the price his country had to pay for him turning the cocaine production and smuggling industry into a ninety billion dollar a year global enterprise.

CHAPTER TWELVE

Police motorcycle outriders stopped traffic at road junctions. The presidential motorcade sped through the evening streets of Austin, Texas. Claudia Cane had left the North American Women in Transport Awards in a hurry. The motorcade drove towards Austin-Bergstrom Airport. The engines of Claudia's plane were coming to life. An eleven mile, thirty minute journey through the city centre, took just sixteen minutes with the aid of police lights and sirens. Pulling up on the runway, Claudia Caine was escorted by her Secret Service detail up the waiting steps and into the fuselage of Airforce Two.

"Good to see you, Mrs President. A full briefing will be ready once we get in the air," her chief of staff said.

"Please God. Billy, I'm not ready for this," replied Claudia.

"It was always the plan in three years anyway, just think of this as a test drive," he said.

The 25th amendment of the constitution of the United States stated that should the POTUS become incapacitated in anyway and unable to fulfil their role, by default the job was transferred to the vice-President. Huey Ace was currently unable to fulfil his role and the country needed a figurehead.

*

Harry ensured the door was pressed tight against its rubber fire seal. The heel of his foot planted on the floor, the toe of that shoe pushing into the door's base. He pushed the door handle down. The lock mechanism was well greased and in good working order. The metal inside the lock didn't scrape or grind together as it moved. No noise. No click. The only sound came from the unavoidable movement of two fire seals sucking in air as they parted company. Harry pulled the door towards him. As before, the light concentration in the corridor went unchanged. The door open only a crack, he listened more than he looked. All clear. The corridors were devoid of people. He could see the landing at the top of the central front staircase. Armchairs and coffee tables sat next to the stairs. There was nobody present. Harry twisted his body and observed the corridor that led back to corner three. He couldn't see any activity there either. No noise. Nothing moving. Nothing there.

The conference rooms on the third floor were all smaller. The fronts of the rooms were constructed with glass. Depending on whether or not the blinds were drawn, an occupant of a room would be able to see movement in the corridor. The room opposite the fire door had its blinds open. It was unoccupied. Pulling the door wider, Harry slipped through the gap. He chose to walk back along the corridor to corner three, to conference rooms where the majority of lights were turned off. To the rooms less likely to be occupied.

He saw thick black cables running along the floor. Midway between corner two and corner three, he noticed a humming noise coming from a conference room to his left. His pace slowed. He crept up to the door. The internal window blinds were drawn, but he wanted to learn what was humming. Making sure the room was empty, he eased the door open. The room held a generator, the cables on the floor feeding from it and out to the corridor. They were powering something. Maybe carrying something too. Information? Data? The cables continued down the corridor to corner three, twisted round and shot off down the back corridor. He headed in that direction. Walking on the carpet he made it safely to corner three. Peering around the corner he looked down the back corridor, towards corner four. Midway between the corners was the top of the duplicate wooden staircase found at the front of the hotel. He watched and listened. No movement, although now he could hear the occasional voice emanating from the floor below. Rolling his feet he walked towards the top of the stairs. Harry strained his ears to hear all he could. Voices came and went. There was lots of activity down there. As he got closer he knelt and then lay down on his front. There was increased electrical noise coming from the open door of the hotel's media suite. A terrorist was visible standing guard at the bottom of the stairs. The green suited x-ray was holding an AK47. Harry stayed where he was. He listened. He observed. He got as much confirmatory information as he could. Soon feeling vulnerable, Harry estimated if anyone came up the stairs, it would take him three to four seconds to get to his feet and run and hide. He dug deep and found a pair. He made the decision to keep low and to crawl past the top of the stairs, towards corner four.

As he crawled forwards he could see straight down the steps and onto the second floor. The more he crept, the more information he was gathering for Schlemmer. He didn't notice his heart beating out of his chest. Adrenaline was coursing through his veins. Harry was putting into practice what he had done in SAS: We Dare We Win. Only this time he wasn't sitting in his bedroom. He thought it would take him years to make use of the skills he had learnt, but it was less than a week since he last played the game.

He could see the x-ray on guard duty more closely. He was no more than twenty feet away. Harry imagined standing next to him, envisaged bringing his knee up to the guard's groin, as he doubled up in agony, smashing the palm of his hand into the terrorist's face breaking his nose, taking hold of his collar, pulling him down and bringing a knee to the face. Grasping his neck he would ram him straight back into the pillar at the edge of the stairs. Terrorist knocked unconscious. Job done. He snapped out of it. He could hear more voices coming along the corridor below him. He needed to cross the wide stairs, get to a point where he was out of sight. Shuffling forward on his elbows, legs straight and dragging behind him, he minimised his movements. He moved forwards to the middle. It was unlikely the guard would turn around and look up the stairs, especially with other terrorists walking along the corridor. The main group of hostages and all the potential threats were a floor below him. The hotel above had been fully cleared of people. Or so the terrorists thought.

Harry stopped and lay on the floor in the open. He tilted his head so his ear was flat to the floor and he could see clearly with both eyes. He halved his ability to hear, but maximised his vision to one hundred percent. Seeing was more important than hearing right now. The front of the mid-sized Indiana Media Suite was teeming with computer monitors. Many more than normal. The cables from the corridor were running into the room. Harry could see what some of the monitors displayed. Written documents that were too far away to be read. Lists of numbers that meant nothing. The terrorist in there was dressed differently. He looked like an office worker. Harry could see him erecting even more flatscreens. Some of the screens already in place displayed images. Moving images. It was the street outside. Harry could see one screen containing an image of the police truck Chief Schlemmer had come out of when he spoke to him on the phone. Voices. He had forgotten about the voices. He could hear them again. Ten feet away and getting closer. Lifting himself onto his elbows he dragged himself away. Once he was at the edge the stairs, he used his legs to propel himself. He quicky moved out of sight, stood up and ran to corner four.

Harry watched the top of the stairs from around the corner. No one climbed the steps. The voices passed. Their sound faded. He needed to move on. Harry padded down the corridor towards the front of the hotel, towards corner one. He passed more rooms with lights switched off. Four conference rooms at the end, either side of the corridor at corner one were bathed in light. He got on his belly again for the last ten feet. Crawling to the first lit room made him feel vulnerable, he made it as quick as possible but feared observing this room might take longer than he wanted.

He could sense movement. Someone kept walking close to the window in front and to his right. He could also hear a noise. A low monotonous drone, like the noise created by many of the same type of machine doing the same task. He edged closer.

Only two rooms to go before he reached corner one of the hotel. Remaining flat and vulnerable, he brought his head to the edge of the occupied room. The blinds were wide open for anyone to look out into the corridor, or into the room. Harry manoeuvred his body so that he lay on his side and faced inwards. He could tell, from the very slight shadow thrown out, at least one person in the room was walking in a circular pattern. What was he walking around? Waiting for the shadow to come close to him again, he started to count. One thousand. Two Thousand. Three thousand and so on. The figure wasn't pacing. Harry counted too high. The figure was walking with little interest at the task at hand. Harry counted to eighty four thousand before he sensed the figure was close again. The terrorist, he guessed, was taking eighty four seconds to walk one loop of the room. Whatever the machines were, they must be making something valuable. Their noise was barely audible, but it was. Just. He waited until the figure had walked twenty one thousands into his new loop. One quarter of a square room. He gave it another two thousands just to be safe. Tilting his head to the left slightly, he could see with one eye what the machines were. Except they weren't machines.

CHAPTER THIRTEEN

The window blinds were open. Harry could see the figure walking in circles around the room. He was dressed the same as the x-ray at the bottom of the stairs. He expected him to have the same style of machine gun. Sitting on the floor were a group of people. A circle of hostages. Their noise, whimpers in unison, had been what sounded like the mellow and monotonous tone of small machines. The room was well sealed. The door closed. The noise had been distorted. He couldn't tell how many hostages were sitting in the circle. He needed elevation. He needed to be higher than the hostages so he could count everyone. Fortunately, Harry's frame afforded him more height than most. Pulling his head back out of sight he waited for the guard to pass again. He restarted his count. Once he hit twenty three thousands, the guard had definitely turned his back. Harry got to his feet. He had to count fast.

He wouldn't be able to hold two counts at the same time. Thousands in his head and people sitting on the floor. In a maths exam Harry was able to get a decent grade, but he was never going to forge a career as a card counter in Las Vegas. One. Two. Three. Four. Five. All the way to sixteen. He needed a closer look at the person at the centre of the circle. It was a strange setup. He was wearing something, a vest of some kind. The guard was about to walk along the third side of the room. He would be able to see Harry out the corner of his eye.

He stood out of view. His back flat to the wall. The terrorist passed with little enthusiasm. Harry began to count the seconds. He looked around once it was safe and was horrified. A male sitting in the centre of the room was wearing a suicide vest. Explosives were packed all around the vest. A control box in the centre. Wires bunched and clipped together fed to detonators which pushed directly into the explosives. The people sitting in a circle around the man wearing the vest were the intended victims. Harry had seen the aftermath of a suicide vest in SAS: We Dare We Win. It wasn't pretty. Victims at the epicentre of the blast had been vaporised. It couldn't be known how many people had been killed. People further out from the epicentre had been killed outright and their limbs and torsos torn apart.

*

Just before midnight, the FBI pulled up at the scene. The Mirimar office had sent two Special Agents. They would be joined by the Special Agent in charge and her assistant. Their hostage negotiator was on vacation. Al Brody was still the number one negotiator.

More people arrived. The streets became livelier. The whole area was awake. It was getting towards midnight, a time when people are asleep, or bedding down for the night. However, Fort Lauderdale wasn't where most people were spending the night.

Not long after the Mirimar Special Agents arrived, a Miami Police SWAT Team parked up. Tank had been on the phone to Miami PD straight away. One of their teams had been loaned to the FLPD until the situation at the Atlantic Grand was resolved. This situation was very real and bigger than any local police force had dealt with before. Everyone wanted to help. Everyone wanted to say they had been involved.

Teonnie had removed her high heels and was walking barefoot around the mobile office.

"I'm ready with the information you requested on Harry, boss," she said.

The chief pulled up a chair opposite Teonnie. She began reading from an impressively large bunch of notes.

"Harry John Fearn. Seventeen years old. Lives on Cloudesley Street. Islington. London. England," she said. "Halfway through his A-Level qualifications, no grades available yet. Studies at Regent High School, King's Cross, London. He's a member of the school cricket team. Here's a photograph of him from the school's website. He must play the drums as well," she said.

Teonnie handed the chief a print out. The boy in the image was sitting behind a drumkit.

"Harry has a mother and a father. He is an only child. The mother doesn't have any siblings and I couldn't find much on the father in my research. Harry has an Instagram account, it hasn't been updated in a year. It's full of photographs of the same boy, just younger. Him and his friends taking pictures, making silly poses and pulling childish faces. His Facebook profile, however, has been accessed and within the last week. A few statuses about coming to Florida and working in the Atlantic Grand. Six photographs of the beach and a few of Fort Lauderdale. The woman in the photos has been tagged as Alison Spencer.

She handed him more printouts.

"Nice," said the chief.

Alison was a good looking woman.

Teonnie laughed.

"She's the aunty and the hotel's general manager," Teonnie said.

She passed the chief another photo.

"There's nothing else to shout about. The others photos are just of him and his friends and family holidays. Now this is interesting. In the very few photographs with his father, his dad's face can't be fully seen. He's wearing sunglasses, even in this one which must have been taken on a cloudy winter's day. There are no leaves on the trees behind them and Harry and his dad are both wearing jackets. Why would his dad be hiding his face?

Harry's profile page says that he's worked at a butcher's shop local to him for the last two years. Then it just mentions the primary school he studied at and lists that he lives in London. His mobile phone number isn't displayed. He doesn't have any other names listed and he isn't in a relationship. He is a non-practising Christian and he's a member of a few groups you would expect a teenage boy to have interest in. Something called LADbible, which is just lads being lads and one about a Russian fighting technique called Systema. He is also a member of two Special Air Service groups and a fan page for the console game, SAS: We Dare We Win. He likes a page that follows our special forces and a group that is about the Israeli Intelligence Agency Mossad. His mother has a business profile on LinkedIn. His father isn't on Facebook, LinkedIn or any form of social media," she added.

Teonnie gulped at her bottle of water and continued.

"This comes from his mother's LinkedIn profile. She runs a lettings agency, also located in Islington. She had a twenty year career with a construction company scoping out new sites for housing development, but left two years ago to get her own slice of the pie. She setup her own company, Cloudesley Lettings," Teonnie said.

She took a breath.

"I took his phone number down and searched that too. It all checks out with what's registered. The phone is on a contract and the network provider is European. I'm waiting to hear about the owner of the credit card that pays his phone contract. It could be Harry's father," she said. Teonnie raised an eyebrow.

"Furthermore," she continued, "I spoke to a man at the Central Intelligence Agency and he can get one of their CIA Teams from the London Station, to observe the house where Harry lives with his parents. A team can be there within the hour," said Teonnie.

She had been talking so quickly she became a little out of breath.

Chris Schlemmer was blown away. Teonnie was a good secretary. A really good secretary, but she had just raised the bar. She was operating at a whole new level. He breathed out a laboured sigh and rubbed his temples. Stress didn't get to him in his job. He was very competent, but he thought having a CIA Team observe Harry's house was international espionage. He needed advice.

Ten minutes later, after speaking with the FBI Agents at the scene, Chris Schlemmer re-entered the command vehicle.

"I think it would be wise to observe Harry's house until we know more about his father. He's obviously hiding something," said Chief Schlemmer.

The chief stepped outside again. His smartphone phone rang in the truck.

Teonnie answered as the phone vibrated across the metal table.

"Chief Schlemmer's phone," she said.

"Is he there?" asked the voice.

"Who's calling?" asked Teonnie.

Teonnie yelled at the top of her lungs, deafening the others in the command truck.

"Chief!"

Chief Schlemmer jogged back towards the truck.

"Yeah," he shouted.

Teonnie handed him the phone.

'Harry,' she mouthed.

"Hello Harry, what can you tell me?" he asked.

Chief Schlemmer told Harry what he was doing and put him on loud speaker. He sat at the table in the command truck. Everyone in a position of seniority crammed into the truck and vied for space around the table. Including the two FBI Agents.

Harry told them exactly what he'd seen. He told them about the two random x-rays he heard in the stairwell. The voices on the third floor before he entered through the fire door. He'd seen an x-ray standing guard at the base of the rear stairs on floor two. Tank busily marked down the known locations of the terrorists. Harry told the chief about the generator he'd seen and the cables running to the Indiana Media Suite, the images on the flatscreens and how the terrorists were able to see movements of the police outside. The chief was concerned there appeared to be surveillance of the street outside. He was worried to know the camera system wasn't running off the hotel's power supply. Most of all, he and everyone in the room wanted to know if the suicide vest they had seen was genuine. Harry thought it was.

"Harry, are you calling the terrorists x-rays?" Chris asked.

"Yeah, it's what the SAS call them, so I'll do the same," he said.

Chief Schlemmer clicked Harry off loudspeaker and thanked him. Harry was told to stay in the upper Porter's Lodge and stay safe. They would have a plan soon and keep Harry updated. He hung up.

"There's more," said Teonnie.

"Hit me with it," he said.

"The affidavit for Harry's cell phone came back. As I said before, it gets paid by credit card, payment is automatically taken each month and it's his dad that pays for it. Harry's father is called John Fearn," Teonnie said.

Chris Schlemmer looked up from his notes.

"I've heard that name before," he said.

"Interesting," Teonnie said, "I'm going to look into the credit card details. Payments in and out and the like."

*

He sat on the bed of boxes and cracked open a new bottle of water. This time he could see what he was doing and chose still water. He switched off the light. Harry didn't want anyone in the corridor thinking it unusual that the light in the Porter's Lodge was switched on. It was past midnight and it should be dark outside. It was, less all the flashing lights of emergency vehicles. Given the time of day, it was strange he wasn't tired. Adrenaline was still running through his veins and his sleep earlier had helped.

When Chief Schlemmer asked him to reconnoitre, he'd been scared. Very scared. Yet at the same time he was confident in his ability. He'd loved every second of his adventure and real life derring-do. His hunger hit him. He needed to eat. He had been able to get down to the third floor of the hotel unseen, therefore it would be easy for him to visit a few bedrooms on the upper floors. Try to get hold of some snacks people had in their rooms.

He realised if he could get into the bedrooms to look for food, he could look for items that would help him. Help the situation. It wasn't in his nature to sit back idly and let anything pass him by. He was a doer, not just a thinker. Why just help the FLPD with recon? He could be a lot more useful. He knew the clothes he would need for covert counter terrorism. He understood how a weapon worked. He had stripped, rebuilt and fired them hundreds of times in SAS: We Dare We Win. The game had also taught him tactics and the skills he would need to fight for real. His mind was set. In the dead of the night he was going to scour bedrooms. Search for kit that would help him to become an SAS trooper.

CHAPTER FOURTEEN

If you were fighting on a battlefield consisting of grassland, wooded areas, ditches and hedges, the standard British Army Disruptive Pattern Material (DPM), or camouflage to the man in the street, was exactly what you needed. If you were fighting in the desert and wanted to remain covert, it was the aptly named Desert DPM that was required. Snowy warfare or clandestine Arctic operations, called for Arctic DPM. Harry wasn't fighting in any of those environments. Not even Urban DPM would help him.

The top brass of the British Army had called urban warfare, FIBUA. Fighting In a Built Up Area. The British Army squaddie had instead coined the term FISH. Fighting In Someone else's House. Harry would still be going fishing, but in someone else's hotel. He would be wearing black. Absolute black, with not a single bit of colour showing. He would be donning all the gear, or the best like for like clothing he could find, that any Special Air Service soldier would wear in a close quarters battle situation. The same gear that his SAS avatar was wearing on the screen in SAS: We Dare We Win. Only this time, his mum wasn't around to quite literally pull the plug. More so, the child in him really wanted to dress up and become the terrorist's version of Friday the thirteenth. This time there was no room for error. He couldn't just restart the level. There was no on off switch. Just an off switch. If he messed up he would die. First though, he needed to find all the clothing and anything else that would help him not die. He already knew the Porter's Lodge was the secure base he would operate from. He just needed to fill it with kit.

Harry used the back service stairwell at corner four. Silently he worked his way down from the nineteenth floor, to the fifteenth floor. As far as he could tell after his preliminary movements around the hotel, the terrorists only populated the bottom floors. All other floors had been cleared by armed men. He just needed to be on the lookout for roaming teams of x-rays who might be patrolling the hotel sporadically. He thanked his lucky stars for his master key.

His master key wasn't a conventional key. All the doors in the hotel, less a few that he had no interest in, worked on RFID. In modern hotels Radio Frequency Identification technology had been the norm for well over a decade. Hotel guests knew this as a key card or swipe card. His swipe card came in the form of a wrist band. All he needed to do was hover his wrist band close to a door mounted card reader and the door would unlock.

Harry silently padded along to the first room he would search. Hotel rooms in a direct line of sight of the elevators were out. Only rooms on corridors that ran from corner one to corner four, or corner two to corner three were searchable, as well as rooms in smaller corridors that criss-crossed the hotel. Rooms near elevators were too high risk. Now on the fifteenth floor he was outside the first room he would search. He steadied himself and took a deep breath.

Harry allowed the card reader a glimpse of his wristband. The card reader now had three options. Flash red. Flash green. Or not at all. A red flash meant access was not granted. Flash green and access was granted. No flash and the battery in the card reader was dead. This was the most unlikely of options. Harry breathed out when the card reader flashed green. Fingers curled around the door handle, he pressed down. The silver lever turned. He felt the mechanism clunk as the internal workings of the lock disengaged. Keeping the lever firmly pressed down, he slowly pushed the door away from him. Stepping into the room he swapped hands and silently closed the door. The room was now secure again. Only a person who had that particular room's key card, or a master key, could enter.

Harry didn't move. He was still and surveyed the bedroom in front of him. Entering from a well-lit corridor he needed to let his eyes readjust to the darkness. He closed his eyes for ten seconds and opened them again. Better. Holding them shut a second time, he opened them to find his sight was on a par with the dimly lit room. He listened for movement in the corridor and worked out what he wanted a closer look at. The curtains of the room weren't drawn, which was good. Light from the surrounding buildings and from the emergency vehicles below, threw up enough light to make the room workable.

The room featured a double bed. A built in wardrobe was opposite. Two armchairs around a coffee table sat next to the window. The bathroom was to his immediate right. Harry moved forwards and headed to the room's mirror coated wardrobe. He looked at the dull reflection. Looking back at him was a seventeen year old kid dressed in black trousers, white shirt and a waistcoat. That was going to change.

He slid the wardrobe open. The room was lived in by a man, the ties on the rail told him as much. He scanned each and every shirt and calculated its usefulness based on its own merits. Ideally all shirts were out, especially white or coloured shirts. Harry had the frame of a lean, thin and tall young man, not the frame of an overweight, average height adult who wore 3XL clothes. Any clothes he found in this room were out. Moving across to the case next to the bed, he pulled it on to its back. Kneeling in front of the zip, Harry pulled it open. Lifting the lid he found the case was empty apart from a pair of black trainers. He picked them out and looked at the size. They were a ten. Harry was a size eleven. Nearly perfect. Beggars can't be choosers. He placed them on the bed.

There were some loose coins on the bedside table. Harry wrapped the coins in toilet paper from the bathroom. Thus ensuring they wouldn't clink together and make a noise. He needed a bag. Preferably a large rucksack. A suitcase would be a hinderance. Searching the bathroom he found a small travel wash bag . It wasn't ideal. The bag was some designer blue thing and small, but it was lockable with a zip. He placed the bundle of coins in the bag. He added a bottle of shower gel to the bag. Changing into the trainers, he placed his cheap faux leather shoes in the wardrobe. He left the room as he found it. No one would ever know he had been there.

Harry's ability to hear any movement out in the corridor had substantially diminished while he had been in the bedroom. There was no way of knowing if there was anyone outside the room in the corridor. He stood facing the door. Open mouthed and listening. Open mouthed because your hearing improved when your mouth was open. He was aware that as time passed, the chances of successfully completing his mission fell. When he searched future rooms, he would work faster. No noise from anywhere. He pushed the metal door lever down and leant into the opening. Nobody there. He stepped out. Closed the door in silence and moved onto the next bedroom.

Harry had scoured many bedrooms with a fine and fast tooth-comb. If he searched every bedroom in the hotel, he would have been searching non-stop for nearly two days. It was now the middle of the night as he walked along the corridors. He stopped dead. He heard Colombian voices. A roaming patrol of x-rays. Sporadic and random. His heart began beating faster. His eyes darted around. He surveyed his options. He backed away in the direction he had come. He heard an elevator. It stopped. The doors opened. The elevator groaned as it strained under the weight of people entering. The footfall he heard told him more than one person had walked inside, two, possibly three people. The doors closed. The elevator whirred away. It moved down. Harry racked his brains trying to think how many different voices he'd heard. He couldn't think. He hoped all the voices had been taken away by the elevator. He moved his head so he could gain just a glimpse of the corridor where he had heard the voices. There was nobody in the corridor. He moved on.

As well as checking all the bedrooms, he looked in every staff cupboard and storeroom. The last room he checked was the linen cupboard for the seventeenth floor. Every floor had them. None of them had so far yielded anything other than bed sheets, towels and pillow cases. But you never know. He crouched next to the linen cupboard door. Harry checked his surroundings. Looking forward and behind. Open mouthed and listening. He was so calm and in tune with his surroundings that after a minute, he could hear the slightest noise. Having heard nothing, he eased the door inwards. He was still crouching as he pushed the door back. He wouldn't open the door standing up. Anyone on the other side of the door with a weapon, could fire at the middle of the door and take him down. Being lower gave him a better chance of survival, a split second warning if the shit were to hit the fan. Harry walked forward into the room in a crouch.

CHAPTER FIFTEEN

Three hours after leaving Austin, Airforce Two landed at Andrews Airforce Base. Less than thirty minutes later, Claudia Caine's Secret Service detail pounded the corridors of the White House and put her safely in the Oval Office.

Claudia's Chief of Staff was with her every step of the way.

"Most of the President's senior staff are hostages at the Atlantic Grand. Steve Easter is here though. He'll be coming by shortly," he said.

"Send him straight through when he gets here, Billy," Claudia said.

She liked Steve Easter. He was Huey Ace's Deputy Communications Director and the man she was lining up to be Communications Director for her own presidential campaign.

*

Standing tall once he was inside the room, Harry pulled the door closed without a sound. He flicked the light switch. The room held the same layout as every other linen cupboard in the hotel. The three usable sides of the room were made up of full length and full height wooden racking. To his left and right, two pools of dried blood lay next to the shelves. Harry's stomach turned. The linen on the bottom three shelves, either side and in front of him, was ripped and torn. Someone had unloaded at few magazines of ammunition. He had to look, but knew what he would find under the sheets. He had to see who the blood belonged to. Hotel workers, he was sure. A guest would never think to hide in a room with no sign on the door. Only his colleagues knew what the room was used for. Steadying his stomach he walked to the first pile of torn sheets.

Gently pulling back ripped and torn sheet after ripped and torn sheet, he saw a head of cropped hair. He pulled the sheets away and got nearer and nearer to what was a body. Harry's fear grew. Pulling the final sheet he uncovered what was beneath. It was the lifeless face of Jay. His eyes were closed, shut tight from the moment he heard the first magazine unloaded. He stayed where he lay. Harry replaced the sheets. He looked untouched and unfound. Listening intently again there wasn't a sound. He moved to the second blood stain. Harry laid the ripped sheets next to him. He exposed a wrist. A female wrist. Another two sheets removed he could see more. Harry removed a final sheet. He closed his eyes and put his head down. A tear trickled down his cheek. The body was female. It was Kim. Harry wasn't religious in the slightest, but he dipped his head and mumbled a prayer. He moved to the middle set of shelves.

He heard a noise. Very slight. Barely audible. His breathing increased. Deeper and faster breaths. His head shot up. Eyes open wide. He expected to see a gunman standing over him. Nothing. Nobody there. Open mouthed Harry quelled his sudden and heavy breathing. He listened harder than ever before. His expectation was for an x-ray to come through the door and for the game to be up. This wasn't SAS: We Dare We Win. He wouldn't be able to restart the level. Nothing happened. He heard the noise again. It was a movement. A very slight scuffing or scraping. A shoe on a wooden shelf. How had the body under this pile of tattered linen survived a hail of bullets. He knew who he hoped it was. He heard the noise again. Then a female's sniffle. Removing the linen from the bottom of the middle shelf he couldn't see anything. The body must have crammed itself right to the back, but there was no one there.

His hope had been destroyed. All that was on the shelf was ripped and torn linen. Sorrowful and despondent Harry put his hand on the shelf above as he began to stand. His head shot up. His hand wasn't on the shelf. He was touching skin. He removed his hand. A leg was pulled back. Forget whoever could hear him. Harry sat back on his heels, squatted and tore at the sheets. The untouched and perfect sheets. She was unscathed and curled into the foetal position, one hand pulled tight over her head, as if to somehow protect herself. Kelsi was perfect before and was still perfect now.

Talking in a low mumbling voice was more effective than whispering. Whispers carried further in the air than a mumbled voice.

"Hello, Kelsi Millicent Maguire," Harry said.

Eyes clamped shut, Kelsi smiled.

She drew her hand away from her head and opened her eyes.

"Harry," she screeched.

She had tears in her eyes.

"Shush," he said.

He clamped his hand over her mouth.

Her eyes watered and formed tears.

Harry spoke in the lowest voice he could manage.

"It's really important that you're quiet, I don't know how close the men with guns are," he said.

Slowly, he removed his hand from her mouth.

She looked at him like a deer caught in the headlights.

"Are you hurt?" he asked.

She shook her head.

"No," she mouthed.

Tears ran down her face, but she started to smile again.

"Come on, let's get you out of here," he mumbled.

He had just gained his accomplice. His comrade. The Robin to his Batman. The Bonnie Parker to his Clyde Barrow. The Juliet to his Romeo, he hoped.

Kelsi was unsteady on her feet. She must have been lying in the same position for over eight hours. Her legs had gone to sleep. Harry held her up. She clung to him. The blood in her legs started to flow again. She looked up at him, smiled and kissed him on the lips. He couldn't imagine the horror she had been through. The sheer terror of having two friends murdered when they lay only feet away. All the time she had kept completely still and not moved. Not made a sound. Not even a cry or whimper. She was made of tough stuff.

"Thank you," she said.

Kelsi smiled, bit her lip and smiled some more. She gave him another kiss.

"Anytime," he smiled.

His arms wrapped around her and he kissed her back.

He held her and she still clung to him. He thought if her hug got any tighter, she would crack one of his ribs. Once she was able to stand on her own, Harry placed the linen back on her shelf and made the area look undisturbed. Harry led the way towards his stronghold. Kelsi followed.

Hand in hand they traversed the corridors to corner four. In the stairwell Harry could hear any door open or close. He would hear in advance the shuffling of feet, the noise of men walking, or running up and down the stairs. A cough would resonate like an echo. The movement of a bolt pulled back on a rifle would be cacophonous and the metallic scraping sound would travel up and down all twenty one floors. The stairs were a good way to travel if you didn't want to be detected, but it would also work against them if they made a noise. Harry showed Kelsi how to roll her footsteps and not let her feet slap down on the tiled floor. He showed her hand signals too.

All the hand signals they would need were done with their right hands. A thumbs up meant all clear. Thumbs down meant the enemy was close by. A flat palm with fingers splayed over his face meant come to me and a balled fist meant halt. No one could hear them. That was why hand signals were vital. They would be able to hear anyone coming. They would have chance to exit into the myriad of corridors.

Harry made good ground back to the Porter's Lodge. Five minutes later they were safely inside. She needed water. Harry gave her a bottle of still. Kelsi lay on the bed of boxes, wrapped up in a duvet of table cloths. Unslinging the rucksack he found in another bedroom, he emptied all the items he had collected on his exploration trip.

*

Four and a half thousand miles away on the other side of the North Atlantic, two innocuous people sat in a car that wasn't anything out of the ordinary for that part of London. It was just an indistinguishable dark blue European hatchback, parked along with two dozen other cars on an unremarkable London street. The occupants of the car were nothing special. Both were in their mid to late thirties, still a couple of years away from reaching forty. They appeared to be of a normal height and weight for their age and gender. The male looked as if he went to the gym to lift weights. Not every day, maybe three times a week. Two fit and healthy adults. Both were Caucasian. The male half of the couple was sitting in the driver's seat and had short cropped blonde hair. He was wearing a black t-shirt and didn't have any distinguishing features. The woman in the front passenger seat had shoulder length brown hair, a birth mark on her left cheek and she sported round glasses. She was wearing a white button up shirt. David couldn't see what they had on their bottom halves, the male was probably in jeans. The woman's white shirt alluded to a pair of black, or dark business trousers. He couldn't tell if they had anything to carry. If they did it would be in the footwell between their feet, or in the pocket of the car door. The pair in the car saw him walk past. Neither marked him as anything special. David was just as average as them. It was possible the occupants of the car were playing a couple, boyfriend and girlfriend, even husband and wife. Neither would get a second glance from anyone. They were similar to many of the street's residents and that was exactly what they wanted.

The car had been parked up with two people inside since the resident woke. As he did every day, he stood far enough back from the front bedroom window so that he could see the street, but so the street couldn't see him. The car wasn't a regular fixture. The resident knew all of his neighbours cars for the two houses either side of his own. As well as the five houses opposite. The non-descript car could have been collecting a colleague from their house to take them to work, but the resident had been watching for fifteen minutes. Either of the pair, the passenger most likely, would have knocked on the colleague's front door by now, or the driver would have blasted the horn. It was now eight o'clock in the morning. The resident decided the car must have parked up some time in the early hours. It hadn't been there when the he had gone to bed. The problem wasn't that the car was a standard sight on a London street, neither was it that the car's occupants were run of the mill. The problem wasn't the street they were parked on, but whose house the occupants were busy looking at while trying to blend in. That was what had prompted the phone call.

A black Range Rover calmly made its way down Cloudesley Street, towards the dark blue hatchback. Ideally there would have been two or three Range Rovers, but time was an issue. The target had to be neutralised. Halfway between the entrance to the street and the forgettable car, the driver of the Range Rover stabbed his foot on the accelerator. The bonnet lifted. The sudden increase in speed wasn't immediately noticed by the occupants of the car. They only noticed a black flash. The SUV smashed into the driver's side of the dark blue hatchback.

Glass shattered. Panels crumpled. The driver's door airbag exploded. The occupants were disorientated. The Volkswagen Golf was pinned between the Range Rover and the kerb. Three men jumped from the SUV. They wore sturdy boots and were dressed in jeans, t-shirts under their bullet proof vests. They swarmed around the car. Two brandished Heckler and Koch MP5k submachine guns. The third aimed a hand gun at the car. The driver of the Range Rover climbed out and paced towards them, his own Browning pistol raised. The men screamed orders at the car's occupants. They were dragged out of the car and placed face down on the pavement.

Because of the unexpected watchers outside his home, the occupant of the house who called for assistance, hadn't the time to switch on the television and watch the morning news.

A white Ford Transit van, one of hundreds of identical vans that would be making deliveries in London at that time of the morning, reversed up the street to the Range Rover's rear bumper. The driver of the van climbed out and opened the side door. He also looked commonplace. Tan work boots, jeans and a blue lumberjack's shirt. He could have been delivering anything. Three men stood with guns trained on the couple. The fourth slipped his Browning hand gun into the back of his jeans. He plasti-cuffed the occupant's hands behind their backs and bound their ankles together. Another plastic tie was used to join hands to ankles. Finally cloth bags were pulled over their heads. Both hog-tied occupants of the common place car were carried towards the waiting Transit van. Two men got in the back of the van with them. The other two men searched the car. They retrieved two handguns. Both were dropped into forensic bags. The pair quickly walked to the van. The driver of the van slid the door shut. Back behind the wheel he turned the ignition key and the van pulled away. The incident had taken less than five minutes.

At the end of the road, the Transit van turned out of the street. A marked Metropolitan Police BMW X5 tore past. It's sirens on and lights illuminated. The Transit van entered the heaving traffic of the nearest main London thoroughfare. The neighbour who had called the emergency services saw the arrival of another marked X5. Armed police officers scoured the area.

On the other side of the road, the householder whose home was being watched shut the front door. He walked away from the police four by fours to the other end of Cloudesley Street. A car was waiting for him. He slipped himself into the passenger seat and David drove away.

CHAPTER SIXTEEN

Harry took a blue tablecloth from a pile in the Porter's Lodge and draped it over the room's wooden desk. He didn't want to make any noise as he emptied the black North Face rucksack. Food had been the primary objective of his search. That objective had quickly been superseded by the need for black clothing. All the same he hadn't disappointed himself. Kelsi sat up on the bed of boxes and she watched him unpack his hoard and carefully place everything on the desk.

Two pre-packed sandwiches were first out of the bag. Harry had taken them out of their plastic carton and wrapped them in paper towel. He saved on space and eradicated the crinkle noise of the cartons crushing. Three bags of sweets, all opened and folded again tightly to expel any air and stop any noise. Two chocolate bars as they were found. Four slips of chewing gum and a whole heap of fruit. She was curious about the next items he removed. She didn't have him down as a thief. He removed a whole washbag of coins from the rucksack, followed by lots of black clothes and they were laid separately on the floor. A black hoodie, emblazoned with a small white logo on the left breast. A black marker pen ensured the logo no longer stood out. The marker pen also did for the logos on the rucksack. Two plain black t-shirts, one long sleeved, one short sleeved and a pair of black gym trousers. He had found a size eleven pair of trainers and had already put them on his feet. The old size tens he kept as spare. They would be too big for Kelsi, but would better than her low work heels. A folding makeup mirror was pulled free and a deck of playing cards. A silent game to stem the boredom of waiting around. He dug deeper and pulled free a ski mask. Skiing wasn't on the conference agenda, maybe the owner of the ski mask hoped to get kinky on their trip away from their wife, or husband. Pulling a charger from the rucksack, he plugged it in and powered up his smartphone. The last items to come from the bag were two small tubes and a sewing tape measure.

"Do you know what these are? They're something to do with allergies I think," Harry said, "I was looking for cans of cola, or bottles of juice, but found these in a bedroom's fridge."

Kelsi scrabbled from the bed and came to the table. He pointed at the two tubes. Picking up a tube, Kelsi lifted it closer to her eyes. The writing on the label was strange. It wasn't written in English, or even in normal letters. She knew it wasn't Chinese or Japanese. It wasn't the Greek Alphabet either, but it looked similar. While Kelsi tried to interpret the hieroglyphic style letters, Harry tapped a few key words into the internet search on his smartphone. He was scrolling through search results when Kelsi struck gold. The word 'insulin' was pretty much the same throughout the world. Certain countries accented the word, or placed a letter E, or A, as the last letter, but they all meant insulin. Written in small letters on the label, hardy distinguishable from the other strange letters, was the word insulin.

"Boys are a nightmare!" Kelsi announced. "Did you even read this?"

"Oh I do say, what a very profound statement to make, young lady," said Harry in a teasing and posh voice. "No I didn't read it."

"It's not me who didn't look at the label, duh!" Kelsi said.

She rolled her eyes.

Harry put his phone down, took the plastic tube from her with a sceptical look and held it close to his face.

"So it contains insulin," he said.

"No shit, Sherlock," said Kelsi.

Harry tilted his head. He looked at her with a blank expression. Kelsi stuck her tongue out. Harry winked.

"Anyway," he said in a flat voice, "the rest of the label is written in Hebrew."

"Isn't that Jewish?" Kelsi asked.

"Yeah, it's what they speak in Israel," Harry answered.

"That's in the Middle East, right? Where they have lots of nuclear weapons?" she asked.

"Yeah, it's in the Middle East, but no, they don't have lots of nuclear weapons," said Harry; "they probably do have some, but won't admit to having nuclear weapons. The country you're thinking of is Iran and the only reason they have nuclear weapons is because you lot helped them with their development in the 1950s."

"Us lot? America, you mean?" she asked.

"Yep," he said.

"And how do you know that, Harry?" Kelsi asked.

"I read books, I know things. I watch the news and I know things. Things like how Huey Ace had one of their military generals, Qasem Soleimani, killed in an airstrike," he replied.

"Okay wise ass, do you know what the tubes do?" Kelsi asked.

"Not got a clue," Harry said.

He put the pen back on the table.

"Something to do with diabetics?" he asked.

"Well it's a good job we aren't all good at geography and history. Some of us actually know real world stuff," Kelsi said.

She continued to tell him how her cousin Elizabeth had some kind of problem with her pancreas when she was only a young child. She needed to have an operation to have it removed. This in turn meant she was diabetic. Kelsi was told how to use her insulin pen in case of an emergency and Lizzie's insulin levels dropped too low and she collapsed. She also told Harry, that if a person without diabetes was injected with insulin, it could cause a pretty quick death and that without an in-depth autopsy, would be hard to trace.

"Ok," he said, "I'm going to put one in my pocket and you're going to put one in yours, if all else fails and we end up meeting a terrorist, we'll stab them with the pens."

"Ok, let me prepare them," Kelsi said.

Harry looked on as Kelsi worked the pens.

She removed the lid and showed Harry the needle. It was tiny and was designed to be hit, or pushed firmly into a person. The device looked just like a real pen. Kelsi replaced the lid and turned the dial to ensure maximum dosage. Therefore, certain death. She put one of the pens in her pocket and handed the other to Harry.

"Well, I don't want to piss you off, do I?" he rhetorically asked.

Harry and Kelsi attacked the bounty of food. Afterwards they collapsed on the ad hoc bed. Kelsi laid her head on his chest and draped an arm over his torso.

He thought of all the skills he had learnt playing SAS: We Dare We Win. He recalled every detail of all the special forces books he had read and how he was going put their tactics to good use. He was going to wage a guerrilla war on the terrorists.

*

The white Transit van used bus lanes and drove through red traffic lights. It quickly passed grid locked London traffic. Pulling off the thoroughfare, the van entered a dark and grimy side street. The driver turned the wheel and the van drove into an industrial unit under a set of railway arches. A woman with shoulder length blonde hair pulled the heavy wooden doors shut. The couple from the indistinguishable car were removed from the van. The driver parked up next to two more identical vans and three more Range Rovers.

The brunette from the average European hatchback, wearing now scratched glasses, pushed them back into place on her nose. She heard the heavy thud of a wooden door closing behind her, followed by a clunk of metal on metal. A clasp was pulled together. A padlock clicked shut. She was relieved to be free of the plastic ties binding her arms and legs. They had started to dig in and cut her wrists and ankles. The men that applied them had been rough. Eyes closed, she rubbed her ankles and rearranged her shirt. Her hood had been pulled free. The intense light she sat in blinded her. The cloth bag had allowed for no light at all. She had been in complete darkness and had relied on hearing to get as much information as possible about her captors. Her ears had been strained, but they hadn't said a word. She was aware she was now sitting on a plastic chair. The type you might find in a school classroom. She blinked her vision back and became aware she was alone in a small room.

Her colleague was missing. She thought he would be close by, probably in a similar setup. She hadn't heard the van leave. There would be more than one room. More than likely the rooms had been constructed inside a larger building as stand-alone units. Her room was no more than ten by ten. She knew nothing about construction, but the room appeared to be new. Not old, anyway. The wooden boarding on the walls was unfinished and free of plaster. Perhaps this was their finished state. Maybe the setup was temporary. It was possible the room where she was now sat, where she was a prisoner, was only used in exceptional circumstances. This was probably as good as it got. She was definitely at a deniable site. She had previously worked in a similar place in Afghanistan. There would almost certainly be some form of metal reinforcement behind the plywood boarding.

She didn't know where she was, but she knew she was still in London. The drive hadn't been long enough to have left the city. The room certainly wasn't a police or prison cell. It was worse. No bed. No toilet. No window. It felt like an interrogation room. An unofficial interrogation room at a deniable site. A place where international law didn't exist and rules weren't followed. The kind of location where waterboarding was practised to get answers. The Geneva Convention wasn't followed in her world. She operated beyond the confines of war. She was a spy. The only feature of the room was a large one way piece of glass directly in front of her.

She was being watched.

The four armed men, the driver of the Transit van and Catherine, the blonde physical surveillance officer from MI5, all looked through the one way glass. Catherine had frisked their prisoner before she cut her free. She had found and removed an identification card tucked into the brunette's bra. She placed the card on a table in front of the one way glass, next to her male counterpart's card. His had been in his sock. If they were operating in a hostile country, they wouldn't even carry identification. Mugs of tea in hand, two of the blades stood at the back of the room. They smoked cigarettes while they waited for their MI5 contact to arrive.

David called ahead. The door to the unit under the arches was pulled open, but only enough to allow the saloon car entry. David was driving. Another man sat in the passenger seat was the more senior of the two. They climbed out of the car as the heavy wooden door was pulled shut. David was dressed casually. The other man was immaculately turned out, dark blue pin striped suit, crisp white shirt and blue patterned tie. This boy was old school.

Looking through the one-way glass at their prisoners, the man in the suit spoke.

"Thank you," he said.

"Their identification cards are on the table, it says they're CIA," said Catherine.

"Is the I.D. genuine?" the suit questioned.

"We think so, but that's something your people will have to check," said the SAS Sergeant. "They fit a CIA profile, both are young, fit and healthy. The fella was probably recruited from the military, most likely top of his class at Fort Bragg. She might have been military, but more likely the woman applied after studying criminology at university."

"Okay, I have a number I can call," the suit said.

He walked out of the viewing room and into the empty arched industrial unit.

The man in the suit made two phone calls. He stepped back into the viewing room with a forlorn look on his face. He'd aged ten years in ten minutes.

"They're CIA and they were looking at me because they don't know who I am and can't find out who I am. More to the point, the Fort Lauderdale Police Department don't know who my son is," he said.

"Your son?" the SAS sergeant asked.

"He's in Fort Lauderdale in Florida and I just found out he's in a hostage situation," Harry's father said.

"Shit!" said the sergeant.

"Untie them, make them a brew. Tell them no hard feelings. Their boss is on his way to collect them. I think they're in for a dressing down," said John Fearn, "David," he continued, "we need to make a move. Our people are booking my wife and I on a flight to Florida. I don't know what time it will be, but I need to get home and pack some clothes."

"I hope your son's alright," the sergeant said.

"Thank you," Harry's dad said

He and David made a beeline for their car.

"Steel badge is still in force," he said.

David drove their car out of the railway arches. Those two words, steel badge, were enough for him to know he was allowed to break speed limits, drive through red lights and force his way past other vehicles while getting to their destination. It was mid-morning by now and the traffic had lessened, but only slightly. They were still in London and battled constant gridlock.

"Sir," said David, "I don't mean to pry, but should you not call your wife?"

"No, I don't want her worrying. I'll call her once we know the flight time. I'm going to second you as my driver for today, feel free to make yourself a cup of tea and watch the television while I pack a suitcase," Harry's father said.

"Thank you, sir," David said

He drove the car as quickly as he could back to Cloudesley Street.

CHAPTER SEVENTEEN

Harry stood in front of a whiteboard in the Porter's Lodge. On it was drawn his plan of action. Outlined in front of him was what he was going to do and how he was going to get it done. Although at the back of his mind was an old military adage, 'No plan survives first contact with the enemy'.

He didn't need to switch the light on. It was bright outside and the sunlight crept around the curtain's edge. To be as effective as possible, Harry would have to wait for darkness. Everyone cut corners and night time was a prime example. Most of the terrorists would be asleep, only a skeleton crew working. If he raised hell once the sun went down he would be fighting a tired and demotivated force. They wouldn't be at their sharpest and that would give him a much better chance of winning. The terrorists wouldn't yet be operating a shift pattern, if they planned to at all.

He didn't know how effective he'd be. He had more or less completed SAS: We Dare We Win, but this was real. What if he was firing a weapon and got a stoppage? What if he couldn't fight hand to hand as well as his avatar? If his hands in real life weren't as good as his hands holding the controller? He and Thomas had spent a week last summer learning about Systema, a Russian Special Forces fighting technique. They had watched countless videos and tutorials on the Internet. Then they'd gone to the park to practise. That had been a good week, but it was only play fighting. He didn't know how he would react if the fighting was real. He was fearful, but fear was good. Fear gave a person an edge. It was to be harnessed and embraced. Fear kept you alive. He picked up his smartphone and called Schlemmer.

His phone vibrated and skittered across the shiny metal desk in the command truck. Chris Schlemmer woke and picked up without looking at the caller I.D.

"Hello," he groggily answered.

"Morning," said a much more vibrant Harry.

Chris lifted his head from the table and looked at his watch.

"Jeez Harry, it's only seven in the morning," he said, "I thought you were lying low?"

"I know, but I've been searching the top floors for the most of the night and I've found loads of stuff, plus another member of the hotel staff," he said.

Schlemmer lifted his head to find most of his fellow police officers in the same situation. The few that were in the truck were either asleep on their desks, or had been woken by the phone call. The only member of his staff who wasn't asleep was Teonnie. She was still working hard.

"That's great Harry, what's his name?" the chief asked.

"Her name, is Kelsi Millicent Maguire," Harry said.

He had thought it best not to mimic her accent.

"Is she safe?" he enquired.

"Yeah, of course, she's in the Porter's Lodge with me," he said.

"Okay, I'll make sure her next of kin is informed," Schlemmer said.

"Two of her colleagues, friends, were also in the room where I found her, both been shot and killed by the x-rays," Harry said.

"Do we know the names of the staff members?" Chris asked.

"Kim and Jay, I think it's short for Jayden," Harry said, "I don't know their surnames."

"That's okay, we can get them from the staffing lists," the Chief said. "Tell her I'm sorry for her loss."

"I'll pass it on," said Harry.

"Listen Harry, the situation down here has changed. The FBI have rolled into town in a big way. They've gone at this with everything they've got and the place is swarming with Special Agents, even the director is in town. They've taken charge of the office block at the back of the hotel," Schlemmer said.

His voice had started to lose its grogginess.

"That's a good thing, surely?" Harry asked.

"It is, but it means I'm no longer in charge, you'll have to start speaking to them," Chris said.

"Not happening", he said, "I know you and trust you, I don't know them at all."

"You've only spoken to me on the phone, Harry. We don't really know each other," Schlemmer replied.

"Yeah, but I've seen you in the street, you look normal, you look like a nice guy. These new people could be anything, or want anything. They're in the same position as you, they can't do anything because they can't get inside the hotel," Harry said.

Now Schlemmer knew Harry really was a switched on kid, he had just repeated the exact same thing him and Tank had spoken about.

"Will you just speak to them and listen to what they have to say, please?" Chris asked.

"Yeah okay, but if I don't like them, they can jog on," he said.

Harry hung up the call.

*

In London, a smartphone vibrated on the duvet as John Fearn packed his suitcase.

It was his Security Service secretary.

"Hello," he answered.

"Hello sir," she said, "I could only manage to get a flight for both you and your wife leaving London at 1600. Also, I could only get economy seating. British Airways have been put on a lot recently by another government agency and are still trying to clear the backlog of their own customers it's created. Will that be okay?"

"That's fine, thank you very much, I have an idea who the other agency will be," John said.

"Okay sir, I've checked you both in online, the tickets are printing off now and I'll get them biked over to your house in the next half hour," she paused, "John," his secretary said, "I hope your son's okay."

She never called him John, it was always sir. He had worked tirelessly for over two decades and his position within MI5 commanded respect, but she felt she needed to call him John. It wasn't work this time, it was personal.

"Thank you, Sophie," he said.

*

The Wavecrest Royal adjacent to the Atlantic Grand also faced the sea. The hotel next door was one block north. It had been built four years earlier than the Grand and wasn't as tall by five storeys. It had been level pegging in terms of star rating, turn-over and prestige. That was until new owners bought the Atlantic Grand and completely refurbished the building. The hotel group who bought the Atlantic Grand spent millions and it was paying off. Big time. Due to aging décor and facilities the Wavecrest Royal, even though it had just as good a seafront location, now only had three stars. Versus the Atlantic Grand's modern and stylish five stars.

The décor of the Wavecrest Royal didn't matter much to the hotel's current residents, they weren't picking up the tab. In less than twelve hours since the Atlantic Grand was stormed by armed men, the Wavecrest had been evacuated because of its proximity to the Grand. Accommodation was needed for all of the elite special forces, whose countries had attendees at the summit, who were now flying in from around the globe. Them, as well as all the American agencies already at the scene, were to be quartered in the Wavecrest Royal.

The SAS has two teams permanently ready this type of event. One on thirty minutes' standby and the other at three hours' notice. They normally responded to national incidents, but now both teams were on their way to Fort Lauderdale, the three hour team readying to move in the next hour. No one could have predicted this attack, nor could they have guessed the scale of the hostage situation. All SAS troopers currently away from base had leave their cancelled and were told to report back to Special Air Service Headquarters at Hereford. The only troopers not recalled were the blades on a mission of a critical importance. The only anti-terrorism teams that remained were the seventy elite troopers scattered around the United Kingdom with their five, two hundred and thirty two mile an hour, 'Blue Thunder' Dauphin helicopters. The teams and their helicopters were often accompanied by an Apache Gunship battlefield helicopter. They were ready to respond to a terrorist attack on the British mainland and they had been utilized on a number of occasions over recent years.

Hereford had a very good relationship with the nation's flag carrier British Airways. They understood their need for speed and secrecy. When eight SAS blades stepped from the business class cabin of a British Airways Boeing 747, they passed straight through the airport terminal with no complications and no holdups. Their route virtually mirrored the one Harry had taken just six days earlier. Suited and booted and dressed like business men, no one batted an eyelid. There would be another eight troopers on the next flight to land and then sixteen more on the two flights after that. That was the first half of the United Kingdom's contribution. In England, the other half of the squadron would soon be making their way to RAF Brize Norton. A passenger plane belonging to the Royal Air Force would fly thirty two men, plus support staff and their equipment directly to Florida.

A Special Air Service Major would be arriving in the city a few hours later, but SAS blades arrived first. When they put their boots on the ground in Fort Lauderdale twelve hours into the siege, it definitely wasn't a case of sit down and shut up. It was the troopers and sergeants in the SAS with all their operational experience, who ran the show. Their expertise in counter terrorism was very welcome. Many special forces units were based on the British model. They were now and always had been regarded as the world's premier, most competent, secretive and well respected special forces unit.

The first incarnation of the Special Air Service had been the Long Range Desert Group in North Africa during the Second World War. Formed in 1941 and under the command of David Stirling, these heavily armed and bearded men, often wearing the attire of a middle eastern native, worked behind enemy lines for weeks at a time. They wreaked havoc on German positions, ultimately proving incredibly effective against the Nazi war machine and successfully carrying out hundreds of missions throughout North Africa and Europe by the end of World War II.

It wasn't until May 1980 and the Iranian Embassy Siege at sixteen Princes Gate, London, that anyone had seen them in action. They were until that point, secret. Clad in black fire retardant clothing and wearing respirators, television news cameras picked up strange men on the embassy's roof. Moments later they were abseiling to the lower balconies, applying explosive charges to the windows, throwing flashbangs through the shattered glass and entering the building. Those strange men were the Special Air Service and that day had won them world recognition and instant worldwide respect. They gained celebrity status both at home and overseas, but no member of the SAS would ever tell anyone what they did for a job. All elite forces around the world worked with the same ideology of secrecy. Members of Seal Team Six and Delta Force were known as 'quiet professionals'. Unfortunately, Hollywood blockbusters had brought them the same fame the SAS had received in 1980. However, if anyone talked they would most likely be blacklisted and kicked from the service.

Margaret Thatcher, the Prime Minister of the United Kingdom at the time of the Iranian Embassy Siege, had specifically ordered the SAS not to use smokescreens to hide their movements. The SAS were secret, but Maggie wanted to show the world what the UK had. The events were televised live on TV all around the world. She had put a big sign up saying, 'This is what we've got, come and have a go if you think you're hard enough'. Very few did after that They had seen how effective the operation in the Iranian Embassy had been.

The world had seen how good the SAS were. Everyone wanted to copy the Britishers. The skills of the Special Air Service were sought after by many foreign governments. For years afterwards and to this day, the SAS is a go to force for the training of troops and implementation of special forces. Before the Iranian Embassy siege, those in the military and police fraternity knew the SAS were the leading unit in the world for counter terrorism. Even back in the seventies, The Regiment had trained many in the art of counter-revolutionary warfare, including helping to create the new German Armed Police force.

As a result of World War II the German state wasn't allowed to have any special forces elements to its army, however the German police force was. Ulrich Wegener, a serving German police officer, knew of only two established counter-terrorism groups at the time. The British had one, the Israelis the other. He went to the SAS. He trained with them and after taking many of their tactics and methods back to Germany, invited the SAS over to craft his new creation, Grenzschutzgruppe9. Back then it had been every other country, now training was mainly conducted in developing nations, many in Africa.

As well as training over this period, the SAS were loaned out and successfully carried out countless missions in Asia, the Middle East and Europe. The black clad blades had even been in action in previous well publicised hostage takings; two of them advising GSG9 in Somalia in 1977, after German airline Lufthansa had an aeroplane and all its the passengers taken hostage. This was in addition to their primary objective of protecting the British Isles and British interests overseas. They were instrumental in The Falkland Isles conflict and the Northern Ireland 'Troubles'. Even today the SAS is focusing on its own development and the creation of its ultra-secretive E Squadron, comprising of the very best veterans from within its ranks.

SAS training was without a doubt the best in the world. They were the most specialised soldiers on the planet. The United Kingdom Special Forces doesn't have the monetary budget of many larger countries. This forced a reliance on ingenuity, adaptability and cunning to mean they were truly unbeatable. If a specialist skill was required, the men of 22 Reg were sent away to units that were experts. Every SAS patrol contained a medic. To gain the high level of skill they needed, troopers would spent months at a time seconded to emergency ambulance crews to learn a full array of skills. If they needed somebody who spoke Italian, firstly they would be taught the language in a classroom. Then they would be sent to live in Italy for a month where they could practise their newly acquired skill.

Having outgrown its base at Stirling Lines, much of SAS training was carried out a matter of miles away at the Pontrilas Army Training Area. What started with the 'Killing House,' had developed into much more.

The House remained, but it had been joined by a street scene with small tower blocks so troopers could practice ladder assaults and abseiling. More items of public transport had been added which it was possible the SAS might need to assault, buses and train carriages. The icing on the cake was a Boeing 747 fuselage that was practised on weekly by the counter-terrorist training teams. Much of the equipment remained unseen in old warehouses left over from when the area was an ammunition storage depot.

The Pontrilas site had seen the construction of an underground training facility, that was more akin to an evil genius' lair from a James Bond movie. Underground tunnels had been constructed to replicate and acclimatize troopers to the cave systems of the northern mountains of Afghanistan. Half a mile of corridors led to all manner of different rooms the special forces may one day have to storm. The underground facility was filled with every gadget available. This was where the SAS could test their ultra-modern weapons in two hundred metre ranges.

CHAPTER EIGHTEEN

After stowing their gear in the Wavecrest Royal, the first eight SAS blades headed down to the FBI operations centre in the office block at the back of the Atlantic Grand.

Having changed from the business suits they wore for travelling into their civvy street clothing in the back of the van as they drove from the airport, they were non-descript. If it wasn't for the unfolding terrorist situation next door, you would never guess they were extraordinary, elite, or special in anyway. Only one of them was over six foot tall and two of them looked like they should still be studying at school. Hair lengths varied. Five of the eight were smoking cigarettes and nobody looked particularly muscular. These men however, were anything but weak and anything but ordinary. They climbed the exterior staircase to the office block that was a hive of activity.

A police officer was manning the door.

"Excuse me, love," the sergeant said, "who's in charge around here?"

"Who are you, sir?" she replied.

"Sorry, we don't carry ID," he said.

The British Army have identification cards, but they only read 'British Army'. They aren't regiment specific. The SAS don't carry any form of identification. Ever.

"Sergeant Stan Lewis, 22 Regiment, United Kingdom Special Forces," he said.

"Pleasure to meet you. You'll have to see someone inside about who's in charge, sorry," she said.

"Thank you," he said.

To become a fully badged member of 22 Regiment Special Air Service, known just as 22 Reg, or 'The Regiment,' to its men and those in the military, prospective troopers had to have served the suggested three years in the British Armed Forces. If you thought you could pass with less experience, you were welcome to apply, but you might not be fit enough, mature enough, or have enough military know how.

After asking permission to apply from the commanding officer of their regiment, soldiers might have to wait for up to two years for a place on selection. Those who didn't spend this time training hard, would instantly regret the decision. Applicants had to undertake a gruelling five month selection process. Only held twice a year, the course was equally hard whether it was taken in summer or winter.

The first week of special forces (SF) selection started with a series of gruelling timed marches over mountainous terrain and really sorted the wheat from the chaff. Day two of SF selection was the 'Fan Dance'. The most gruelling timed march of all. Replicating a tactical advance to battle, it was carried out over the Brecon Beacons highest peak, Pen y Fan. Carrying a 45lb bergen (rucksack) on their back, water bottle, military webbing belt and rifle, the candidates covered a fifteen mile route. The pace of the march was brutal. Applicants dropped like flies. The first week of selection whittled out many of the less prepared and capable students. Of the two hundred applicants, up to one hundred would be returned to their original units. Tough beyond belief, marching in the unforgiving Welsh mountains meant men had died while attempting this first phase of selection.

The Special Air Service and Special Boat Service of the United Kingdom run a dual initial selection process. They wanted immensely fit applicants. The members of both the SAS and SBS needed to excel in fitness. The human brain was unable to make minor cognitive decisions when the body's heartbeat exceeded one hundred and forty five beats per minute. When on operations their hearts would regularly beat above this limit. They would still need to operate just as effectively as if they had just been out for a gentle stroll and not endured a five mile run while carrying a bergen, equipment and rifle weighing a further fourteen stone.

It wasn't just their fitness levels that were tested. Applicant's mental fortitude was continually under pressure. The physical element was hard. The students were pushed to their limits and had their mental weaknesses exposed. As a result, ninety per cent of applicants were cut. What the directing staff (DS) of the course wanted to see was that candidates will to keep going with their grit and determination to carry on.

The would-be members of the Special Air Service who passed the first phase of selection then endured twenty four weeks of competency testing. Even if a soldier passed initial selection and passed all of the other elements, they still might not make it. If they threw into doubt their mentality, not fitting in with The Regiment, they were returned to their original unit. Those that passed the first week would spend the majority of the next five months training in the jungle. That was the real reckoner. Many applicants wouldn't make it through the jungle stage. It was harder than the first week. In the jungle they would learn special forces tactics, techniques and procedures, as well as how to use many SF weapons. If an applicant got through all that, then came the escape and evasion (E+E) and interrogation phase.

During escape and evasion an applicant could either throw in the towel themselves, or get binned by the DS. Mental fortitude to carry on just didn't make the grade. The SAS wanted the best and therefore E+E was one of the most difficult stages. It started with a briefing. The student was told they would be living off the land for a period of time and weren't allowed any contact with anyone else. Dartmoor National Park in Devon was one of the sites used for E+E. Every farm in the vast moorland was well accustomed to these training exercises. They knew that if anyone should approach them and ask for food, or help, they were to report the incident. They did report these incidents and it had proven the downfall of a good number of applicants in the past.

Before an applicant attempted E+E, they were first stripped naked. Every body cavity was searched to ensure they weren't attempting to bring anything onto the exercise with them. They were given a pair of old army lace up boots, minus the laces; green army overalls, army greatcoat, a military cap comforter and a standard issue army clasp knife. They were not allowed socks or underpants. Once dressed in their minimal clothing, the few remaining applicants were hooded and loaded onto four tonne army trucks. Driven from basecamp to various locations for over two hours, they had no idea where they were. The individual was then dropped at a location known only by the DS. They were told they must rendezvous with an agent every twenty four hours. A student was expected to live off the land by hunting, fishing and foraging and to make a shelter and fire if possible. Even when asleep there was no let-up in the hunt for them. The hunter force consisting of commando or parachute regiment members, searched twenty four seven. The force wouldn't be given details of the applicant's location or drop off point. They would have to find the applicant as if they were any other enemy. If caught, the potential SAS trooper would be treated as a prisoner. If not caught in the first twenty four hours, the applicant would meet with their agent who was one of the directing staff. The DS would check them over to make sure they weren't dying, give them a block of cheese and a lump bread and send them off to meet with another agent the next day. Contact would be minimal. This continued for four to six days depending on the weather conditions, the success rate of the hunter force, or until an applicant was captured. If a student made it to his final RV with their agent, they would be captured near to that location.

The next phase was conducted by interrogators from the British Army Intelligence Corps. It was designed to replicate the treatment they could receive at the hands of a real enemy. Trained by the Joint Service Intelligence Wing, the males and females that carried out this phase knew everything there was to know about interrogation. They gave the applicants hell. The interrogation was twofold. The questioning was also two fold and the interrogators would play good cop, bad cop. The interrogator would treat them well and speak to them nicely, ask them about their families and what they were doing when they were caught. Talk about their background and where they were from. They would also make their questions as complex as possible. The intelligence officers grilling the students would give them an emotional reward, a pat on the back if they said something important. They might tell them something bad was to happen to them, but that could be avoided if they were truthful. They would say things like, 'Just be honest with us and we will ensure nothing bad happens'. The interrogator wanted to appear as they were helping the applicant. That was a lie. If they didn't get their way and the interrogators knew the applicant was avoiding answering questions, refusing to answer, or downright was lying to them, they would tear into him, attempt to trip the student up and find holes in their story, they would coerce the applicant into saying certain things that would later prove incriminating. Students were often required to stand naked in front of female investigators and take all manner of criticism. They were picked on and bullied, made to feel inadequate and feeble. Their prowess as a man was thrown into doubt. They were mocked. The interrogators laughed at them. Many soldiers and later applicants to the SAS had hard, uncomfortable upbringings. They had joined the army at sixteen as a way to get out of that situation. This was an item the interrogators paid close attention to and used as a tool to dig on the SAS students. All the students had to remember was that as a member of the UKSF that had been captured by an enemy force, there would always be someone mounting a rescue mission. It wasn't going to last forever.

After World War II, the Geneva Convention was significantly updated and covered topics including the humane treatment of prisoners of war. Many of the warring factions and terrorist groups the SAS would likely face, didn't follow the Geneva Convention. The interrogation they received during this final phase of selection had to closely follow this, yet not step over the line. Even so, under the laws of the Geneva Convention a captured soldier only had to tell his captors three things: his surname, his rank, his army serial number. Applicants would keep to this for as long as possible, despite all manner of trickery from the interrogators. Eventually students would give a cover story, but never let slip the real reason for their being there. This was harder for some students than others.

The second fold of interrogation was just as demanding as the questioning and allowed for no let-up in the process. When not being interrogated, applicants would be held in stress positions - made to lean against walls in a demanding position. Squat for long periods of time, or sit on the floor with their legs out and arms raised above their heads. They wouldn't be allowed any sleep. They would be subjected to loud noises, a baby crying constantly via a speaker system, loud clangs of metal beating like a drum, have running chainsaws waved precariously near to them. All of this was conducted while they were wearing blackout goggles. They would then be subjected to white noise played through headphones while they were tied up and unable to remove their sensory deprivation equipment. Then they were hauled back into questioning. This could last up to four days and like the escape and evasion phase, applicants could throw in the towel at any point.

If an applicant to the SAS passed that final stage and didn't quit, they were in. The few remaining applicants of the two hundred that started five months earlier in the Brecon Beacons were handed the coveted sand coloured beret and given their winged dagger cap badge. The regiment's motto 'Who Dares Wins,' wasn't tattooed across their chests, it was engraved on their hearts. If you failed the course at any stage, you could try for selection again, but only once.

Stan's troopers followed him through the door and into the office.

"Who's in charge please, mate?" Stan asked.

A young lad looked up from tapping on his laptop, boredom on his face. He must have known he was a glorified concierge.

"Well that's George Katz, the Director of the FBI. He flew in from Washington D.C, arrived a couple of hours before you guys," he said.

The lad pointed into the spacious room overflowing with FBI Special Agents.

The room was busy and noisy. Agents were tapping on laptops like himself, others pouring over reports. Many were in conversation which each other, some walking around the room on their smartphones. A group in the centre of the room were talking with George Katz.

"Who are you looking for?" he asked.

"Are there any SF guys here?" Stan counter asked.

"SF?" the lad questioned.

He was probably fresh out of training at the FBI Academy at Qauntico.

"Special Forces, British," Stan said.

"Ahh, you'll be wanting the Ops Room," he said.

CHAPTER NINETEEN

Taking an internal staircase, the FBI staffer walked to an identical office downstairs. He knocked on the door of the hastily put together Ops Room (Operations Room) and stepped back. A man in a New York Mets baseball shirt pulled the door from the inside.

"These men are British Special forces," the lad said.

"Thanks," said the New Yorker.

Once the FBI staffer was out of earshot, the guy introduced himself.

"Senior Chief Petty Officer Tommy Moore, Seal Team Six," he said with a thick accent, "Nice to have you here fellas, come on in."

Seal Team Six was no longer their official title. The Naval Special Warfare Development Group (DEVGRU), was the unit's official name. Seal Team Six was their previous title and the one they commonly used. People knew that name and knew that along with Delta Force, they were America's tier one anti-terrorism unit. Once they were inside and the door was pulled, Tommy walked to the centre of the room.

There had been a long standing collaboration between Seal Teams, Delta Force and the SAS. More recently an SAS trooper was in Nairobi, Kenya and mentoring and training Kenyan Troops in January 2019. Four al-Shabaab Islamic jihadists, along with a suicide bomber, attacked an office complex and hotel. A Seal Team was conducting the Kenyan's training and the SAS blade was officially under their command. They hadn't yet been given the green light to intervene and asked the off duty trooper for his help.

The eighteen year veteran of the SAS was shopping in the city. Having all of his equipment in the trunk of his car, he made his way to the incident. People were dying. There was only one man present who could make a difference. After a quick phone call to the British High Commission, he was given permission to intervene. The trooper first coordinated the Kenyan Army's efforts. Donning a Balaclava to hide his identity and wearing his off duty civvies and hastily put on light body armour, he entered the complex. The blade carried a C8 assault rifle and Glock pistol. Twenty one civilians had already been killed by the insurgents. The trooper, with total disregard for his own safety and knowing that there wasn't any backup, killed two of the four jihadists. Next was an evacuation of the civilians. He helped ensure the safety of seven hundred workers and guests at the complex. The last two jihadists were shot and killed by Kenyan Forces. The magnitude of the actions of the SAS trooper earned him Britain's second highest medal, the Conspicuous Gallantry Cross, only superseded by the Victoria Cross. His story went down in Special Air Service history and gave him legendary status.

"I'm glad to have you guys here. One Seal Team Squadron is operational elsewhere and half of another is training in the Arctic Circle. We're about seventy men down. How many guys you got coming in?" Tommy asked.

"I'm not entirely sure, a full squadron I think. I also heard the Australian SAS are on their way with sixteen troopers," answered Stan.

"We got word the Canadians are sending twenty men down, including a few support staff," Tommy said. "Should be quite the party."

The room's window blinds were all pulled shut, but it was daytime outside and the sun was throwing out plenty of light.

A large group of guys came to the centre of the room to meet the new arrivals.

Tommy shook hands with all the Brits. The other guys did the same. Stan was happy with his US counterpart. His rank meant he had joined the military as a private. He was normal.

"Dave, 22 Reg," Dickinson said.

"John Perez, Seal Team Six," said an American.

"Ross Denton, SAS," said the six footer.

"Rodney Camack, Delta Force Master Sergeant," said his equally tall counterpart.

"Scally, The Regiment," said the heavily accented Scouser.

He shook hands with another Delta Force guy.

The introductions carried on for five minutes until Stan asked if anyone round here had ever heard of a kettle? That got a laugh from the Americans. Soon they were all standing round chewing the fat with mugs of coffee.

"When I get home, I'll send you a box of teabags," Stan said.

Stan, Tommy and Rodney talked.

They took a walk around the room while the others chatted. Stan was impressed with the set-up. There wasn't much he would have done differently. All three were sergeants and experts in their field. Between them they had over thirty five years special forces' experience. Stan had the most operational experience of the three sergeants and had recently returned from a successful hostage rescue in Burundi.

Land locked in East Africa, the Republic of Burundi was the African continents smallest and most unstable nation. A militant anti-British faction had taken over the British Embassy in the country's largest city, Bujumbura. They were threatening to murder all of the staff unless their demands were met. The British Government doesn't negotiate with terrorists. The Prime Minister didn't hesitate in sending half an SAS Squadron to resolve the situation. An SAS Officer, Stan and a further thirty one men were in the country within twenty four hours of the siege starting. Forty eight hours after the siege started, all seven terrorists were dead and the safety of eighteen British Embassy staff had been secured. That was only three weeks ago.

With that recent and successful operation in mind, the US Sergeants offered Stan the role of operation commander. Stan told them that the Atlantic Grand being on American soil meant it should be an American led operation. Tommy was the more experienced of the two Americans and had taken a lead role in Operation Neptune Spear, the mission that ended the hunt for and killed Osama Bin Laden. He was to take command of the operation.

Rodney, the lean and mean African-American Delta Force Master Sergeant, had been involved in the training of Kurdish Forces in Syria and had taken part in numerous raids to eradicate ISIS. He was the operation's second-in-command. They both agreed to have Stan come along as senior advisor and his men as advisors. Advisors or not, they knew they would be getting their hands dirty.

*

Once he had properly woken, he made his way to the ad hoc FBI office. Chief Schlemmer stood with George Katz and Tank Bolling. Surrounding them was an entourage of FBI Special Agents. Specialists in hostage rescue and specialists in hostage negotiation. Dressed in a black three piece suit, a thin and ageing George Katz picked up the phone. He dialled Harry's number and passed the phone to Chief Schlemmer.

He slept, but with the smartphone next to his face. His eyes would sense the flashing light as the phone rang. The ringtone was muted and vibrations turned off. The phone flashed. Harry's senses kicked into gear and his eyes opened. The phone in front of him displayed a withheld number. Schlemmer? The 911 dispatcher? The FBI? Picking up the phone Harry looked at the screen. In his heart of hearts, he knew it was the FBI coming to ruin his day. He reluctantly answered the call.

Chief Schlemmer spoke first and they had a brief discussion. Harry asked Schlemmer to call him back, in private, after the phone call. Schlemmer handed the phone to George Katz. The call lasted no more than three minutes and went exactly as Harry thought. Sit tight. Stay safe. Don't get involved. No more running around the hotel. The big boys are here now and we're making a plan. There wasn't even a thank you for what he had already done.

"Righto," Harry said.

He rather impudently clicked off the call.

His smartphone lit up again exactly twelve minutes after the initial call ended. It was the chief. After their brief discussion and Harry reiterating to him how they wouldn't be able to plan anything, because they were in the exact same situation as the police had been, he said, 'Tell them to jog on'.

"Listen Harry," said Chris, "the FBI might think they are all that, but there are bigger boys arriving here all the time and some of them are from the console game you play. All I ask, is you don't get anyone killed and you don't get yourself killed. Just be really careful."

"I will," he replied.

*

"Can we have a chat in private?" Stan asked.

Facts and details about the situation needed to be learnt. Everybody involved would need to know all of those facts, but first they had to get hold of them and for that, they would need a quieter room away from the much busier and nosier main Ops Room.

"One step ahead of you," Tommy said.

He had already chosen a senior planning room. The three sergeants entered a smaller glass fronted office. A hand written note had been taped to the door. It read, 'Knock before entering'.

'We've covered most bases already," Rodney said, "but tell us what you want to know, so we can make sure we haven't missed anything."

Stan nodded and sat down with another mug of coffee. He didn't need to write out a list of what he wanted to know, he had been a counter-terrorism specialist for fifteen years.

"First things first, have the terrorists killed anyone yet?" asked Stan.

"We know at least four conference guests were killed in the initial armed takeover of the hotel. We are also aware that two staff members were shot and killed while trying to evade capture. We don't think anyone has been killed since," Rodney answered.

Stan pondered his thoughts.

"Who were they?" he asked.

"The staff?" Rodney asked, answering his own question, "Two kids who worked in the hotel, there are two more to discuss, but we'll get to them shortly."

"The terrorists stormed the hotel. One conference guest was killed because he fought back and at the same time local PD took three 911 calls. The callers were shot and killed. The first one I knew personally, he used to be my boss when I was a search and rescue diver for the navy. The first man they murdered was Larry Knowles, the Commandant of the United States Coastguard," Tommy said, "I really want to get the bastard that pulled the trigger."

"You will," Stan said. "Who's next?"

Tommy took the lead for the next two victims as well.

"A lady called Roisin O'Leary, secretary to the Irish Prime Minister. Next was a guy called Felix Schleck, a reporter from Luxembourg," he said.

"Totally random killings, they were just doing something the terrorists didn't like. Do we think there has been anyone else killed since then? Stan asked.

"Not apart from the staff," Tommy said.

"Then there's Harry," Rodney said.

"Harry?" Stan asked, "who's Harry?"

"The hotel manager's nephew, seventeen years old, apparently working in the hotel for the summer. He was working at the time of the assault and somehow managed to dodge capture. The FLPD Chief has been talking to him, we'll take a walk over to see him when we get chance," Rodney said.

"So things have quietened down a little?" Stan asked.

"Yeah," said Tommy. "After the initial television broadcast the terrorists made, we haven't heard anymore gunshots. We think it's all quiet."

Stan thought some more and nodded his head.

"So no demands, or threats have been made by the x-rays?" questioned Stan.

"None at all," said Tommy.

"Okay, so if they aren't killing hostages indiscriminately, there is no need for an immediate response. We've got time to plan," Stan said. "Have you got a quick reaction force (QRF) in place?"

"Yeah, we got some guys from the Seals and Delta next door, all kitted out and ready to go," Tommy said.

Stan slid his smartphone out of his pocket and made a call.

"Dave, get four of the lads get dressed up and have them join the QRF next door."

"Will do," Dickinson said.

Stan clicked of the call.

"Second thing," Stan said, "I want the medical history of every hostage, whether they're a guest or a staff member."

"We have people speaking to the governments of those attending, they're fetching them for us," said Tommy. "The medical records will be here in the next few hours."

"The staff will prove easier," said Rodney, "the vast majority of them were released just after the hostage taking, only the general manager of the hotel remains, plus a couple of staff who were never found by the terrorists. An eighteen year old female was hiding in a storeroom with the two hotel workers who were shot and killed. Harry found her alive and unharmed, she's now hiding with him."

"What's Harry's deal?" Stan asked.

"He's over from England, according to the PD Chief, he's a special forces geek," Rodney answered.

"Interesting. Get the general manager's medical records, I want the medical records of the two kids as well," said Stan.

It was highly likely that one or more hostages caught up in the terrorist action may be suffering from an illness or condition. Their well-being could depend on them regularly taking prescribed drugs. Diabetes was one such condition. A type one sufferer was insulin dependent and their situation would grow progressively worse if they didn't regularly receive doses of insulin. Other conditions common in hostage situations were angina and asthma. If the special forces knew about this, they could arrange for the x-rays to pass those required drugs to the hostage. Clued up terrorists knew that deliberately stopping this from happening only shortened the time it took the special forces to make an armed assault.

"They also have a surveillance system in place, cameras on all sides of the building looking at the street. What's more concerning is that it appears to be powered by a separate power source, not the hotel's own," Tommy said.

"Bollocks, if we cut the hotel's power before we assault, they're still going to know we're coming," Stan said.

Tommy and Rodney nodded their heads.

"In the immediate I want a team going over the TV broadcast the terrorists made, everyone needs to watch it. Someone might pick up on something that others will miss," said Stan, "I also want all the CCTV videos from every building and street surrounding the hotel. Let's see how these bastards got in. Once they've watched it, they need to watch it again. We need anything, a gesture, a look. Get one of our interrogators to do the same, they spend their lives looking for the 'tell'."

Rodney and Tommy nodded their heads.

"We have the hotel's architect plans on file, they're printing off and we'll have them in the hour," Tommy said.

"How accurate are they?" Stan asked.

"We presume some internal walls have changed, but structurally nothing's altered, Rodney has sent for a couple of the hotel's maintenance men," Tommy said.

"Excellent, as soon as they get here, have new plans drawn up and bin the old, make sure they do not get mixed up," said Stan. "Who's providing overwatch right now?"

"FLPD posted snipers to the rooftops as soon as they got here," said Rodney. "The SWAT commander is a guy called Tank, he's a good guy, but not ex-military, we put Delta snipers alongside them."

"Top work," said Stan.

No military outfit would question information fed back to them by military serving personnel, their thought processes are focused and pristine. Other agencies were unknown quantities with different priorities and unknown influences, promotion, trouble at home, anything that could be a factor to a missed parameter, or lack of focus. There had to be a military presence observing the situation. SWAT teams weren't trained to feedback the same level of detail as an SF operator.

A police sniper might communicate back to the Ops Room saying the suspect is writing. A special forces soldier would feedback information saying the suspect is writing with his left hand, using a ballpoint pen. The pen has a blue plastic tip. He's picking his nose at the same time, but hasn't looked up from his paperwork once. Details mattered. A lot more information other than just a simple task could be amassed on a suspect. In this instance the individual was left-handed. That could be a 'tell'. Hundreds of known terrorists could be eliminated. Only a few known left handed terrorists remained. The SF were closer to knowing who they were up against. The information also told the SF the x-ray was studious, but easily distracted by trivial matters. All details would be passed to the 'special forces liaison'.

Information could be collated and related back as intelligence. The present giving foresight into the future and ergo, the edge. If the sniper could see clearly enough to read the note that was being written, he might be able to pick out a name. If the name was passed to the special forces liaison, he might be able to deduct who the terror organisation was. Most terrorists and their associates were known to military intelligence.

"I don't know who you have in place at the moment, but our Badger was on a flight a few hours after ours," Stan said. "He'll be here shortly."

"Your what?" Rodney asked.

"Badger," Stan said.

"Your what?" Rodney asked again.

Stan had a glint in his eye.

"Badger. A thick set nocturnal mammal of the weasel family. Typically has grey and black coat," Stan said.

"Stan, we know what a fucking badger is," Rodney said.

All three started to laugh.

"The Badger's our special forces liaison. He's the interface between intelligence, in this case eyes on intel and the SAS troops on the ground," Stan said. "Even the UK High Command don't know where we are. The Badger is the only person that knows the location of an SAS team and is the only person in communication with forward troops. However, in this instance every educated man or woman in the world, with even the slightest degree of comprehension of anything, will know there are special forces operational in Fort Lauderdale. But we still need our Badger. Most badgers you poke with a stick will snarl at you. This one will take your fucking arm off and ram the stick up your arse before you know he's moved."

"We've got one of them too," Tommy said. "Our Badger's a man called Steve."

"Funnily enough, ours is too," said Stan.

*

After his phone call with the FBI and later Chief Schlemmer, Harry dozed sporadically until later in the day. Occasionally he would wake, climb off the bed, make some notes and have a sip of water. He didn't want to have too much, drinking meant peeing. That meant making noise. He didn't have a set of eyes in the corridor to see if anybody would hear him. Instead he would wake and suck a boiled sweet. He would make more notes and iron out the finer details of his plan. Kelsi slept. Every so often she would wake. Usually induced by a nightmare about her recent experience. Harry would get back on the bed if he wasn't already there and give her a hug. He'd comfort her until her eyes closed again and she drifted off to sleep.

He woke properly at ten in the evening. Curled up, lying next to him, Kelsi slept like a baby. She must have been awake and fearing for her life the whole time she had been in the linen cupboard, scared to make an involuntary noise if she fell asleep. He peered through a gap in the curtains. Nothing had changed. The police were still outside, The FLPD command truck, the SWAT truck, a couple of Ford Expeditions and Dodge Chargers sat idle with lines of parked up fire tenders and ambulances. The food truck had a steady stream of emergency service personnel placing orders. As well as the odd figure in a black suit. FBI for sure. Harry wished he could be there, standing in the queue, ordering a burger, or taco. All he had was the fruit he'd scavenged. The sandwiches were long gone.

He wondered if the x-rays had a shift pattern yet. If they did, how did it work over a twenty four hour period. Was it three eight hour shifts, or two twelve hour shifts? Three eight hour shifts meant more men would be needed, or the number of men on shift would be fewer. Two twelve hour shifts meant fewer men sleeping, or sitting idle for less time overall. It also meant the terrorists would be working for longer and could be more susceptible to fatigue. Harry reckoned on two twelve hour shifts. His next question was when would the shifts change? It would be sensible for there to be a day shift and a night shift, changing over at six or seven in the evening, then exactly twelve hours later in the morning. Both those times had already passed. The shift would have changed. The time was right. Dressing in his new black clothes he left a note for Kelsi. Harry checked all his pockets and ensured nothing on his person would make a noise as he walked. She stirred from her slumber. She knew where he was going. They'd talked about it.

"Are you ready?" she asked.

"I was born ready," he answered.

Kelsi smiled and tried not to laugh. Seconds later, she fell asleep with a smile on her face. He headed to the door and listened for movement in the corridor.

*

Alejandro Diego Munoz and Marie Thouvenin hadn't seen each other for over a year. On the first evening, the Wednesday, Bothrops Atrox didn't sleep. He had had plenty of chance to do exactly that whilst waiting at Opa-Locka Airfield. Marie Thouvenin did sleep that night, but only for four hours. She slept late and rose early. All to support her lover. The next day had been long, but not challenging. By ten in the evening of the Thursday, Bothrops and Marie were both ready for their sleep. They wanted to share a bed. They wanted to share each other.

They ascended the hotel taking the grand front staircase. Bothrops wanted to check on the men he hadn't yet seen. Surveying the kitchen that was feeding his men, he spoke briefly

with the chef he had brought on the mission. The chef offered
to cook them a steak dinner. He politely refused. There were another two stops to make before he was on his own with Marie.

Dressed differently to the rest of Bothrop's force, in office
attire, his tech guy was maybe the only terrorist who would get
out alive, as well as Bothrops and his loved ones. The tech guy
was lounging back in a reclining leather swivel chair, watching
images on four large flatscreens, when he and Marie reached the
Indiana Media Suite.

"Don't get up," Bothrops said.

"I wasn't going to," said his tech guy.

Normally a person showing such insolence would receive
a beating. Not delivered by Bothrops, his days of giving beat-
ings were long gone. He would select men for the task. In this
instance, the churlish attitude of the tech guy was appreciated.
He and Bothrops had been born a few doors apart in the same
slum. They only differed a couple of years in age.

His friend and tech guy was an occasional employee. He
was chosen for this task and paid even more handsomely than
the foot soldiers. His regular job as a senior telecommunica-
tions engineer for Colombia's main telephone network provider
had taught him the skills he would need for the most important
task to come.

"When do you start setting up?" Bothrops asked.

"Tomorrow morning, when the Wavecrest Royal has started filling up nicely. Do you still plan to attack tomorrow evening?" the tech guy asked.

"No," Bothrops said, "a couple of nights from now, in the
late evening when the hotel is full of special forces, that's when
we will rock them to the core and show them our real strength."

They left the tech guy observing the surveillance cameras.

Climbing the last flight of stairs at the rear of the hotel,
Bothrops and Marie walked to the second room holding his
hostages. The room containing the POTUS. He didn't radio
ahead. He didn't announce his coming. He wanted to be able

to surprise the guard on duty and check on the welfare of the hostages. They were all important people and they should be treated fairly.

They were being treated correctly. One at a time, the hostages were being allowed to shuffle on the floor to a water dispenser and have a drink from half-filled plastic cups at the base of the fountain. They were watched by the armed guard every inch of the way. Another guard arrived every hour to bring food and escort hostages to the toilet. Bothrops stood out of view to everyone in the room. He observed. If there was nothing wrong, he didn't plan to intervene. He didn't have to.

They took the elevator to a suite on the twentieth floor. It was the largest in the hotel. As well as containing four bedrooms, it enjoyed a large living area with sea view and kitchenette. Bothrops Atrox took great pleasure in spending the night with his mistress, in the suite originally allocated to Huey Ace.

*

Working in a quieter corner of the main Ops Room for the last half hour, Rodney wrapped the door with his knuckles. Stan and Tommy looked up from poring over plans of storm drains in the streets surrounding the Atlantic Grand. Rodney entered.

"Good news," he said.

"Shoot," said Tommy, in his quick fire New York tongue.

"The architect of the Wavecrest Royal next door sold his business, but the architecture firm that bought it is right here in Fort Lauderdale. They've emailed over some plans. I've had a quick look at them and a lot of the room sizes aren't that different to the rooms in the Atlantic Grand. It will be perfect to use as a practice building. The bedroom layout will be different, but we can work with that," Rodney said.

Special forces were extremely competent because in their down time when they weren't operational, they practised. Everything from storming a house, office, aeroplane, covert surveillance of a target moving through a city, vehicle borne raids, helicopter extraction, to simply moving at speed while carrying full kit and weapons. They practised all they could, but once they were heading out an operational mission, or had certain facts about their target confirmed, they practised explicitly for that task. Their target was known. It was the Atlantic Grand. They hadn't yet received orders to assault the target building, but they were sure they would and when they did, they wanted to be as prepared as possible. Rodney had now secured a facility close by, in which they could do exactly that.

"Brilliant," Stan said. "Get working on a programme so that every man here gets numerous hours practise. Alternate the lads between practising and QRF duties."

CHAPTER TWENTY

Harry left Kelsi in the Porter's Lodge. That's where she would be safest. The terrorists had no reason to believe there would be anyone up there, it was just a storeroom.

All he had to be wary of were x-rays randomly patrolling the hotel. Harry thought the terrorists' state of mind should work in his favour. The hotel had been taken captive. It was theirs. As far as they were concerned, they wouldn't need to do anymore taking. There was no one else other than the hostages in the hotel. As a result they weren't looking for anyone as they policed the corridors, hallways and passageways. When they roamed around the hotel they would be in pairs, a three, or four. They would be relaxed. Their guard would be down. Their task would be reactionary. There would be no need for them to creep around the hotel using stealth and cunning. They would talk to each other, not conceal their movements or speech. That would be Harry's early warning system.

He was in a state of high alert. He was in a place he wasn't meant to be and doing something he shouldn't. He was tuned into his surroundings as he silently tracked around the hotel. He used all the guile he could assemble. He would hear any x-rays a mile off and be given enough time, however small, to hide. Maybe even counter attack and ambush. He made his way down to the bottom basement floor, the maintenance department.

Harry took the same stairs as the first time. Creeping quietly he used all the skills he had played and read about. He made it to the third floor of the hotel undetected. Unlike the recon mission he had carried out for Schlemmer, he didn't need to exit the stairwell on this floor. Harry didn't think it possible to be more careful than he already had been, but he was. His pace slowed. He took care with his footwork. Slow was smooth. Smooth was fast. He was both.

He continued descending to the landing of the second floor. It was the same story on floor two. As far as he knew, the only room that was occupied was the Indiana Media Suite at the back of the hotel. He moved on, open-mouthed, his back turned to the outer wall of the stairwell. Ears strained, he listened hard. Diligently he placed one foot in front of the other as he made his way to the first floor.

Two steps from the main landing of the first floor, he heard voices in the corridor. Harry froze with fear. It felt like a lifetime. In reality he was only prone for a second. He weighed up his options. Stay where he was and get captured, or shot and die, or move and hide. He chose the last option. In less time than it took him to think about it, it was done. Harry stood flat to the wall, in the gap behind where the door would end up if it opened. He didn't know what he would do if it did open. The best escape plan would be to slip through the opened door as the terrorists walked to the stairs. Get out of sight before they got to the mid landing and saw him. Once through the door, he would have to deal with anyone on the first floor who saw him. If that happened he would give it legs and attempt to evade capture, or death, or both. The voices got louder, then dissipated. They had turned the corner. The voices were travelling away from him. He breathed out and moved on.

On the first basement floor he couldn't hear any voices. He took the opportunity to look at the staff entrance. The door wasn't rigged with explosives like he would have imagined and it wasn't how Tank had thought either. They both expected a light wooden frame charge to have been attached to the inside of the door, industrial grade adhesive tape holding the device in place, charges and detonators on the hinges and lock. Instead a

Claymore anti-personal mine had been placed ten feet in front of the staff entrance. Normally two spikes protruded from the bottom so the mine could be pushed into the mud, or grass, or any soft surface. This one sat a foot from the floor on a purpose built metal stand with four legs.

A Claymore could be operated in two ways. When the enemy was within range of the device, it could be triggered by a soldier with eyes on the target, or it could be triggered by the victim unwittingly activating a tripwire. In this instance the tripwire was hooked up to the external door. When someone pulled from outside, the Claymore would explode. If you were in the firing line and weren't killed by the pound and a half of C4 explosive, the seven hundred metal ball bearings that were ejected when the C4 detonated, would surely see you off.

He was familiar with the Claymore anti-personal mine, he'd used them on SAS: We Dare We Win. He knew how effective they could be and also how destructive. Console games he'd played in the past always seemed to lessen the effect of the C4 explosive, but the SAS video game had hit the nail on the head and it tallied with what he'd read about them in real-life accounts. The explosion was much bigger than the previous games had made out. A Claymore weighed only thirty grams more than four grenades. The explosion was comparably larger.

There were sensors present on the doors too. A simple type that was commonplace to find on the front doors of shops, offices and industrial units. One half attached to the door, no bigger than two packets of chewing gum, its counterpart device directly opposite and fixed to the door frame. When the door opened and the two parted company, an electric doorbell would be set off. The only difference was this device didn't ring a bell, it triggered a suicide vest worn by the most important man in the world.

Turning around, he headed back to the stairs and didn't hear any sound from the second basement floor. On the mid-landing between basement two and three, he saw a problem. A pile of cigarette butts lay on the floor of the bottom landing. Harry couldn't be sure, but he would bet it was terrorists and not hotel staff who left them there. The lights were turned on in the room leading from the stairwell. That was definitely a bad thing. He hadn't been down to Maintenance in his extensive three days as an employee. He didn't know and couldn't imagine how the floor would be laid out. He knew that the bottom basement floor of the hotel contained the maintenance department workshop, their tools and supplies, as well as the other door he needed to check. The Goods In door was a roller shutter door. He didn't know what that would look like. The dirty linen chutes also terminated there. He guessed piles of bedsheets and a big garage door. He continued down the stairs and towards the light.

The air was undisturbed, voiceless, soundless. He looked through the safety glass in the door. The lights were on. Nobody in the room. The evidence on the floor told him someone had been recently. They might come back soon. Harry cracked on.

The door opened straight into the maintenance department. Racks of tools and cabinets, like the ones mechanics use, lined the walls. Work benches sat in the centre of the room, much like the layout of his woodwork classroom at school. The back right corner of the room, corner four, was where the loading bay door was located. He walked there first.

The roller shutter loading bay door echoed the same story as the staff entrance two floors above, but this time there were five Claymores, all stood two feet apart. Behind the loading bay at corner four was where the other service stairwell terminated. Next to that was a big pile of used linen. Above it was the linen chute. Forward of the shutter door and standing in the goods-in area, was a large open ended metal box. Attached to the box was a flatscreen and operator's control panel. Long hanging plastic strips filled the gaps at each end. The industrial x-ray machine, *for sure*. Just like the machines at the airport, only ten times bigger. It was time he found what he had come for.

*

Once they were in the suite, they showered separately. Bothrops in the main bedroom's bathroom and his puta in another. She had previously ordered a small suitcase to be sent to the suite. This was now the case she chose from. She finished applying makeup and dressed again, this time in lacy black lingerie. Marie slipped on a pair of patent black high heels and sauntered to the main bedroom to greet her sweetheart.

*

Another British Airway's 747 landed at Miami International Airport late in the evening. Mr and Mrs Fearn didn't know anyone on their flight. The Badger did. He walked separately to the eight SAS troopers, it was operational procedure, even if they were on friendly turf. The Badger took the keys for the van that had been pre-arranged for him, as well as the eight troopers. Harry's father stood at the other end of the rental company's desk.

At short notice the only car the rental company had available was a sports utility vehicle. It was huge and far bigger than they required, but John Fearn still signed the paperwork and took the keys. He needed to get to Fort Lauderdale.

As Harry's parents drove the hour north to Fort Lauderdale, an unmarked rental van overtook them. John Fearn was given light relief from his wife's sobbing, she was fast asleep in the passenger seat. All he could imagine was the last time he'd seen his son. He had shook his hand at Heathrow. Now he wished he'd hugged him.

*

As Harry hunted around in the maintenance department for items he would need, Bothrops and Marie lay in a post coital tangle of sweaty bodies. They talked about the unfolding situation and he explained how the missile strike would work.

"You see my dear," Bothrops said, "I have had my people study many sieges over the last forty years to see how the world has reacted. The prime example is how the SAS of the United Kingdom set the standard at the Iranian Embassy in 1980. Almost every, if not every country, now has a special forces capability. They are all based in some way on the Special Air Service. At the Iranian Embassy Siege they made their temporary base in the Royal College of General Practitioners, right next door to the embassy. I have no reason to believe that the FBI outside won't do exactly the same."

"How do you know the FBI are outside?" Marie asked.

"They always are with big incidents like this. They will send their very top people. Never in the history of the world, has something like this been done. The Americans will send their special forces too. When they arrive, they will need somewhere to sleep. All the hotel guests will be told to leave the Wavecrest Royal and everyone will sleep there. FBI. Special forces. All of them," he said.

"How do you know that?" she asked.

"Because they will want them as close to here as possible," he said. "They will want them on the scene. Everyone copies what the SAS did in 1980."

Marie thought for a moment. She didn't speak. Just laid her head on his chest.

"When the American special forces arrive," he said, "they will realise how big the task is and they won't want to bite off more than they can chew. They will ask the British for help."

"Why will they?" she asked.

"Because the Special Air Service are the best in the world. When they arrive they will stay in the same hotel," he said.

Once again Marie didn't speak. She straddled her lover and kissed his neck.

*

Harry looked around the room. He searched for the items he needed. Some of the items were controlled substances. They would be locked away in a steel cupboard, or cage. Mentally he made a route. The shortest route he would need to walk to acquire what he needed.

Staying low and out of sight to anyone who might enter the maintenance department, Harry moved around efficiently. He found the headtorch he required and then worked back to front. Picking from shelves and opening drawers. The task of finding what he needed didn't take long. He managed to squeeze everything, less the container of gasoline, into his rucksack. Harry moved towards the exit, but the possible problem he had seen earlier had materialised.

CHAPTER TWENTY ONE

Stan coordinated the new arrivals. The blades that had just arrived from the airport were sent straight to the Wavecrest Royal. They were to link up with Rodney and start practising for an assault. He introduced Steve to Steve. They worked together to assess all of the information fed back to them from the snipers.

*

His wife was still asleep in the passenger seat. The SUV Harry's dad drove, passed a sign welcoming him to Fort Lauderdale. The in-car satellite navigation system directed him towards the Atlantic Grand. Towards his son. John had spent years in the service of MI5, making snap decisions and devising plans that had to hold firm. He was doing no different now. However, in all his years with military intelligence section five, he'd never been in a situation where his family was involved. That was a game changer. He was so tired he was falling asleep at the wheel, but he had to stay awake. He needed to speak to the Fort Lauderdale Police Department.

*

Harry was ready to leave. Looking through the safety glass in the fire door, he could see an x-ray was puffing away as if his life depended on it. Maybe he had some special skill that set him out from the rest. A slight upper hand? A family connection?

Possibly. Had he once worked in a hotel? Or been a mechanic, or carpenter, could that be why he was down in the maintenance department? Harry didn't want to find out.

He could hide behind a workbench. There were plenty and he could hide like that for hours, a constant game of cat and mouse as he moved around the workshop to stay hidden from the terrorist. He could hide in the x-ray scanner and probably never be found, but if a curious terrorist looked inside, he wouldn't have anywhere to run. Maybe the best place to hide out of sight would be to his left, corner one, in a pile of dirty linen. The x-ray in the stairwell dropped the cigarette. Stamping it flat, he turned towards the door.

The door was pushed forcefully open. Harry breathed in and closed his eyes. The terrorist stormed into the room and kept walking towards the workbenches. He was pissed about something. That was it. Game over. Standing flat against the wall, Harry felt the faintest touch as the door brushed against his nose. It had reached the end of its range of movement. The x-ray's footsteps grew quieter. Opening his eyes, Harry saw the x-ray storming deeper into the room. He grabbed the rucksack's top handle with one hand, the jerrycan of gas with the other. Squeezing through the gap in the closing door, he only just made it. Harry stopped in the stairwell and threw the rucksack's straps over his shoulders. He drew them tight so the black bag wouldn't move or shift as he walked. He reaffirmed his grip on the jerrycan and got the flock out of dodge.

Back at the Porter's Lodge, Kelsi was still fast asleep. By the look of things, she hadn't woken while he was gone. He stashed the gas can under the table and did the same with the rucksack. Taking a bottle of still water, he took gulp and he headed back out for more reconnaissance, this time for himself.

Harry didn't know if the hostages were being fed. He guessed they were. One thing was for certain, the x-rays definitely would be. The hotel had three different sized restaurants. The terrorists wouldn't need the largest. Or even the second largest. He headed to the smallest restaurant. It could still seat fifty people at once and serve one hundred and fifty diners in one service, three times a day.

Reaching the second floor and traversing the corridors to the restaurant, he could hear voices. Hidden behind four indoor plants, he could see a group of six terrorists, seated with dirty plates and bowls in front of them. Saying something in his own language, an x-ray entered the restaurant. The others wiped their mouths and took a last swig of their drink. They stood. Picked up their weapons and headed for the door. Harry looked on with curiosity. The lone terrorist started to clear away the used plates and bowls. He was surprised. They had good discipline. Maybe they weren't going to be such a pushover after all. Three minutes passed. Five different x-rays joined the lone terrorist. More terrorists, but different ones. Another sitting. Harry clocked the time.

*

Coffee in hand, two FLPD motorcycle officers stood on a gas station forecourt. A sports utility vehicle passed them. The vehicle came close to veering off the road, the driver forced to wrench at the wheel to stop the SUV careering into the median. Their coffee was binned. Two Harley Davidson engines roared to life and the police officers left the forecourt. Two black Police Road Kings illuminated the night sky with flashing lights. The vehicle pulled over. Stopping behind the SUV, one of the pair kicked his bike onto its stand and walked to the driver's window. His holster unclipped, he was ready to draw down on the occupants if they resisted.

"Licence and registration, please sir," said the officer.

John buzzed down the window and handed the officer his driving licence.

The noise of two police sirens kept him awake for the final two miles. The crowd parted at the outer cordon. The barrier lifted. Harry's father drove through and parked up. It had been twenty hours since he had woken that morning. He was now four and a half thousand miles away and had felt sick since he had spoken to the CIA Station Chief in London. He wanted a bed. First he needed to find out what he could.

John Fearn ran from his car to the first visible point of authority, the FLPD Tactical Operations Command Vehicle. He sprinted past lines and lines of fire trucks sat at the kerb. Even more parked up ambulances sat opposite. The roads between the outer and inner cordon were devoid of members of the public. All he could see were emergency service personnel and their vehicles. He ran towards the next roadblock. Wooden barriers blocked his way. He was intent on vaulting them, but a policeman stood in his path and told him to stop. He didn't. The FLPD Officer put his right hand to his holster and clasped his sidearm, left arm raised, palm out. For a second time he shouted at the man running towards him. 'Stop'. The runner halted and stood ten feet short of the blockade.

"State your business," said the officer. Hand on his weapon.

He had only sprinted a few hundred feet. In his heyday John could have run like that all day and it wouldn't have touched him. Twenty years on, he now worked behind a desk. The sprint had taken its toll. Hands on his hips and drawing air to his lungs, he tried to speak. The officer was growing impatient and raised his voice.

"Sir, state your business," he said.

"My name… is John Fearn," he breathlessly said, "My son is in the hotel… and is a hostage. Your people want to know… who I am."

The officer got on his radio and waited for a reply.

"I have to escort you to the command vehicle sir," the police officer said.

They were about to set off. Harry's mum caught up with her husband and they walked the last of the way with the officer.

John pointed to the lines of black sedans and SUVs. All parked nose in to the kerb.

"FBI?" he asked.

"Yes sir, how did you know?" asked the officer.

"I know how you guys operate," he said, "I talk with the CIA on occasion."

"Who are you," the officer asked, "a reporter?"

"No, I work for the Security Service of the United Kingdom. As well as my son, my boss is in the hotel," John said.

Not wanting to let on that he didn't know what the Security Service was, the officer didn't ask any more questions. He led John and his wife to the command truck. Asking them to wait outside, he entered the truck and made contact. The chief came straight outside with an outstretched hand.

"Chris Schlemmer, Fort Lauderdale Chief of Police," he said.

He shook John's hand.

"John Fearn, Harry's dad," he said in reply, "This is my wife, Harry's mother, Elizabeth Fearn." Chris shook her hand.

"Please, come inside," Chris said.

*

Nineteen floors above them, Harry hunted around bedrooms. He searched for clothing for his accomplice. He needed help. He needed Kelsi. She really was about to become the Bonnie Parker to his Clyde Barrow. If he could find her a black outfit, she'd have it. She had told him some of her stats. Apart from her bra size, which was very impressive, they meant nothing. He just needed small, medium and large. The nineteenth floor wasn't providing him with anything suitable. He thought he'd have more luck a floor or two down. He was right. The seventeenth and eighteenth floor provided him with plenty. By the time he was back at the Porter's Lodge, his rucksack was bursting at the seams. There were plenty of clothes for Kelsi to choose from.

CHAPTER TWENTY TWO

"Do you know what the situation is?" the chief asked.

"I know bits, but all of that's hearsay. News channels have the habit of twisting the simplest fact, I'd like to hear it from the horse's mouth, please," said John Fearn.

"At 1917 on Wednesday, a number of armed men took control of the Atlantic Grand in a violent takeover," Chief Schlemmer said.

Elizabeth Fearn whimpered and put a finger to her eye. She stopped the water forming there from developing into a tear. Teonnie brought box of tissues over. She pulled up a chair and draped an arm around Elizabeth. Chris Schlemmer continued.

"They made hostages of nearly five hundred governmental employees at the DW30 Summit, including the President of the United States. Reporters and hotel staff were also taken captive. We believe the President's Secret Service detail were taken by surprise and incapacitated, we're not sure to what extent. The terrorists then released one hundred and eight of the hotel staff, thirty two media staff and two hundred and fourteen governmental employees. The building is now in the terrorists' control. As of yet, we have no way of safely accessing the building," Chris Schlemmer said.

Elizabeth Fearn was visibly distressed.

"Why wasn't Harry released" she asked, "with the rest of the staff?"

"He wasn't directly caught up in the terrorists' initial assault, the first thing I knew about him still being in the hotel was when my dispatchers called me and said they had a young man stuck on the nineteenth floor," answered Chris.

"Do we know for certain which organisation the terrorists represent?" John asked.

"The hostage taker is Bothrops Atrox," Chris said, "the drug lord. He made a televised address to the world via NBC, have you seen it?"

"No, but my people told me about it," John said.

"If I may momentarily interject, who are your people and what do you do for a living Mr Fearn?" Chris asked.

"My people are my staff and the reason you couldn't find out who I am, is because I have to be very good at protecting my identity for my family's sake. For over two decades I've worked for the Security Service of the United Kingdom. MI5 if you would rather, but that hasn't been our name since 1929. I'm the Director of 'A' Branch, who cover all forms of surveillance. This could be physical surveillance, basically having one of our people pretending to be someone they're not, whilst in close proximity to the person that has been highlighted to us, a lone terrorist, or terror group for example. While we're in the area of interest, we gather as much information on them as possible. We can covertly gain entry to your house or workplace, we'll steal confidential documents, or photograph them, put listening devices in your building or telephone, or bugs and trackers in your car. You'll never know we're there and we'll know everything you're doing at any time of the day. We will learn everything about you. We protect the realm of the United Kingdom from terrorism, rogue nations wanting to steal our military technology, spies and everything else in between," said John.

"Seems to me," Chris said, "you're very good at your job, even the CIA couldn't find out who you are."

"I know everything about that street," he said, "Every resident, every resident's car, their job and their children, I know one of my neighbours has three mortgages on his house and is facing bankruptcy and another has an illegitimate child by a woman in Wales."

Elizabeth looked up when she heard illegitimate child. She looked at her husband. He looked back.

"No chance," he said.

John Fearn looked at Chief Schlemmer.

"I have to know who's living near me. I have to see the threat it before it rings the doorbell," John said, "The problem the CIA had, was that they stood out because they were trying too hard to blend in."

"Do we know if Harry's safe in the hotel?" Elizabeth asked.

"I believe he is, I have spoken to him on the phone a number of times," Chris answered.

Elizabeth Fearn let out the breath she seemed to have been holding since she had left London.

"He says he has found a colleague alive as well, a young lady called Kelsi Maguire," he added.

"Oh good, at least he isn't alone," said his mum.

"So is he in hiding?" John Fearn asked.

"I would hope so, but initially we needed confirmation on a number of items Bothrops Atrox indicated to in his NBC address. I asked Harry if he was confident enough to check these for us and he said yes," Chris said.

"So you're using Harry as a pawn in your horrible game? You're putting my little boy in harm's way!" Elizabeth said angrily.

John put his hand on Elizabeth's arm.

"Did he agree to this?" he asked.

Chris nodded.

"It's all because of that bloody game he plays," John said, "He wants to think he's in the SAS."

*

He needed to tell Schlemmer what he'd seen. He hit the recent call button on his smartphone. Kelsi used the knife function on the Swiss Army Knife Harry had found and cut the remainder of the fruit into pieces, to try and make some kind of fruit salad. The food situation was getting pretty bad, Harry needed to raid the fridges in hotel bedrooms again.

Schlemmer answered the call.

"Harry," Chris said.

"Hey," Harry replied.

"How are things going up there, buddy?" asked Chris.

"Pretty much the same, we're running out of food, but I'll find some more. I've done what you asked and checked the staff entrance door and roller shutter goods-in door," Harry said.

"And?" the chief asked.

"It's not what we thought. They're using Claymores," he said.

"Using what?" Chris asked.

"Claymores are just a modern style of landmine, permissible under the Mine Ban Treaty if command detonated, but not if they're victim-activated," Tank added.

"He's right," said Harry, "and these are victim-activated, set to explode if the door is opened from the outside."

"Shit. What about the car park fire exits and ground floor windows?" Chris asked.

"They're next on my to-do list," he said.

"Okay, be careful. What are you up to now?" Chris asked.

"Bit of this, bit of that, checking fire exits, staying out of trouble, you know how it is," he said.

"Okay, make sure you stay out a trouble a bit longer please, Harry," said Chris.

Chris knew what he had just said would go in one ear and out of the other, but he liked Harry and his attitude. He liked his sass.

"Harry," Chris said, "your parents were just here, they want to speak to you, shall I call them back?"

"No. I don't want to speak to them, it'll fuck with my mind and right now I need a clear head," he said.

He hung up.

Harry went back to work and Kelsi sat up on the makeshift bed in the Porter's Lodge. He rubbed out some notes he had written on the whiteboard and made new ones. His plan was constantly evolving. Better and more practical thoughts were entering his head.

Kelsi pointed to the pile of stolen equipment on the table.

"What are the silver bags?" Kelsi asked.

"Rat poison. I'm going to drop the pellets in the terrorists' food and take them out, or at least render them useless," he said.

"All of them?" She asked.

"No," he said, "just some of them. They won't all eat at the same time. After I'd been to Maintenance I had a quick look around at the comings and goings of the terrorists. I saw that about five, or six of them eat at the second floor restaurant at once. I took a note of the meal times. Each meal time lasts about half an hour, leaving the rest of the bad guys free to do what they're meant to be doing. Being bad, guarding hostages, or whatever. I stuck around for a bit and saw another two groups of terrorists eating. Presumably it will be a similar set-up in the morning."

Kelsi didn't look horrified. He thought she might.

"Okay," she said.

"I got loads of things from Maintenance that'll help, but at some point I'm going to have to get hold of a weapon," he said, "Until I can get my hands on one, I'm going to use anything that will hurt them. I'll need to get into the second floor kitchen and I need you to show me how, I don't know all the nooks and crannies like you."

She scrambled from the bed. Her head was filled with mental images of the hotel, its second floor and how to access the kitchen.

"Bear in mind there will most likely be terrorists moving around on the second floor, we need to be as fast as possible, use corridors running between the main walkways," Harry said.

Kelsi put her hand up. She mouthed the words, 'Hang on'.

"I'm assuming there will be a chef in the kitchen, cooking the food?" she asked.

"At least one, maybe two, but no more than that," he answered.

"Why not more than two?" she asked again.

"It doesn't take two chefs to cook five or six people a meal," he said.

"Fair point," she said.

Kelsi pursed her lips and thought some more.

"What if the terrorists are eating burgers and fries? How are you going to hide the pellets then?" she asked.

"They won't be eating burgers. Think about it. I presume the chef is an x-ray as well. He's cooking food for numerous terrorists three times a day, his job will be more or less constant. He'll cook something he can batch prepare, batch cook and serve all in one go," Harry said, "if on the other hand he makes burgers, or hotdogs, or something labour intensive like that, he'll be there all day, cutting the buns in half, putting on the cheese and the tomato and lettuce. See what I mean?"

"That's really clever, how did you figure that out?" she asked.

"I guess I'm just made for this," he said.

Harry neglected to mention he saw the terrorists with bowls of stew and then it all just made sense in his head.

"Hang on, if they're eating breakfast, won't it be something like toast?" she asked.

"Could be, but they have a chef there for a reason. Any idiot can cook toast, maybe they will have a full Colombian, like a full English," Harry replied.

"What's a full English?" she asked.

"A traditional cooked breakfast. Bacon, sausage, eggs, beans, hash browns, maybe, fried bread and black pudding," he said.

"Beans, they'll be there for sure, everyone likes beans," she said, "What's black pudding?"

"Pig's blood, in a Pattie-type arrangement," he answered.

"That's disgusting," she replied.

"Nah, you'd love it," he said.

A very sceptical look crossed Kelsi's face. Harry smirked.

"Okay, so here's what you're going to do," she said, "if we get past the chef and into the dishwasher area, we can access the ventilation duct that travels directly above the cookers, you can drop the pellets through the vent right above the pot of beans on the stove."

"Smart girl, thank you," Harry said.

Kelsi looked as proud as punch.

"There's only one problem," she said.

"What?" Harry asked.

"I've seen the duct loads of times and I don't think it will take your weight, how much do you weigh?" she asked.

"Fourteen stone," Harry answered.

Kelsi looked past him, staring at the wall.

"What are you doing?" he asked.

"Putting it into American. You weigh one hundred and ninety six pounds. I only weigh one hundred and eighteen pounds, that's five and a half stone less than you," she said, "I'll do it."

"But you can't," Harry said.

"Why not?" Kelsi asked.

"Because you're a girl, a female, a woman," he said.

Kelsi had an exasperated look on her face.

"Great, another naive man," she said.

"What I'm saying is, you have motherly instincts, you're meant to be a life-giver, not a life-taker," Harry answered.

Angrily, Kelsi threw her arms in the air and stood up to get in Harry's face.

"Oh spare me the cliched, overused bull crap, Harry," she said.

"Shush," Harry said.

He put a finger to his lips.

Kelsi looked sheepish.

"Sorry," she said and looked into his soul.

She spoke more softly this time.

"I told you my daddy was killed in a bar fight, except it didn't happen in a bar, it took place outside the bar and it was murder, do you think I don't know more about it than that?"

Harry didn't reply.

"Three men kicked my daddy in the head until he was dead. Jason O'Hare, Kevin Brewski and Michael Carter. Do you know why they did it?"

This time Harry couldn't reply.

"Sixty dollars. My daddy was murdered because of three twenty dollar bets he won. They said they had the money in their car, when they all went outside to get it, the three men dragged him down an alleyway and kicked his head in. That's murder in the first degree. Michigan State law doesn't permit the death penalty, but murder in the first means life imprisonment, without the chance of parole. The entirety of three people's lives incarcerated," Kelsi said.

Harry felt like a proper bastard.

"Is that what happened, are they in prison?" he asked.

"No, they got off on a technicality. All three of them walked free. Do you not think I've thought about those men every single day of my life. I hate them with every fibre of my being. They took my daddy away from me when I was only two months old. Do you know your daddy, Harry?" she asked.

He looked up. He hated himself. He answered her question with a nod.

"I never knew my daddy, the same way Kim's little boy is never going to properly know his mom. The men that killed her, the men that killed my daddy and the men that have killed people in this hotel, all deserve to die. So like I said, I'll crawl through the air vent, it might not take your weight," she said.

Harry nodded.

Silence.

They both looked at each other's shoes.

Kelsi looked up first and wrapped her arms around him.

"I'm sorry for shouting at you," Kelsi said.

A tear ran down her face.

"I don't want to have to shout at you ever again," she said.

Harry held her and wiped the tear from her cheek.

"It's just going to be me and you against the terrorists, babe," he said.

Kelsi hugged him even tighter.

"It'll be dark in the duct," she said.

"Good job I took a headtorch from Maintenance then," he said.

Kelsi smiled.

"I need to get dressed properly," she said.

Harry averted his gaze. Kelsi dressed in the clothes he'd scavenged for her. Before putting them on, she held them up so she could get a better look. He had done a surprisingly good job. The black trousers he pinched were the bottom half of a black tracksuit. A man's tracksuit. A small man at that. They were still a little large, but at least they weren't too small. There was also a woman's long sleeved black t-shirt that was nigh on the exact right size and black hoodie.

Harry had his back turned and inspected the hoard on the desk, his eyes locked onto the clam shaped makeup mirror. He slid his hand across the table in the clam's direction. Very carefully, he used his thumb to depress the clasp holding the two parts together. When the holding-lever wouldn't push down anymore, he forced his forefinger between the two components and prised them apart. Harry made a few slight adjustments to obtain the angle he wished. Using a finger pushed flat on the bottom half of the clam, he moved the mirror away from him and to his left.

Just in time, he saw Kelsi with her back turned. She placed her shoes to one side. Unzipped the back of her skirt and allowed it to fall to the floor. 'Fuck,' he mouthed. His eyes widened. He saw her bend over to pick the skirt from the floor. Her lacy white underwear tightened. Her legs seemed to have gained ten inches. Then there was her ass, tanned and delightful. She squatted. *For sure.* Placing her skirt on the bed, she unbuttoned her blouse and let it slip from her shoulders. Her bra matched her knickers, white and lacy. Her shoulders were also tanned and perfect. He was looking directly into the mirror when she turned around to pick up her tracksuit bottoms. 'Shit,' they're massive. This time and he got a full frontal view. She was better developed than the girls at his school that studied A-Level Physical Education. Sitting back on the bed, Kelsi pulled-on the tracksuit bottoms. She picked-up the long sleeved t-shirt and slipped her arms into the sleeves. Lifting her arms in the air, she popped her head through the neck hole and delicately rolled the black fabric over her body. Harry's eyes bulged. Her chest was as beautiful as her ass. She had a perfect hourglass figure.

She sat on the bed. Harry closed the mirror. He didn't want another moment like the one with Alison on the beach. Harry thought he'd got away with it. Kelsi smiled to herself. She had seen the mirror as soon as she turned around. He was trying to be the perfect English gent, which he was, but occasionally he slipped up. She smiled. Maybe she had teased him and taken her time pulling the t-shirt over her head.

Harry finished bagging-up the rat poison. The hundred gram bag he had taken from Maintenance contained a pair of latex gloves, the blue skin tight type a surgeon would use. He followed the instructions on the packet and wore them to handle the poison. Having decanted the bag of pellets from the rustling air sealed plastic bag to a clear plastic zip-lock bag, he set about reading the warning label.

The label on the rat poison read Brodifacoum. He didn't know what that was. The label also said that Brodifacoum was four times stronger than Bromadiolone. He didn't know what that was either, but he was happy in the knowledge that the poison he had picked-up was the good stuff. He read the bottom of the label. 'The strongest and most effective rat poison that you can buy'. Perfect. He was careful not to nick, or tear the latex gloves as he removed them from his hands. Kelsi would be needing them next. The gloves went in the same zip-lock bag, but with the tops of the gloves exposed so that she didn't have to delve into the bag and fish them out. He turned and looked at Kelsi. She was looking at him with a grin on her face.

"What?" he said.

Kelsi's face broke into a smile.

"So you approve of my underwear then?" she asked.

Shit! She'd seen him. He gulped and turned away. Not wanting to make eye contact, he continued packing the rucksack and the pockets of his combat trousers.

"It's okay, it would be stranger if you didn't want to look at me getting changed. I'm glad you find me sexy," she said.

Harry turned around and blushed when she blew him a kiss. How was he ever going to live this moment down. He did. It came pretty easily when Kelsi asked him to come and join her for a snooze. They needed to waste a few hours till breakfast anyway.

CHAPTER TWENTY THREE

Harry woke from his snooze and rolled over to Kelsi. She wasn't there. His heart started pumping.

"We need to have a hot drink when we wake up, don't you think?" she asked.

"For fuck's sake, I wondered where you were then," he said, "No we don't need a hot drink, that'd be classed as a luxury."

"There are kids in Africa who've got more than we have in here," she said.

Harry snorted.

He climbed from the bed and checked his trouser pockets, ensured the buttons were fastened. The contents secure and the main compartment of his rucksack closed. He slung it on his back and shuffled. Nothing moved. He passed the rat poison to Kelsi.

"Have you got everything? Are you ready?" Harry asked.

Kelsi finished tying the laces on her black trainers and pulled the new hoodie over her head. She stood up and looked him in the eye. Her face was expressionless.

"I was ready before you were born," she replied.

She forced her hand over Harry's mouth and stifled his laughter.

He halted his silent guffaw. She could tell he was smiling. She felt his lips widen against the palm of her hand. Kelsi smiled back. She removed her hand. Their lips collided. She reached up to hold his face. He pulled her closer and her foot lifted from the floor, knee bent as they kissed. Harry held her like that for what seemed like an age. He stood her up and looked down at her trainers.

"Hang on," he said.

Harry got to one knee and she dreamt of him proposing. Right at that moment she would have said yes, but he wasn't proposing. He lifted up her right foot and Kelsi was forced to hop on her left foot until she found her balance. He pulled. The trainer wouldn't come free. The laces were too tight.

"You need to slip these off easily, you'll have to remove them before you climb into the extraction duct. Wearing them will cause too much noise, someone'll hear you," he said.

She placed a hand on Harry's head to get some stability.

Kelsi put on her best royal accent.

"Undo them then, Jeeves," she said.

He untied the knot in the trainer. Then he did the same for her left foot. She sat on the bed and retied the laces so the trainers could be easily slipped off. They were ready.

"Come on," he said, "there's work to be done."

*

Most of the American operators and British troopers were either practising for an assault in the Wavecrest Royal, or sitting ready for action as part of the QRF. Notwithstanding that, the Ops Room was now brimming with guys as more and more special forces personnel had shown up. The latest unit to knock on the door were commandos from Brazil. They followed elite soldiers from the Danish Jaegar Corp, Irish Army Ranger Wing, Israeli Unit 621, who were known for being particularly vicious and unforgiving, as well as the Korps Commandotroepen from the Netherlands. The eleven different nations present all had governmental leaders held hostage at the DW30. Sounds of work and chatter filled the Ops Room, people on phones, laptop computers, operators skimming through technical manuals and quiet professionals in conversation. The three elite sergeants continued to hammer out plans in their side meeting room.

They had to find roles for all the different special forces in attendance. At the same time they had a golden opportunity. Never before in the history of the world had so many elite special forces soldiers from different countries, been available for a single operation.

"We'll call the operation, 'Joint Venture,'" Tommy said.

Stan was staring into space. Lost in thought.

"Hey, Stan," Tommy said, "we'll call the operation Joint Venture, what do you think?"

Still, Stan remained deep in thought.

"Stan, are you with us?" Tommy asked.

"Yeah, sounds good, I like it," Stan said, "but first we need to contact all the local airports."

"Why? Going home because you haven't got any tea to drink?" Tommy said.

He laughed at his own joke.

"No, but I know exactly how we're going to get so many men into the hotel at the same time," said Stan.

He pointed to a wall mounted television screen in the outer bullpen. Tommy craned his neck to see what Stan was talking about.

"More importantly," Stan said, "that's how we're going to get hundreds of hostages out of the hotel, without compromising the exit doors."

Every television news channel in the country and most of the world, was showing rolling footage of the Atlantic Grand. Aerial footage of the hotel. Police officers standing at roadblocks. The coming and goings of the FBI, or strange figures hiding their identity with baseball caps and sunglasses. The muted news channel that was on a screen in the Ops Room however, was running a story about a budget airline. Images of the airline's owner flashed over the screen, alongside videos of queues at check in desks, a video of one of the company's passenger jets at a smaller airport loading bags and boarding passengers. The passengers were climbing a mobile staircase on the back of a small truck, up towards the waiting jet.

"We'll use mobile airport ladders, I like it," said Tommy, "Good man, Stan."

"Bearing in mind we think most, if not all of the exits and entrances are rigged with explosive charges," Stan said, "we should enter the building above the first floor. Floors two or three would be best. All the windows on the first floor might be fitted with sensors too. Have your snipers reported anything to that conclusion?" Stan asked.

"I was talking to the Steves earlier, they think there might be some form of sensory equipment on the windows," Tommy said. "I'll get word to Schlemmer and ask him if Harry can confirm, or deny."

Stan nodded.

There was a knock on the door.

"Come in," he shouted.

"Speak of the devil," said Tommy.

"We've just been to see the FLPD," American Steve said, "Then we went to get the FBI's perspective."

"Harry's been doing more recon for Chief Schlemmer. The explosive on the staff door isn't a frame charge, it's a Claymore," added English Steve.

"That's an SAS tactic," Stan said.

The Steves nodded.

"Do you think one of our own has gone rogue? English Steve asked.

Stan shook his head.

"They wouldn't be stupid enough," he said.

Stan looked at Tommy.

"The SF group other than yourselves and Delta who use that, are the Germans," Stan said.

"Why the Germans?" American Steve asked.

"Because we taught them," Stan said.

"Looks like we've got some highly skilled GSG9 mercenaries in the hotel boys," American Steve said.

"Also," English Steve added, "the door is rigged with pretty generic sensory stuff. The type that rings a bell when the door is opened, but wired up to the president."

"The FBI think that's bullshit by the way," American Steve said, "They said Bothrops wouldn't risk killing his own men if they were in proximity of the suicide vest."

"The FBI don't know shit" Tommy said, "Bothrops Atrox hasn't got to where he is today, without being ruthless and not giving a damn about his people."

Nods all round.

"Therefore," added Stan, "he must be planning to get out somehow, there must already be a plan in place. We just need to work out what it is. Everyone needs to start thinking like him, how would we escape from that building? Either before, or after we assault."

In the next room along the corridor, operators from two nations and three different special forces comprised the Quick Reaction Force. They strolled around their room and looked at photographs of Bothrops Atrox, his sons, his known associates. They sat together, watched films and played cards. One of the Americans had brought his games console and four of the tier one operators sat playing the most comprehensive first person shooter of the decade. SAS: We Dare We Win.

Thirty two men from Delta Force and Seal Team Six, sat with sixteen Special Air Service troopers. They were fully kitted-up and ready to move to immediately assault the hotel. The cupboards of the kitchenette were packed with sandwiches and snacks, microwave meals and coffee-making facilities. The guys of the QRF needed to be kept topped-up and ready for action. Most importantly, one of the Britishers had pulled a packet of teabags from his Bergen.

No sooner had the Steves left, there was another knock on the meeting room door. After a shout of 'Enter,' an SAS Major along with a Seal Team Lieutenant Commander walked into the room.

"Hello Stan," said the cheerful and very well-spoken British Major, "I've been pondering how we should go about assaulting the hotel on the flight over and I think…"

Stan cut him off.

"…with respect Sir, sit down and shut up," said Stan. "We know what we're doing."

The major hadn't long been assigned to 22 Reg and although he was as keen as mustard to get involved, he didn't have enough operational experience.

The British Major and American Lieutenant sat with them. Tommy and Stan continued to discuss practicalities and impracticalities of the assault. As time ticked on and the hours passed, a more detailed plan could be developed. SF intelligence-gathering increased and went from strength to strength. The initiative lost by the hostage-takers was gained by the special forces. The hostages chance of survival increased. The terrorists chance of getting out alive decreased.

They agreed on the need for the quick processing of hostages once they were outside the hotel. A folder of photographs and names of all the hostages would be best. Just one folder, not two or three. More than one would build in the possibility for error. People could be missed. Under the photographs of the conference attendees would also be their age and job title, as well as the country they represented. The same folder would also contain similar information for the few staff that remained in the hotel. The list would be alphabetised to enable speed of processing. Doing it this way they would get it right first time. Tommy left the room to set a few of the Dutch with their impeccably good English, on the task right away.

When he came back, he mentioned the need for increased noise before the attack.

"Definitely,' Stan said.

"What do you think, should I give Miami International a call?" Tommy said.

"Yeah, we did the same thing at the Embassy in eighties," Stan said. "Get a whole flight path to shift its course so it flies directly over the hotel, that's going to be hundreds of planes, ask them to fly a couple of thousand feet lower too."

An increased amount of noise would serve to unnerve the terrorists in the hotel, disrupting their ability to fight back effectively.

*

Harry and Kelsi reached the second floor landing. He went through his drill of checking a door. There wasn't anyone present.

After carefully tracking around the second floor, twice hiding from terrorists, they reached a small off shoot passageway. From there they would enter the kitchen. There was a stationary x-ray at the far end of the corridor, corner four. If he stayed where he was, he wouldn't prove a problem. Was he making a patrol of the second floor? Did he just traverse along the back corridor? Harry hoped it was the latter.

They were near to corner one of the hotel. The off shoot corridor they were in only contained one door after the kitchen door. Kelsi told him that it led to a small walk-in cupboard, no bigger than a water closet. It contained nothing of interest to the terrorists. After the cupboard the corridor terminated at the exterior glass wall of the hotel, a view of the car park was visible, as was a little of the road at the front of the hotel.

The Fort Lauderdale Beach Boulevard was deserted. Kelsi looked out and could just about see a police roadblock further up the highway. Wooden blockades and police tape were stopping anyone coming closer. Harry peered into the kitchen through the same safety glass that was in the stairwell fire exits. Beyond the kitchen was the restaurant where the terrorists would eat their ill-fated meal. Past the kitchen, but before the restaurant, was the place they could access that duct's service hatch. Harry ducked his head back when saw movement in the kitchen. Whoever it was, they were making one hell of a noise. Knowing they were concentrating on something else and not looking at the door, he raised his head.

A chef. Just one. A tubby little man with a mop of sweaty black hair. Kelsi had a look and didn't recognise him. He wasn't one of the regular chefs, but he was dressed like one. He looked Colombian, or South American at least. Harry thought it impossible that a hotel employee would be allowed to move around unguarded. Was he likely to be armed? Probably not. He might have a weapon in another room, but Harry thought it unlikely he would have an AK47 stuffed down his chef's trousers. The chef was making a racket. He wasn't delicate and didn't appear to have any designs on being quiet. For only one man, he made nearly as much noise as an entire kitchen full of chefs.

Kelsi covered Harry and watched the x-ray at corner four. Harry observed the chef for five minutes, watching him work, walking between the main part of the kitchen and a smaller ante-room. The main kitchen was made up of polished metal worktops running around the edge of the room. The walls were clad from floor to ceiling with white tiles, the ovens and stoves built into two freestanding sections, four feet wide and twenty feet long. They ran left to right, lengthways in front of them, one behind the other with five feet between them. Above them ran the extraction ducts that eradicated the fumes. A pattern had developed. Harry thought there would be a maximum of thirty second's grace for him and Kelsi to get across the kitchen floor, into the back-of-house pot wash area and to the access-plate for the duct. Kelsi tapped him on the shoulder. She gestured with her fingers that the x-ray at corner four was walking in their direction.

The chef disappeared into the ante-room. Harry pushed the handle less door inwards. Holding it open for Kelsi, she crawled through on all fours and hid behind the first row of stoves. Crouching down himself, he entered the kitchen and eased the door back towards its frame. It was the type of door that was only a push door. It would open inwards to the kitchen, or out into the corridor, perfect for waiters and waitresses carrying trays for room service with both hands, not ideal for sneaking into a room undetected. If Harry let go of the door, it would swish back and forth until it finally came to rest. The chef would know someone had entered his kitchen and would go looking. Harry could hear the footsteps of the terrorist walking down corridor. With a split second to spare, he eased the door closed. He joined Kelsi sitting behind the unused stove block nearest to the door. Mouth open, he listened.

It was apparent why the chef kept disappearing. In the background Harry could hear a football match. The chef must be watching the game in the next room. Maybe he had a tablet PC. The game must be a repeat, sports matches weren't played in the morning. It wasn't an English Premier League football match. It wasn't a US Major League Soccer game. Or even an Italian Serie A game. From the fanatical commentator, Harry presumed it must be a couple of Colombian teams playing. Someone had just scored a goal. The Spanish speaking commentator went wild, ranting fast and loud. To Harry, the commentator's voice just blurred into one incomprehensible drone.

The chef stormed back to the main kitchen in a rage.

"Malditos bastardos inutiles," he shouted.

It wasn't the chefs team who had scored.

A wooden spoon flew over the unused stove top and came within inches of Kelsi's head. Smashing against the tiled wall next to the door, the pair were covered in tiny specks of whatever the chef was cooking. Harry put a finger to Kelsi's face, wiped off a splat of food and placed it on his tongue. He leant over.

"Beans," he muttered.

Kelsi smiled.

The chef shouted some more. Harry got onto his belly and crept in front of Kelsi. Peering around the corner he couldn't see the chef and crawled over to the next stove block. Two stoves were switched on. The first one contained a frying pan. The second, a deep pot. The beans. He reached into his leg pocket and pulled free the clam mirror. Taking a ladle from the bottom shelf opposite and affixing the mirror using the chewing gum he pulled from his mouth, Harry eased the mirror out. He could see the chef. Luckily he was still watching the football match. Harry motioned for Kelsi to come and join him. She got on her stomach and crawled over.

Suddenly the fanatical commentator started shouting. In the mirror Harry saw the tubby chef cheering and dancing around.

"Goooooool!" he cried.

Tubby waved his arms in the air.

"Excelente gol, brillante me gusta Asprilla, bien hecho," he cried.

If the chef's team were performing well, he was likely to spend more time watching the game and less time at the stove. He was less likely to compromise Harry and Kelsi.

In the reflection, Harry could see the room the chef stood in. It was no more than a food preparation area, probably where the potatoes were peeled and the veg was cut. On the back wall, leaning against the white tiles was a tablet PC. Tubby had his back turned. Bent over and keeping low, Harry and Kelsi snuck into the dishwashing area. He could still hear the football game, but they were no longer in the same room as the chef. However the risks were still extremely high.

Harry wanted to check on the chef. He padded to the corner of the pot wash room where it met the kitchen. There wasn't a door, just an opening. Poking the mirror around the wall, he could see the chef still watching the football match. The chef turned. Harry pulled the mirror back out of sight. His heart immediately began beating out of his chest. He didn't know what to do. Had the chef seen him? *No plan survives first contact with the enemy.* What matters is how quickly you are able to adapt. Shit. Infront of him was a stack of unwashed plates, utensils and some huge kitchen knives. Harry picked up a knife with a serrated edge. Tearing with a rough edge, as well as penetrating with a stabbing action would cause the most damage and more than likely make the wound impossible to fix before the chef bled out. If tubby came around the corner, the knife was going straight into his heart. Harry heard the chef shuffle his feet. He'd stopped moving. Harry looked around the corner with the mirror. Tubby was stirring the pot of simmering beans.

Harry visually inspected the vent's access hatch. He pulled a multitool from his leg pocket and stood on a discarded milk crate. The access hatch was the size and shape of a piece of A4 paper. It was laid on its side in a landscape formation and held in by six bolts, three equidistant along the top and three directly below along the bottom edge. Harry was forced to use the multitool's knife and jiggle out dirt and grime from the heads of the bolts, before the Allen attachment key would fit. Leaning over an industrial glass washer, he unscrewed the bolts of the service hatch. The bolts were only stiff for the first turn, then they unscrewed easily.

It was a most fortuitous decision of Kelsi's to crawl along the ventilation duct rather than Harry. Even if the duct had been able to hold his weight, he wouldn't have been able to fit, let alone get through the hatch. He looked at the size of the duct and wondered how even Kelsi was going to fit.

She removed her trainers as the hatch was unscrewed, then swapped positions. Even though she was stood on the milk crate, she required a leg-up to get to the duct. Her body contorted and somehow she squeezed through the gap that had been created. As soon as Kelsi was in the duct, Harry replaced four corner bolts that held the hatch in place. If for whatever reason anybody came into the pot wash area, the duct had to look untouched. Harry made a space for himself under a large stainless steel draining board and climbed to the back. He replaced the bottles of detergent on the bottom shelf. He was completely hidden and nobody would be able to tell he was there.

CHAPTER TWENTY FOUR

The ventilation duct was smaller than it looked from the outside. Getting stuck scared the life out of her. She was surprised she had volunteered for the task in the first place. One thing spurred her on, she imagined the men who were to eat the poison were the men who had killed her dad.

If she wasn't wearing the headtorch, Kelsi wouldn't be able to see anything. She felt the front pocket of her hoodie. The rat poison was still there. Forward she crawled, hoping she wasn't making any noise to the outside world. It should have been a straightforward crawl, then a left turn at the tee junction in the duct. It wasn't.

Kelsi had only crawled a few feet when Harry screwed the access hatch back into place. She wanted to turn left, but she couldn't. A mesh grill blocked her way. She pulled at it with her hands, but it wouldn't budge. She was afraid to pull harder in case she made a noise and the chef heard. She just hoped there weren't going to be more grills preventing her progress if she went the long way around.

Her new plan was to turn right instead. Then take four left turns. She turned right. Kelsi crawled forward an inch or two at a time. Her hands were getting covered in dirt. Steam was sucked up through the vent and into the duct. At the same time it carried with it tiny particles of food too small for the eye to see. The bottom of the duct and now Kelsi's clothes were covered in greasy food residue. Reaching the next junction in the duct, she lifted herself onto her side and squeezed herself around, methodically inching a limb forward at a time, then shuffling her torso in the same direction. She repeated the motion eleven times until she was free.

The next junction was another left turn. She rounded it with just as much difficulty, if not a little more. Kelsi looked at her watch. She had been in the duct for ten minutes. The next section of duct was twenty feet long. She needed to hurry. It wouldn't be long before the terrorists sat down to eat. If she got above the vent and the cooking pot wasn't there, she would be wasting her time and Harry's. The grease and debris became worse as she inched towards two unused vents. Kelsi was getting caked in gunge and slimy grease deposits. She was sliding around in the vent and it was becoming impossible to move with any speed. For every foot she crawled, she exerted as much energy as if she had crawled five. She was acutely aware that any rough parts of the vents she was now crawling over, could snag on her clothes, meaning the thin metal of the duct would ripple and make a noise. Her captivity or death would then became a certainty.

She crawled above the extraction vents for the unused cookers. She was a mere stone's throw from where she wanted to be, but it seemed it would take her an age to get there. Fortunately nothing snagged. She made it to the third left turn. Turning herself onto her right hand side, she inched around and covered the next section of duct more quickly. Squeezing herself around the final left turn, her torch illuminated the vents she needed and the metal grill that had hampered her progress in the first instance.

She crawled forward ten feet and was forced to lie over a vent in order to reach the next one. The one where the pot of beans simmered. Kelsi was hit in the face by the rising vapour. The beans must have been spiced. The vapours made her want to sneeze. She held her nose. Her body convulsed and eyes watered. Reaching under herself, she pulled the clear plastic ziplock bag from the pocket of her hoodie. Without putting her hand into the bag, she delicately slid her fingers into the latex glove protruding from the top. Kelsi didn't know where the chef was, she couldn't hear him. She needed to glove up her left hand, but she wouldn't be able to hold her nose. As soon as her hand was removed, she felt a sneeze building. She held it at bay for as long as possible, but she couldn't hold back the tide. Sneezing, she made a small yelping noise. The chef was on his way from the football game to the stove. He stopped dead in his tracks. He instantly began looking for the origin of the noise.

Harry heard the chef pacing around, heard metallic scrapes as he removed pots and pans from metal shelves. He saw tubby's bottom half striding into the pot wash. He was looking for something. Harry was poised and ready with the kitchen knife he had taken earlier. Ready to jab the blade straight into the chef's face if he bent down to look on his shelf.

Kelsi couldn't see the chef at all, but over the noise of the football match, she could hear clangs of metal. She lay deadly still until the sounds stopped. The chef had resumed his position in the ante-room watching his tablet.

Turning onto one side, she shielded her face from the vapours. The fanatical football match commentator was shouting again. The chef was cheering. His team had scored another goal. He appeared to have forgotten about her earlier indiscretion, or satisfied himself that there was nobody else in the kitchen. He hadn't looked up. He mustn't have thought it possible the noise could have come from above. He would stay to watch the replays of the goal. Surely? This was it. Her best opportunity. The pellets fitted through the vent easily. But if her aim wasn't exactly right, the chef would notice pellets on the floor. He would look up and see a pair of eyes staring back. All it would take would be for him to run, grab his weapon and fire. That would mean the end for her. She wasn't moving anywhere fast.

Her eyes watered. She tried not to sneeze again as she positioned herself directly over the cooking pot. Kelsi dropped the first pellet. Her heart stopped. It hit the edge of the pot and seemed to take and age to decide which way it would fall. Into the beans, or onto the kitchen floor? Eventually the pellet fell into the beans. The next pellet was dropped from three slats further back and was almost a direct hit. The pellet after that, she dropped from one slat back again. That was as good as it was going to get. Kelsi knew she had to get quicker. She didn't know how long she had been in the duct since she last looked at her watch. Surely the meal was ready by now?

She went deadly still when she heard more Colombian voices and footsteps. These must be the men who had come to eat. She saw the tubby, sweaty chef walk below to greet the men. This was her last opportunity. She dropped the pellets as quickly as she could. Every single one landed on target and was quickly dissolved. A door swung open. The chef took a ladle and gave the pot a stir. He also took a teaspoon and gave the beans a taste. Kelsi smiled. 'Serves you right you fat bastard,' she thought. He disappeared and came back with a stack of white bowls and began filling them with beans. Kelsi breathed out. She had done it. Just.

Making sure her head torch wouldn't shine between the slats of the vent, she looked at her watch. She had been in the vent for thirty two minutes. Harry had told her that it would only take ten minutes. He hadn't known about the metal grill forcing her to take the long way around. She removed her gloves and started moving. He would be worried.

Inching herself backwards, yet remaining quiet, was a slow and laborious process. Kelsi couldn't use her feet to get a purchase on anything. There was nothing to grab hold of and she was coated in food detritus. The four right hand turns, formerly left hand turns, were however aided by the grease that had now become a part of her. She slipped around them more easily than before. She was exhausted. She wanted to lie where she was and sleep for a week, but she knew she couldn't. She had to get out of this duct. There would be plenty of time for sleep after. Hopefully in Harry's arms.

*

The noise level in the Ops Room suddenly increased. The Australian SAS were back from an early morning practise session in the Wavecrest Royal. They were coming to do their stint on the QRF. Having left their headquarters at Campbell Barracks on the outskirts of Perth, they spent twenty nine hours travelling. Flying east across Australia to Sydney, they then had a two hour layover before flying to Miami International. After schlepping up the east coast in three vans they hired, they arrived in Fort Lauderdale raring to go and have a crack at the terrorists.

When Tommy and Stan stepped out of the smaller meeting room, they saw the main office coming along nicely. The walls were now adorned with schematics of every floor in the hotel. One entire wall was plastered with A4 photographs of Alejandro Diego Munoz , his sons and known associates.

"Hey Tommy, come 'ere," called Frank Hofmann.

"What's up Frank?" Tommy said.

His fellow New Yorker was sat around a TV with a group of Seals, reviewing the NBC footage of Bothrops' initial address.

"See this guy here, the one at the back of the room," Frank said.

He pointed to the screen.

"He's dressed differently and he moves like a pro," Tommy said.

"Hey, pause the video a sec, guys," Frank asked.

The screen stopped moving. Tommy peered in for a closer look.

Frank smiled.

"Now look at the boots he's wearin,'" he said.

"Black boots," Tommy said.

"Not any black boots," Frank said, "Remember when I went to Germany to seek out my family history?" Frank didn't wait for a reply, "Well that guy is wearin' the same damn boots as those GSG9 fellas I saw. Remember I told you I saw them while I was sitting outside a café one time?"

"Yeah, yeah, I remember you telling me," Tommy said.

"Well those boots are identical, I'm telling you, he's a GSG9 mercenary," Frank said.

Tommy smiled and looked at Stan. He was smiling even more.

"Good work guys, replay the video over and over, see what else you can find out. Have you looked at the CCTV from the cameras on the streets surrounding the hotel yet?" Tommy asked.

"Yeah, there was nothing until I went out for a walk and looked for extra cameras that weren't in the usual spots. I found one on the back of this office block. I think it's been knocked by something, nobody would normally point their security camera at someone else's hotel, but it's worked in our favour," Frank said.

Tommy looked expectant.

"Tell me more Frank," he said.

"So while dinner was being eaten at the DW30, a truck backed up and loads of terrorists climbed out," he said "We could only get a partial glimpse of the x-rays, no face shots and we could only see their right shoulder and part of their head, but we've slowed the tape right down and counted what we saw. Me and the guys estimate there are at least fifty six terrorists that entered the hotel."

Tommy patted Frank on the back and made his way outside.

Over a cigarette and a coffee while stood at the back of the office complex, they looked at the camera that had detected the terrorists. Tommy and Stan chatted. The merc, or mercs were confirmed as German. They were surprised however, by the amount of terrorists that had entered the building. Over fifty six x-rays was a very high number for an operation of this size. Ten would be more than adequate. Why did they have that many men? What were they planning? They walked back around to the front. A cop approached with two men, both in their fifties or older.

"These two gentlemen work in the maintenance depart of the hotel, they know the place inside out, I thought you might like a chat with them?" the cop said.

"I'd love a chat with these guys, thank you," Tommy said.

The guys from the hotel's maintenance department were introduced to a few operators from The Unit. The maintenance guys walked around and inspected the floor plans stuck to the walls. They suggested alterations. Two Delta Force operators followed them around the room with black marker pens.

Once the hotel became a reality and was inhabited, it became apparent certain elements of the floor plan weren't practical, or could be better. Alison had called the carpenters in and a few doors had been removed, new partitions and stud walls constructed, old ones torn down. Large workbenches in the maintenance department were marked down, as well as the location of any large pieces of furniture that might hinder the SF when they assaulted the hotel. That was the level of detail they worked to. Once done, the maintenance guys went over the building plans again and again until they had added as much detail as possible.

*

Harry heard slight movements above. Relief washed over him in abundance. Kelsi had been gone a lot longer than expected. He crawled out from his hide and was exhilarated when he saw bulges in the ventilation duct.

He removed the access hatch and helped a slimy and greasy Kelsi climb down. After screwing in the bolts and ensuring the hatch was firmly back in place, he pulled her trainers back on and the pair made their getaway.

They travelled up the hotel. With Harry acting as a lookout, Kelsi made a quick search of a few bedrooms. She sought clothes to replace her current ones. She also grabbed two packets of wet wipes for a rubdown shower. Harry wouldn't like it when she went into the bathroom to have a wash, but if she stayed in view of him, she feared he might have a heart attack. She found a bag of her own and filled it with neatly folded clothes.

Back in the Porter's Lodge Kelsi pulled her new outfits from the bag she'd taken. It appeared even top fashion designers made plain black rucksacks and this one didn't require attacking with the black marker pen.

"Meant to say, I got some more food when you were up in the duct," Harry said.

"Really?" she asked.

Harry began pulling new items from his rucksack: knives, forks, spoons, bread rolls, sachets of sauce, salt and pepper. Yet more fruit and a plastic container full of meats and cheeses. A chocolate cake and a spray can of whipped cream. He even pulled out a plastic container of beans.

"The chef went for a piss, so I took my chance. I thought you might want some," Harry said.

"Hasn't that got rat poison in it?" she asked.

He shook his head.

"I spooned it out after ten minutes, long before you dropped anything through the vents," he smiled.

"Awesome, got some bread rolls?" she asked.

Kelsi rubbed her body down with the wet wipes, in the bathroom much to Harry's dismay. They sat on the floor, cross-legged and facing each other. Not seeing her rub herself down had been a disappointment, but Harry thought her choice of clothing was a good substitute. She sat opposite him in a skin tight blue sports bra and pair of black yoga pants that made her thighs look like they could crush watermelons. They sat with the plastic container of cold beans between them. Harry salted and seasoned the food. Kelsi got two spoons and tore a bread roll in half. For breakfast that morning and considering the circumstances, they dined like a king and queen.

CHAPTER TWENTY FIVE

Almost twenty four hours later, Harry returned to the same floor. He looked through the glass in the fire door from the service stairwell. He was unable to see anything. He had used the service stairwell at corner four this time. The floors of the hotel holding bedrooms had roughly the same floor plan. As the hotels floor usage changed from floors of bedrooms, to floors of conference rooms and restaurants, the floor plans altered. All Harry could see was a dimly lit corridor and a windowless wall directly in front of him. He wished he was playing SAS: We Dare We Win. He would be able to refer back to the floorplan on his game player's dashboard. There was no dashboard now. Only memory. His knowledge of this floor was minimal. He hadn't spent much time here. Hell, he hadn't spent much time in the hotel. He could remember the wall in front was the far end of a conference room that ran all the way from the Indiana Media Suite to corner four.

Opening the fire door a notch, he listened. Voices laughing at a story another voice had told. Two, three, or more voices, all coming from the Media Suite. He stepped through the door.

To the right was the glass wall that formed the rear of the hotel. He was stood on the corridor that ran to the rear wall of the restaurant. One of the other differences of this floor was the floor covering. Carpet had been replaced with highly polished stone floor tiles. His plan would work beautifully. Walking away from the rear of the hotel and edging his head around the righthand corner, he could see the bottom steps of the rear staircase. A different sentry to last time, but everything about him was the same.

Harry had thought long and hard about his next step. He wasn't going to be killing anonymously with poison. Not even at a distance with a sniper rifle. This was going to be face to face combat, killing up close and personal. He needed to up his game to be effective. He needed to do the work the police and the SF couldn't. The only way to obtain weapons was to think outside the box. He had to use whatever he could get his hands on. He would see the moment a man died. Harry would see the pain and suffering in the x-ray's face. His death would be an immediate reaction to his own action. He didn't know how he would feel having blood on his hands. Terrorists still bled. But they had brought violence and death on innocent people. By being in the hotel they remained steadfast in their want to do more harm.

Harry waited for a window of opportunity. It wasn't long before he got one. The guard at the bottom of the stairs was called forward to the media suite. For a matter of seconds the corridor was empty. Harry made his way to the inside of corner four. He made it to safety unseen and unheard. He rolled his feet down the corridor in the direction of corner one. The restaurant was to his left. He could see the entrance up ahead and bathed in light. Was anyone about to walk through from the kitchen to the restaurant? Or vice versa?

He stopped and listened. The double entrance doors in front and to his left were open. He could hear clearly. There wasn't any conventional restaurant noise. There weren't any people talking and there wasn't any cutlery scraping on plates. Harry couldn't hear footsteps, or noise from a football match either. He stepped closer and eyed the restaurant. Nobody there. Harry bent double as he edged forward and passed the half height restaurant window. He reached the entrance and ducked out of sight, knelt behind the maître d' stand and took stock of the situation. He made another noise and sound check. Nothing. He got to his feet, but still remained hunched over and stayed as low as he could. One hand grasped the handle at the top, another supported the thick red tube. Harry pulled upwards. It wouldn't budge. He stood tall. With one big pull the fire extinguisher came free.

Quietly he retreated back in the direction he had come and stayed close to the wall. He didn't hug the wall as Hollywood movies would suggest. If a person stayed right next to a wall, it was possible to be hit by a projectile as it bounced off and skittered down the structure. Harry stayed a foot out from the wall and stopped every twenty feet to check behind him. Nothing. Ten feet from corner four.

He placed the fire extinguisher on the left of the corridor. There was no room for error now. He moved forward again until he was five feet from the corridor's turn. Waiting and listening, everything was silent. He shuffled forward five more feet and pulled a bottle of clear shower gel from his leg pocket. The tube was upside down. The contents couldn't be spilt. Harry had cut off the squeezy bottle's cap in the Porter's Lodge. He didn't want to risk making the sound of the cap being popped open. That was the level of care the SAS took and Harry had learnt from the best. Squatting down, he pressed hard on the tube. The shower gel was squeezed all over the floor. The lines of opaque shower gel he made were similar to those a farmer created as he ploughed a field. He took care. The slippery gel could prove deadly if he got it on his feet. Leaving a small gap just wide enough for him to walk along, directly in line with the fire extinguisher and on the inside of the corridor, he backed away. He readied himself. Pumped himself up and mentally prepared for any outcome. *No plan survives first contact with the enemy*, but this just might. His only real plan if the shit hit the fan, was to run in the other direction. Harry took a deep breath and exhaled. He was going to do something he had so far avoided. He was about to go face to face with a terrorist.

Carefully manoeuvring forward past the shower gel, Harry ensured not a globule of the viscous liquid touched his feet. He peered around the corner and could see the sentry at the bottom of the stairs. AK47 hanging loosely from the strap draped over his shoulder, not held in his hands. Harry saw him yawn and bring a hand to his mouth. He wasn't fully alert. All this played in Harry's favour. Standing straight as if he was were standing to attention, Harry put a smile on his face and briskly rounded the corner. There was a good distance between him and the x-ray. He scuffed his feet on the floor so the terrorist would hear him. If the sentry didn't notice him until he got closer, his plan wouldn't work.

The sentry heard him and turned, shouted a warning and waved his AK47 at Harry. A hip shooter, not a pro. This fella didn't have a Scooby-Doo. Harry turned and ran back to the corner. The x-ray holding a silenced AK47 gave chase. A silenced weapon would help Harry later. The x-ray wanted to take him alive, wanted to drag the hostage back to his boss like a dog brings a ball back to its owner. Harry overshot the corner and turned to face the sentry. Realising that Harry wasn't going to give himself up, the sentry began wildly firing from the hip. Fucking amateur. Harry navigated around the shower gel. Once past, he broke into a sprint. His legs exploded and he charged towards the fire extinguisher. Grabbing the handle he back tracked the way he had come. He could hear the sentry running towards the corner, the x-ray not exercising any caution as he made the turn was an error. A fatal error. He had under estimated Harry Fearn.

The sentry didn't have time to see the wet floor. His foot hit the shower gel and slid away. His upper body followed. The x-ray's second leg hit the gel. He fell heavily on the tiled floor. Banging his head, momentarily stunned but not unconscious. The sentry expected to see the kids heels as he ran away.

The underside of a fire extinguisher was the last thing he ever saw. Harry smashed the butt of the extinguisher down on the terrorist's head. The first blow was delivered with so much force the x-ray was knocked unconscious. Harry's blows didn't stop. The attack was quick, frantic and violent. He repeatedly smashed the fire extinguisher down on the sentry's head. The extinguisher was heavy and awkward. Adrenaline fuelled Harry. His stomach turned when the x-ray's skull shattered. He didn't have time to think about it. Placing the cannister on the floor, he leant against the wall. He drew deep breaths. The attack had been harefooted. Harry had expelled all of his energy. His eye sight was going fuzzy. Breathing hard he gulped down enough oxygen for him to feel normal again. His eyes refocused. He wiped his forehead with the back of his hand. It was now covered in red smears. Harry wanted to throw-up. Blood from the terrorist's head had spattered on his hands as he pulverised the x-ray. He had to get a move on, but he was still careful as he searched the terrorist. He reH

Harry took the silenced AK47, two belts of ammunition, four magazines and two grenades from the dead body. A shout came from the media suite. It was the x-ray's mates asking if he was okay. They probably thought the random hostage wasn't a match. Harry Fearn wasn't random. He draped the two belts of ammunition around his neck. He wanted to look like a soldier from 2 Para he had seen in a photo. Hard as nails and ready for a fight.

He heard the sound of office chairs pushed back. The two leg pockets of his black trousers took the four loaded magazines. He slipped one of the grenades into his hoodie. He needed the other. He heard more voices, concerned voices. Two people calling their mate. Two people worried about their friend.

A film about the Vietnam War had taught him his next move. More importantly it was the Viet Cong's tactics during the Vietnam War. He had to move quickly. Those concerned voices had turned into footsteps and they were heading his way. Taking hold of the second grenade, he pressed the handle down and pulled the pin free. Crouching next to the sentry, Harry's fingers grabbed at the man's bloody and sticky hair. He pulled the x-ray's head forward and slid the grenade under the body's neck. Lowering the terrorist's head back down, Harry gently released the grenade's handle. He let the weight of the body take up the pressure. The footsteps coming towards him were no more than thirty feet away.

CHAPTER TWENTY SIX

Harry left the booby trapped body and quickly retreated down the corridor towards corner one. He needed to hide, more x-rays might be responding to the sound of gunfire. Hiding behind the restaurant's maître d' lectern again, he kept his eyes on corner four.

He could no longer hear the footsteps, but he knew they were getting closer. He heard them again as they broke into a jog. Reaching the corner the footsteps came to a sudden halt. They slowly entered Harry's view. One x-ray frantically said something in Spanish. The men spoke to the dead sentry as they moved nearer. The x-ray not talking took out his smartphone. The other moved towards the body on the floor. He was still talking to him as he got on one knee. The x-ray on the phone stood over the body and relayed information to whoever had picked up the call. The terrorist on one knee wiped a tear from his face. Touching the dead man he started to cry. Maybe the dead sentry was a relative. A brother? A cousin? His body dropped. He cradled the dead man's head and pulled his body towards him. Harry winced. The grenade under the sentry let out a thunderous roar.

A grenade detonating inside a building was terrifying. The immediate area was decimated. Glass walls shattered, stud walls ripped apart. At corner four a bomb really had gone off. Still complete parts of the wall were spattered with blood and dirt. Tiles had been torn from the floor. A small crater sat in the centre of the corridor.

The head of the sentry was ripped from his body as the grenade detonated. The man attempting to cradle the body was blown upwards by the blast. His dead body lay face down. Blackened and badly burnt. Both hands had been vaporised and were no longer attached to his arms. The terrorist who had been on his smartphone was blown back against what was left of the internal wall of corner four. He was also dead. His feet and legs taking the brunt of the explosion. Boots blown apart. Ripped and torn. They hung from his feet. Harry looked and thought he could make out bone amongst the mess of blood and flesh. He could hear another pair of feet running. A shout of urgency. The feet rushed towards the sound of the explosion. It was time for Harry to extricate himself from the area.

*

Bothrops Atrox heard three bursts of gunfire. His smartphone rang. It was one of his men. His man on the second floor said something about a sentry lying dead. The first floor of the building shook. The phone went dead. Bothrops waved Klaus over. They set off for the scene of the explosion.

They arrived less than a minute after the call had abruptly ended. Knowing the risks of approaching such an incident, Klaus asked Bothrops to stay back while he cleared the area. The only man alive at the scene of the explosion was Bothrop's tech guy. He was unscathed by the explosion. It soon became apparent why. Not a front line fighter, he had stayed with the surveillance cameras in case an attack from outside was imminent. He had only come out from the Indiana Media Suite after the explosion.

Bothrops was livid. He began ranting like a mad man. His curly black hair, soon soaked slick. His plan was going wrong. He had been hesitant when employing some of his men, but they had performed well under direction from Klaus and Christian. He relented and allowed them to pass the basic selection process for his small army. Now his initial thoughts were proving to be correct. Some of his men were and always had been, idiots. Too stupid to have been allowed to join his mighty organisation.

He had no organisation to join when he was a boy. Now he ran his enterprise like a Fortune 500 company. It was the biggest cocaine cartel in history. Bigger than the Cali Cartel and any Mexican cartel. His enterprising had made his cartel global.

Born to a jobless father and a mother who did a little cleaning work, he was the definition of poverty in Colombia. His schooling was even poorer than his family. No money. No education. No prospects. The only way out and the only way to get ahead in life was to turn to crime. His chosen profession was smuggling. He started as the only employee of his operation. Now he had thousands of employees and his business was global. His organisation spent millions of dollars a year on payoffs and bribes. He had spies everywhere: police stations, container ports, airports and hospitals. Deep within the Colombian Government, Bothrops tapped phones and eavesdropped on everyone. He even had moles at the US Embassy in Bogota. Notwithstanding this, he still had 'idiotas' working for him.

"Get this cleaned up," he demanded of his tech guy.

Bothrop's childhood friend looked at him in disbelief. He couldn't believe what he was being asked to do.

"Get this cleaned up, bag up the body parts, dump them in the basement," Bothrops said again.

"But I don't..." the tech guy was saying.

He was cut off.

"You do whatever I tell you to do, I pay your fucking wage," Bothrops shouted.

He slapped his chest.

"You work for me! Me! Now get it done and don't question me again," he yelled.

"Sorry," the tech guy said. "Where do I get bags from?"

Bothrops screamed at the top of his voice.

"Idiota! Use your brain you imbecile, maybe in the kitchen," he shouted.

His hands shook in a rage, much like a toddler having a strop. Bothrop's felt behind his back and pulled free a gold plated Desert Eagle. The most powerful magazine fed semi-automatic pistol in the world. Aiming the weapon single handed at his childhood friend, he strode towards him. The colour drained from his tech guy's face.

"If you weren't so valuable, you'd be joining those idiotas down there," he said.

He flicked the gold pistol at the bloody mess on the floor.

"Now get it cleaned up," he ranted.

Bothrops called Klaus back from checking the restaurant and kitchen. They headed back to the California Great Hall.

"Why did I bring these idiotas with me Klaus?" Bothrops asked.

Klaus hoped it was a rhetorical question and avoided annoying Bothrops with his honest opinion.

"They are fooling around and killing each other," Bothrops said. "Get all the men together, I need to talk to them."

*

The butt of the new rifle in his shoulder, Harry extracted himself from the scene of the blast. Sporadically pausing and hiding behind sofas and tables, he checked the path in front of him was clear, as well as ensuring nobody was on his tail. He slowly moved up seventeen floors. There wasn't anyone behind him and he didn't want to give an x-ray the opportunity to follow him back to his stronghold. He entered the fourteenth floor via the service stairwell at corner two and headed along the front of the hotel to corner one. He stopped and edged around the corner. Nobody there. Pacing towards corner four he made a sudden left turn down a smaller passageway and headed towards the building's south side. Reaching the end of the hallway he turned right and headed towards corner three. Giving the bedroom at the end of the corridor a flash of his master key wrist band, he entered and lay on the floor.

Weapon pointed towards corner two, he lay open mouthed, listening, watching, waiting. He was lying in a good, near perfect position for zeroing the AK47 to his eye. After a sleep he would come back and zero his automatic rifle in a setup like this.

*

Officer 243 lifted the tape of the police cordon and let Chief Schlemmer's car pass. He parked up and jumped out of his car with the vigour only a sleep, shower and new set of clothes could achieve.

Climbing the steps to the command vehicle he was surprised to see Teonnie already back at work. He had sent her home just before himself and he had returned a mere six hours later.

"These two gentlemen from the military have just arrived to see you," she said.

"Chris Schlemmer?" Rodney asked.

"Yes guys, how can I help?" the chief asked.

"We'd like a chat," Stan said.

Chris nodded.

"This way please," the chief said.

He showed them to the kitchenette in the mobile office. Once inside the small kitchen he asked if they'd like a coffee.

"That'd be great man, thank you," Rodney said.

"Got any tea bags?" Stan asked.

"We might have a bottle of iced tea somewhere?" said Chris.

"Nah, I was after hot tea," replied Stan.

"Afraid not," Chris answered.

"Bloody Americans," Stan said. "White coffee, three sugars."

They all laughed.

"So, you guys are with the army?" Chris asked as he handed out the drinks.

"Yeah, Delta Force and the British SAS," Rodney answered.

"What can I help you with?" Chief Schlemmer asked.

"The young lad in the building, Harry, we understand you've been talking to him?" Stan asked.

"Yeah," Chris said.

"What do you know about him?" Stan said.

Chris told the sergeants how Harry had called 911 and then he had called Harry. They spoke about the hostage taking and how Harry hadn't been taken captive. Harry had snuck around the hotel at his request and confirmed the presence of Claymores and sensors on the external doors, the location and status of the President of the United States and that he was wearing a suicide vest.

He looked directly at Stan when he told the pair how Harry kept referring to the video game, SAS: We Dare We Win. Stan chuckled to himself.

"A lot of the younger lads in The Regiment play the game. Whoever helped the game developer was undoubtedly an ex-regiment man, a lot of information about our training was absolutely spot on, but they kept the important stuff secret. Apparently it's really good," Stan said.

"What do you know about his background?" Rodney asked.

"Harry John Fearn lives with his parents in Islington, London. He's a seventeen year old student studying for his A-Levels. Plays the drums and plays for the school's cricket team. His mother runs a real estate agency. We couldn't find anything on his father, he's very elusive. In the photographs on Harry's social media, he's always wearing sunglasses," Schlemmer said. "consequently I managed to get two CIA guys to sit outside his home, to find out what they could about his father. They were snatched."

"How do you mean?" Stan asked.

"I spoke to Harry's mother and father last night, the father arranged it," the chief said.

"Who the hell is this guy?" Rodney asked.

"He's MI5, Harry doesn't know. He's the head of department called A-Branch," Chris answered.

Stan was smiling.

"Fearn," he pondered, "I knew that sounded familiar, is his dad called John?"

Chris nodded.

"My squadron was on anti-terrorism rotation a couple of years ago," Stan said. "We were based in London and worked as strike teams, dealing with anything that required a specialist armed response. I had daily interaction with many of his physical surveillance operators. Those men and women are absolutely brilliant at their jobs. I never met the man in question, but we had plenty of dealings with his MI5 guys. Did a black Range Rover drive into their car?"

"That's what I hear, do you know the guys who did it?" Chris asked.

"Probably not. I might recognise them from around camp, but they'll be in a different squadron. We'll say hello to each other, but generally keep ourselves to ourselves," Stan said.

"Does Harry like you?" Rodney asked, "personally I mean?"

"I guess," Chris said.

"Ok," said Stan, "we want you to keep talking to him. You can tell him we're here and we're coming up with a plan of action. Tell him we might need him to help us. Okay?"

"Yeah, sure," said Chris.

"Thanks," said Rodney.

The two SF sergeants made their way out of the kitchen.

Chris was left wondering if he really had been talking to the special forces. Sure, they looked like they could handle themselves, but they both looked incredibly normal. He wouldn't look at them twice if he passed them in the street, but maybe their normality is what made them extraordinary.

CHAPTER TWENTY SEVEN

Kelsi tried to stay awake. She shouldn't have been tired, she had slept for a whole day. Harry had taken longer than she expected. She didn't know how long it would take. She didn't even know what he had gone to do. He had just said he was going to inconvenience the x-rays. She fought to keep her eyes open for as long as possible.

She was woken. There was someone at the door. The lock mechanism clicked. Her heart pounded. Whoever opened the door hadn't flicked the light switch. The closed curtains made the entranceway pitch black. She couldn't see who it was. A dark figure moved in front of her. The shape had something with them. A really long weapon.

She felt under the hoodie she was using as a pillow. Her fingers touched the insulin pen. Her fist clamped the tube and she moved into a crouch. The x-ray was now in front of her. His back turned, he looked around the room. It was only going to be a matter of seconds before he turned around and saw her. She stood up on the bed, her fist raised above her head, ready to jab the insulin pen into the terrorist's neck. Kelsi's shallow breaths increased. Her body lunged forward.

Kelsi must be sleeping. He didn't want to wake her by switching on the bright lights. Harry sat on the edge of the bed so he could untie his trainers. A tumbling body fell over his right shoulder. He kicked whoever it was in the head. The figure screamed. How had the terrorists found his stronghold? Where was Kelsi? What had they done with her? He stood up to put the boot in again. The scream hadn't come from a terrorist.

It was Kelsi. Shit! He had just kicked her in the head, but she was still conscious. He managed to retract his foot so she didn't receive another kick to the temple.

"I'm sorry, I'm so sorry," he said.

Harry got to his knees. Took her in his arms.

She lay on the carpet with the insulin pen in her hand. She must have thought he was an x-ray. Next time he would turn the light on and wake her. A tired and grumpy Kelsi, was better than a dead Harry.

Her eyes were closed. She had pulled her arms over her head, ready to receive a kicking.

"Hey," he whispered.

She scrunched her eyes tighter.

"Hey, it's Harry," he urged.

He kissed her lips.

"I'm so sorry, I thought you were a terrorist," he said.

Her eyes opened and she looked at him, still struggling to make out the figure in front of her. Maybe she was concussed, more likely stunned and confused. He didn't think the kick to her head had been that powerful. It had literally been a kneejerk reaction.

"Harry," she groggily said, "is it really you?"

"Yes babe, let me turn the light on," he said.

He made his way to the light switch.

Once flicked, he could see her properly. Lying on the floor and looking as cute as ever. His lips arced. She smiled back.

"I'm so sorry," he said.

"Don't be, I was about to stab you with the insulin pen. Thank god you sat down," she said.

Harry lifted her onto the bed.

Stepping into the bathroom he used two of Kelsi's wet wipes to remove the remaining specks of blood from his face and hands. He hoped she hadn't seen them. There would be questions otherwise. If there were, he would just tell her she was imagining things because of the kick to her head. He walked back into the main room and took the silenced weapon that lay at the base of the bed.

"I need to do this now," he said, "sorry about the light."

The light didn't matter. The boot to the head had woken her. Clearing a space on the table in front of him, he went to work on the automatic rifle.

Harry wasn't surprised the terrorists were using Kalashnikovs. That particular weapon would have been chosen for them with good reason. The AK47 was virtually idiot proof. Its design was incredibly simple, pretty much just point and shoot. The simplicity of the weapon meant it rarely went wrong. If the vast majority of the terrorists were using AKs, all the magazines would be interchangeable. All of the rounds were of a 7.62 calibre. They could pick up any magazine, or any belt of ammunition and it would be perfect for their weapon.

For crowd control, the weapon looked brutal and that in itself, was half the battle won. Serious looking weapons, meant the hostages took their holders seriously. The AK47 wasn't known for its accuracy, it was known for packing a punch and having great stopping power. It was also loud and noisy when fired. Being noisy in a firefight was just as effective as being accurate, it kept people's heads down and kept them scared. Harry's weapon was the only AK47 he had seen that had a silencer. For what he was planning, it would be perfect.

There were a number of incarnations of the AK47. The type the terrorists were using was the version with the folding metal stock, perfect for close quarters combat. It was short and wieldy. This was ideal for the grunts who were hip shooters trying to impersonate Rambo. They might think they looked like their idols on the Hollywood screen, but their aim would be woeful. They wouldn't be looking cool when Harry laid down some properly aimed rounds that brought them to the floor.

Designed in 1947, the AK47 was a simple and cheap rifle to manufacture. Its design had been replicated world over, many times and it had stood the test of time. The original design had lasted over half a century and didn't show signs of becoming weaker with age. The long stroke gas system on the Kalashnikov meant it was particularly reliable in arduous conditions, perfect for a long, hard Russian winter, or for use in the depths of the Colombian rainforest.

No matter how arduous a weapon was, it was only as good as its maintenance. Harry didn't want to hear a deadman's click when he pulled the trigger, especially if faced with some blood thirsty x-rays. There was only one thing to be done, the weapon needed to be stripped back to its component form to ensure everything was working as it should.

The first task of dismantling the Kalashnikov, or any weapon, was to ensure it wasn't loaded. Harry knew this weapon was loaded. It had been fired at him. Off the top of his head he couldn't remember how many rounds had been fired, but it wasn't a full magazine. There was definitely a round in the chamber.

Not long after he had started playing SAS: We Dare We Win, there was a level all about weapon recognition and weapon care. To be an effective SAS soldier, one had to be able to pick up any weapon anywhere in the world and know how to use it. New weapons and old weapons, handguns, automatic rifles, general purpose machine guns and sniper rifles. Even mortars, surface to air missiles and anti-tank weapons needed to be understood. The AK47 had been one such weapon on that level. Harry had been required to strip it down and give it a thorough clean, before putting it back together again. The game player was to do that in a timed test before progressing to the next level. Like many levels on the game, Harry didn't pass first time, but when he did he was at the top of his class.

He unscrewed the silencer and pulled the loaded magazine free of the rifle. Laid it flat on the table and pushed the safety selector down. Harry took a look in the chamber. One bullet loaded and ready to fire. He removed the projectile and slid the cleaning rod out from under the barrel. The top strap was next.

The upper most cover of the rifle came free and exposed the recoil spring. Pushing the spring forwards and lifting the component up, he allowed it to push back on itself and removed the spring and guide rod.

Kelsi looked on in amazement.

"You look like you've done that before," she said.

Harry smiled.

"I kind of have," he said.

"Are you a member of a gun club?" she asked.

"Can't say I've ever been to a gun club," he answered.

"Are you actually a spy? Like a real Fearn, Harry Fearn?" Kelsi asked.

"Afraid not," he said.

His eyes peered back to the weapon and concentrated on delicate movements.

"You wouldn't tell me if you were a spy, would you?" she questioned.

Harry chuckled.

"No," he said firmly, letting her know she needed to be quiet.

Fingers gripping the carrier bolt group at the top of the weapon, he slid it back and up. The weapon was either brand new, or very well maintained. His bet lay on the AK47 being new. Placing the bolt group on the table, the bolt was pushed back, rotated and pulled free. Finally, the gas tube was removed from the top of the rifle.

"There you have it, rifle stripped," he said.

He threw Kelsi a wink.

"That's taken you less than two minutes," she said.

"How much less?" he asked.

"I don't know, more than one, but less than two," she answered.

Harry tutted.

"Don't you tut at me, Mister! What's up?" Kelsi asked.

"I'd just like to know, my best time for stripping an AK47 is one minute, thirty four seconds," he said.

Kelsi wiped the grin from his face.

"You'd better get some more practise then, champ." Kelsi said.

She winked back at him and stuck her tongue out.

"You've got to put it back to together now," she laughed.

Harry started to rebuild the rifle.

He really fancied Kelsi and although she didn't know it, sticking her tongue out at him and winking, had given him an idea.

Harry was on his way to join Kelsi on the bed. A note on the whiteboard caught his eye. No time like the present to get things done, this was an important one, a lifesaver if he ran out of ammunition.

He took two bottles of sparkling water and emptied the contents down toilet. He asked Kelsi to help. She hunted around for a pair of scissors and set to work cutting three, foot wide strips from a tablecloth. Harry dragged out the jerrycan he had stolen from Maintenance. Unscrewing the lid, his nostrils were filled with the volatile odour of gasoline.

He unpinned a laminated sign from the wall, rolled it into a funnel shape and inserted the tip into an empty glass bottle. Hunched over he decanted the gasoline into the waiting bottle. He repeated the process until both bottles were filled. By the time he was done, Kelsi was also finished. She had cut the table cloth into strips. Taking two pieces of cloth, he asked her to cut the remaining cloth into two, one foot square pieces. Once she was done, he tightly rolled those squares into foot long cloth cylinders. Taking one at a time he forced the cloth cylinder into the top of each gasoline filled bottle. They fitted tightly. The gas wouldn't seep out. The odours of the gas stayed in the bottles. Eight inches of cloth projected from the top. The other end was soaked in the gasoline. Gradually the gas would creep up and soak the cloths protruding from the top. Taking each bottle separately, Harry rolled the homemade incendiary devices in the remaining two, four foot long, foot wide, table cloth strips.

The outer cloth covering ensured the bottles wouldn't clang together, break or leak when they were tightly squeezed into his rucksack. He had just armed himself with two Molotov Cocktails. They would cause destruction on an unprecedented scale if things came down to the wire and he ran out of ammunition.

Finishing up, he flicked the light switch and joined Kelsi on the bed.

Harry didn't have the best sleep. He couldn't stop thinking about the men he had killed. The first terrorist had been murdered in a horrific way. His death had been a direct result of Harry's actions. Harry kept reliving the moment he felt the skull give way. The next two x-rays to die had been killed in the grenade explosion, he thought of this as more of an indirect consequence of his actions. Ultimately however, he knew it was his placement of the grenade that had caused their deaths. Knowing he had three men's blood on his hands wasn't nice. The thought didn't want to make him vomit, he just didn't feel right and he was unable to stop thinking about the incident. It played on his conscience constantly. He relived the frantic attack and saw the grenade's detonation in his mind over and over again. He had deprived someone of their son, children a father. Someone had lost an uncle, brothers and sisters were now without a sibling. There would be crying and wailing when the news reached them.

Kelsi's hands felt out for him. She wasn't able to touch him. Harry wasn't lying in bed. Her eyes opened and she sat up. She could see his silhouette by the window. He had pulled the curtains open a notch and was looking at the police activity on the street below. She crawled from the bed and walked barefoot to the window.

"Hey," she said.

He liked her delicate and feminine voice.

She wrapped her arms around his waist, but there was no response from Harry.

"Are you okay, baby?" she asked.

Lifting his arm she snuggled underneath and pressed her body into his side. She loved his cuddles. She was safe and protected.

"Yeah, I'm okay," he said.

"Why can't you sleep?" she asked.

"Because I just killed three men," he said.

"Oh my God, how?" she asked.

"Trust me, you don't want to know," he said.

"I do," Kelsi insisted.

"Well I'm not telling you," Harry replied.

The English gentleman appeared again. He didn't want to expose her to, or worry her over anything. They were silent. She let him gather his thoughts. She showered his chest in delicate kisses.

"Harry, just remember why you're doing this," she said.

She tightened her hugging arms around his waist. He kissed her on the top of the head. "Come and get in bed, I need holding and I think you do too," she said.

Letting go of his waist she closed the gap in the curtains. The room dark again, she took his hand and he reluctantly allowed her to pull him back to bed.

CHAPTER TWENTY EIGHT

Apart from the terrorists watching over hostages, Bothrops called all of his men together at shift change. Those who had just finished their nightshift were ready for their beds. Those starting their shifts were still yawning and rubbing their eyes. In the Texas Ballroom they lined up in a role call formation, just as they had in the warehouse before they came to America. There was someone missing, Ademir wasn't in attendance. One of his men was already AWOL. This incensed the boss.

He stood in front of the two ranks of men and took a harsh line from the off. He was irate. His temper was getting the better of him. He was berating his men for something they hadn't done, but nobody was aware Harry was operational as an opposing force in the hotel. According to Bothrops, the incompetence, blundering and stupidity of his men had led to the deaths of three of their colleagues, their brothers in arms. When one of the men's noses started pouring out blood, the boss' anger boiled over.

"What is wrong with you idiotas?" he screamed. "Why can't you be normal?"

He looked at the men who stood before him, not helping their colleague with a bleeding nose. What was wrong with these morons? The boss was rapidly beginning to regret his decision to employ such imbeciles. But what choice did he have? Any man with even the slightest schooling wouldn't have entertained the idea of coming on such a futile suicide mission.

"Help him, help him," the boss screamed.

Flecks of saliva left his mouth.

"Get some cloth for him," he said.

Unless ingested, rat poison was relatively harmless to humans. If it was ingested it could cause a plethora of side effects, just one of them was bleeding. Nose bleeds for no apparent reason. Bleeding from the gums, blood in urine and bloody diarrhoea. Brodifacoum had a long life span once it was ingested into the human body and could remain present for several months. If untreated it could further cause a shortness of breath and other respiratory disorders, as well as extreme fatigue. The x-ray who was not present at the morning's roll call was incapacitated and in bed. Ademir had only ingested a small amount of the poison with his breakfast. He would be in agony for days.

Bothrops hadn't envisaged encountering problems with his men's health, no provisions for sickbays had been made. Additionally, there was no medical expertise in the hotel. More men would die. He just didn't know it yet.

*

Harry had woken with a clear head. Most of the previous day had passed by while he slept. He had ended three men's lives the previous night, but they were terrorists, no good x-rays who had brought death and captivity upon innocent people. It was a big step to take another life. It had consequences for everyone. Although the SAS books he had read and the way soldiers rationalised it all made sense to him. He was fighting evil. They were evil. He knew he would kill again.

With only eight moving parts and all of them well-oiled and moving freely, the AK47 was going to go bang every time. Now he had to zero the automatic rifle to his eye. Harry needed to make sure that when it went bang, it went bang at what he aimed at. Easier said than done when you didn't have access to a shooting range. A long hotel corridor would have to suffice.

He made a target for when he zeroed the rifle. Kelsi watched Harry with curiosity. His black marker pen flicked over the large sheet of white flip chart paper. She knew he wasn't drawing a conventional target. His target had something. It wasn't artistic flair, but it was unique. When finished, the cap was snapped onto the marker pen. He held his target up for her to see. She laughed her head off. It was funny. Harry was a genius.

She looked at him and smiled.

"I bet Van Gogh's shitting himself," Kelsi said.

Harry couldn't help but let out a snort.

He was glad the AK47 had a silencer attachment, but a silencer only brought the noise of the weapon firing down to one hundred and forty three decibels. Still above, but only just, the safe hearing zone.

None of the terrorist rifles he had seen had aftermarket sights. For the type of environment in which the terrorists were operating, the standard iron sights on the AK47 would suffice. Combat within a range of fifty metres didn't require anything more. At that distance weapons wouldn't need zeroing either. Only a complete idiot would miss at that range with a capable weapon.

The hotel was extra-long and for those shots, Harry wanted to be accurate. He wanted to be more accurate than the terrorists. He wanted to be able to take them out at a distance. Only a stupid man would wait for a target to get closer and come into range. Only a very stupid man, didn't do all he could to prepare. Harry intended to survive by living out the mantra of 'prior planning and preparation, prevents piss poor performance'. If the x-ray's weapons weren't zeroed, he would make sure his weapon was. He would be better than them. He wanted to be able to put terrorists on the floor before they could get in range of him. Primarily he would have a much better success rate and secondly, he would have a far superior survival rate. A man only had to mess up once and bang goes his survival rate.

Harry chose the seventeenth floor again. The corridor between corners one and four would be his rifle range. He checked the service stairwells and ensured there weren't any terrorists nearby that could react to the sound of his AK firing.

He positioned himself at corner one of the hotel. Harry flashed his wristband and backed into the corner bedroom. He took the sewing tape measure from his bag and was gutted at first glance. The tape wasn't in centimetres. Of course it would be in inches, he was in America now. Everything in Europe was in the metric system, kilos, litres, metres. The only imperial measurements he could think of that England still used were stones and pounds for a person's weight, miles not kilometres for distance, as well as pints for beer and milk. He unravelled the tape and breathed out. There were centimetres marked out on the other side of the tape. It must have come from the bag of a European staying at the hotel.

He laid the tape measure out flat and removed a shoe. Using it as a weight at the far end of the tape. Harry measured the distance of the entire corridor. The corridor was eight and a half metres shy of what he would have liked. He could work with that. He tacked the target to the end wall. After he replaced his shoe, Harry strode back down the corridor to his firing position in the bedroom. The door needed to be held open, Harry stuffed a towel under the door's bottom edge. Nothing was visible from the landing on corner two.

In an ideal world when a rifle was zeroed to a user's eye, five to ten shots would be fired. The sights of the rifle would then be adjusted to compensate for any deviation made by the bullet while it was travelling to the target. After observation another five to ten shots would be fired, more adjustments of the sights made and a third time five to ten shots fired. Hopefully they would land on target. The process of zeroing a weapon should take as long as it takes. It should not be rushed or hurried. The shooter firing the weapon should be absolutely calm and in a prone state, lying or kneeling.

Harry lay flat. The metal rifle butt unfolded so that the full length of the weapon was made available. More length, more accuracy. The butt of the rifle pressed snugly into his shoulder, his cheek rested on the stock, he could see the whole target with the whole of his vision. Up until this point, the terrorists didn't know there was anyone loose in the hotel. When he fired shots to zero the rifle, that might all change. The terrorists would go on the offensive to find the culprit.

He lay there, prone and immobile. While he regulated his breathing and heartrate, he put himself in their position. Who would the x-rays think they were up against? A special forces soldier? A close protection officer? Did they believe they were fighting a regular soldier? Or might they think they were battling a law enforcement officer, or even a retired law enforcement officer who was now a private security guard? Who was the have a go hero destroying their plans? Who was the rather painful thorn in their side? It wouldn't take them long to put two and two together and work out that the other two incidents had been orchestrated by the illegal alien running amok in the hotel. The last thing they would expect was a seventeen year old schoolboy. A gamer with a love for first person shooters and a geeky obsession with the SAS.

It was nerve racking stuff. Harry wanted it to be over as soon as possible. He wanted to get back to Kelsi and the safe haven that was the Porter's Lodge. No. They would have to move as soon as he was back. The terrorists would be out and looking for the person that fired the weapon. He thought he might as well leave the target where it was. Leave it and give a big middle finger to the x-rays. He would have to find a smarter hide. He had just the place in mind.

CHAPTER TWENTY NINE

The bottom of the magazine was resting on the carpet, beneath was a concrete floor. Firm shooting bases didn't get much better than that. Harry's breathing was steady, so was his heartrate. He was in a good place. He flicked the selector switch to single shot mode and pulled the trigger. He settled down from the recoil, then a second time. He checked for sound and movement. Nothing. He got to his feet and moved towards the target. Harry inspected where his shots had landed.

Two pulls of the trigger, two bullet holes. Both had landed on the target. That was a good start. The two rounds had pierced the paper directly under the centre mark, an even better start. He gauged how much the sight was out and darted back to his firing position.

Ideally a sight tool would be used to move the sights. He didn't have one. All Harry had was two flat head screwdrivers stolen from Maintenance. To get his aim spot on, he would need to move the front sight down, so his aim moved upwards. Harry estimated half a turn of the sight would be enough. He straddled the rifle the way it pointed. The weapon pinned between his thighs, he inserted the flatheads into the notches on the rifle sight. He twisted half a turn to the right. There was no windage movement of the rounds he had fired and there wouldn't be any in the confines of the hotel. He didn't make any adjustments to the horizontal aim of the AK.

He lay flat behind the Kalashnikov and let his heartbeat and breathing fall again. If his calculations were correct, this time the rounds fired would land on target. He fired, then fired again. This time when he reached the target he was a little too high. He would have to move the sight a quarter turn back to the left.

He was conscious of time and the terrorists having maybe heard his shots. Reaching his firing position he went through the same procedure as before, but only moved the rifle sight a quarter to the left. He fired again. This time when he checked, his shots had landed in the centre of the target.

He would leave the target where it was. Harry hadn't drawn a conventional target, not even the outline of a soldier. He had drawn, aimed and shot at an emoji. The one with the winking face and tongue sticking out. Leaving it in place would serve to unnerve the terrorists, as well as saying, 'Fuck you, I've got a weapon now'.

He returned to the Porter's Lodge without incident, but wishing he had thought of the need to move before he left.

He opened the door.

"We need to move and quickly," he said.

Kelsi looked up.

"Why?" she asked.

"They probably just heard me firing the rifle, they'll come looking for us," he said.

Kelsi looked surprised.

"I didn't hear you," she said.

"Really?" he asked.

"Yeah, not a peep," Kelsi said, "I wasn't expecting you back until I'd heard some gun shots."

"Okay, that's good, but we still need to move," Harry said.

"Why?" she asked.

He imagined her mind working overtime.

"Hang on," she said, "we need to move because there might have been a terrorist nearer to you than I was and he might be reporting the gun shots right now!"

She looked pleased as punch.

Harry smiled.

"Correct," he said.

If she was looking pleased before, she now positively beamed. Her smile. Her white teeth all in perfect formation and her full and youthful lips destroyed him. Harry strode over, took hold of her face and kissed her.

"Ten minutes and I want to be out of here," he said.

Notwithstanding what the 911 dispatcher had told him, Harry needed the vibration function of his smartphone turned on, or he wouldn't know about an incoming call. Vibrations in his trouser pocket woke him. Without opening an eye, he dug around with his fingers and pulled the device free. He opened an eye and saw the caller ID.

"How early?," he muttered.

"You sound a bit tired Harry, have I woken you up?" Chief Schlemmer asked.

"You know you have, I didn't get to sleep until the early hours and even then I kept waking up, I'm so tired," Harry hushed.

He didn't want to wake Kelsi.

"Ahh, that's a damn shame," Chris said, "that's payback for when you woke me up early."

"What do you want, anyway?" asked Harry.

"The special forces guys have been to see me. They need to know if there are sensors and booby traps on the first floor of the hotel. They want you to check the windows and fire exits," Chris said.

"Alright, calm down, I'll do it in a bit," Harry said.

"Promise?" asked Chris.

"Do you want me to pinkie promise?" Harry facetiously asked.

"I don't want you to do anything, it would just be very helpful if you could," Chris said.

"Yes I promise, now let me get some sleep," Harry said.

"Harry, do me a favour," Chris said, "when you go to look this time?"

"What am I doing?" Harry bluntly asked.

"Being careful, that's what you're doing, I want you to be really careful, please," Chris said.

"They won't even know I'm there," Harry said.

He clicked off the call and tried to snuggle his head against the cold metal once more.

Fortunately, the service elevator car Harry and Kelsi were hiding on top of hadn't moved in the night, but sleeping comfortably had been a challenge. Cables fed from the top of the elevator car to the giant mechanism on the top of the hotel. Gizmos, boxes of mechanics and electronics had prevented either of them from getting a decent sleep. They were sat in upright positions. Legs lying awkwardly around the cars whirring parts. Harry had got cramp twice during the night. Their upper bodies and heads were propped against the cold, uncoated metal. Kelsi stirred.

"Hey, good morning Mister," Kelsi greeted.

"Hello sleepy," Harry said.

Kelsi realised she didn't know if it was morning. The elevator shaft was pitch black and only allowed for tiny slivers of light.

"Actually, what time is it?" she asked.

"It's morning, but too early," Harry said.

He yawned and put a hand over his mouth.

"Go back to sleep and try and get another few hours," he said.

He blew her a kiss.

Kelsi smiled and caught the kiss, pressing it into her heart.

*

Ademir had dragged himself out of bed, forced his body to work. He struggled to dress himself, let alone shower. A quick facial wash and half-hearted brush of his teeth was all he managed. The blood in the toothpaste he spat back into the bowl went unnoticed. He didn't want to be late. The boss hadn't been happy when he didn't show up to shift change the other day. He hadn't felt half as ill then, as he did now. Stumbling down the corridor he felt as if he was crying blood.

Ademir collapsed outside the California Great Hall. He was the last terrorist to die of the ill-fated meal. Having only ingested a microscopic amount of rat poison, the chemicals had taken their time to work. His ill health had grown progressively worse as the organs in his body deteriorated and finally stopped working. He had been crying blood.

*

It was daytime. The hotel was alive. Previously when he had operated the hotel had been quieter. A skeleton shift of x-rays had been working minimally, now the larger dayshift of terrorists was working. They would be doing things, he didn't know what, but he knew they would up to something. He would undoubtedly see green boiler suits. He needed to remain hidden. Harry had to use all of the cumulative fibres of shrewdness every special forces book he had ever read had instilled in him. He had to utilise all of the elite skills SAS: We Dare We Win had taught him. His mind was going into overdrive. He needed to stop and calm himself down.

A few minutes of deep and calm breathing passed over him. Harry illuminated the area with the torch on his smartphone. He gathered his things and made sure he was fully kitted out, weapon, ammo, grenade and this time, ski mask. He listened hard, strained his ears and attempted to hear movement beyond the elevator car. He couldn't hear anything. Drawing down large glugs of water, he handed Kelsi the bottle. He told her to stay hydrated.

"What if I need to pee?" she asked.

"There are four floors below us, plus three basement floors," he said. "Squat off the side."

"That's disgusting," she said.

Harry shrugged.

"Needs must. People do extraordinary things in times of war, you're just having a pee. Get on with it, you'll be alright," he said.

"I suppose," she said. "Where are you going?"

"The special forces want to know if there are booby traps, or sensors on the ground floor," he told her, "I'm going to check them out."

"Can I come?" she asked.

"No, it's too dangerous," Harry said.

"But…" she started.

"NO," Harry forcefully told her, "we're going to live through this, but sometimes I have to do things on my own, it's safer that way."

Kelsi pulled a sad face and blew Harry her own kiss. She lifted the access hatch on top of the elevator.

Silently he dropped into the steel box below and she passed down his equipment. Once his rucksack was tight on his back, he mouthed. 'See you later'.

Kelsi lowered the hatch.

Then it opened again.

"What if someone uses the elevator?" she asked.

"Just stay out the way of the moving parts," he said.

"No," she said, "I mean, how will you find me?"

"I'll walk up and down the stairwell until I find the elevator, don't worry, I PROMISE I WON'T LEAVE YOU HERE," he said.

Kelsi smiled and closed the steel hatch.

Harry still couldn't hear anyone and now, looking through the small viewing window in the elevator doors, he couldn't see anyone either. He pulled the ski mask over his head.

*

Bothrops ordered two boiler suits to clear away Ademir's body. They didn't want to do it, they didn't want to become infected with whatever Barrio disease Ademir had brought with him to America. They thought it could be the AIDS disease, or any other of a multiple amount of infections it was possible to gain from living where they lived. He was the seventh body that had been placed in the ad hoc mortuary. All the men in there had died from bleeding. The men lying in that room had been covered in blood. It had come out of their faces, mouths, noses, eyes and ears. Their fingertips had been coated in blood as it had run from their nails. One of the bodies even had a blood stained crotch.

They were quick and efficient. The x-ray holding the legs backed up to the inward opening door. Once they were inside they held their breath and hastily placed the body of their friend Ademir on the floor. They left the room as quickly as they entered, they didn't want to be in that room a second longer than necessary.

*

Stan and Tommy and a handful of essential planning and support staff, were all that remained in the Ops Room. The training in the hotel next door was constant and relentless.

The two sergeants looked at a street plan taped to a wall.

"Black Country ay we," the voice behind them said.

Tommy looked puzzled and spun around to see what the deep voice was talking about. Stan burst out laughing. Before turning around, he knew who it was.

"Well bugger me, Tony Hill, I haven't heard that saying for years!" Stan said.

"How are you doing, mate?" Tony asked, in his dull Black Country accent.

Him and Stan firmly shook hands.

"Good, really good, why are you here?" asked Stan.

"Me and my Brick were in Mexico on a job…" Tony said.

"A Brick? Is this going turn out to be like a Badger?" Tommy interjected.

Stan laughed.

"Like Stan and his ugly bunch, we work in teams of four. Our teams of four are known as Bricks. Anyway, as I was saying we were in Mexico City on a job when news of this situation broke. We couldn't finish the job quick enough to be honest, but we had to wait for a meeting to take place between the chap we were watching and his Mexican contact. After the meeting and our man had got on an aeroplane back to England, I made a phone call, spoke to the Ops Room in Hereford and waited for a call back. After an hour of no call back, I decided we'd just make a move. We hired a car and took shifts at the wheel to get here as soon as we could. It's over two thousand miles from Mexico City to Fort Lauderdale," Tony said.

"Why didn't you just get a flight?" Tommy asked.

"We've got some equipment with us that nobody needs to know about. British Airways are the only airline we can fly with when we've got it, so we put it in the boot of the car. Anything we can do to lend a hand?" Tony asked, in his deep tones.

Tony hailed from the Black Country in England, so called because of its rich history as being one of the smog filled heartlands of British industry and the first place to successfully harness the power of steam. Stan knew Tony from his days in the regular army. The pair had served together in Afghanistan and Iraq, but he hadn't seen Tony since he passed selection for the SAS. As he found out, his old colleague hadn't done too badly for himself either. He was now a member of the third branch of the United Kingdom's Special Forces tree. The highly secretive Special Reconnaissance Regiment (SRR).

The SRR was created in 2005, over sixty years after both the Special Air Service and the Special Boat Service. It was the only special forces regiment in the United Kingdom to recruit women and it took its applicants from all three branches of the armed services. The selection process to join the SRR was immensely hard, physically demanding, emotionally draining and intellectually challenging. It left room for only the best of the best. A small regiment of around one hundred and sixty members, it was a very important jewel in the crown of the British Army's capabilities. It formed the frontline against international terrorism. The SRR was borne out of the Force Research Unit, a top secret special forces unit established in Northern Ireland in 1982. Their role was to obtain intelligence by deeply penetrating the Irish Republican Army (IRA) and their terrorist movements and plans. Part of the British Army Intelligence Corps, their role was fact finding, as well as running double agents and informants.

The SRR was continually operational with its operators being scattered all over the planet, but a large amount of their work was on home soil and their fight was currently against the terrorism gripping many westernised nations around the globe. When they were at home the men and women of the SRR were stationed with the SAS at Stirling Lines. Nobody on camp even knew who was SRR and who was SAS. No one asked questions and the members of the elite regiments just went about their day to day business. The SRR specialised in the unseen. It specialised in the undetected and while it was doing these two things, it was busy gathering as much information on its target as possible. However, if it was called for the SRR was capable of being just as devastatingly lethal as its two older brothers. They were the best in the world at what they did. There was not a method they didn't use, or a terrorist on the planet who could outfox them. Stan smiled and looked up at the six foot six, brown haired, Third Dan kickboxing sergeant.

"Good to have you on board Tone, how does some reconnaissance sound?" asked Stan.

"It's what we do best, mate," Tony replied.

After a concise thirty minute briefing, the tall athletic frame of the SRR sergeant was making his way out of the room with a new tasking.

CHAPTER THIRTY

Once he was on the landing, he listened open mouthed. Nothing. Harry didn't know why, but he wondered how long it would take for a door to close, with a door closer's resistance holding it back. He looked to his left and fully opened the door, brought his watch into view and let go. Twelve seconds was all it took, thirteen maybe until the door was sat snugly in the frame. Harry stored the information in the back of his mind and made a downward path.

He was in the service stairwell at corner four, midway between the second and first floor. He waited and listened. The stairwell was quiet. Then he heard it. Three men coming up the stairs from below. He couldn't tell which floor they had come from, but there were only three floors below him. They weren't tearing up the stairs in a sprint, more of a leisurely jog. No real urgency in their movements. Harry backtracked up to the second floor. He desperately wanted to try his new silenced AK47, but not in the cavernous stairwell. He positioned himself far enough back that none of the x-rays were able to see him, but he would be able to shoot them before they laid eyes him. He never got chance. They exited the stairwell on the floor below him, the first floor.

There was a good reason why he couldn't try out the zeroed AK47, this mission for Schlemmer was meant to be a clandestine op. He would remain hidden wherever possible. Easy come, easy go. Just slip in and slip out. Undetected. He pondered where the three men had just come from. Had they come from the maintenance department? He doubted it was the gym and there was nothing of interest to them in the offices. He decided they must have come up from the maintenance department, but why? He thought he should at least see if there were better options of accessing the first floor.

The reason why the terrorists might be using the maintenance department festered in his mind as he traversed the hotel. Harry visited the front and back main staircase, as well as the corner two service stairwell. The rear service stairwell was still the most viable option, the reception area had been brimming with x-rays, all doing something or other and all would want to fill him with holes.

Making it back to corner four, he nestled himself into a prone position on the mid landing. This time there was nothing to see, nothing to hear. Harry made his way to the fire door on the main landing. The situation was now critical. If he was found, the mission would be blown. He would be shot on sight. The lives of a few hundred people and the leader of the free world hung on his next move. He still couldn't see or hear anyone. He moved down to the first floor and pulled the door handle and allowed himself into the corridor. Immediately he saw an x-ray.

The terrorist had his back turned and was walking towards the lobby. He must have exited from a meeting room further down the hallway. Harry heard more voices. They were coming his way. He padded down the corridor in the direction of the terrorist he had just seen. Choosing an internal room on the right of the corridor, he entered and hoped the terrorists coming his way didn't want that particular room. Pulling the cord to close the blinds at the front of the room, Harry slowly allowed the door back into its frame. The voices were only metres away. He didn't dare let the door shut completely, the terrorists would hear the door catch engage. He held the door open a crack. The x-rays, three of them, walked by without incident. He wanted to see where they were heading.

Slowly opening the door, he used one eye to peer down the corridor. The terrorists stopped outside one of the larger conference rooms. It was either the Michigan or Georgia room, he couldn't remember which. His ears picked up movement behind him. A door was closing. Twelve, maybe thirteen seconds till it was shut. The person coming towards him wouldn't take that long. He closed his door to just a crack again and noticed the x-ray was pushing something as he passed. Opening the door, he saw the terrorist pushing a large black case on wheels, the type a rock band might use when they were on tour. He watched the x-ray with curiosity. He knocked and entered the same room as the last three x-rays. Two tasks had just been added to Harry's operation. He wanted to find out what was in the box and what was happening in that room. To look now would be suicide. He'd have a look once they'd gone.

Stepping out of the room, he paced across the corridor in one fluid and fast movement and entered the meeting room opposite. No one saw. No one heard. He was covert. He was clandestine. This room was one of the smallest rooms on the ground floor. He couldn't remember the name of the room and he hadn't wasted time glancing at the door's nameplate. The room only had seating for ten people. This time the room's corridor window blinds were closed, but it reminded him that he hadn't opened the blinds in the room opposite when he exited. Harry hoped none of the terrorists would be switched on enough to notice. Turning around raised his curiosity. He didn't know what it was until her got closer, but he guessed it was a sensor for the car park facing window.

Harry could see a white box fixed to the wall at the very edge of the large glass window. The box was small, maybe three or four inches high and no more than an inch in both width and depth. It must have been fixed to the wall with small screws. Velcro sticky pads could be used, but they weren't as effective, the pads would absorb the smaller vibrations. Whoever fitted it had received professional training, or had been in the military and used it themselves previously. If all the boxes were in the same position, a sniper running visual surveillance couldn't see them. Harry moved closer.

He knew that he had used the same type of device on SAS: We Dare We Win. It was a Viper shock sensor. They were commercially available. He knew that because he had thought about fitting one to his bedroom door when his dad's mate, wife and their young children had come to stay last Christmas. He needed more visual confirmation though. Just seeing one Viper in one room wasn't enough. The SF would want more.

Following the same protocol as before, he opened the door and made it into the corridor. He headed in the direction of corner one. This time there was nobody in the corridor, but it was still a high risk move. He was out in the open with no real exit options. He could run along a corridor, but the chances of escape were slim. He would get gunned down in the process. As he paced past, Harry was able to gain visual confirmation that the fire door mid-way along the corridor was rigged with a sensor and Claymore. It was sat back in the corridor opening, far back enough that an elevated sniper wouldn't be able to detect it. He knew what he was looking for this time and it hadn't required more than a quick glance to his left. The SF would have to take that one exit being a replica of all the exits. He'd checked two doors and was damned if he was going to check all the others.

The room after the fire door had its window blinds closed. Too dangerous, anyone could be inside and he wasn't about to find out who. He was able to see there was nobody in the room after that, so he entered. Pulling the window blinds temporarily closed, he darted to the left hand side of the full height window. It was another Viper, same box, same position. A door slammed shut. Harry crouched behind the table and chairs in the centre of the room and ensured three round burst had been selected on his AK. He was ready to punch some holes in terrorists. They were talking loudly as they walked, but the voices faded. Harry guessed it would be the four x-rays he had seen earlier.

A minute counted down in his head. He opened the door. Harry peered one eye down the corridor, but could only see towards the lobby. He relied on his hearing to check behind him. There was nobody present. Two items of four ticked off his mission list. Two more to go. He opened the window blinds. Harry went to have a look what was going on in the room next door and what was in the wheeled box.

The room turned out to be the Michigan Conference Room. Easing the door open, he entered with weapon raised. Stretching from the middle of the hotel's north side, it ran down to the lobby at corner one. Rectangular in shape, a polished oak conference table normally ran down its centre. That was normally. This wasn't. All of the table's sections had been pushed to the wall and the chairs now sat on top. What was in the centre of the room was the polar opposite to the norm.

Harry's mouth was agape from the second he realised what was in place of the table. The consequences suddenly dawned on him. It was bad. Very, very bad.

"Shit!" he said.

All those people, not just any people. The SF. The FBI. Lots more. All their lives were in danger. He could see missiles, but he didn't know what type. That didn't matter. The attack would be devastating. The death toll massive!

*

An hour after leaving the Ops Room, Tony was stood at an FLPD roadblock. He blended in with the other tourists perfectly. His Brick hadn't checked into the Wavecrest Royal with the other special operators. If anyone saw them leaving the hotel, they would be clocked and marked as SF. Instead, they had found a room and booked themselves into a hellish backstreet hovel purporting to be a hotel. Tony didn't know if the guest house had a star rating, but he thought they would be lucky if they weren't in negative figures.

After four independently taken shopping trips, two men of the SRR were now dressed as locals, shorts and t-shirts. Tony, as a tourist with a locally bought Florida emblazoned t-shirt and Renee, one of the only women who could hack the pace in the elite regiment, posing as an office worker. She stood in heels, grey pencil skirt, white blouse and glasses. They had placed themselves at pre-determined positions in the streets surrounding the Atlantic Grand and had been tasked with seeking out any dickers the terrorists may have on the outside running counter surveillance.

'Dicker' was a term the British Army had come to use in Northern Ireland. In layman's terms it meant 'watcher'. The IRA had lots of dickers all conforming to the Irish Republican Army ideology. They wanted the British out of Northern Ireland and the country reunified and ran from Dublin. Ireland was a Catholic country and when the English invaded in the 12th century, they had instilled many colonists loyal to the English Crown. This was further exacerbated by the settlement of Protestants many years later. After a centuries long war the IRA had become a very proficient force. They secured the independence of twenty six of the thirty two Irish Counties, in the form of the Irish Free State in 1921, but the British wanted to keep a safe haven for the Protestants they had instilled in the country. That sanctuary was the remaining six counties and became Northern Ireland.

The two religions living within it hated each other. There were now more Protestants than Catholics in uppermost part of the country. The IRA wanted full reunification and the only way they could achieve this was through violence and terrorism. IRA dickers looked out for British Army movement throughout the towns and fields of Northern Ireland, they then alerted the IRA to their presence. The IRA had hundreds of hidden weapons caches throughout Ireland, especially in fields that bordered with the Republic of Ireland. Despite the dicker's best efforts, the British Army found these reserves of weapons on a regular basis in the rolling fields of South Armagh. The British Army wouldn't tell news outlets because it would give the IRA press they didn't deserve and enhance their image as a fighting force. The general public living in Northern Ireland were kept in the dark about the powder keg in which they were living.

The IRA weren't the only people who used dickers. They were synonymous throughout the world for many different organisations: military, governmental, legal and illegal. In Somalia during the Battle for Mogadishu in 1993, Somali militiamen in control of the city used young children with cell phones as dickers, to forewarn them of impending American military action. What Tony and his three SRR operators were now looking for, were signs of dickers working for the terrorists inside the hotel. He had been told of the terrorist's three hundred and sixty degree camera surveillance system, but cameras behind a piece of glass couldn't see everything in the surrounding streets, nor could they hear the street. He, as well as those in the Ops Room, were convinced they would find one or more dickers on the outside.

*

The Michigan Room must have held thirty black boxes on wheels, all pushed under the table. Thirty missiles should be laid out on the floor, but a visual scan told Harry there were more than that. He counted sixty.

Harry's head was sweating and he felt as if he couldn't breathe. He lowered his hood and removed his ski mask. All of the missiles were in front of the window. Snipers wouldn't be able to see into the room because the exterior window blinds were closed. He moved closer and knelt next to the nearest tube.

"Fuck," Harry said.

The lethal tubes were Javelin anti-tank missiles. There being no tanks for miles to see, he knew the target had to be the Wavecrest Royal. His eyes also picked up twenty discs with handles.

Moving further into the room, Harry stood over the round discs. He realised he'd seen them before, when workmen were changing the glass shopfront at his mum's lettings agency. They were suction cups to hold panes of glass. If the job needed twenty of them, it must be a seriously big pane. Then it clicked. The terrorists were going to remove the pane of glass from this room and fire the missiles at the Wavecrest Royal. The hotel would be decimated. Hundreds of Seal Team Six, SAS, Delta Force and FBI dead, then they would replace the glass. He noticed two Vipers sitting on the floor next to the window, they were to seal the hotel tight after the deadly barrage of missiles had been fired.

"Bastards," he muttered.

The door behind him opened.

CHAPTER THIRTY ONE

Every half hour the operators of the SRR changed their appearance. Turned a baseball cap around. Shrugged on the grey jacket for a business suit, or pulled their sunglasses over their nose. They also moved to a new area of operation. To stay any longer in the streets surrounding the hotel, when all of the other onlookers had moved on, would arouse suspicion in a dicker who had knowledge of counter-surveillance. The operators were now in their third area of operation after starting surveillance of the crowds at the police cordons.

The FLPD construction of an inner and outer cordon had hindered any dicker, but reconnaissance was still possible, even from a street away. The smartphone in Tony's pocket vibrated with a Whatsapp Message. It was Renee:

'Birch Road. Building opposite corner three of hotel, above hair salon. Possible static dicker location. RA'.

Tony didn't need to ask why she thought a dicker was hiding at that location. Renee was a switched on girl. She had heaps more knowledge than him when he was only twenty five years old.

Tony had news of his own. He had noticed the same Hispanic male at both of his previous locations. He wasn't browsing the street scene as all the other onlookers were, nor did he come across as relaxed and looking at the impressive set-up of the FLPD. Crowds were good for anyone conducting physical surveillance. An operator could get to within a metre of the person of interest without being noticed. Tony had seen the

Hispanic guy using the zoom facility on his smartphone. He was getting a closer look at the police inner cordon, vehicles and personnel, paying an unhealthy amount of attention to the external office staircase the FBI and SF were using. To an average Joe this was just a normal man with an inquisitive nature. To the SRR this was lethal behaviour. The Dicker hadn't seen Tony or his operators and now he was pushing through the crowd to get to the front.

Tony exchanged pleasantries with an American couple and their young children. He was handed an invaluable opportunity of cover. Two of the children started squabbling and soon enough, it got physical. One pushed the other and the father intervened. Tony got to one knee, looped an arm around the second child and calmed him down. To anyone running counter-surveillance for the Dicker, Tony was a family friend, a trustworthy, genuine bloke. Not a highly skilled, lethal surveillance operator.

The kids stopped arguing. Tony found himself stood next to the Dicker. Getting this close was a big no no. He was breaking the cardinal rule of physical surveillance, he was making himself memorable to the suspect. He was so close to him, they were rubbing shoulders. The crowd at the FLPD roadblock was at least five onlookers deep and stretched right across the road. Tony's height was working in his favour, he towered over the Hispanic. He knew he would have to take a back seat on observing this dicker from now on, but this opportunity was too golden to miss.

He could see the suspect constructing a message on his smartphone. He was also using Whatsapp. Tony was sure he was using it for exactly the same reason as the SRR. Whatsapp was a secure messaging app. Messages sent were encrypted end to end. That meant only the sender and recipient were able to read them. They were incredibly secure. The message the Hispanic male was creating included a zoomed in photograph of the SWAT truck with its rear door open and was accompanied by a paragraph of text. Tony couldn't speak the suspect's language fluently, but from time spent in Colombia observing drug manufacturing plants, he knew enough. He knew the important words. The words in the suspects message were throwing up all manner of red flags. He was singling himself out as a dicker. Tony was positive he was working for the terrorists so he backed away.

He was well placed to track the Dicker as he moved away from the outer cordon. He walked down Riomar Street, towards the beach and the entrance of the Wavecrest Royal. Tony followed forty feet behind on the other side of the street. Reaching the Beach Boulevard, the Dicker met up with a South American woman. Years of observing people had made Tony an expert in human behaviour patterns. He knew what was about to happen. They turned and he and his female accomplice looked back up Riomar. Good counter surveillance skills, but a rookie mistake. She had associated herself with him the moment they hooked up. Looking to see if anyone was following him was now pointless. Tony was out of sight to the pair and in a café just before they turned to look up the street.

Inside the café a comely waitress took Tony's order. He observed from behind a half height frosted glass window. Sat at his new observation point he contacted his colleagues, sending a message to the Brick group chat. He could see a member of his crew was instantly typing a message in reply. Baggers already had eyes on the female Dicker and as far as he could tell, she was keeping count on the numbers of service personnel in the Wavecrest Royal. She was completely random and looked exactly like she was meant to be there. Nobody would notice her, or the device she was using to keep count. Sat on a bench across the street, her back turned to the sea, she was keeping tabs like manned door security at a club would with a clicker. She was counting people in and out of the hotel.

The whole terrorist action was much more elaborate than anyone had previously imagined. Everyone was at risk. All the

information was presumably being processed through the static
location Renee had noticed. Tony was handed a Cappuccino as
he sent a message to his team:

'Hold fast, remain in position. TH'.

He sent another to the Ops Room. Stan's smartphone pinged
with a new message:

'Three dickers. One; in building opposite corner three. Two;
on foot and observing hotel and FLPD from outer cordons.
Three; has eyes on the military and FBI entering and exiting
the Wavecrest Royal. TH'.

Stan replied:

'Standby'.

*

Harry froze. He didn't know what to do. A split second was all
it took. His brain kicked into gear. He spun around on his heel.
Three of the four terrorists he had seen earlier had walked back
into the room. Before they went for their weapons, Harry knew
he had to put them all on the floor.

Two seconds was all it took. It was as if he was playing SAS:
We Dare We Win. Bringing the silenced AK47 up to eye level,
he moved his head a millimetre closer to the rifle sights. The first
x-ray shouted something he didn't understand. The AK's safety catch was already off. One pull of the trigger. Three rounds.
Two pulls of the trigger. Six rounds. The first two terrorists were
hit in the chest and dropped to the floor. The last man through
the door was left wondering what was going on. A third pull on
the trigger and rounds seven, eight and nine, thudded into him.
The silencer hadn't lessened the gunfire much at all. Hollywood

bullshit. Harry got to his feet and ran to the still closing door. He knew the whole action had taken about eleven seconds. His fingers grasped the door just before it met the frame.

In the corridor Harry looked to the left towards the lobby. A pair of terrorists were staring down the corridor. Sudden shouting and hand movements followed. They beckoned more boiler suits to follow them. Standing prone he brought the rifle to aim. Harry let off another three round burst. Both x-rays fell to the floor. He realised he'd left his ski mask on the floor next to the missiles. Too late to go back for it now.

Harry turned and ran towards corner four. His covert operation was skewed. He could hear voices behind him. He didn't take the stairs. He thought about turning left and running along the back passageways to corner three, that looked like his only option. He turned left and stopped dead in his tracks. A better escape route came to mind. Out of sight of the x-rays, Harry pulled free the last grenade from his hoodie and pulled the pin.

He released the grenade and rolled it under arm, up the passageway, in the direction of the boiler suits charging down the corridor. Waiting three seconds for the grenade to detonate felt like the three hours. The x-rays were getting nearer and his chances of survival were decreasing. The grenade detonated. It was as perfect as he could have hoped.

Glass shattered. Carpet was ripped up. Stud walls were blown apart. Ceiling tiles crashed down and x-rays fell. Firing the remaining rounds of his AK down the passageway, he heard a deadman's click. He used the confusion to his advantage. He opened the door at the end of the corridor and took hold of the doorframe. Harry heaved himself up and jumped into the linen chute.

He fell feet first. To fall headfirst would have been suicide. He would almost certainly break his neck when he landed. The fall was fast. It didn't last long. Harry only had three basement floors until the chute terminated. He couldn't see anything. It was pitch black.

The mountain of linen at corner four of the maintenance department was momentarily disturbed. A free falling object ploughed into its peak. Harry came to a halt and scrabbled free of the dirty sheets. He checked himself over and made sure he had everything he fell with. Running from the heap of linen and passing the giant x-ray scanner, he vaulted up onto the workbenches and ran across them. Leaping between benches he made his route as linear as possible. Harry pulled the spent magazine free of the AK and reached into his leg pocket for another. Jumping down from the last workbench, he slammed the mag into the weapon just as he reached the door to the service stairwell at corner two. He hoped he got there before any x-rays made it down to the maintenance department. He had, but as he pulled the door in front of him, the door at corner four opened.

The terrorists had seen him, however he knew it would take them longer to traverse the maintenance department. It wasn't straightforward. The route criss-crossed. The workbenches in the centre would hinder them. His sprint, albeit now on an incline, was straight up the stairs. Harry ran and ran. He fished his smartphone out of his pocket and called Schlemmer. The call was answered after two rings. Harry didn't wait for Chris to speak.

"You have to evacuate the Wavecrest Royal," Harry urged.

He was breathing hard.

"Slow down Harry, what are you talking about?" Chris asked.

Harry spoke slowly and deliberately, trying to offset his breathlessness.

"Evacuate... Wavecrest Royal.. terrorist… missile… strike… imminent," he said.

He continued up the stairs.

"I don't understand what you mean, Harry," said the Chief.

Hearing a door open below, Harry fired down the stairwell. Fire and move. In the command truck the chief winced as the sound of rifle fire tore down the phoneline. He held the phone away from his ear until the noise subsided. Harry's weapon stopped firing. The AK had jammed. Stoppage. On his console game he always had a back-up weapon. He would drop to one knee and draw his handgun, but this time he didn't have one. Stuffing his phone in an empty pocket, Harry ripped the magazine from the rifle and dropped it on the floor.

"Hang on Chris," he shouted. Loud enough so the phone in his pocket would hear.

He pulled back the bolt and opened up the rifle. A spent shell casing was stuck in the chamber. The AK was well greased, it shouldn't have jammed. Harry didn't know why it had. Maybe it was a dodgy round, he thought. He tried to prise the casing out with his fingers. It was hopeless. It was stuck fast and wasn't going anywhere. Fuck. Harry's heart was racing. The chances of getting caught were multiplying. Holding the chamber open and turning the rifle upside down, he tapped the weapon on the handrail of the stairs. Nothing, it wasn't budging. Double fuck. He tapped harder. Then out and out bashed the AK47 on the rail. The spent shell casing wasn't coming out. Lifting it above his head, Harry threw the weapon down the centre of the stairwell. He hoped the x-rays still had their heads down and weren't making up any ground. He relayed his message to Chris loudly and clearly.

"TERRORISTS HAVE JAVELIN ANTI-TANK MIS-SILES TO FIRE AT THE WAVECREST ROYAL. EVACU-ATE NOW. I REPEAT. EVACTUATE THE WAVECREST ROYAL," shouted Harry.

He jogged up the next flight of stairs.

"Doors are all sealed with Claymores, sensors too, there are Vipers on the ground floor windows," he added.

"Shit," said Chris, "keep safe, I'll ask them to assault the hotel as soon as possible."

"ROGER. OUT," Harry said.

*

Teonnie saw the chief jump to his feet. He darted out of the command truck. On the street Chris Schlemmer ran as hard as he could towards the offices at the back of the Atlantic Grand. Running straight across the grass he headed for the stairs.

The FLPD Officer manning the door was startled.

Head down, he raced up the steps.

"Move," Chris shouted.

The occupant of the desk in the corridor looked up.

"Where's the Ops Room?" the chief asked.

The lad at the desk pointed.

Chris darted down the internal staircase and raced along the corridor. The Ops Room wasn't locked and he ignored the sign on the door.

Only a few faces at desks. He saw Stan in a side room. He didn't recognise the other man. Racing past desks and chairs and drawing the attention of those in the office, he burst into the room.

"Harry's been on the phone, the terrorists have a rocket system in place to blow the Wavecrest Royal to kingdom come," the chief breathlessly said.

"Slow down, collect your thoughts and tell me again," Stan told him.

After Chris had relayed his information calmly, Tommy radioed the Delta Force snipers that were in place on the surrounding rooftops.

Chris was leaning against a filing cabinet and had almost recovered from his breathlessness. Stan passed him a cup of water.

"Are you okay?" he asked.

"Yeah, yeah. I'm good," Chris said, "I just thought you should know the score as quickly as possible."

"It's appreciated, thank you," Stan said.

"You need to evacuate the Wavecrest," Chris urged.

Finishing up on the radio, Tommy looked over.

"We can't," he said. "The terrorists have their own people on the outside, they're keeping count of the numbers of special forces entering and exiting the Wavecrest. They're waiting to get the maximum number of service personnel in the hotel before they strike."

"Shit," said Chris. "What are you going to do?"

Stan looked at him.

"Take the dickers out. If it looks like the siege is going to last longer, we can feed the x-rays in the hotel disinformation using their phones," he said calmly. "It's what we're good at."

Chris liked their style.

"Any word on the ground floor doors and windows?" Tommy asked.

"Yes, Harry said they have Claymores and sensors in place, they also have something to do with snakes on the windows?" he said.

He knew that wasn't what Harry had said, but right then that was all he could think of.

"Vipers?" Tommy asked.

"Yeah, that's it, Vipers on the ground floor windows," Chris confirmed.

"Shit," Stan said.

"Are they bad?" Chris asked.

"Well they don't make an assault any easier," Stan said.

There were three types of sensors for glass. The best of these sensors was the Viper. The Viper was a vibration sensor that worked on detecting shockwaves. When a vibration big enough was detected, the alarm was activated.

CHAPTER THIRTY TWO

"A child? A fucking child?" Bothrops ranted.

Nicolas, the man who told the boss about the intruder interfering with their plans, was only two years older than Harry. He trembled with fear as he stood before the boss. He was growing angrier than Nicolas had ever seen him.

He was renowned in their country as a great business man, but one who had an incredibly violent temper and a destructive vengeance. It was commonplace for Nicolas to be walking through the slum where he lived, only to see people that had crossed Bothrops Atrox, dead and hanging from telegraph poles. His friend's older brother had once crossed him and he was found dead in the same way. He had been tortured until his death. Two days later, Nicolas' friend and his whole family went missing never to be seen again. Everyone knew Bothrops had arranged for the family to be wiped out. That was the evil of his vindictiveness. Now he thought Bothrops Atrox would do the same to his family.

"Yes sir, that is what I hear," he replied.

"All the rooms were searched, why was he not found?" Bothrops asked.

"I don't know, sir," he said.

Nicolas was trembling and wanted to cower in the corner of the room.

"Go back to what you were doing," Bothrops said.

"I was watching over the hosta…" Nicolas said.

"Well fucking get on with it," Bothrops raged.

He snapped his fingers at his son.

"Pablo," Bothrops commanded.

Pablo came to his father straight away. As a youngster he had found out what would happen if he was disobedient.

"You said every room in the hotel had been searched, is that not correct?" Bothrops said.

"Yes, every room," replied Pablo.

Bothrops exploded. Fury gripping his whole body.

"Well that is clearly not the case you fucking imbecile," he cried out. "Find the child, go and find el chico," he said.

*

Harry was running up the stairwell and he realised why he had timed a door closing. The terrorists should be tactically clearing each flight of stairs, but they weren't. They were just legging it after him. Harry was running hard, but still exercising a little caution. He could turn and lie in wait for them. He would be able to take them all out easily if he had a weapon. Still not showing any care, the x-rays were taking less than six seconds to fully climb a floor. Their lack of caution was perfect. The thought of someone giving them resistance obviously didn't figure into Bothrops' plans. They hadn't been taught how to tactically pursue an assailant. Harry slowed even more. It took a lot of nerve, but he knew what he was doing. At least he hoped he did. Running up one more flight of stairs to the tenth floor, he opened the fire door fully. He stopped and unhooked his rucksack, opening the straps to the top compartment. He could hear the boiler suits below and judged it was time to move.

Entering the tenth floor without a weapon, Harry immediately turned left. By the time he had ran to the first smaller corridor on his right, he had opened his bag fully. He pulled one of the Molotov cocktails free and placed the bottle of gasoline just out of sight in the corridor's T-junction. Running along the new passageway and away from the bottle of gas, he only had seconds to spare. The x-rays would know where he had gone. It wouldn't have taken them twelve seconds to climb two floors. The door closer resisted for thirteen seconds.

He ran halfway down the corridor and pulled the second Molotov cocktail from his bag. After a quick rummage in the top compartment of the rucksack, he found the lighter he had pinched.

At home in England, Harry was on the Islington High School Cricket Team. He was a bowler and the best the school had. He was such a good bowler his team mates had nicknamed him 'The Assassin'. During one cricket match, he had taken out the first four opposing batsmen with the initial eleven balls of the game. Batsmen three and four came one after the other. He was so good at bowling balls at the opposing team because when he wasn't playing SAS: We Dare We Win, he was practising his technique in the school's cricket nets. He was a fast bowler and his pace and aim were exceptional. Deadly accuracy was his friend and that was exactly what he relied on now.

He knew his aim would be spot on, but the gas filled bottle was heavier and weighted differently at either end. It was a world apart from a smooth and perfectly round cricket ball. It would spin and twist as it flew through the air. Harry countered this. He would throw the bottle differently. He took up a stance similar to that of a knife thrower in a circus show. He wanted to throw the botte while he faced forward and not twist his body and possibly skew his aim.

Harry turned around and could see the other Molotov Cocktail in front of him. He moved closer until the gas filled bottle was twenty two yards away, or sixty six feet. Exactly the same as the distance between stumps on a cricket wicket. He heard the terrorists enter the floor. They had seen the door closing. His plan was holding up. Harry flicked the lighter three times. It spouted a flame and he lit the rag protruding from the top of the gas filled bottle in his hand. The x-rays split. That wasn't part of his plan. Two of them had turned left as the entered the floor and were running down the same corridor he had taken. The third x-ray had ran straight through the door and was heading across the front of the hotel towards corner one. When he turned left it would only be seconds before he saw Harry. It was a classic pincer movement and exactly what Harry would have done. He had to think on his feet.

He backed up again before he bent forwards, then shuffling his feet in the bottle's direction, he jogged ten paces to build his speed. Above his shoulder and ready to throw, his right arm held the flaming bottle by the neck. He could feel the heat. The flames were burning the hairs on his hand. His left arm was outstretched and the tips of his fingers pointed directly at the other bottle. He could hear the two of the x-rays pounding down the corridor. His aim was spot on. He released the bottle. End over end it somersaulted towards the target. Harry could see the flames spouting from the rag with every rotation. He saw a green boiler suit reach the T-junction. The x-ray raised his weapon. At the same moment the bottle found its target, the second terrorist arrived.

The glass bottles shattered causing a fireball. The two terrorists were covered in flames. He didn't have time to turn and run in the opposite direction, Harry dived on the carpet and missed the ball of flame by inches. It consumed his corridor and licked up the walls. The gasoline vapours burnt easily. As quickly as it started, the fire was over. Harry had another issue, the third terrorist would be behind him any second.

He crawled forward as quickly as he could, the carpet beneath him burnt to a crisp and still smouldering. He scrabbled forward like a lizard over hot desert sand. Moving as fast as possible, his elbows and knees bore the brunt as he tried to hold his body away from the intense heat. Both terrorists were dead, charred and blackened by the fireball. The SAS books he had read told him the smell of pork that currently consumed the area was the smell of burnt flesh. Harry reached the first body, the x-ray who had attempted to fire his AK. The strap holding the weapon to the terrorist was scorched to nothing. He pulled the weapon free with ease, but fuck it was hot. Red hot. Harry rolled onto his back and sat up. He could hear footsteps getting louder. The third x-ray was close. Harry re-arranged his arms in his hoodie. His right arm pulled back and his sleeve on the trigger, the barrel of the AK resting on his covered left forearm. Fucking hell, it was still really hot. The x-ray turned the corner. Harry saw him. Even with his sleeve acting as a barrier, the red hot trigger burnt his finger. The previous owner of the rifle had it set to fully automatic. An amateurs move, but on this occasion it was his friend. He anticipated it and aimed low. The kick of the rifle caused it to rise up and round after round ripped vertically through the terrorists body. The x-ray got a few rounds off. They all went into the walls and ceiling as Harry hit his target. He fired the weapon until it ran dry. The terrorist lay on the floor, peppered with 7.62 rounds. Harry's arse felt like it was on fire and he quickly got to his feet. It was time to rearm and reload.

*

Tony's Brick had rotated. From the bench next to hers and directly opposite the Wavecrest Royal, he now watched the female Dicker. Further up the Beach Boulevard and waiting in the wings was Renee. She remained unseen and unnoticed. Andy followed the Hispanic male. Baggers had eyes on the Dicker room. A blue light on Tony's phone flashed. He opened the message from Stan.

'Disable Dickers two and three. Bring their phones to Ops Room. Immediate action required. Out'.

Tony had to think fast. The Hispanic male could be taken out easily enough, dragged into a bush, or down an alleyway. Better than that, two of his men could get really close in the crowd at a roadblock. The female sitting on the bench was going to prove a bit of a headache. She was in broad daylight and highly visible. The sun was blazing, it was a hot day even for Fort Lauderdale. She had to drink to stay hydrated. He could see a bottle of water to her left, it was nearly empty. She's either going to need to use the bathroom, or to buy another bottle of water. That was going to be their window of opportunity.

*

Harry was sweating and not just because of the fireball. The terrorists would come in force to hunt him down. He took what he needed. Both Molotov's used, he binned the rucksack and got the hell out of the hot zone. He moved away from the scene, towards the service stairwell at corner four. Peering through the safety glass, he expected something, but he saw nothing. Opening the door a notch the story was the same. Still nothing. Harry headed up the stairs and entered the twelfth floor.

*

Andy and Baggers joined the group WhatsApp call. Via their discretely positioned microphones, all of the Brick team members could communicate with each other. Now stood two metres apart and two metres behind the Dicker, they were amongst the horde of onlookers at the roadblock where Tony last noticed the suspicious Hispanic male. They were ready for immediate action, but word had to come from their gaffer. They didn't talk to each other. They didn't need to, they knew exactly what each other was going to do. They didn't make eye contact, but they both looked towards one man. They were eyes on. Everything now hinged on the female Dicker.

Sucking the last dregs of water from the bottle, she dropped her phone and clicker into her bag.

Tony discreetly spoke into his mic.

"RA, move in," he said.

That was Renee Allen's airwave handle. The operators of the SRR, exactly like their spy game counterparts in MI5 and MI6, never used real names over the net. Acronyms were used. The safety of their families was paramount.

Hearing this, Andy and Baggers moved closer. Now only a metre from their man, their part of the takedown would be slick and fast.

Even though many people now used handsfree kits, it was still possible to stand out and be marked as police. It was far safer and more effective to have a well concealed open microphone. An open mic also meant that nobody had to do anything suspicious like hold their collar when they spoke. The SRR and every other undercover intelligence outfit used them.

The female Dicker stood up and crossed the Beach Boulevard. She was heading away from the ocean and into Fort Lauderdale. Tony didn't move. Renee was moving in her direction.

"Turing right, right, onto Riomar Street, have visual," Renee said.

"Have that," said Tony, "I'll be fifty feet behind you, opposite side of the street."

They covered both sides of the street, mitigating the need for Renee to cross the road should the Dicker do the same. If the she did cross, Tony would simply pick up the follow and Renee would back him up. If all four of the Brick were on the same follow, they could keep it up all day.

"Heading west on Riomar. Takeaway food shop ahead on the right, she may enter. Am I disabling her if she does?" Renee asked.

The reply was instant.

"Affirmative," Tony said, "AP, KB, standby, standby."

Andy and Baggers looked at the people between themselves and the Dicker, at the path they would take. One metre was all. The whole thing would be over in a matter of seconds. Baggers' knew exactly what he was going to do. Andy's hands were free and ready for action.

"Dicker slowing, I may need to walk past if she stops," Renee said.

"I can follow, if needed," Tony said.

"Dicker now entering takeaway restaurant, I'll follow," Renee said.

Tony crossed the road in a jog and he saw Renee enter the takeaway sandwich shop. He needed to support her and have eyes on confirmation of the takedown. He drew level with the glass shopfront and could see Renee. In front of her, the female was making her way to the disabled bathroom at the back of the store. She was slowly meandering through the queue with Renee two steps behind. Pulling the door handle, Renee made her move.

The Dicker stepped inside the cubicle. Renee's hands thumped the Hispanic woman in the back. She lost her balance and fell. She didn't have time to break her fall.

Tony entered and fought his way through the developing crowd.

"British Army, make way," he shouted.

Tony reached the door and pushed a do-gooder out of the way. He was just in time to see Renee plasti-cuffing the female dicker. He tilted his head towards his concealed mic and spoke with speed and urgency.

"Go. Go. Go," Tony said.

They both came up from behind and pulled the last of the crowd out of the way. Baggers' clenched fist landed a massive sweeping uppercut to the lower ribs of the dicker. A second punch struck his kidney. The Dicker instinctively turned and began to fall to the floor. Baggers caught him again with a blow to the throat. Andy snatched the phone from his hands as he fell. It was done. The phone was slipped into Andy's pocket. Nobody saw. It lasted less than three seconds. So quickly nobody had time to register what they were seeing. The Dicker was on the floor. People realised what was happening and the screaming started. Somebody shouted, 'gun'. The crowd scattered. Curled into the foetal position on the floor, the Dicker was immobile and not going anywhere. Andy and Baggers hooked an arm each under the Dicker's arm pits and fought through the scattering crowd to drag him to the sidewalk and plasti-cuff him.

The crowd ran in any direction, just as long as it was away from the incident. FLPD officers at the roadblock saw nothing, but heard everything. They moved in. Weapons drawn, they couldn't see what they were aiming at. Officer 269 hooked his arm into his patrol car and his grabbed Colt AR15 automatic rifle.

"British Army, police STAND BACK!" Baggers shouted.

"Stop what you are doing and step away from the body," 269 shouted.

The street was now devoid of onlookers. The only people that remained, were one half of the SRR Brick, the Hispanic male and five FLPD officers. They were now all pointing their weapons at Andy and Baggers.

"British Army, police STAND BACK!" Baggers shouted again.

Andy finished plasti-cuffing the dicker.

"Stop what you're doing, or I will fire my weapon," officer 269 repeated.

"No you fucking won't! BRITISH ARMY, STAND BACK!" Baggers shouted a third time.

Officer 312 had her sidearm drawn and watched the two men on the floor disobey her colleague. The radio on her belt sprang to life and she listened to the message.

"Mike, it's okay, they're good guys," she said.

"Stand up and move away," 269 persisted.

Andy looked at the officer with the automatic rifle.

"BRITISH FUCKING ARMY, LOWER YOUR WEAPON, OR I'LL PUT IT SOMEWHERE A SKILLED SURGEON, WOULD HAVE TROUBLE FINDING IT!" he hissed through gritted teeth.

He pulled the plasti-cuffed detainee to his knees.

269 lowered his weapon. The police radios sprang into life once more. There were two terrorists they needed to take into custody. The Brick needed to be freed up, there were more important things for them to do.

CHAPTER THIRTY THREE

Harry made good ground from his fireball ambush. He routed himself randomly around the hotel, up a floor, across, down a floor. Across and up another floor. He made it impossible for anyone to predict where he would next appear. He was back on the sixth floor. Back where he had left Kelsi sitting on the elevator. The car hadn't moved. It was still in the same place, but four terrorists stood on the landing. Armed to the teeth and he was certain, looking for him. The landing of the sixth floor was a target rich environment, but Harry decided against another gun battle. At some point, everyone's luck ran out.

Tracking around the sixth floor to the rear service stairwell, he made his way up the hotel until he judged he was far enough away from x-rays. He hoped they wouldn't hear any of the small scraping noises he might make. Then he cursed his stupidity. He had chucked his rucksack after the Molotov attack and faced with the new problem of rendezvousing with Kelsi, he regretted the decision sorely. He needed the tools that were in his rucksack. Harry had taken more than he needed from Maintenance. The duplicates were in the Porter's Lodge.

He made it to the Lodge and entered with a flash of the wristband. They hadn't yet searched the room. Harry went straight to his hidden stash of tools. He was quick and thorough and picked out the crowbar he wanted. Foresight was great. Hindsight could be a bitch. Harry had just been struck by a brilliant bit of former. He pocketed a ball of string.

Now on the seventeenth floor, he had made it to the elevator shaft Kelsi was in. He couldn't pull the outer elevator concertina door. The door would have some type of lock in place that only allowed the door to open when the elevator car was present. Secondly, yanking at the door handle would just create noise. The terrorists below would know where he was.

Harry gently pulled the concertina door as far as he could until the locking system engaged. A small gap had been created between the door and the edge of the metal frame, it was locked in place and wouldn't pull anymore. Pulling back the door handle with his left hand and pushing the tip of the crowbar into the gap with his right, he made inaudible scraping noises. The tip of the crowbar was now in. He forced and jimmied entry until the thickest part of the crowbar sat in the gap. He breathed in, listened and went through his sound check routine. Nothing. He could hear the terrorists below. Stationary. Still stood on the landing, their conversation cloaking his insignificant noises.

Pushing the crowbar into the gap until it wouldn't push any further, he wrenched back and applied all the pressure he could. The lock was resisting his movement. He pulled on the crowbar hard and applied maximum pressure. Harry was red in the face, but it wasn't enough. Turning his body so his left flank was next to the door, he lifted his right leg and placed his foot on the doorframe. He gave his movement more energy. He pulled again.

"Come on you bastard," he muttered.

Harry pulled with both arms and pushed with his right leg. Nothing. He was putting everything in and getting nothing back. His eyes closed and a grimace spread across his face. He eked out the last of his energy. Snap. The lock popped. Harry fell backwards and hit his head on the floor. He could see stars, but he was in.

His head was pounding, but he caught his breath and the stars dissipated. He listened again. The voices had stopped talking. They must have heard the metal snap. He had landed on the floor with a thud, but had kept hold of the crowbar. An x-ray shouted something, but he couldn't hear any footsteps. It was critical he didn't make any more noise. It would rouse the interest of the terrorists and they were bound to come looking for him. The noise he made had just been a random metallic snap. Metal structures made these noises sometimes, he didn't know why. Maybe it was to do with the expansion and contraction of metal structures on a hot day. Harry smelt cigarette smoke. That was why the x-rays were on the landing. Now access to the shaft had been granted, it was time to get moving.

The elevator car was on the sixth floor. He had eleven floors to climb down. Harry silently pulled the door back enough to allow him entry. A shoulder's width was all he needed. The elevator shaft was so dark he couldn't see more than two floors below. He didn't want to shout down, or even whisper to Kelsi. There was only one thing for it.

The rifles strap had been burnt to nothing by the fireball, that was why he had put a ball of string in his pocket. Needing both hands to be free as he climbed down the elevator shaft, Harry looped the string again and again, between the two hooks on the rifle. He pulled the new strap around his chest and the AK nestled tightly against his back. Squeezing his body through the gap, he placed the crowbar on the strip of floor behind the door. Pulling the door closed to less than inch, he began his descent. If he fell, he would die. No questions. Depending on where he landed, he figured there was a 50/50 chance of killing Kelsi. The thought of either scared the shit out of him.

There were horizontal bars inside the shaft like rungs on a ladder. Although this particular ladder wasn't like something you could buy at Home Depot, the gaps between bars weren't a uniform distance apart, nor were they easy to climb. Harry didn't know what the distance between rungs on a ladder were meant to be, but he knew this ladder didn't have them. The darkness also made his descent nigh on impossible.

He had been on a school outdoor pursuits week in the mountains of Wales and had done relatively well the day his class went rock climbing. This wasn't anything like that. It was much harder. He didn't have a safety harness, safety rope, or helmet. This was different to any climbing he had done before. His legs and arms were forced to reach far beyond their limits, as he struggled to find the next hand or foothold. Harry's foot slipped. The force it placed on his other foot caused that to slip too. Only the tight grip he maintained kept him from falling. He smashed his face against a steel girder. His breathing was frantic. He hung by his arms, his feet flailing as they tried to find a new foothold. By the time he found new purchase, he was trembling with fear. Scared to move another inch. He wanted to climb back to safety, but he couldn't. He had to get to Kelsi. He had made her a promise. He needed to help her climb up the elevator shaft. If he was finding it tricky, she would find it damn near impossible. Harry composed himself. His breathing found a steady rhythm. He looked down. He still couldn't see anything. Looking up he could just a slither of light from the barely open concertina door. That light was virtually non-existent and he knew it was only going to get smaller. He began his descent once more.

Harry realised the irregularly spaced bars and handholes were the in same position on each floor. After descending two more floors, he got a little more sure of where the rungs would be and he remembered the foothold that had caused him to slip. He avoided it. In the centre of the shaft hung the two thick metal cables, the cables that pulled the elevator car up or down. They could aid his progress, he would be able to use the thick metal wire like the army ropes, the same as he used in SAS: We Dare We Win. They were the fast ropes that the elite troops used when they needed to quickly exfil from a helicopter. He didn't have any gloves to prevent rope burns, so he wouldn't move as rapidly as them. Even if he was slower, it would be quicker and safer than climbing down the elevator shaft.

He took hold of the cable with one hand, then the other. His feet were still planted on the steel frame. With great care he moved a foot across to the cable. He hooked his leg around the thick metal wire, so the vamp of his trainer was pushing on the cable. When he moved his other leg, his foot would sit opposite, his lower legs would be crossed and when pressed together, they would act as a brake. He had to get the balls together and just go for it. He took a deep breath and found the bottle. Harry readied himself for a fall, to see the last seconds of his life flash by. His hands gripped tightly and he removed his foot. Nothing happened. He stayed where he was. Harry breathed out. He had to get a shift on. If any of the x-rays saw the partially open concertina door, they would know it was him. He would be a dead man.

His body was pulled tight against the cables. He shuffled his hands down, an inch at a time until they were lower than his chest. His feet and body moved down until his arms were above his head. He repeated the movement, getting quicker and moving down a metre each time. Sooner than he thought, he was twenty feet from Kelsi. She looked up as she heard the scuffing movement above her.

'Harry,' she screeched.

"Shush," he urged. "Get your things, you need to come with me."

Kelsi didn't question him. She did exactly what he had asked.

She didn't have much to bring and what she did have, fitted into the pocket of her hoodie. She left the empty bottle of water. Replicating his positioning on the thick cable, she tried to heave herself up. After the eighth try, it became apparent she didn't have the strength to lift her own body. Harry smirked.

'If I had those tits, I'd struggle too,' he thought.

How the hell was he going to get her out of here? Then he heard the concertina door rattle and scrape. His heart skipped a beat. The x-rays stepped into the car. The cable he was holding was pulled taught. He didn't know if he clung to a cable that travelled up, or down. He willed the top hatch of the elevator not to open. Involuntarily Harry moved upwards. So did she.

"Don't speak," he said, "don't worry, I'm getting you out of here."

Harry was moving upwards. Twenty feet before the car and fifteen feet something before her. That didn't give him much time, but it would be enough. Just. He begged the elevator car would take him to at least the seventeenth floor and keep going. He didn't want it to stop on a floor below, or stop on that floor. Harry looked up and saw the sliver of light fast approaching. He knew what he wanted to achieve, doing it successfully was another matter entirely. Before he knew it, it was time.

With the deftness of a poker player shuffling a deck of cards, his left hand moved away from the cable and his fingers slid into the sliver of light. His right hand followed and both feet quickly after that. The elevator car racing up the hotel gave him no room for error. He twisted his body and forced the inch wide gap between the door and the frame further apart. Turning around, both his hands delved back into the darkness and felt for Kelsi. Harry grabbed her wrists and heaved with all of his might. She came with him. He heard the crowbar clang as it fell into the dark abyss. Harry dragged her from the shaft. Both of them landed on the floor, her on top of him. She had tears streaming down her face. The elevator stopped on that floor.

*

In the Ops Room both Dicker's smartphones had been pinging with messages for the last ten minutes. The dickers hadn't sent a sit-rep for thirty minutes. Looking back through the messages Tony deciphered them as best he could and before the phones rang and no one answered, he needed to reply. He sent a standard answer they had been using. He sent the female's reply first. 'Ningún cambio'. Waiting five minutes, he replied on the male's phone. 'Ningún cambio'. There was no change at either location.

*

"Porters Lodge," he said in a hurried voice, "take this and hide behind the chairs."

Harry thrust the master key wristband towards her.

Kelsi jumped up and ran. He heard her tear up the stairs. He knew he had to slow the x-rays and let her get a head start. He was sat where he fell, cross legged with the gap in the door in front. Harry slung the AK from his back. The safety catch wasn't on. The interior door shuddered. An x-ray took up his grip on the doorhandle. It opened an inch and the barrel of Harry's AK pushed into the gap created. He gave the trigger a pull. It must have been knocked onto fully automatic as he fell backwards onto the landing. There was an extended burst of fire. He could hear screams from inside the car. Flicking the AK to three round burst as he ran, he gave it legs up the first flight of stairs, only stopping on the mid-way landing to cover his retreat. He let the elevator have three more rounds.

He scarpered. As he was running, he heard the elevator door open and a Germanic voice shouting. He didn't know what was said, but he knew they must be hurried orders. The German would be telling the boiler suits to chase after him. Harry thought as he ran. There had been four x-rays on the landing of the sixth floor, he hoped they had all taken a round from his AK, but more than likely he had only peppered one. The x-ray pulling the door.

He kept running, up the stairwell to the twentieth floor, passing the Porter's Lodge on the nineteenth, attempting to throw the terrorist hunter party off the scent and away from Kelsi. He could hear their footsteps. Harry exited the stairwell and entered the twentieth floor. Twelve, maybe thirteen seconds was all he had before they were on him. The corridors were laid out differently on the top floor. The rooms were all suites and contained multiple bedrooms. He raced along a passageway and turned left. Harry was fast, but he wasn't Olympic one hundred metre standard. He would never reach the end of the corridor before the terrorists were able to shoot at him. He ran as far as he could before he had to fire back.

CHAPTER THIRTY FOUR

The terrorists knew they were after a child, but the child had already inflicted serious damage. El chico had skills. Christian knew he was more than a match for the kid, but the two Colombians weren't. That had already been proven. Their mate lay dead inside the elevator. Christian wanted to be the man who ended the life of the stone in his boss's shoe. El chico could not be allowed to live. Screw what Bothrops had said about bringing him in alive. He was a slippery little shit and Christian knew the only way was to shoot him on sight. Now they were getting close to achieving that goal. El chico was cornering himself. On the twentieth floor he would die. Christian planned on pulling the trigger. They saw him running down a corridor to the back of the hotel. He was running away. All the x-rays fired.

Harry knew they were behind him, he could hear them giving chase. He ducked into an alcove to check his weapon over. Bullets zipped past him. He pulled the magazine free of the rifle and pressed on the top projectile. The 7.62mm round pushed halfway into the mag. He knew he only had fifteen rounds remaining, sixteen at best. He had to give the hunters a final burst of fire to keep their heads down. He would be given a few seconds' advantage. He pulled the trigger. Then a second time. Three rounds went left. Three rounds went right. The hunters' position at the end of the corridor was peppered with projectiles. About eight 7.62 rounds remained.

Harry gave it legs and ran down the last of the corridor towards corner three. Sixty feet from the end and the hunters' heads were no longer down. Rounds were ripping past him. They were getting closer. He could hear the hunters, the German shouting in Spanish, 'Moverse'. If he turned left at the end of the passageway he would run towards a large suite on the twentieth floor. Thirty feet to go. Turning right would send him down another corridor. Towards corner four. More bursts of fire from the x-rays. 'Moverse. Moverse'. Wallpaper was torn as rounds embedded themselves in the walls. Plaster fell from the ceiling. Harry's surroundings were decimated. A light fitting ahead exploded as it was struck by a 7.62 round.

Harry gasped and grimaced as he inhaled. He could feel a searing pain on the right of his torso. A round had clipped him just below the ribs. It hurt like fuck. A lucky shot, not an aimed shot. The only problem with luck was that it attracted more luck. He knew the Colombian's aim wouldn't be effective at their current distance, but they might get lucky again. Or the German might fire.

Ignoring the pain he kept running, waiting to feel another round hit him. Waiting to drop to the floor as a vital organ stopped working. Ten feet from the end and the rear guest elevator on the hotel's back corridor sounded. The choice had just been made for him. He turned left and saw locked doors. No longer having his wristband he raised the AK to his eyeline. He moved forward. Harry twice pulled the trigger. The lock was struck with two bursts. The double doors flew open. One round remained for his AK47. If he had two then it was a bonus.

Charging through the doorway he entered a large living area, the room from which all other rooms led. Sofas and a coffee table sat in the centre. The wall on the right beyond the furniture housed two bedrooms. Two doors. Both closed. Two options. A smaller bedroom door was open to his immediate left. Three options. He ran forwards to the open doorway on the other side of the living area. The fourth option.

Entering the suite's main bathroom he slammed the door behind him. The hunters would hear the door slam. He hoped with three closed doors, he would be given enough time to hide. The bathroom door was immediately filled with holes. The x-rays fired around the corner and down the passageway. He heard their footfall again as they entered the suite. Hearing them shooting out locks, he visualised the scene. Twenty seconds passed. The group of three realised where he was. The bathroom lock was filled with rounds. The door burst open. A grenade was thrown in and skittered across the tiled floor. One, two, three seconds before it detonated.

The explosion tore through the bathroom. Tiles on the floor splintered. The toilet fragmented and lethal shards of vitreous China flew through the air and hit everything. The floor to ceiling glass window shattered. Glass blew out into the open air. Window blinds tattered, they fluttered as the room was filled with a light breeze. More AK rounds were fired into the room. Harry's ears were ringing. He only just heard the two thuds as gravity took two empty magazines to the floor and two clicks as both weapons were reloaded. Two boiler suits stood in the doorway and unloaded two more full magazines. They backed away and into the living area. Another two thuds and two more clicks as they reloaded.

Edging through the threshold into the bathroom the hunters could see nothing but devastation. The room was shell shocked. Everything broken and busted. They inched forwards into the room. The vigilante they hunted wasn't there. The only place the little rat could have gone was out of the window.

Harry was lying down in the thick and heavy metal bathtub next to the glassless window. He sat up and fired his last round. The left hunter of the pair dropped. Harry heard his own deadman's click. He lay back and was out of sight in time to miss the second hunter unloading a full magazine. Stepping forward to the bathtub with weapon raised, the hunter saw Harry lying in the tub. With rage in his eyes, a smile spread across his face. The x-ray moved forward and the barrel of his red hot AK sat inches from Harry's head. He jammed the searing hot tip of the rifle into Harry's temple.

The pain was instant and caused Harry to pull away and screw his face up. The muzzle of the rifle followed his head and was still pressed against his skin. Harry's twisted and contorted face changed. He was confident. Pain was temporary. The wound would heal. He smiled back at the terrorist. Dead was forever. Enraged the hunter pulled the trigger. His smile was lost when he heard the click. Disbelief on the hunter's face.

Surging upwards, Harry threw his arms forwards and took hold of the hunter's boiler suit. He rolled to the right, dragging the hunter over the bathtub head first. The side of the tub stopped Harry. There wasn't any glass to stop the hunter. Harry released him as his forward motion was enough to drag him into the open air. The last noise Harry heard were screams as the hunter fell twenty floors to his death.

He leapt from the tub and searched the first hunter's body for more ammunition. Pulling free a magazine filled with 7.62 rounds, he pressed the top projectile. The spring didn't compress. He swapped the full magazine with the empty mag in his AK. He took another magazine. Checking it was full, Harry pushed the mag into his leg pocket.

The German was somewhere in the suite. Excluding the bathroom, he could be in anyone of three rooms. If Harry was in his position he would have placed himself in the small bedroom just off the living area. The vigilante would have to pass the room to get out and it was the closest room to the exit. The best room from which to give chase. Harry had an idea. He removed his shoes.

Christian could hear movement. He wasn't sure who it was. He knew one of the Colombians was dead. He heard his screams as he fell to his death. The noise was getting closer. Somebody was inching along the other side of the wall in front of him. Christian moved to the back wall of the smallest bedroom and knelt behind the bed. Weapon raised, he waited for his prey to walk into his cross hairs. It was the boy. It was el chico dressed in black. The figure backed into the doorway, covering all other rooms in the suite. He had forgotten the most important room. He was no match for Christian. He waited until the prey had fully exposed his mass, but a split second before his head came into view and he was able to turn and look over his shoulder, Christian pulled the trigger. Three rounds hit him in the back. The boy fell forwards into the living area.

Christian stood up and walked to the doorway to finish the job. The boy who had been raising hell had fallen awkwardly. El chico's body lay face down and twisted. Christian slid the action back on his MP5 and checked there was a projectile in the chamber. He knew there was and knew there were plenty more in the magazine. He had time to check. The boy wasn't going anywhere. He looked down at el chico. The body had black hair, the boy didn't.

A burst of fully automatic fire ripped through the boy's body. Rounds hit him in the neck. Blood and flesh followed the 7.62 rounds as they drove themselves into the door casing behind. Christian fell down and slumped against the bedroom wall. Gargling and grabbing with his hands, he attempted to halt blood flowing from his neck.

Wriggling out from underneath the dead Colombian's body, who was wearing Harry's clothes, he took hold of his AK. Harry got to his feet and selected single shot mode. He pulled the trigger just once. Christian stopped gargling.

He would come back for Christian's weapon as soon as he could. He wanted his clothes too. In the immediate he needed to find the passengers who were aboard the elevator. AK pointed wherever he looked, Harry checked the other two bedrooms in the suite. Nothing. He walked into the corridor. Nobody there.

Returning, he laid the AK within reach and patted down his lookalike. He wanted to ensure he hadn't missed anything in the transfer of clothes and weapons. Knelt over the body, his right hand searching the left leg pockets. He swapped and his left hand search the right leg. Harry sensed something wasn't as it should be. Someone was close.

"Don't reach for your weapon," the female voice said.

The faintest hint of a French accent.

"Stand up slowly," she added.

Harry froze. For fuck's sake, how had he missed it? It was game over. His fingertips touched something in the body's leg pocket. His trousers. His magazine pocket. It wasn't a magazine. His fingers slowly wrapped around the object. He raised his head to see who the voice belonged to. Harry knew it would be Amanda, or whatever she was now calling herself. She was dressed differently to when he had seen her last. She was now in khaki combat trousers and a white strappy top. Her own AK was pointed towards him. His fingers moved ever so slightly and ever so slowly inside the pocket.

"Stand up, now," she commanded.

Harry dropped his head, he wasn't in a position to argue. Caught. Captured. The game over. Resigned to probable torture at the very least, an assassination maybe, a round to the forehead, or back of the head as he knelt before the main group of hostages. They would want to reiterate their initial message: *if you try to fight us or to escape, we will end your lives.* Maybe they would beat him to death. Entirely plausible. They wanted revenge for all the damage he had inflicted. They would want retribution. There would be plenty of terrorists willing to administer the punishment, there would probably be a queue. Maybe they would find a pair of pliers and remove his toenails, remove his teeth and press on the exposed nerve endings to inflict as much pain as possible. Harry was fully aware that was how prisoners of war had been treated in past conflicts. He thought the terrorist's treatment would be even worse. His fingers finished rolling from side to side.

"Up," she said again.

The beating was going to hurt, but not as much as this was about to hurt her.

Emptying the air from his lungs loudly enough for her to hear, he took a sudden a deep gasp to ensure the optimal performance of his muscles. His body rose at an angle and fast. Lurching forward he rammed his shoulder into her abdomen. Amanda's arms were thrown up and she fell backwards. She kept hold of her AK, but the weapon's aim was knocked up and a burst of fire arced into the ceiling. Harry continued surging forwards. She fell backwards. He landed on top of her. The lid of the insulin pen had been removed in his magazine pocket. Now clenched in his fist, he rammed the small plastic cylinder into Amanda's neck. Her face was a picture of complete shock.

Harry gritted his teeth.

"Bitch," he said.

She convulsed. Insulin flooded her body.

There were no dying gasps. He didn't see her eyes close. Amanda twitched as her body fought the chemical ravaging her veins, arteries and ultimately her heart. He held the pen in place until she was dead. Harry pressed two fingers into her neck and didn't feel a pulse. His face contorted with his own pain. The gunshot wound to his side was throbbing and stinging. He had never felt pain like it. His fingers remained on Amanda's neck for ten seconds. He wanted to make sure she was dead. She was.

He had to get out of the suite and fast. If the terrorists didn't hear anything back over the radio. If el chico had taken down five x-rays and one of them a highly trained mercenary, they would send more. First though, he took all the weapons and ammunition he could.

He searched the three bodies in the suite and removed Christian's clothes and boots. They would prove significantly better than his old clothes, let alone the boiler suit he currently wore. Christian's clothes were designed exactly for the type of situation he was in. Leaving the MP5 to one side, he found a grey gym holdall and filled it. Magazines, pistols, AK47s, Christian's clothes. He could change into them later. It was time to move.

After tightening the shoulder strap and slinging the holdall around his back, he took hold of the MP5 and made his way down one floor to the Porter's Lodge. Ideally he would have zeroed the MP5. However he didn't have time for such luxuries anymore. The Heckler and Koch MP5 was a good and precise weapon. Harry moved. He carried a permanent contortion on his face. The first order of business would be to get Kelsi to clean and dress his wound.

When he came up to his stronghold, his heart sunk. The door was wide open. The wood of the door's casing was splintered and scattered all around. The lock of the Porter's Lodge door had been shot out. He raised his newly acquired MP5 and listened. He couldn't hear anything. Edging around the corner he couldn't see anything either. *Slow is smooth. Smooth is fast.* Weapon trained down the corridor, he looked towards corner two. Nobody there.

There were, like all the hallways in the hotel, pieces of furniture in alcoves to make the place seem more homely. A chaise longue or the bust of a great US figure. George Washington, Amelia Earhart, or simply a table with a vase holding flowers. The vase in front of him lay on the floor, smashed into dozens of pieces and flowers scattered all around. He knew straight away, or at least he hoped that it was Kelsi's doing. She was a smart girl. She was leaving him a trail of damage and destruction. She was telling him where she had been taken. He hoped she had thrashed out some more and left him more tell-tale signs. He wanted her back. Nobody was allowed to hurt her. He removed the holdall and lay it at the edge of the corridor.

Weapon aimed wherever he looked, he edged towards the open doorway. He expected the terrorists to be lying in wait. If he had one, he would have thrown a flashbang into the Porter's Lodge before entering. He didn't have one. He had to think outside the box. He backed up to the wall opposite the door opening. Pushing off the wall Harry moved quickly and fell forwards tucking his neck in. He fell into a forward roll and entered the room low and fast. Coming to a stop half sitting, half squatting. MP5 scanning the room for targets. There was no one in there alive. There was one body.

CHAPTER THIRTY FIVE

The body was male, Colombian, wearing a green boiler suit and slumped next to a stack of chairs. The insulin pen Harry had given to Kelsi was hanging from the body's left bicep. She'd put the tip straight through his green suit. Kelsi wasn't going to go down without a fight. Harry needed to move. It wasn't safe here any longer, his stronghold had been compromised. He gathered all the items he would need and placed them on the table. He couldn't take everything, he needed to thin out his equipment. First he tended to the desperately painful wound on the right flank. Even though it had been pillaged by all and sundry, there was a first aid kit in the Porter's Lodge.

Harry perched on a table. He faced the entrance to the Lodge. Un-popping the studs holding the top half of the boiler suit together, he shrugged it from his shoulders. The MP5 was never more than an arm's length away. Wincing and grimacing, he removed his t-shirt and exposed his wound. *A lucky shot.* He picked up the MP5, held it with his right hand and aimed at the door. The silver packet he removed from the first aid kit was in his left hand. Bringing it to his mouth, he bit down on the top and tore open the sterile packet. Harry wiped the wound and the surrounding skin with the only antiseptic wipe left. He winced even more and said 'shit,' a dozen times. Two bandages left in the box, he took both. Fresh blood began to seep from the centre of the wound, but the 7.62 round that clipped him had been moving so quickly, the majority of the wound had cauterized itself. The blood began to clot.

Harry covered the wound with the smallest bandage, it was more of a band aid. It was square and to be effective, it needed to be rectangular. Part of the sticky edge pressed onto the wound. It was going to hurt when it was removed. The second bandage was cotton, stretchy and rectangular. It was far too big. He folded the bandage in half and wrapped it around his torso. He was wrapping himself up like an Egyptian mummy, but it did the job and covered the band aid. The last thing he needed was for the wound to get infected. There weren't any pain killers in the first aid kit, but he knew he'd taken a couple of packets from hotel bedrooms. Grabbing a box, Harry stuffed four into his mouth. He drew down glugs of water from the first bottle of water he came to. *He bloody hated sparkling water.* He unlaced his shoes and removed the rest of the dead grunt's boiler suit. He dressed in Christian's clothes, even his gloves.

Dressed head to toe in black, he knelt and tied the laces on the mercenary's boots. The trousers were a bit tight around the thighs. Christian didn't cycle as a hobby and he had to loosen the straps on the leg holster for the 9mm Hecker and Koch USP sidearm. Before holstering the pistol, he checked the working parts. Perfect. The weapon fit snugly into the holster.

He filled the mercenary's tactical ops vest with his equipment. Harry stuffed the pockets with magazines of ammunition and clipped on all the grenades. He applied the ops vest to his torso like a waistcoat. He swapped the old and battered AK with a fresh one from the holdall. The last thing he did was to pull the mercenary's black ski mask over his head. It felt a little sweaty, but soon he wouldn't even notice. Only his eyes could be seen. He felt the part and looked the part. He was the part. He was his avatar in SAS: We Dare We Win. An object glinted and caught his eye. He must have dislodged it when he removed the first aid kit. He smiled and slipped it between his tactical vest and t-shirt. He had just found something as good as a flashbang. Better than that, it would also double as a silencer.

Harry slung the MP5 on his back and used the new AK47 as his main weapon. He needed all the firepower he could get. Harry binned the holdall, he couldn't move quickly enough with it. Carrying all the magazines for the two weapons, as well as the sidearm strapped to his leg, his combat trousers weighed him down. Harry tightened the trouser belt. The one thing the SAS: We Dare We Win hadn't prepared him for was the weight. Thank goodness he wasn't wearing full body armour and a respirator, else he wouldn't be able to move. 'Let's do this Harry,' he told himself.

*

Alison heard the shouting. The screaming. The torrent of abuse directed at her captors. A female was being dragged kicking and screaming towards the California Great Hall. She could hear the woman lashing out and kicking at everything she could. The voice grew nearer. She recognised the Mississippi accent and high pitched scream. Alison gasped and tears of joy ran down her face when Kelsi was dragged into the room. She was being treated appallingly, but she wasn't dead. That was what Alison feared when she hadn't seen her in captivity with the other staff. Kelsi being alive was all that mattered right then.

A terrorist placed a chair in the centre of the room. Kelsi was forced to sit. A more senior terrorist. A sergeant, or corporal, or something, walked closer and a selected a squad of four. They gathered round. The rest of the terrorists in the room, the ones watching the hostages, made the mistake of looking towards the centre. They were berated in Spanish. Alison could only surmise to what was said based on her limited Spanish skills, but she guessed it was along the lines of, 'Look at the hostages, not us,' followed by a string of words she knew were Spanish curse words.

"NO," Alison screamed.

Kelsi received the first hand of her beating. A backhand to the face that split her lip and knocked her free of the chair. The hostage next to Alison, a man she knew was called Hans and from The Netherlands, got to his feet to intervene. He was hopelessly outnumbered and facing a force of armed men. The butt of an AK47 hit him in the head. He tumbled back to the floor and another terrorist ejected a full magazine of 7.62 into the ceiling. That ensured no more have a go heroes attempted to get to their feet. The terrorist changed the magazine for his weapon.

"We need a first aid kit. NOW," Alison demanded.

Hans, now slumped next to her, was bleeding profusely from the head.

The sergeant, or corporal, or whatever, looked at the grunt who had hit the older gentleman. He flicked his head to the door and told him to go and find a first aid kit.

Kelsi was lifted back onto the chair and her beating continued.

"Where is el chico?" the senior terrorist asked.

Kelsi looked up. Blood seeping down her face and tears in her eyes.

"Go to hell," she said.

He slapped her again.

*

From the nineteenth floor to the second floor, Kelsi had left a trail of damage. To the terrorists, she was just feisty and defiant, a girl attempting to be a heroine, not a clued up young woman who was telling Harry where she had been taken. He followed the trail of destruction. Smashed vases, kicked over tables, scuffed wallpaper, sofas that had been knocked about. The final clue she left for Harry was a snapped baluster on the front main staircase. He was sure she would be held in the California Great Hall.

It was too risky to take the main front staircase down to the reception desk. The previously x-ray busy reception area was now empty of terrorists, they were all searching for him. But there were so many places someone could hide and lie in wait, remain hidden and ambush him as he tracked Kelsi. *His accomplice. His comrade. The Robin to his Batman. The Juliet to his Romeo.* The girl he liked more than he had ever liked any girl. She was something else. A cute, hot, tough little cookie. She had a perfect body and face. He liked everything about her. He thought for the first time in his life he was in love. He was going to save her. If it meant going face to face with terrorists, lots of them, then he would do it. If it meant he died in the process, then so be it. As long as she lived.

A CD was the glinting object that had caught his eye in the Porter's Lodge. The artists were a Norwegian Thrash Metal group. Not Harry's type of music, but it would double as a very effective flashbang and silencer. His hand felt between the tac vest and his t-shirt. The disc was still there. He needed to get into the Audio Visual (AV) cupboard. The AV cupboard wasn't just a room where the CD player was stored. It was the room that controlled everything that went through the speakers in the California Great Hall, as well as everything displayed on the large video screen at the front of the room. It was the type of setup you would find at music concerts, or in a recording studio.

From his position at the top of the stairs, he could hear her screams. Harry wanted to rush down the main front staircase with all guns blazing, come to her rescue and stop whoever was beating her. The slaps Kelsi were getting weren't because of anything she'd done, it was all down to him. He was el chico. She wasn't la chica. Harry needed to play this one smart. He had to outfox the terrorists. Backing away from the landing he turned his back, weapon raised he traversed from the front of the hotel, to corner two. Taking the service stairwell he headed down to the first basement floor, past the small standalone offices and into the back office, lots of unused desks and computer terminals. Harry was as quiet and cautious as he dared, but speed was necessary. Saving Kelsi was what counted. Creeping through the office, he came to the small staircase that led to the back of the reception desk. There could be a terrorist hiding behind the desk, lying in wait for him. Now they had Kelsi, they knew he would come. If they didn't, they underestimated him.

He crept up the carpeted steps. He could see the back of the reception desk. Underneath the glossy countertop lay shelves filled with hotel writing paper, printers and computer stuff. His sixth sense kicked in. There was someone behind the reception desk. Harry pulled the out the clam mirror and opened it up. He held the glass in front of his face. He looked weary, generally battered and tired. He needed a rest, but he had to rescue Kelsi. He could sleep when he was dead. Edging out the mirror he could see the back of an x-ray, hidden and perfectly placed to shoot him. He looked at the shelves. The wires for the printers had given him an idea.

Harry slowed his movements down. *Slow is smooth, smooth is fast.* He backed down the stairs. Moving to the back of the office he knelt behind a desk. He looked around and saw what he needed. Looking forward again, AK47 aimed at the bottom of the stairs, he felt for what he had just seen. His fingers found the end and touched the USB component of the cable. With slight movements he wiggled it free of the rear of the computer. Working blind, his fingers felt their way along the cable and towards the printer on the desk. He wiggled that USB out of the device as well. Coiling up his new garrotte, he slid the cable into his tac vest. Harry stepped back to the bottom of the stairs. He laid the AK47 on the floor. The MP5 that hung from his back was laid alongside. He couldn't make a sound.

Masked up and all in black, Harry crept to the top of the stairs. The terrorist was still crouched facing the exit and the end of the reception desk. Bent over, he kept his eyes on the man who was intent on gunning him down. Harry's fingers felt inside his Tac Vest. Pulling free the USB Cable, he loosened the coil. His hands found the middle of the cable and he widened them until they were a foot apart. He clenched tightly.

Harry crept closer, aware of his footwork and surroundings. He couldn't hear any voices. He didn't think anyone was watching. If they were, they would have raised the alarm by now. Feet closer became inches closer. Harry got so close he could hear the terrorist breathing. That was tough. This was a harder kill than when he used the fire extinguisher. He was close enough. He snapped the cable forward and over the head of the terrorist.

The cable brushed past the x-ray's windpipe. Harry pulled back. The x-ray dropped his AK and felt behind his head. Loosening his right fist, Harry allowed the cable to run through his hand and whipped it over the terrorist's head and made a loop. The x-ray stood up. Harry was forced to stand with him. The shorter terrorist bucked and fought. Harry loosened the fist in his left hand and made another loop. He tightened his grip and pulled with all the strength he had. The cable tightened. The boiler suit thrashed out even more. His right foot kicked out. That was a fatal mistake. As the x-ray's right leg thrashed out, Harry kicked his left leg. The cable tightened and by the time the x-ray hit the deck, he was in the final throes of death. Harry was pulled down with him. The x-ray's body twitched and bucked as he made a last effort for survival. Harry kept the cable tight and counted to ten. The incident had taken no more than fifteen seconds. He couldn't leave the corpse of a terrorist lying around. It was a sure sign he had been there.

Harry crawled to the reception area exit. He couldn't see anyone. Rigor mortis was still three hours away and he was able to move the body with ease. Pulling back by the shoulders, he turned the x-ray to one side and dragged the corpse around the bend and down the stairs.

He chose a large metal cupboard as the hiding place for the body. After removing a shed load of ring binders and placing them on top of the cabinet, he removed a shelf and pushed the cadaver inside, shut the doors and turned the key. Finally, he threw the key in waste paper basket.

Getting back to his weapons cache at the foot of the stairs, Harry removed his black mask and wiped the sweat from his face. Moving the dead body had been hard work. Before continuing his mission to snatch Kelsi back, he searched the key cabinet in the back office.

It wasn't good protocol to leave a key cabinet unlocked, but it was fixed to the wall behind the desk of the hotel's operations manager, the person in charge of the hotel when Alison wasn't present. He was the type of man you didn't cross. Nobody dared to take a key from the cabinet without his permission, fortunately Harry did. He found the AV cupboard key within seconds.

Harry was back in the game. He pulled the mask over his head and adorned himself with his weapons. He slung the AK47 on his back and used the MP5 as his primary weapon. The MP5 was around fifteen decibels quieter. A narrow margin, but in the game he was going to play, margins mattered. He checked the CD was still tucked behind his tac vest. It had to be there, it was pivotal in what was going to happen next. It was.

Harry ascended the carpeted stairs and kept low as he snook behind the reception desk. He paused and listened. Nothing. Remaining low, he moved out. He made his way through hallways until he was at corner two of the hotel. Halfway along the corridor between corners two and three, was the AV cupboard. Slowly and smoothly, quickly yet quietly, Harry moved towards corner three. To anyone watching, he moved like a seasoned quiet professional. A soldier who had been subject to many hours of practice and who had taken part in numerous covert missions. The last thing anyone would have thought, was that he was just a seventeen year old kid with a passion for video games and the special forces. Safely reaching the AV cupboard door he checked behind him. Nothing. He slid the key into the lock and stepped into the dark.

CHAPTER THIRTY SIX

Harry found the light switch and illuminated the room. A complex setup, panels of knobs, dials and switches everywhere. He stood back and took in the view. His eyes found the power switch. The control desk illuminated, the AV cupboard soon started to heat up with the power running. Sweat was running into his eyes. Harry removed his ski mask and rubbed his face. Scanning the desk he found a stack of five disc drives, one on top of the other. He chose the top drive. Pressing a button, a drawer opened. Placing the CD on the shelf, he pressed the same button and the CD was swallowed.

He flicked the selector on the MP5 to single shot. He didn't want to use bursts of three, he might not have chance to reload. Harry pulled the ski mask over his head and slid the volume knob to maximum. The next step was crucial. He had to be quick. Easing the door back he checked the corridor. Nobody there. Moving a small lever, Harry ensured the room's door would lock as soon as it slammed shut. He didn't want anyone getting into the room quickly and switching off the music. Harry braced his eardrums and pressed the button that read play. The noise was instant.

Leaping out of the AV cupboard, Harry slammed the door and ran towards corner three. The whole ground floor was consumed by the noise. The music was so loud he only just heard the slam of a different door and the running footsteps in time. Bolting inside the nearest conference room, he closed the door behind him. A running figure dashed past. Harry was back in the corridor. Taking a glance to his right, he saw the x-ray was heading for the AV cupboard. He had to get a move on. He might not have long until the music stopped. Weapon raised, he headed for corner three. Turning right and rounding the corner, he vigilantly neared the Great Hall's entrance.

*

Alison was deafened. Her hands cupped her ears. The California Great Hall was overcome by a deafening and instant noise. It was music, but not how the vast majority of people think of music. There was just a thunderous beat. The voice in the song wasn't singing the lyrics. He was screaming every single word. Some might call it music, but Alison thought it to be obscene. The noise was excruciatingly loud and violating her ears. She knew exactly where the sound was coming from. The California Great Hall's audio system. Speakers behind the walls, the sound came out of a narrow slit below the ceiling.

At the same time as the music had started, the white wall at the end of the room came alive. The music video for the song was projected onto the wall. Every hostage in the room, less Alison who was looking at the situation with Kelsi, looked at the music video.

The sergeant, or corporal, or whatever, screamed. He used hand signals to get his message across. He told the other terrorists to keep their eyes on the hostages and not to look to the centre of the room. The terrorists that beat Kelsi had stopped and the squad of four's eyes scoured the lines of hostages. They were looking for whoever had caused this interjection to proceedings. The more senior terrorist left the room.

A few seconds later a man dressed all in black and wearing a mask entered. He looked like the men who carried out the raid on the Iranian Embassy. Weapon raised, he darted to the centre of the room. One green suit in the centre of the room saw him, he raised his weapon. It didn't get further than elbow level. The figure in black shot him through throat and the terrorist fell to the floor. The deafening racket masked the sound of gunfire.

Margins mattered. The black clad figure came forward another pace and stopped. Kelsi was looking at the floor, but the two green suits either side of her chair looked out at the hostages. The man in black shot them. Less than a second between the pair. They both fell to the floor. The last green suit of the four spun around, gun at his waist. That terrorist was hit by a double tap to the chest by the man in black. He ran forwards and stood prone over the body, aimed at the terrorist's head and pulled the trigger. The music was still deafening. The terrorists watching the hostages hadn't even heard the man shoot dead four of their fellows. The majority of hostages were mesmerised by the gothic rock band imagery on screen. Those who did see the figure, knew he must be a good guy.

The man reached the centre of the room and Kelsi who had been stunned from her beating. Alison realised she knew the stride of the man in black. She had seen that gait before. She had played with the black clothed figure when he was a child and she recognised the outline of the man. Except it wasn't a man. It was a young man at most, a mere teenager. The terrorists were calling him el chico. They were correct. He was a boy. It was Harry. Suddenly relief washed over her. At the same time a deep sense of dread and concern for him consumed her.

Harry reached Kelsi and spoke, his mouth next to her ear. He took her hand and pulled her from the chair. She removed the pistol strapped to his leg. Kelsi watched the front, pistol pointing towards the door. He watched the rest of the room and covered their retreat. Their exit. Their getaway. Kelsi walked forwards and Harry walked backwards. They got to the door and then they were gone.

The music stopped and the video projection went blank. The corporal stepped into the room and saw a scene of death and destruction. Four of his men lay dead and la chica was gone.

"Qué mierda ha pasado aquí idiota?" he roared.

The green suited slime turned around and saw the same as the corporal. Their faces were dumbstruck.

Turning left out of the California Great Hall, Harry headed back the same way he had come. His right hand aimed the MP5. His left hand held Kelsi's. A left hand turn in the corridor was up ahead. The music stopped. Harry pulled Kelsi into a meeting room.

The interior and exterior window blinds were drawn, the room dimly lit. He put his fingers to her face. Kelsi smiled, burst into tears and threw her arms around Harry. They hugged and he showered her in kisses. He quietened her down. Harry had one eye on the corridor, on the small gap of light between the closed blinds and the floor.

Kelsi was silent. Content. She was safe and protected again. He heard footsteps. A man walking quickly, but not running, not as much urgency in his stride. The strip of light went momentarily dark as the figure moved right to left, towards the California Great Hall. Harry counted to ten in his head and opened the door. Peering into the corridor, he saw no one. The passageway was empty. If the next phase of their extraction went well, 'Operation Snatch Kelsi back' would be perfectly planned and executed. Taking her hand and mouthing, 'Quietly,' they ran away from the Great Hall. Harry saw the AV cupboard as they rushed past. The lock had been shot out. They headed for the stairwell at corner two.

They climbed the stairs, Harry watching the front, vigilant and ready, Kelsi playing tail end Charlie and watching their asses. On every landing they stopped for three seconds, silent and listening. Nobody behind them. Nobody ahead of them. They made it to Harry's preselected floor and bedroom. Harry had chosen the sixteenth floor. He guessed the terrorists would first go back to where they knew Kelsi had been hiding and search the Porter's Lodge. That was now as good as out of bounds. He guessed their second play would then be to search the hotel from the ground up. He thought they would hope whoever snatched Kelsi would have gone to ground as soon as possible. Thus, they would search the lower floors first. The terrorists evidently didn't know what her wrist band did. She still had it. He gave the card reader a glimpse and depressed the door handle.

The bedroom was smaller than most on that floor and situated on a corridor that criss-crossed the hotel. He hoped it would be one of the last rooms to be searched in the event of another hunter party. Harry edged the door shut and heard the click of the locking mechanism.

Ideally he would lay a wardrobe on its side and push it up against the door, but all the wardrobes were built into the walls. The dressing table was fixed to the wall as well. He no longer had the rucksack containing his screwdrivers. Although the bedside cabinets were moveable, they wouldn't do anything to stop someone gaining access. He took a chair from around the coffee table and wedged it under the door handle. That would act as a security device, as well as an early warning system should anybody try to get at them.

He ripped the ski mask from his head. This time there were no gentle kisses. Kelsi pressed her body into his. Their mouths met and tongues twisted. Hands ravaging each other's bodies. Harry lifted her up. Kelsi hooked her legs around his waist, arms around his neck. Their kisses slowed, passionate and meaningful, tender and gentle. Loving. They fell back on the bed and continued the kiss. Her hands roamed through his hair and over his chest. She removed her hoodie and t-shirt and threw them to the floor. His hands squeezed her boobs through her blue sports bra. She pushed him flat on the bed and straddled him.

"We can't," he said.

"I know," she said.

Harry's face dropped. She brushed her hand against his cheek.

"What's up, babe?" she asked.

"I want to have sex with you, believe me I do, but we can't, not here and especially not now," he said.

"Let's wait till this is over to get under the covers and make it special," she said, "and I need a shower."

"That sounds beautiful and we will, but you can't have a shower," Harry said.

"Why?" she asked.

"It's too risky," Harry said, "you'll make too much noise."

"I suppose," Kelsi replied.

She stuck her bottom lip out and winced as it split again.

"Fill the sink and have a wash, but no running water once you've filled the bowl," he said.

"Good thinking, Batman," she said.

He checked himself over. Checked weapons and magazines. He heard the running tap and the sound of water change from water splashing onto a sink, to water filling a bowl. Kelsi stepped out of the bathroom and Harry really didn't want to go anywhere. She was naked from head to toe. Kelsi's face had started to bruise from the slapping she had received, but that didn't detract from her beauty. She had the body of a Goddess. A big peachy ass with long legs and nice thighs. Big, firm breasts. A toned and sporty body. God he wanted to stay. She was perfect. He had to force himself to stand up.

"Where are you going?" she asked.

"To pick a fight," he said, "but I'd rather stay here with you."

"Understandable," she said.

She smiled most radiant of smiles.

"Sonofa bitch," she said. Kelsi put a finger to her lip to feel for the damage.

Harry smiled back. She was beautiful in every way.

"Please be careful. I want you Harry Fearn," she said.

"Absolutely ditto, Kelsi Millicent Maguire," he replied.

Their kiss was gentle and smooth, slow and controlled. Her naked body pressed against his. He took the opportunity to hold her naked ass.

"How long will you be?" she asked him.

"Probably about an hour," he said, "I'll double tap the door three times and then give it a single tap, so you know it's me."

She smiled, winced and nodded. They kissed.

"Put the chair back under the door handle when I've gone," he said.

"Okay," she said.

She straightened his ski mask after he'd pulled it over his head.

"Wait," she said.

Kelsi rushed back to the bed.

"Do you want this?" she asked.

She was holding his USP.

"Keep it, I know what you can do with just a diabetes pen," Harry said.

He let himself out.

*

The five star US Army General left. She sat quietly with the office doors closed, her staff given instruction that nobody was to enter, or knock. Claudia read the papers in front of her, took in the information on which she had just been briefed.

Her head was all over the place. She didn't have the military experience of her colleague, her boss. The man who she had fought a party leadership battle against and the man whose vice-President she had been until recently. She was now the President of The United States of America. Claudia Cane had taken up the role by default. That wasn't how she had wanted to become the POTUS. Even though the role and the impending military action she now dealt with was new to her, she wanted to make the best of her Presidency, no matter how short it turned out to be. Her aim was to fill the President's shoes more than her boss had. She could still be the people's President even if they hadn't voted her into office. She knew she could show them who they should have voted for and who they would want as their President, when President Ace's tenure ended. Everything came down to how she dealt with the situation in Fort Lauderdale. She needed advice from three people, two of them were right here in same room.

Claudia stood up. Her eyes travelled away from the desk, beyond the two sofas in the centre of the room and looked at the painting on the wall. She wondered how George Washington would have handled this situation.

She looked to her left, at the sideboard holding fresh flowers in a vase. The item alongside the vase had been there since 1945. It signified the importance of the special relationship. How one country interacts with another, how the newer of the two nations works with what many thought of as its mother, how they both strived to form a greater bond, greater ties. Each great nation had the other's back. The bust of Winston Churchill did just that for Claudia, more so than her boss. Picking up the phone she spoke to Huey's secretary in the room next to the Oval Office. She asked to be put through to Ten Downing Street. It was time to speak to the third person who could advise her.

Henry Bryce answered. The nature of the special relationship afforded them a direct line that would always be answered.

"Good afternoon, Mrs President," Henry said.

"Good evening, Prime Minister, how are you?" Claudia asked.

"Better if I'd had chance to eat my dinner at home," he chuckled, " but needs must and the wellbeing of two great nations hang in the balance."

"Yes. Sorry about that Prime Minister," replied Claudia.

She had only met Henry Bryce once, during a state visit he had made to America the previous year. She had liked him. He was much older than her and she thought of him a bit like she had thought of her grandad, wise and with years of experience. She would much prefer to have been his vice-President.

"I'm told the Special Air Service have been of great help to our own special forces. All the units have worked towards a viable plan of action, they are now ready to carry out an assault to retake control of the hotel. I wanted to ask you about it first," Claudia said.

"Not a problem. Thank you for extending me the courtesy. I'm looking over the same information on which I presume you've just been briefed?" he asked.

"Yes, Prime Minister," she answered.

"The plan is a robust and workable," he said, "I don't foresee any problems with its implementation. I have every faith in the SAS and your own special forces. I believe they'll be successful."

"The other item I wanted clarification on, was the young man at the centre of it all. Harry Fearn," she said.

"Yes. I've heard this young man is being of the most extraordinary use. According to information fed back to me, he started confirming what the police asked about the whereabouts of President Ace and the security measures of the terrorists. Apparently he's been putting himself in danger and killing terrorists?" he asked.

"I had heard the exact same thing Prime Minister," Claudia said.

"I've never met his father, but read his personnel file and spoke to him on the phone a short while ago. His father works our Security Service you see. He's the director of A Branch. He has had a most distinguished career. If Harry's anything like his father, he will have proven a most invaluable asset.

His father says he's been playing a computer game of some kind, SAS: We Dare We Win. He's quite good at the game and they have had a number of conversations regarding it in the past. John said he had a bash at it once and as you would say in America, Harry 'whooped his ass'. He's certain that as Harry has already done so much for your people, he is sure he will be able to help aid the assault," Henry Bryce said.

"Thank you Prime Minister. I believe we should extend the same courtesy I gave to you, to all the nations present at DW30. I don't however, want to jeopardise operational security. When shall we call them?" she asked.

"When it's over, Claudia. When it's over," Henry said.

"Thank you Henry," Claudia said.

She put the handset back in its holder.

She respected his viewpoint. He was the second most successful Prime Minister of the United Kingdom of all time. He had been Prime Minister for the last eighteen years.

CHAPTER THIRTY SEVEN

Harry negotiated his way down the hotel, floor sixteen down to fifteen at corner four. He tracked around the fifteenth floor to corner two. He heard a door open below him. Bothrops must have sent out more hunter squads. Harry moved back into the corridors. MP5 raised, he worked his way across the floor and back to corner four. He descended to thirteen. Another door opened a few floors below him. The terrorists must be seriously pissed off. Whoever had opened that door was now running up the stairs, more than one person. They were coming for him in force. He had to think fast. He couldn't run in the stairwell, he would be heard. He could hide in one of the bedrooms, but whoever was running towards him would see the door closing. He didn't want to run and hide. He was up for a fight. Harry spun around. Lady luck was on his side. The service elevator was on the thirteenth floor. He quickly and silently entered.

He could hear the x-rays on the landing two floors below. They didn't break their stride. They were still coming for him and they were quick. It was possible they were searching the hotel top down and bottom up simultaneously. He had to stop them. They would find Kelsi. He was behind the elevator doors. They couldn't see him, but he could see them and he was protected by two metal doors.

He wanted to save ammunition for the MP5. Harry made the AK47 his primary weapon. Pushing the tip of the barrel against the Perspex viewing hatch at the front of the elevator, he was just in time to see the hunter party. Two x-rays with

Antoni, or Pablo as he had learnt, a step behind. Harry fingered the small lever on the side of his weapon to fully automatic. The AK's rate of fire was six hundred rounds per minute. Pulling the trigger he unleashed hell and emptied a full magazine of thirty 7.62 rounds, in just over three seconds.

Lowering his weapon, he peered through the now non-existent viewing hatch. Two boiler suits lay mangled on the stairs. The first had been hit in the chest and had fallen back to the midpoint landing. The other had been hit in the face and neck. He'd fallen back as well, but was wrapped up in the stair's metal banister. Where was Pablo?

Harry moved an eye closer to the viewing window. The elevator shuddered and lurched upwards. He had to think. Pablo was a floor above, moving the elevator car to his own territory. That wasn't where Harry wanted to be. The Perspex of the viewing window on the new floor was very much intact, that was until Pablo shot it out and pushed the muzzle of his AK through the hole.

Pablo unloaded an entire magazine. The noise was deafening and intense. Rounds flew around the elevator like kernels in a popcorn popper, only one hundred times louder and infinitely deadlier. Not withdrawing the muzzle, he twice changed his magazine and unloaded another sixty rounds into the elevator.

Pablo's laugh was evil.

"Let's look at you now, chico!" he shouted.

He heaved the external and internal elevator doors back to see a lifeless Harry, bleeding and riddled with rounds of ammunition. That wasn't what he saw. He couldn't believe his eyes, how had he evaded him?

Harry felt the elevator move as Pablo stepped into the metal box. All four steel sides of the tin can were pot marked and dented. The inside looked like the bottom of a thousand egg cartons and the floor was covered in ninety expended rounds. Pablo looked up at the roof.

The butt of Harry's AK smashed him in the head. Letting out a primeval scream, Pablo dropped his own AK. He put his hands to his face and staggered backwards onto the landing. He was stunned and dazed. He felt for his nose. It wasn't there. He could only feel broken cartilage and blood. Pablo was furious. He drew his sidearm and flicked the safety catch. Storming into the elevator, he pushed his Beretta 92 pistol through the hatch in the roof. Pulling the trigger and twisting his hand, he sprayed the whole magazine until his weapon ran dry. He hadn't heard the thud of a body falling down, nor had he heard the cries like that of an injured animal. He looked to his left and got another rifle butt in the face. The sidearm was dropped. He let out a noise of pure rage. When Pablo was on the landing, Harry had taken the time to lower himself from the access hatch. He hid out of view, in the corner of the elevator.

Harry had never had a fight in his life, not a real one, not a proper one. Not a fight with a protagonist and antagonist. He had fought his mates, of course, but that was only play fighting at school, acting out scenes they had seen on television the night before. Those fights were just school boys having fun.

He stepped out of the elevator to see Pablo scrabbling around on the floor, stunned and holding his face. A pretty boy with muscles wasn't either once he wasn't good looking. He was just an ugly lump heaving around a body, that looked like ten pounds of shit in a five pound bag. Harry grabbed Pablo's feet and dragged him to the centre of the landing. He lay him down on his back so Pablo could see the moment Harry won. Kneeling at Pablo's feet he reached for his cable ties. Harry was instantly aware he had made a mistake. Pablo had strength left. He kicked Harry in the chest. Falling backwards Harry landed with a thud against the fire door and slid to the floor. He was up and instantly back on his feet. Back in the game. No way was this scumbag going to win. Apart from his current role in the hostage taking, he'd hurt Kelsi. That was wrong in Harry's book.

Pablo reached behind himself and came at Harry with another handgun. The one he had just pulled from his belt. Why the hell hadn't Harry frisked him? He knew he had to stop making mistakes.

The pistol was the same as Pablo's fathers. A Desert Eagle. Still the most powerful magazine fed semi-automatic pistol in the world, but this time it was silver plated. Pistol, sidearm, handgun, whatever people called it wasn't an accurate description, the thing was akin to an anti-aircraft gun. Its stopping power like that of an artillery shell.

Pablo stepped towards Harry. The distance between them closed to four feet. With his right arm outstretched, the pistol was a little less than two feet from Harry's chest. Bad move. Harry jerked his right hand across his body and took hold of Pablo's gun hand, pushing the weapon offline and away from his chest. Harry took a step forwards and brought the heel of his right foot down on Pablo's left kneecap. He screamed a third time. His patella struck, his upper and lower legs were forced apart. Bones pressed against each other. Tendons were pushed to breaking point and snapped. Harry's heel kicked out half a dozen more times and Pablo fell to the floor. Still having hold of his gun hand, Harry was forced to the floor with him. His body twisted in the fall and he landed with his back on Pablo's chest, but Harry's grip remained tight on Pablo's wrist. The Desert Eagle waved in the air. They fought against each other. Pablo was stronger than Harry. He had known that since they first met in the manager's office. Pablo overpowered Harry and turned his wrist in. Harry knew that sooner or later this would have grave consequences. He raised his left arm to join the battle against the Desert Eagle. It never got there. Harry brought his elbow back down, fast. Pablo's face was already split and busted, but Harry was playing for a knockout. Over and over, Harry smashed his elbow into Pablo's face until his gun hand fell limp. Taking the weighty Desert Eagle, Harry wriggled free in time to see Pablo trying to get to his feet. Harry smashed the butt of the pistol down on his head. This time he knelt at the side of Pablo as he applied the cable ties.

*

The assault plan devised by the US and UK Special Forces had been signed off by a five star US General. It involved every member of an elite force present in Fort Lauderdale. Operation Joint Venture planned to bring an overwhelming force into the Atlantic Grand at the same time and completely swamp the inhabited floors of the building. The terrorists would be given no time to react and nowhere to hide. Moments before the assault, Harry would cut the terrorists' video surveillance and take out any x-rays while he secured the US President and the room he was in. He would remove the suicide vest worn by Huey Ace and attempt to hold hostage room two until SF teams arrived at his location.

The SF directly involved were chosen for their operational experience and would be English speakers. English being their first language. Clear communication was key. Any remaining SF were to be utilised to secure the mounting up point half a mile away, as well as the route to the hotel taken by the first of the assault teams. They, as well as further teams, would then be used to secure and search the hostages in the hotel's car park.

Once the mobile steps acquired from local airports were next to the second and third floor windows, the man at the top of the mobile ladders would press an explosive shaped charge against the hotel. Glass having been shattered, teams assaulting the north and south sides of the hotel would enter and commence their own individual missions.

The area around the hotel would be covered by Delta Force snipers on rooftops. A US Coastguard vessel laden with Seal Team snipers would be a quarter mile out to sea. The roof of the Atlantic Grand would also be covered by Delta Force snipers in the air, with helicopters provided by the 160th Special

Operations Aviation Regiment. The 'Night Stalkers' were the US Army's dedicated special forces helicopter aviation unit.

The plan was simple, but incredibly durable. Only the FBI Hostage Rescue Teams (HRT) were carrying handcuffs, all other assault teams would put a round straight into the forehead of a terrorist. All teams however, carried plasti-cuffs. Every single person in the hotel would be treated as a threat and plasti-cuffed until they could be officially identified as a hostage. The assault involving two hundred and eighty two special forces operators was to be the largest joint special forces operation in the history of the world.

*

Dragging an unconscious Pablo along the corridor was more difficult than Harry imagined. Already breathless from the fight, he found that Pablo was a big, heavy, dead weight. He thought about lifting him over his shoulder in a fireman's carry, but if Pablo became conscious, the last place Harry wanted him was around his neck. Halfway down the corridor Pablo stirred and lashed out. Harry kicked Pablo in the head and sent him back to sleep. That one was for Kelsi he told himself. He continued and dragged him into the Porter's Lodge.

Harry grabbed a roll of duct tape and placed it over his mouth, nicking the tape on his lips so he could breath, that was if Pablo's busted open nose didn't allow for it already. He wrapped his ankles and wrists in tape as well, making it impossible for him to escape, then quickly prepared the area where he would leave Pablo.

Once he had frisked him, he made another stash of weaponry. Hooking his hands under Pablo's armpits, he dragged him into the bathroom. Harry struggled, but heaved him into the tub and laid him on all the discarded porter's junk. His head sat at the tap end and his feet nearest the door. Rushing back to the fresh weapons cache in the main room, he picked out

Pablo's discarded smartphone. Returning to the bathroom, he took hold of Pablo's hand and used his thumb to unlock the device. He scrolled through the recent calls. He was looking for a certain name and a frequently called number. One contact had been called three times that day already, six times yesterday and a whole heap of times throughout the last week. He used the phone and took a photograph of Pablo, tied up and in the bathtub. He sent it to the number that was saved as 'Papa'.

Harry was checking himself over at a table in the main room when Pablo's smartphone rang. The caller I.D. flashed up as Papa. Harry answered. Papa spoke immediately.

"Pablo eres una idiota estupida, no es la hora de jugar juegos infantiles. Debes pensar en lo que haces. Dónde está el chico?"Bothrops ranted.

Harry didn't speak.

"Pablo porque estas siendo tan estupido?" Papa urged.

"This isn't Pablo," Harry said.

Bothrops spoke. English this time.

"Who is this? Where is Pablo?" he asked.

"This, is el chico," Harry answered.

"You hurt my son and I will finish you," Bothrops said.

Harry laughed.

"You couldn't finish your fucking dinner," he replied.

Clicking off the call Harry dropped the smartphone in the toilet bowl. He roughly placed a strip of duct tape over Pablo's eyes.

He had to move. The Porter's Lodge was unsafe. Grabbing his new hoard of weapons and grenades, he made a beeline back to Kelsi.

CHAPTER THIRTY EIGHT

Tommy's phone rang. The room went quiet. Everyone in the Ops Room had been waiting for this call. He walked to the corner of the room to answer.

"Hello?" he said.

Everyone was on tenterhooks.

Stan looked up.

No sooner had Tommy answered the call, he'd hung up.

He walked closer to the elite soldiers from all around the world. The room was packed. Everyone had returned from their practice drills in the Wavecrest Royal. A crowd of faces looked at him. He pulled a chair from under a desk and used it to climb onto a table. He needed to address the men.

"That was the president," he said. "We assault the hotel in two hours."

Excited chatter filled the room. The time 1400.

"Most of you," he said. He waited for the crowd to grow quiet once more.

"Most of you have waited your whole lives for an opportunity like this. Operation Joint Venture is of an unprecedented scale and an operation this large, with this many different units involved, has never been attempted before.

You may be fearful, but the enemy will be terrified. You have received the very best training your nations can offer and that training has been the best in the world. You, are the very best in the world.

Conduct yourselves with the upmost professionalism and deadly accuracy. There will no doubt be television news cameras watching you. There will be no smokescreen to shield your movements. The eyes of the world will be upon you.

We are to bring about the terrorist's rightful destruction. Show them no quarter. They chose to die when they forced an armed entry to the hotel.

For some of you here, this will be your last fight. You will leave your units afterwards and maybe have your memoirs published. Remember, what we do is secret and that if you choose to embellish the truth, it is the men standing either side of you that will bear the brunt.

I fully intend to bring each and every one of you out of that hotel alive. So fight hard and if you are ferocious in battle, remember to be magnanimous in victory. Thank you," said Tommy.

He stepped down from the table.

Two Australians were busy in conversation.

"What's the trigger, mate?" one shouted.

The trigger was the word that would initiate action. The word that meant go! Every trigger was decided on the operational commanders brief. The most common trigger was 'Seven,' said three times. Seven is the first number with only two syllables. That meant it could be whispered, or muttered, without being misunderstood. On the third seven, everyone sprang into action. A trigger didn't have to be verbal. A gentle tap to the helmet from the operation commander could be the trigger. If everyone was poised and ready, a squeeze of the shoulder of the entry man at the front of the breach would do the trick. He would then action his shotgun. Tommy was the operation's commander, so it had to come from him, but everything had been so hectic in the latter planning stages, even Rodney and Stan had also overlooked the need for a trigger word. Tommy leapt back onto the table. No need for a chair to aid his ascent this time.

"Good question," said Tommy. "The x-rays are going to know we're there as soon as the first entry explosion is made, so unless there is a need for absolute silence, we'll use 'Go, go, go'. If there is a need for silence, I've always found three taps to the helmet to be just as effective as any other trigger."

"Thanks, mate," shouted up the question asker.

Stan also took to the table.

"I want a final run through of the operation so everyone knows what they are going to do. Sit down gentlemen and get comfortable, this is your time in history and two hours from now, you're going to rock the world," said Stan.

All the operators took their positions again, sitting on chairs, the edges of desks, leant against walls. A few were crouching at the front. They listened intently to Stan. He was from the United Kingdom Special Forces. Every operator in the room afforded him and the other blades the respect they deserved. There was just something different about them.

The three sergeants had assigned themselves roles. Stan was to command the assault to the north side of the hotel, Rodney the south side. Tommy was to take overall charge of the operation. Stan climbed down and all three men paced between white boards, balsa wood models of floor plans, blue prints and schematics charts on the walls. At the same time they asked questions of the team leaders of each separate squad. Which staircases they were going to use? What rooms they were going to clear. What was the order in which they were going to clear them? Every special forces soldier in the room, regardless of rank or unit, wanted to be involved in an operation like the storming of the Iranian Embassy. This operation was going to be their Embassy and it was bigger than anyone could have dreamt.

The inception for Delta Force had come about after a US Army Special Forces Captain was sent on an officer exchange programme to England to work with the Special Air Service. He commanded 3 Troop A Squadron and conducted guerrilla operations with them in Malaya. On his return to the US he pushed for their need for an SAS type unit and believed the

USA was left vulnerable without a similar set-up to the British-ers. It wasn't until a decade later when he had been back to Viet-nam twice, to command US Special Forces and the increased threat of international terrorism had been seen first-hand, that he got his way.

The selection for a soldier to become an operator in The Unit, had striking similarities with that of the selection of an SAS trooper: Initial fitness testing, marches and an incremen-tally increasing weight of what is carried in an applicant's Ber-gen; map and compass work; the traversing of hills and moun-tains during the day and night. When an applicant reached their rendezvous point with the course directing staff, they were only told the gird reference of the next RV Point. The DS would say, 'Have a good un'. All this served to whittle out the applicants who weren't one hundred percent committed. The bigger and heavier guys were up against it, their bulk meant that many of the tasks didn't come easily. Those left were av-erage and shorter, like Stan's SAS troopers who walked from the Wavecrest Royal, they blended in perfectly. If the Delta applicants successfully completed the final stress phase and a forty mile hike across mountains and between RV points, they were subjected to yet more interviewing and questions on top of the questions and essays they had already written.

The SAS pioneered and developed a fighting technique called Close Quarter Battle at their CQB training ground, the 'Killing House'. All the special forces present had a similar set-up based on the original model. Realism was everything in the Killing House. Live bullets were used. Real flashbangs and gre-nades. Watermelons were even used as the heads of mannequins impersonating terrorists. The building itself was a constantly improving training platform. The English Monarchy were from time to time, sent down to Hereford to experience the Killing House and how the SAS would rescue them should they ever be snatched by terrorists. Delta Force have the 'Shooting House,' it operated in exactly the same way.

Finally, Stan unrolled an A1 sized photograph and tacked it to a notice board.

"This is Harry who we have all been talking about. He will be armed. Dressed in black and may be wearing a mask of some kind. He will be in hostage room two at the time of the assault. Learn his face and do not shoot him!" he commanded.

The men in the room who were on the first wave of the assault assembled around the photograph. They learnt Harry's face and any of his distinguishing features. Hair colour and style. The colour of his eyes and any minute imperfections they contained. Eyes were almost unique and could be relied on for good identification. They learnt his dimples, freckles, or any tiny scars his face held.

*

1415

Troopers, operators, commandos and quiet professionals made shaped charges with enough explosive to penetrate the high tensile 4ply laminate glass of the hotel's exterior. Tommy, Rodney and Stan, dressed in their black fire retardant assault suits, made their way to the FLPD command truck. The route they took from the Ops Room ensured they were never visible to the dicker in the static location. Chris was at the top of the steps when they arrived.

"Ahh gents, come in force I see," Chief Schlemmer said.

He had also received a similar phone call from the President.

"Would you like to come inside, I don't think you would like the media to see pieces of paper being signed," he added.

"You took the words right out of my mouth," Tommy said.

Chris asked his staff in the mobile office to vacate for a few minutes. Only Teonnie stayed. Chris wanted minutes of the meeting taken. Years in the job had taught him to cover his own ass.

The police, the ruling authority in Fort Lauderdale, were required to handover control to the armed forces in a situation like this. There was nothing written in law that allowed the military to carry out their duties, anywhere outside of an army base, or warzone. The FLPD was top dog. Only in times of national emergency, was it necessary for the army to intervene. The only time the military are allowed to be involved is when someone is carrying out an act of terror. Lives have to be in imminent danger. They were and the President of the United States had given permission for the special forces to assault the hotel.

It was up to the Chief of Police to decide when the handover of powers took place. Chris wrote the handover permissions on a piece A4 paper pulled from the back of a printer. It was signed by Tommy. At 1549 all control of the surrounding area would pass from the FLPD to the special forces. The police would stay in place until the assault on the hotel commenced, so as not to spook the terrorists who they knew were operating a camera surveillance system. All the police would need to ensure was the placement of assault columns of airport ladders, access to their entry points at the north and south sides of the hotel. Tommy also asked if an FLPD SWAT team could be temporarily loaned to the SRR. Chris agreed. The hand written piece of paper was signed and slipped into Tommy's pocket.

1420

He pulled his smartphone from the bedside table when he heard three buzzes. It was Schlemmer:

'The special forces will you call soon, they need your help. Chris'.

"Shit," Harry said.

He said shit in such a way, anyone that heard him would think whatever the shit was about, must be a big deal. Kelsi lay next to him on the bed. They looked into each other's eyes as they spoke. They talked about the WhatsApp, about the situation coming to an end. They spoke about what they would do in the days after the siege and how their lives would return to normal.

Ten minutes later, Harry was sat up on the bed, a pillow propped behind him. Kelsi sat between his legs. He ran his finger through her hair. His smartphone vibrated. As before when the FBI called him, the caller I.D. showed a withheld number. He would answer the call. Harry trusted Schlemmer. If he said he needed to speak to these guys, he needed to speak to them.

He put the phone to his ear.

"Hello?" he said.

A thick and heavy New York accent spoke to him.

"Hey dude, is that Harry?" the voice asked.

"Yeah," replied Harry.

"Good to finally speak to you man, I've been hearing a lot of good things about you. My name's Tommy, I'm down here at the back of the hotel in the office complex. I'm with Seal Team Six," he said.

Harry's eyes widened. He knew exactly who they were, basically the American cousins of the SAS.

"Hi," Harry said.

Tommy thought it should be Stan who spoke to the kid. An English accent might be better for him, especially after all they'd heard from Tank and the kid's love of the SAS.

"I got a fella here called Stan, from the Special Air Service, say's wants to talk to you for a minute or two. Can he do that?" Tommy asked.

Harry would have done anything for the SAS at that moment. They were his idols. In his eyes, they were gods.

There was a long pause and Tommy had to ask again.

"Harry, is that okay?"

"Yeah, yeah, he can do that. Yeah sure, that's fine," he said.

"Hello Harry," a British voice said.

Harry was so excited he was shaking like a shitting dog. This was incredible, how the hell had he ended up talking to one of his heroes?

"Err yeah. Hi. This err is, Harry. Who's this?" he asked.

He was completely starstruck.

"I'm Sergeant Stan Lewis from B Squadron, the Special Air Service. We'd like to thank you for everything you've done so far in the hotel," Stan said.

It was a blade. A real life member of the world's most elite military force. *Some seventeen year olds have footballers as their idols. Some have pop stars or movie stars, but this was Harry's type of idol.*

Harry tried to play it cool.

"No problem," he replied.

"Me and a few Seal Team Six guys and some more Delta Force fellas, have come up with a plan of how we're going to get into the hotel. We'd like you to help?" Stan asked.

Harry didn't have to think about this for more than a nano second. If the SAS had asked Harry to jump off a cliff, he wouldn't have asked if there was a safety net. He would have asked if they wanted him to walk, or run as he jumped off the edge.

"Yeah, that's fine," Harry replied.

Stan talked through the plan with Harry. He told him how many special forces operators were involved. Explained exactly how they were going to enter the building. What each SF team were going to do once they were in the hotel and what Harry needed to do to enable all of that to happen. He asked Harry to talk it back to him so it was straight in both their minds.

"Firstly, I cut the terrorist's video surveillance so they can't see you coming," Harry said. "The SF will be mounting up on mobile airport steps half a mile away. The drive to the hotel should take approximately one minute. During that drive the power to the hotel will be cut and the backup generators disabled, the mobile staircases split at the road junction of Bayshore and Birch. Special forces operators attack on two sides of the hotel," Harry said.

"Which sides?" Stan asked.

"The north side and the south side, the sides of the hotel between corners one and four and two and three," he replied. "The teams hitting the north side of the hotel will enter the car park via the Beach Boulevard. The south side teams will come down Granada Street and the assault will take place from there."

"Correct. Carry on," Stan said.

"Thirty seconds before you get here I will have finished securing Huey Ace. I'll have entered the room in which he is being held, neutralised any x-rays and removed the suicide vest. I'll then lay the vest out of the way in the corner of the room. Anyone that tries to come through that door will also be neutralised," Harry said.

"Good," Stan said. "Personally I'd have just shot them rather than neutralise them, but I guess there's more than one way of skinning a cat."

Stan got a laugh from Harry and put him at ease.

"I meant to say, I'll probably have a girl with me too," Harry said.

"Bloody hell, Harry. How have you had time to go pulling women?" Stan jokingly asked.

Harry chuckled.

Lying on the bed, Kelsi blew him a kiss.

"Okay, what happens next?" Stan asked.

"Ten mobile staircases carrying one hundred and fifty four operators from Delta Force, Seal Team Six, FBI HRT and the SAS will attack either side of the hotel. Placing frame charges on the glass sidewalls at equidistant points on the second and third floors, they blow the glass. You'll all enter the hotel. The hotel's power will be down so you'll all be using weapon mounted torches," Harry said.

No professional organisation used red dot laser technology. If a gunman saw a red dot on him, or on a piece of furniture, he would just need to aim at the other end of the laser and the bullet would hit two inches from the scope.

"Splitting into four and eight man teams, you'll clear rooms on the first six floors of the hotel and secure the hostages and…" Harry waited for a second and made a point of saying, "…shoot any terrorists."

This time it was Stan's turn to laugh.

"Which floors do we clear?" he asked.

"Floors one, two and three, as well as basement floor one, basement two and basement three," Harry said, "and FBI Hostage Rescue Teams will start clearing floors four and up."

"You said floors two and three, who enters on which floors?" Stan asked.

"The SAS and FBI Hostage Rescue, enter on the third floor, Seal Team Six and Delta Force enter on the second floor," Harry said.

"Then what happens?" Stan questioned.

"At 1605 a second wave of ninety six SF will run across from their hidden positions and enter the hotel via the staircases used by the first wave. They rendezvous with the FBI HRT and search every other room in the hotel. Once the situation on the first three floors and three basement floors is secure, any SF not doing a job imperative to hostage evacuation will join the second wave in searching the rest of the hotel for x-rays and hostages," Harry said.

"What else is going on by this point?" Stan asked.

"The SF will secure all exits to the hotel and wait for US Army bomb disposal. Hostages will be evacuated and checked to make sure they're not a terrorist, then they'll be checked again by the SF outside in the hotel's car park. They will only be released from their plasti-cuffs once they have been matched to an actual person and job title, from there the FBI take over and do investigative stuff," Harry said.

He took a breath.

"Then I'm going to come and find you and shake your hand," Stan said.

Stan couldn't see it over the phone, but Harry was grinning like a Cheshire Cat.

"Harry," Stan said, "we need to synchronise our watches. I want you to dial yours in to 1429 hours when I say."

A few seconds ticked by.

"Ready," said Harry.

"Hold, hold, now," said Stan.

"Got it," said Harry.

"That was good, now let's go over and over the plan again until I don't need to prompt you," said Stan.

CHAPTER THIRTY NINE

1430

Land to build on was at a premium in Fort Lauderdale; however a small piece of untouched grassland sat half a mile north west of the Atlantic Grand. This was where the special forces chose to mount up prior to the assault. The eight soldiers of the Austrian Jagdkommando and the four Forsvarets Spesialkommando from Norway, were sent to secure the area as soon as the operation was given the green light. Not long after, ten mobile steps from local airports arrived on the back of five semi-trucks.

*

1500

Kelsi knew Harry's demeanour had changed. He was on edge. She thought he might be struggling. He had told her what the SAS man had asked. It was a lot. He was a seventeen year old kid for Christ's sake. She was a kid too, if she was being honest. They were just two kids who liked each other, but they were in an adult's world, playing adult games.

Kelsi knew who the SAS were. They were like Seal Team Six, or Delta Force. She knew what they did was really dangerous. Bearing that in mind and although she wouldn't dream of telling Harry, she thought it wrong of the men he idolised to ask him to put himself in danger. If they were asking a seventeen year old boy to help, there must be no other option. They must really need him. He had put himself in so much danger already. It was a lot of stress and strain for a young man. He had done things nobody, let alone anybody his age, should ever have to do.

Harry sat on the edge of the bed, concentrating on an imaginary dot on the wall. He ran through the plan in his head. Not the SF plan, his plan. If he fucked this up and didn't get things done his end, people would die. The breathing through his nose intensified. He psyched himself up. *He was pumped up and ready to go ballistic.* Kelsi worried, she had to tell him what she was thinking.

"It's not too late to call it a day," she said.

Harry looked at his watch and stood up. He dragged the ski mask over his head, turned his covered face and looked at her.

"I'll call it nothing," he said, "Success is not final, failure is not fatal. It's the courage to continue that counts."

"Wow!," she said.

Kelsi touched his hand.

"Winston Churchill said it first," Harry said.

"I don't care who said it, you meant it," she said.

Harry wrapped her hand in his, squeezed and kissed her.

He checked his pockets. Ammunition, grenades and for the hundredth time, checked there was a round in the chamber of his MP5.

"Do you still want to come?" he asked.

She nodded. The safest place in the hotel was two paces behind him.

"Okay, first we need to go to the Porter's Lodge," he said.

"What for?" she asked. "You said that's out of bounds!"

"It is, but I need a weight," Harry said.

"A weight?" she asked.

"Yeah, to hold something down, but it needs to get lighter and lighter," he said.

He knew exactly what he wanted.

Kelsi looked confused.

"Don't worry, I've got this," he said.

Harry passed her the AK47.

He slid the USP into his leg holster and stuffed Pablo's pistol into the back of his belt. If he made it out of the hotel, the silver plated Desert Eagle would make a pretty cool souvenir.

She followed behind. He moved up stairwells, padded down corridors and tracked around the hotel. Harry's instincts were so high, unless she spotted an x-ray, she wouldn't speak to him. Then it clicked, he wasn't on edge, or struggling. The boy she met when he started working in the hotel had become a man. He was hard as nails and he was hers.

'My man,' Kelsi mouthed.

Near to the Porter's Lodge Harry halted, prone in a corridor alcove with Kelsi behind him. Nothing came or went. They moved forward.

He entered tactically in case there was anyone lying in wait. There wasn't. Harry poured the remaining gasoline from the jerrycan down the toilet. Pablo smelt the gas. He squirmed, made muffled yelps and pissed himself. Harry refilled the metal container with water.

Kelsi edged backwards into the Lodge, her AK trained into the corridor. Once he filled the jerrycan, Harry screwed the cap on tightly. Kelsi slung her AK on her back and picked up the can. He needed to be able to react.

Half way down the hallway Harry slowed. He raised his hand in a fist. Kelsi stopped and covered them.

"I need to go back, I forgot something," he muttered.

Kelsi nodded. She understood. Harry entered the Lodge to get what he needed. Leaving the room, he didn't appear to have picked anything up.

"What did you get?" she asked.

"You'll see," was all he said.

They set off.

1540

In the stairwell at corner two, they reached the third floor. He knew what he had to do next. If he was to knock out every camera individually, it would take him forever. The x-rays would know about it before he'd finished, not to mention he would be forewarning the terrorists of an impending assault on the hotel. The best way to go about the task was a sudden shutdown of all the cameras. If you poured water on anything electrical, it would go bang. Or hiss and smoke. Either way, it would be rendered useless and wouldn't work anymore.

He pointed at the conference room opposite the stairwell's fire door.

"That's where you need to be. Shoot anyone who comes through this door, or anyone who walks past your position. I'll hear and come out as backup," Harry said.

No movement. No noise. Harry and Kelsi stepped through the door. He left Kelsi and moved along the corridor, towards the generator. The room was on the left, facing the street. Interior and exterior window blinds drawn, lights turned off. Only the available daylight lit the room. That was enough for him to see what he was doing. If the door hadn't been held open by the cables in the first instance, he wouldn't have even noticed the generator was there. You could quite easily have a conversation while stood next to the thing.

The tables and chairs were still in the centre of the room. The generator sat on top. The control panel faced the door, he needed the controls facing up. Harry grabbed a bottle of sparkling water from the table. He liked the idea of sparkling water fucking something else over, other than just himself. He pulled the generator onto its side.

Harry pulled the cables that fed into the machine outwards a notch. Enough so the generator still delivered power, but enough to allow water to creep in. Unscrewing the cap with a hiss, he began to pour. The water found a path and commenced seeping into the generator. He didn't know what the reaction of the machine would be. Not an explosion. He hoped for hissing noises. The electrical parts of the generator fried, maybe a bit of smoke. Sure enough, it started to hiss. A flash of light. Bang. More smoke. The generators hum stopped. It had been fried. The x-ray in the media suite would come looking. He pulled the generator back onto its belly, dried the control panel with two doilies from glasses on the table and made his getaway.

*

1548

Half a mile northwest of the hotel, ten mobile airport ladders sat on the grassy area off Bayshore Drive. A police cordon had been instated. A crowd had developed to watch the unfolding events. More and more residents came out of their homes when they saw four large Greyhound Coaches pull up. Over one hundred and fifty men, all dressed in black and carrying submachine guns disembarked. They were ready for something big. Everyone in the crowd had a smartphone. All of their devices were fitted with a high quality zoom enabled camera. Every SF operator had their face covered with a mask, their identities had to be protected. When the time was right, they would remove their face covering and don their respirator. They couldn't wear anything underneath. The respirator had to form a vacuum around the face. They would do this out of sight to anyone watching.

The route the SF convoy was to take had been shut down. Police vehicles blocked every side road. At the mounting up point Stan Lewis stood with his fifteen blades at the base of their mobile ladder.

The point man on each staircase checked and double checked his explosive shaped charge. The demolition of the glass entry points to the hotel needed to be perfect. The rest of the SF team checked the pockets of their bullet proof vests.

They ensured they had everything they needed. They pulled their respirators tightly onto their faces. Stan heard a whistle and looked up.

It was Tommy.

"You good?" he shouted.

After checking with his men, Stan waved a thumbs up. Tommy checked all ten of the ladders had given the same state of readiness. The last man up each staircase was at the wheel of the truck. Everyone wanted to hear the SRR detonate their frame charge.

Control of the area passed from the Fort Lauderdale Police Department, to the special forces.

1550

The Dicker room was located on Birch Road, opposite Granada Street and corner three of the hotel. The room's position on the third floor, above a hairdressing salon and office space, meant the Dicker could see the FLPD command truck, as well as the entrance to the offices at the rear of the Atlantic Grand that the FBI and the SF were using and all their comings and goings. When the SF left and headed to the mounting up point, they had done so covertly, leaving by a side door. Anyone inside that location would also be able to see them return and assault the south side of the hotel. They would be able to give a split second warning to the terrorists. This amplified the ability of the hostage takers to start executing their captives, or to start preparing defences. Either would prove bad news. The Dicker needed taking out before the assault could begin.

The SRR did more than just reconnaissance. *If it was called for, it was capable of being just as devastatingly lethal as its two older brothers.* With the entirety of the SF presence in Fort Lauderdale currently mounting up, there wasn't anyone else that could carry out a raid on the potential dicker's location. The SRR would do it themselves.

The hairdressing salon two stories below the terrorist observation post hadn't been occupied since the arrival of the FLPD. The front doors of the building were locked and although the SRR were trained at picking locks to the same level as a professional locksmith, the front doors would take too long to pick. Extra time would be added and the whole operation may compromised. A forced entry from the external rear fire escape stairwell was the only option.

In silence, Tony and his Brick climbed the metal fire escape. Three operators covering one operator. Slowly and methodically they moved. Operation Joint Venture hinged on their success. Dressed in black assault suits they wore respirators and carried MP5s. They made it to the third floor. They would gain access via a fire door. An explosive entry was needed. Renee, the fourth Brick member up the stairs, carried the explosive shaped charge. With the speed they needed to move, they wouldn't have time to clear the other rooms on that floor. An FLPD SWAT team led by Tank Bolling, waited one floor below the SRR. They would follow the SRR into the building and clear the rest of the floor of any potential threats.

They couldn't make a noise. They couldn't speak via the radio, the inhabitants of the third floor might hear them. Only being half a mile away, the SF at the mounting up point would hear the explosion. The team crouched out of sight. The plans of the building told them the passageway the other side of the fire door ran towards the front, towards the Dicker's location. It met with another corridor running left to right. When the SRR reached the T-junction, they were to turn right. The first door they came to on their left was the room they wanted.

A black clad figure stood up from her crouch. Using an extendable pole, Renee pressed the shaped charge against the fire door. Tony checked his watch. He looked at Renee and nodded. She waited for him to lower his head, checked her team were out of the line of the explosion and activated the remote trigger. The birds in the trees were shocked and startled into life. Once the door was blown, a flashbang was thrown into the hallway. The Brick raced into the third floor of the building.

The daylight created by the blowing of the fire door illuminated the passageway. They rushed past three closed doors, three potential threats to their safety. Reaching the end of the hallway the Brick turned right and reached the target room. The third man in the team had his MP5 slung over his back and carried a Remington 870 shotgun. Two solid rubber slugs were fired at the two hinges in the front door and one at the lock.

The occupant of the room was an unarmed Hispanic male in his late twenties.

Tony was first through the door and had his weapon trained on him.

"On the floor, on the floor," he shouted.

The other members of the Brick flooded in and dominated the room. The occupant didn't comply. Stood in front of four operators dressed in black, he froze.

"On the fucking floor," Baggers shouted.

Still nothing. Things were getting desperate. Why wouldn't he get on the floor? He was dressed in jeans and a pullover. In this hot weather it was unusual. Was he cold? Was the pullover concealing a weapon, or a suicide device? Three seconds ticked by. The whole team was thinking the same thing. They were all looking at his hands. Did he have a remote trigger for the device? The petit frame of Renee stepped forward. She swung at him and the Dicker's nose met with her right fist. He was on the floor. Renee rolled him over and plasti-cuffed his arms behind his back.

Shouts of, 'Clear,' could be heard from Tank's SWAT Team as they searched the other apartments on that floor. A bag was thrown over the Dicker's head and he was hoisted to his feet. He would be taken for interrogation and the room sealed and preserved as evidence for later investigation by the FBI.

1552

Harry and Kelsi headed to corner one. They entered the conference room that backed onto hostage room two. The POTUS
and fifteen high ranking politicians were metres away. Ensuring the window blinds at the front of the room were drawn,
Kelsi knelt and positioned herself ready to shoot anybody that
entered. Harry walked over to the stud wall that backed onto
hostage room two. Removing the Stanley knife he had taken
from the Lodge at the last minute, he began to cut into the wall.

This was classic covert entry. Something he had practised
many times on SAS: We Dare We Win. He worked more quickly than he wanted, but his cuts were still silent, his movements
precise. He cut a four foot by two foot hole. Scoring the outline
gently with the knife, he worked the blade deeper each time. After fifteen cuts of each side, he removed his room's section of stud
wall. All that remained was the hostage room wall. He started to
cut and only made ten cuts on each side. Anyone who could see
the wall from hostage room two, would think it was untouched.

Telling Kelsi he would be back in a minute, Harry grabbed
the water filled jerrycan. On his return he'd tap the door as
before. He didn't want a trigger happy Kelsi filling him with
7.62. He was at corner one. He needed to get to corner four,
but he couldn't walk there directly. The hostage room was in
the way. They would see him. He took the long way around.
He only hoped he didn't bump into the x-ray watching over
the surveillance cameras, if he hadn't already checked on the
generator. Harry made his way through the corridors and passageways. MP5 in his right hand. Safety catch off, three round
burst selected, jerrycan in his left hand. He halted at the rear
main staircase and got to his knees. The CCTV monitors in
the Indiana Media Suite were blank. Reaching corner four he
placed the jerrycan in the centre of the corridor.

Dropping to one knee, Harry laid the submachine gun
within easy reach on the floor. He took a grenade from his tac

vest. A bead of sweat ran down the inside of his ski mask. He placed the grenade on the floor and manoeuvred the jerrycan so that it was in a landscape setup, the outlet at the bottom and pointing towards corner one. He lifted that corner and slid the grenade underneath. More sweat ran down his face stinging his eyes. He held his breath and removed the pin from the grenade. The weight of the water in the jerrycan held the handle down. Harry twisted the can's screwcap and instantly water seeped out. With his left hand holding the top left corner of the jerrycan, his right hand made more twists. The more he turned the cap, the more water spilled out. He judged it would take two minutes for the weight ratios to change. The grenade's handle would become stronger than the water in the jerrycan pressing down. The process could take three minutes, but no longer. More than that and the SF would be making entry. People would die. Removing his stabilising left hand and getting to both feet, Harry breathed out. He watched the jerrycan. It didn't move. The grenade didn't roll out from underneath. He didn't need to run anywhere. The grenade's handle was sufficiently pressurised for the time being. That wouldn't be the case forever. He needed to get back to Kelsi.

Picking up his MP5 he backed away and headed towards corner one.

Following the procedure he'd laid out with Kelsi, he gave the door the slightest of taps. He held his breath as he turned the handle.

*

1555

Everyone had heard the SRR charge detonate. Crowds of onlookers stood at the sidewalk. They saw a convoy of armed men preparing to move. The crowd held up their smartphones and videoed the trucks. They wouldn't be able to instantly upload, or send their new video, cell phone signal coverage for the whole of Broward County had been shut down for two hours. Stan heard over the comms that the hotel's power had been cut and the backup generator disabled.

He looked to his blades.

"We're on," he said.

CHAPTER FORTY

Harry entered the conference room. Kelsi was crouched down aiming her AK47 at him. Without warning the lights went out. He switched the weapon mounted torch on and checked his watch. Anytime now enough water would have chugged out of the jerrycan. The weight pushing on the grenade's handle would exert less force than the handle itself.

1556

He thought back to being in his bedroom on the last day of the school. He never completed SAS: We Dare We Win. His mum had literally pulled the plug. He had thought he was being packed off to Florida for the summer to work in a hotel. It had been so much better than that. Harry had dreamed of this type of situation ever since he had started playing first person shooters on his console. The reality was terrifying. At the same time it was thrilling. So much better than sitting playing a video game in his bedroom. His body ached. He had taken a battering. He had nearly fallen to his death. He'd been in fights. Ran harder and faster and pushed himself more than ever before. He had been shot. Pain had coursed through his veins. He had wanted to cry, but he wouldn't change any of it for the world. He wanted to join the British Army more than ever.

Enough water had glugged out of the jerrycan. The grenade's handle released. The handle lifting released a spring. The spring allowed the striker to hurtle down the interior of the grenade to the percussion cap. The impact of the striker hitting the percussion cap caused a spark. That spark lit the fuse. In turn the fuse lit the detonator and caused a small explosion inside the grenade. The small explosion caused another much bigger explosion. The grenade detonated and the metal that formed the grenade's shell flew in every direction.

Harry was expecting it and had closed the conference room door. The noise caused his heart to beat faster. Screams and whimpers came from the adjacent room. Those screams were going to get a lot louder in the next thirty seconds. He waited five seconds for the x-ray in the next room to walk to the door. Harry imagined him opening it and peering through, looking where the explosion had come from. Harry walked to the stud wall. One foot away from the hole, his MP5 was set to three round burst. *He was pumped up and ready to go ballistic*. He drew back his right foot. Taking a big gulp of air he drove his heel forwards.

No single word was tangible as the screaming, shrieking and crying got as loud as it could. The hostages were under attack from all angles. MP5 raised, Harry stepped through the hole.

One hostage. Two hostages. Then a third. All saw a man dressed in black, weapon mounted torch leading the way. The group on the floor screamed, cried, huddled together. Pack mentality, safety in numbers. Harry's aim filtered through the crowd and lit up their faces. The front door was open. The terrorist had fled towards the diversionary blast. No one to fight. Only seconds before the terrorist returned to his post. Harry had to make sure there wasn't another terrorist packed in with the hostages. The terrified screams subsided. He heard movement in the corridor, running footsteps. His aim swung away from the hostages. A boiler suit rounded the corner.

The barrel's torch illuminated the doorway. Bang. Bang. Bang. In quick succession. Three rounds hit the x-ray. The screaming, shrieking, crying and sobbing was back and as loud as ever. Harry strode towards the body he had just dropped.

Stood over the crumpled mess on the floor, he aimed at his head. One pull of the trigger and three rounds blew the terrorist apart.

Harry sensed Kelsi moving behind him. She had stayed out of the line of fire until the room was clear. She set herself up to provide overwatch. She would have his back as he spoke to the hostages and removed the President's suicide vest. She sat on the floor, separate to the group of hostages, right knee bent, she used it as a platform for her AK. She aimed the at the doorway.

The hostages didn't know who Harry and Kelsi were, but they were evidently on their side. Umpteen thoughts were running through the heads of the sixteen hostages. Some of them knew more about this type of situation than others. The ones that knew more had one question. Why had the military sent only one man and a young woman?

Harry didn't flick the MP5 to safety. The submachine gun hung loosely to the side of his person. Should he need to start putting more rounds down, this was the best option. He spoke loudly and clearly. With the exception of the POTUS, all the hostages turned around, or craned their necks to see the figure in black speak.

"Please don't panic," Harry urged, "I am a friendly and I am facilitating the special forces outside. My name is Harry Fearn, I am a British worker in this hotel. I have been liaising with and helping the police and special forces since the start. They will be here very shortly."

He removed his ski mask and stuffed it in a leg pocket. There were gasps of shock as the hostages realised how young he was.

"Your cooperation is needed now, more than ever. I need you to make a path for me to the President," he said.

Words uttered from the hostages in a multitude of languages. He guessed all the voices were saying the same basic thing. 'A child. He's just a boy. Jesus. What the… so young!'

Five hostages shuffled to the side. He stepped forward and spoke again.

"Over there is Kelsi," he said as he pointed, "She is also a friendly and is a US Citizen working in the hotel."

He moved towards the POTUS.

Harry knew he needed to talk to the casualty. The POTUS appeared to have withdrawn deep inside himself, he was in some kind of solitary state. From what Harry had seen on television and heard about the current President of the United States, he, like all the people who hadn't voted for him and the majority of the people around the world, thought he was loose cannon. A renegade. A shyster who deceived the US voters to obtain the presidency. Builders and contractors had cowboys. Stock market traders had rogues and every other profession had individuals who didn't do their job properly. The world of politics had Huey Ace.

"Huey, I'm going to remove your vest now, I'm going to cut you out and take it off intact. Okay?" he asked.

The POTUS didn't reply. A hostage sitting next to him, maybe a senior advisor to Huey Ace, told him that he was required to call him Mr President. Harry smirked.

"Yeah?" he said. "Well I'm not, so deal with it."

Harry glanced at his watch. He was pressed for time. Getting to one knee he withdrew Christian's knife. More whimpering and gasps of shock from the hostages. Harry carefully began to cut the straps holding the vest in place.

He was at his most vulnerable, he had his back turned to the door. An AK47 fired. The shock caused more wailing and screaming. Huey Ace didn't even flinch. It was like his senses and reactions didn't exist anymore. Dropping the knife and taking hold of his weapon, Harry back rolled and trained his MP5 on the fresh body of a terrorist. Standing up and aiming his weapon at the newer of the two x-rays, Harry paced to the doorway and pulled the trigger. The POTUS was the highest value hostage the terrorist's had. He thought they would send more men his way. He looked towards Kelsi.

"You okay?" he asked.

She was shocked by her own actions, but she managed to nod back while keeping her AK trained at the door.

"Expect more to come, get that door shut, draw the blinds drawn," he said. "If they can't see us, they can't shoot us."

Instantly Kelsi was on her feet to do what he asked. She flung the door and it nestled itself shut with a bang. The crowd on the floor jumped.

Time was really pressing now. Harry darted back to the PO-TUS. Getting to one knee, he picked up the knife and roughly cut the straps of the suicide vest. Time was of the essence. He couldn't give a rat's ass about delicacy towards Huey Ace. The vest cut, he raised it free of the president and stood tall.

*

1559

The convoy reached the junction of Bayshore and Birch. Tommy's lead staircase turned right. Four trucks followed. Stan's mobile set of steps and the four behind him, drove straight until the ocean forced a right turn. They headed down Fort Lauderdale Beach Boulevard. Between the palm trees and hotels, Stan could see the last vehicle of Tommy's convoy. Perfect. They would arrive at precisely the same time. The plan was to attack at 1600 hours, plus a handful of seconds, it was going to be exactly that. The usually packed beach was deserted, it had been part of the exclusion zone since the first police roadblocks were instated. Less the odd police Mustang, the area was cloaked in a post-apocalyptic eeriness.

Four helicopters hovered in the air above the cordon. Two FBI helos, an FLPD chopper and a Nightstalker helo providing operational support in the form of snipers. Eighteen thousand feet higher, a drone fed video footage back to the support staff in the Ops Room. The same video was displayed on screen in the White House Situation Room and COBRA in London. Stan turned to his men.

"Ten seconds," he said.

*

The operation was played out in front of her, the live video footage coming from a Wasp III unmanned aerial vehicle. Claudia Cane watched two wall mounted television screens in the Situation Room, both showing faultless high resolution images. The first image showed a three block by three area of operation, the convoy of mobile ladders snaking their way through Fort Lauderdale. The second image was much closer. Claudia could see individual men clinging to the mobile stairs. Half of the convoy headed through the city, the other five mobile steps drove alongside the beach. They rumbled forward. As they came closer to the Atlantic Grand, Claudia's heartrate increased more and more. By the time the convoy swerved sharply into Granada Street and the other into the hotel car park, her heart was in her mouth. Before today she had never made a military decision and she had just made the most important decision any president may ever have to make. Now watching the reaction to her action, she dreaded the possibility of men dying, her having sent them to their deaths. She hated it. She wanted it to be over. Claudia Cane wanted to fast forward a couple of hours and know the result. She couldn't. She watched the five mobile airport ladders of the north side assault scatter like ants on a patio. They raced through the car park to their respective breaching positions.

*

Stan's lead truck had turned sharply into the car park of the Atlantic Grand. Scally, the staircase's driver, looked for a marker to identify the glass panel his team were to attack. Two more trucks bristling with SF guys drove past. Their staircases pulled up outside their entry points. Sixteen Delta Force operators assaulted at corner four of the hotel on the second floor. Between them and him, ten FBI HRT operators took another part of the glass wall. To his left another sixteen SAS blades struck. Further still at corner one, floor two, a Seal Team Six operator would place his shaped charge against their glass panel. Feathering the gas, Scally peered up and saw the edge of the stairs above him inch towards the correct glass panel. He stopped and pulled the handbrake. Engine off, he grabbed his MP5. Jumping from the cab, he darted to the bottom of the steps. Dave had already scrambled to the top of the staircase. He held a pole pressing the large explosive shaped charge against the glass. It was now eight seconds after 1600 hours.

Stan spoke into his comms.

"Team north three, placing shaped charge now," he said.

In the Ops Room Hollie's mic came alive.

"Have that," she replied.

Stan's team was north three because they attacked the north side of the hotel and were the third team from the front of the building. She marked the team's position on the white board that held a layout of the third floor.

Captain Hollie Hogan made up only part of the Special Air Service's unsung support team. Gaining a first class honour's degree in the history of war, meant Sandhurst snapped her up when she applied to be an officer in the British Army. Any team movement, regardless of nationality or branch of the military, on the north side of the hotel and the third floor was her bag. She marked all movements on the whiteboard in front of her. Captain Sue Graham of the Australian SAS worked the south side of the third floor. When the five white boards to her right came alive, Delta Force support staff would go to work. The three white boards to her left were managed by three Seal Team support staff. Those boards were taking care of floors four, through twenty one. Hollie's earpiece would then come alive again as all the operators, troopers and hostages left the building by the same point - North side, third floor, middle staircase.

'Stand by, stand by,' Stan said.

The troopers on the steps put their heads down. Stan heard an explosion emanate from the other side of the hotel.

"Go. Go. Go," he said.

Dave activated the remote trigger. The explosion fractured the thick glass panel and sent thousands of fragments of glass crashing into the room. He dropped the remains of the pole onto the car park floor and stood back as troopers rushed past him into the office room. At twelve seconds past 1600, the men from Hereford stepped into a boardroom.

The first man in scanned the room, the barrel of his MP5 following his line of sight and illuminating the area. He moved to the right, towards the door. The second man broke left as he entered the room. The third man walked briskly and calmly to the centre. More explosions sounded, the north side of the hotel this time. There wasn't a terrorist in the room. Stan entered and headed for the closed door. Shaken loose by the explosion, a swift kick with the flat of his boot ensured it fell into the corridor. He took a mirror from his leg pocket and surveyed the corridor. Nothing in either direction. Two flashbangs were thrown into the corridor anyway, one to the left, one to the right. Smoke filled the area. Standing back and slapping the man to his right on the shoulder, Stan sent the trigger to move.

*

1600

The building was shaken by the first deafening and destructive entry explosion.

"Everyone stay where you are," Harry commanded, *"Kelsi, leave your weapon, come and join the group."*

Another explosion sounded, nearer this time.

She did. A third explosion thundered. All the hostages sidled up and huddled together. Solidarity. Mutual comfort. Herd mentality. *Safety in numbers.*

"They're here, stay where you are, don't stand up, it's going to be okay," he shouted.

Harry strode to the back right corner of the room. More explosions shook the building. The retake of the hotel was on. He laid down the suicide vest and stepped away. Harry sat with his back to the wall he had entered from and ten feet from the vest. He removed his weapon and laid it on the floor next to him, far enough away not to be thought of as a threat to the SF, but close enough to take hold of and fire back if another terrorist appeared.

CHAPTER FORTY ONE

The first blade stepped through the door casing. MP5 in his shoulder, two magazines clipped together ensured a fast reload. He turned right, the second man turned left. Stan turned left and tapped the man in front on the shoulder. The team split. Eight right, eight left. In Stan's team, eight torches shone brightly as they paced down the corridor. The point man on the right, Stan two paces behind him on the left. They covered the corridor with two pairs of eyes. An internal door flew open and a boiler suit stepped out. The point man and Stan fired. The x-ray dropped before he had chance to get a round off. They both stood over the fresh body and both fired. Ahead, a figure to their left appeared. The point man stopped, raising his left fist. It was the second SAS team to assault on the north side of the hotel. A trooper entered the corridor.

One floor below, Seal Team Six guys were doing the same. Everyone moved forward again. Stan's team moved down the corridor, straight towards hostage room two. More teams of blades cleared and secured the other rooms on the third floor. The door to each cleared room was marked with a chalk X, the door then closed and the corridor kept secure. They heard the last of the entry explosions. Everyone was now inside the hotel. For a brief moment the corridors on the second and third floors were flooded with troopers and operators. They all had designated jobs, all knew what they were doing. Just as quickly, the corridor emptied. Fifteen seconds after the initial explosion and the SAS and FBI HRT had filled the corridor, only Stan's team and his fifteen blades remained in the hallway. His team continued towards corner one, to the POTUS and the other fifteen hostages.

Stan neared hostage room two. His team gathered outside. He checked the edge of the entry door for explosives. They weren't taking any chances with this room. The door could be booby trapped. A blade stepped from the rear of the pack. Strung over his body armour on a bungee cord was a Remington 870 shotgun. He fired three solid rubber slugs into the door, one into each of the hinges and one into the lock. The door fell into the room. He stood back. A flashbang was thrown. One loud bang. The room filled with smoke. Troopers rushed in.

One trooper through the door, two through the door. Stan burst through the door. The bodies of two x-rays lay on the floor. Stan added his own rounds to each body. The troopers verbally dominated the hostages.

"Down, down,' they shouted.

"On the floor, fucking get on the floor," Dave shouted.

A hostage tried to get to her feet. Dave's fist thumped her in the chest. She sat down. The troopers wanted everyone face down. Those that didn't comply were manhandled and forced to eat carpet. A trooper walked to the end of the room, his weapon trained on the hole Harry had made. He saw more blades enter that room via the front door. The room was cleared.

Stan's vision fought through the smoke filled the room. He counted the hostages and came back with a count of seventeen, one more person than there should be. Scanning the room with weapons raised, the troopers searched for a seventeenth person, the hostage that shouldn't be there. A terrorist impersonating a politician. Stan's eyes found Harry, tears streaming down his face. He wasn't upset, the smoke from a flashbang stung like a bitch. Harry pointed to the President's suicide device. A trooper stood guard over the vest. Nobody could go near. With weapons raised, more troopers strode around the room. Pulling the heads of hostages back, they needed to see their faces.

"Who's the seventeenth hostage?" Stan shouted.

Harry looked up and dried his eyes with the back of his hand.

He couldn't make out Stan's question. His respirator had distorted what he said. Stan came closer.

Crouching, he put a hand on Harry's shoulder.

"Who is the seventeenth hostage?" he shouted.

"My friend, the one I found in the linen cupboard," Harry shouted back.

"Where is she?" Stan shouted.

Kelsi raised her arm.

Two of Harry's heroes dragged her from the group. One patted her down and checked her for weapons. The other stood with his weapon aimed at her head.

The trooper gave a thumbs up.

"Clear," he shouted.

At 1604 Stan spoke into his mouthpiece again.

"POTUS secure. I repeat POTUS is secure. He is not, not, in need of urgent medical attention. Suicide vest not yet made safe, but is protected," said Stan, "Two x-rays down in gold hostage room, one more in the corridor between corners four and one."

Hollie placed three black stickers on three red magnets.

"Have that," said Captain Hogan.

She pressed a yellow sticker onto a gold magnet on the white board.

The POTUS had just been marked as safe.

Taking plasti-cuffs clipped to their belts, troopers organised the hostages. Harry took hold of his weapon. He got to his feet.

"Can I help?" he asked.

He pointed towards the plastic cuffs on Stan's belt.

"Yes," Stan said.

He passed him a handful.

Harry told Kelsi that he would come and find her when the operation had finished. Tears ran from Kelsi's eyes. He took her wrist and applied a plasti-cuff.

"Why are you upset?" he asked.

Kelsi stared at him like he should know why.

"The flash thing and you said I was just your friend that you found in the linen cupboard," Kelsi sniffed.

"Yeah?" Harry asked.

"I don't want to be, just your friend," she said.

Harry pulled her other wrist in front of her and zipped the plastic ties together. He kissed her. Harder, more passionately and meaningful than a gentle kiss on the lips.

"If I didn't want the same, I would have tied your hands behind your back," he said.

Harry winked and smiled and his face held a big grin.

He kissed her again.

"Harry," shouted Stan.

"What?" returned Harry.

"If you're helping, fucking get on with it," Stan ordered.

He moved onto the next hostage and left Kelsi smiling. Harry plasti-cuffed three more hostages. He added them to the line Stan's blades had started. Another trooper stood guard at the door.

"I'll see you in a bit," Harry muttered in Kelsi's ear.

As the hostages were led out of the room, Harry pulled his ski mask back over his head.

The seventeen hostages were passed from Stan to trooper, trooper to trooper, Harry to trooper. The blades were joined by their other teams. A chain to process the hostages towards the mobile steps was made. Each trooper looked over each hostage. Looked deep into their eyes. Were they hiding anything? Did they have a weapon on their person? Did they recognise them from the terrorist photos? A split second decision whether or not to allow them to pass was made. SF operators needed the brains of a judge and the heart of a lion. The hostages reached team North Three's entry point. They were pushed out of the hotel and down the staircase into the car park. Met on the tarmac by more SF operators, they were forced to the floor again. Stan hadn't got time to stand around and watch. He knew what was going to happen. The process seemed harsh, but it was thorough and kept everyone safe.

He turned to Harry.

"Are you coming with us, or going with them?" he asked.

Stan flicked his head to the car park.

It was the easiest choice Harry had ever made.

"I'm coming with you," he said.

*

Delta Force were assaulting the south and north side of the hotel, Granada Street, corner three, car park, corner four. Their explosive entry was made at sixteen and seventeen seconds past 1600.

The rooms they made entry to the hotel from were clear of x-ray activity. Thirty two quiet professionals made their way into their respective corridors.

Like almost all special forces worldwide, Delta Force operators chose the weapons they carried. In a hostage rescue CQB situation, no weapon came as close as the Heckler & Koch MP5. Weapons raised and torches shining brightly, they advanced in a fighting formation down to the three basement floors.

The Unit's thirty two operators broke into smaller squads. Some operators were continuing down the stairwell to the second and third basement floors. The team taking the first basement floor quickly moved to the front of the hotel. They neared corner two. An x-ray darted in front of them. Three operators fired. He died six feet before he reached the staff entrance, the Claymore and the sensors to the President's suicide vest. Eight men stormed the back office. Two, four man teams assaulted the staff canteen and standalone offices. Delta operators met no resistance on the other two basement floors. Leaving men to guard entry and exit doors, the remaining operators headed up to the first floor.

*

As the SAS had been plasti-cuffing their hostages on the third floor, Tommy's sixteen man Seal Team neared the main entrance to the California Great Hall. Highly alert and determined, they paced down the corridor. Weapons raised, flashlights illuminating the way. One operator on the left. One on the right. Two operators behind them. Reaching a blind corner, Tommy took out his mirror. He signalled to his men that there were three x-rays in the corridor outside the California Great Hall's entrance.

The terrorists were nervous. They were right to be so. They were about to get smoked. The x-rays could hear violence all around them. Chaos was coming their way. They were trigger happy. That was the nail in their coffin. Seal Team Six hit them hard.

Another four men from Six came in behind, ready for a final push. A flashbang was thrown around the corner. The terrorists started shooting as soon as they saw it roll towards them. Boom. They were blinded by the light. The x-rays unloaded a full magazine. The reload time was all Seal Team Six needed. Four operators, backed by another four, swung around the corner and came out shooting. Automatic rifle fire reverberated down the corridor. The terrorists were dead before they got chance to finish reloading. Two seconds and it was done. All three had bullet holes in their foreheads. Six pulls of the trigger. Six entry holes. Three dead x-rays. Ensuring they were dead, operators stood over the terrorists and unloaded more rounds into their chests. They secured the entrance to the California Great Hall. More Team Six operators flooded the area.

Tommy got on the radio.

"Three x-rays down, rear corridor outside silver hostage room," he said.

Their position and the dead terrorists position was marked on the first floor white board.

Two Team Six men came to the front with their shotguns. They stood ready at the solid wooden doors. Operators positioned themselves ready for a final assault. The California Great Hall had more exits and entrances than just the main doors. Seal Team members stood ready at all four exterior corners of the room. Ready to take out any terrorists who attempted to make a run for it.

The air waves fell silent. Everyone was poised and ready. Tommy balled his right hand into a fist. He moved his fist towards his helmet. The pack tightened. 'Tap. Tap. Tap'.

On the first tap, operators took up a solid stance. On the second tap they aimed. On the third tap, the two operators with shotguns unloaded rubber slugs into the door's hinges. They fired a further two rubber rounds at the locking mechanism. Two kicks. The wooden doors fell forwards and into the hall. Operators threw flashbangs to pre-determined points in the room. One flashbang went left, one went right, two more were thrown further down the Great Hall. The first flashbangs thrown were exploding. Their thunderous roar boomed through the building. Another two flashbangs were thrown to the rear of the room. The sound from outside the entrance was awesome. Two loud bangs and a flash of light, followed by two more and two more. The screaming and wailing of the hostages was instant. Crying and incomprehensible noise filled the room. It didn't matter if the hostages were male or female, both were crying, both were screaming. All were very scared. The shouts and cries worsened when the gunfire started. It was mayhem. To Seal Team Six operators, it was their kind of havoc.

Operators were lined up behind one another in the corridor. A split second after the last flashbang went off, the first operators entered the room. Whilst still moving. *Slow is smooth. Smooth is fast.* They fired their weapons. Two bewildered and shocked terrorists stood twenty feet into the room. Both were double tapped. Both dropped. The first two men kept moving, one went left, one went right. They were followed by two more operators who went left and right, then another two. The entry of Seal Team Six operators was like goods coming off a production line, constant and smooth. Two more operators stood at the blown door with weapons trained straight down the California Great Hall. Every inch of the vast function room was covered by an operator's aim.

The Great Hall was too big for a conventional assault. Seal Team Six relied on the disorientation the steady stream of flashbangs had caused. *Prior planning and preparation, prevents piss poor performance.* Operators swarmed from the back to the front, from the main entrance, to the stage area. They moved like a line of infantry troops would have marched forward at the Battle of Waterloo in 1815, but this time their line resembled an inverted V.

The two operators stood in the doorway were the last to walk forward. The first operators to enter were already twenty feet into the room. Moving forward, the operators headed towards where the last flashbangs landed, each man pulling the trigger of his weapon at targets stunned and shocked by the flashbangs. All of the hostages were eating carpet, that made it easier to pick out the terrorists. Operators left and right fired. Terrorists fell down. An x-ray managed to escape down a back corridor, the same passageway a 911 caller had tried to escape through. The operators didn't chase him. They were dedicated to their task and kept moving forward. A barrage of automatic weapon fire was heard. Seal Team Six operators in the southside corridor had seen the x-ray. They all fired on him. The escapee had been stopped.

The eight operators in the Great Hall conducting a thorough, but quick search, disposed of six terrorists. They were backed by another sixteen operators. Working in pairs, one pulled the dipped and hiding heads of hostages back so identification could be made, their partner covered them. A terrorist kneeling behind a group of hostages jumped up to fire on the operators. He didn't get to one knee before he was killed by twenty eight rounds from various submachine guns. This caused more screaming and wailing. There was no point shouting back at the hostages, ordering them to be quiet was futile. There were just too many frightened civilians in the room. Only shouts of 'Down, stay down,' or 'On the floor,' were used. The occasional forceful hand of an operator encouraged a hostage to remain on the floor.

An operator in the search team had his weapon trained on a hostage while his buddy searched the captives. He felt something pull his trouser leg. A hostage looked up and pointed to his next door but one neighbour. Without a second thought, the operator stepped forward and kicked his boot into the hunched over body. Falling backwards the figure's automatic rifle was exposed. The gunfire was sudden and terrifying. The operator fired and ended the x-ray. Kicking aside the body, a discarded green boiler suit lay visible on the floor.

At the same time as the main assault on the California Great Hall, the remaining rooms on that floor of the hotel were searched by more Seal Team operators. In addition to the sound of rifle fire in the Great Hall, sporadic bursts of gunfire could be heard all over the first floor. In the Ops Room on the first floor white board, more red magnets had black stickers applied. When those operators in the hotel finished their room search, the first floor fell silent. The only noise remaining was from the whimpering and sniffling of hostages.

*

The two FBI Hostage Rescue Teams that were north four and south four, made their explosive entry to the hotel at twenty four seconds past 1600 and twenty eight seconds past 1600. They entered the corridor of the third floor and found the passageway already littered with blades. Making their presence known with shouts of, 'FBI,' they joined the controlled chaos and made their way to the service stairwell at corner four. An HRT operator aimed his submachine gun up the flight of stairs. HRT specialists passed him. This was repeated over and over. The twenty men already in north and south side assaulting teams split. They created four separate teams of five men. The fourth floor was cleared successfully with zero resistance. No hostages were found. The HRT made their way to the fifth floor.

CHAPTER FORTY TWO

1605

Ninety six operators from Delta Force, Seal Team Six, the Australian Special Air Service and the Special Operations Regiment of Canada, hitherto remaining out of sight, ran from the Wavecrest Royal and hidden positions south of Granada Street and assaulted the Atlantic Grand. Using the mobile staircases already in place, they headed to the front and back service stairwells. Moving up the hotel they commenced clearing rooms in the same fashion as the FBI. Rooms upwards of floor four were cleared rapidly. Five floors were cleared at a time by the various different special forces. The fast pace of their work ensured that within an hour, they were nearing the top of the hotel.

1658

On the eighteenth floor the FBI HRT prepared to assault a bedroom on the back corridor of the hotel. The HRT trained continually for hostage incidents, prison uprisings and armed situations. This was their bread and butter work and something they were very skilled in.

Following the deaths of seventeen people at the Munich Olympics, the FBI created their own hostage rescue team. The idea from conception was to have a unit far more skilled than any SWAT Team and for it to be ready for the 1984 Los Angeles Olympics. Although not a secret unit, they were still professionals who got the job done. The majority of their members were not military. Their ranks consisted of university graduates and every day folk who wanted to make a difference to society, former office clerks and accountants who felt a yearning for law enforcement. After serving a minimum of three years as an FBI Special Agent, they could apply for the HRT. Then they were subjected to two weeks of extreme physical training to ensure they could make the grade. Although not trained in the many disciplines of a Delta operator or Seal Team member, they were experts in hostage rescue. This situation was what they practised for constantly in their Tactical Firearms Facility (TFF), or its informal name, the 'Shoot House'. In the TFF they were able to practise assaults on all manner of buildings. More importantly, they learned to identify threats in a split second. An old lady looks like an old lady, but if she had a firearm at her side, she was a threat. A man in a bandana, camouflaged trousers and a t-shirt holding his hands up, might be a hostage, or a terrorist surrendering.

It was impractical for the assault teams to make an explosive entry to every bedroom, there were too many. An HRT operator stood ready with his dynamic hammer. The dynamic hammer would smash against the lock and shatter the mechanism with one blow. The force from the hammer then continued, forcing the door from the frame. Lined up opposite the hammer man, four HRT operators stood ready to assault the next bedroom. Bedroom one or one hundred, the threat was the same. There could still be an enemy behind the door. The first operator held his fist out. The hammer man saw him clearly. The fist sprang a thumb. The hammer was raised. Then a finger and the hammer was drawn back. Another. The hammer was flung towards the bedroom door. The first operator had his hand back on his weapon and was ready to enter the moment the lock gave way. Smash. Four men entered. The last operator dropped his hammer and entered the room. He headed straight into the bathroom.

"Clear," he shouted.

The HRT continued their search and entered the next bedroom. Two gunshots rang out. The shots were close. The urgency of the situation increased. The pace quickened. The countdown with the fingers was gone, doors were just smashed open. All other training remained intact. It became a case of clearing rooms as quickly as possible. Their fear was they had heard the execution of a hostage, or maybe two. The possibility that they would hear more gunshots was entirely plausible. They moved quickly. Weapons raised, they entered another bedroom.

There was blood spatter in the room. It lay on the ceiling next to the bed. A terrorist lay beneath. He had placed the muzzle of his AK beneath his chin and pulled the trigger. Having pierced his skin, the 7.62 round missed his jawbone and travelled through his tongue. Penetrating the soft and hard palate at the roof of the mouth, it continued into his brain. He was killed instantly. The round hadn't stopped there. It kept travelling through his brain. A large piece of the back of his head was missing. The round had taken with it brain and skull. A pink mist of blood and brain marked the ceiling. Any remaining mist had settled on the carpet and gave the beige colour a red hue.

The second body in the room was slumped against the wall opposite the bed. The x-ray had placed the muzzle of an AK47 in his mouth and pulled the trigger. The round of ammunition discharged from the weapon travelled through his neck, missing the brain entirely. The round instantly severed the spinal cord, shutting down the signals the brain sent in its dying second of life. That exit wound wasn't large and didn't include any bone or brain, just blood, the staining on the wall was centred by a 7.62 diameter hole drilled through the stud wall. The round travelled into the bedroom next door and into the bedroom beyond that, before enough momentum had been lost and the projectile had been halted.

There was nobody else in the room apart from the two cadavers. Both bodies were dead terrorists and both had taken their own lives. They probably knew they wouldn't survive. They were being hunted by experts. There was no need for anyone from the HRT to check for pulses. The x-ray's weapons were placed in clear plastic bags for FBI Forensics. The hostage rescue team continued their search.

*

1704

On the floors above, the gunshots were clearly audible to the Australian SAS and Canadian Special Forces. The Australians presumed the room they were entering was just another hotel bedroom. They found a storeroom full of bottles of water. A whiteboard marked with scribbles and diagrams leant against a wall. They were Quick Battle Orders. A makeshift bed had been constructed. A dead x-ray lay on the floor next to a stack of chairs, a syringe of some sort protruded from his arm. They knew instantly this must be the room Harry was using as his base of operations.

Another blade yelled from the bathroom. He had found the body of a man. Bound, blindfolded and gagged. The duct tape blindfold pulled from his face, he was immediately identified as Pablo Munoz. An Australian trooper spoke into the mic in his respirator.

"Pablo Munoz in custody."

*

The last few remaining hostages were leaving the California Great Hall. It took a while to get over two hundred hostages out of the hotel. They were pulled to their feet and pushed towards the rear central staircase. Passed between operators standing only five feet apart, each was given a quick look over. A more in depth check would be made in the car park. Delta Force, Seal Team Six, Harry and the SAS looked into their eyes. They were satisfied they didn't recognise them from the known terrorist photographs. The line of hostages passed between SF operators stretched from the California Great Hall, up the rear staircase and onto the corridor that led to the north three entry point.

*

In the basement that was home to Cabinet Office Briefing Room Alpha (COBRA), thirteen people watched the live footage. All were senior security officers and government ministers. All had colleagues involved in the hostage situation. British Prime Minister Henry Bryce watched the drone footage. Hostages were manhandled out of the hotel. The special forces at the scene needed all the men they could get their hands on. After an already rigorous checking process the hostages were not escorted down the stairs, they were allowed to walk themselves. This action was twofold. It freed up SF soldiers to carry out another task, it also acted as an opportunity for a terrorist to show themselves. If they had so far evaded capture and made it this far, the thought that they might make it out alive was possible. This was the turning point. They would be able to see how thorough the search continued to be. They wouldn't be able to free themselves. They could try to pull a weapon, unlikely considering every one of them had been plasti-cuffed. More likely, they could try to run. That eventuality had been covered. At the bottom of the stairs, six Israeli Commandos from Unit 621 stood with their weapons trained on the hostages as they walked down the steps.

From the bottom of the stairs the hostages walked straight into the hands of Brazilian 1st Commandos. They were passed to Irish Rangers and the Danish Jaegar Corp. Forced to the ground, they were interrogated by the Dutch Kords Commandos.

Henry smiled as he stood next to the UK Director of Special Forces.

"Bloody good job and extremely well executed," he said. "Who's in charge down there from our side?"

"Officially, Major Richard Greenfield, but I think we both know it's an SAS sergeant called Stan Lewis," said the director.

The Prime Minister collected his thoughts for a moment.

"I think we owe him a medal, his men too," the Prime Minister said.

A Minister urgently called.

"Sir," he said.

The Prime Minister was about to leave the room.

"Look."

The young man pointed towards the magnified drone image. A scene of commotion was unfolding.

Three of the Kords Commandos targeted one hostage on the floor. Two commandos furiously flicked through the book of hostage profiles. Their job, nationality, photograph. They couldn't find the male hostage in the book. One of the commandos appeared to be asking the other hostages if they knew him. The commandos were lifting the hostages' heads from the floor and pointing towards the unknown man. The aerial video was so clear, Henry could see the other hostages shake their heads. More plasti-cuffs appeared. The unidentified hostage had his feet bound. He was carried away by Irish Rangers.

*

The heat of a Florida summer's afternoon was beginning to take its toll on the hostages waiting to be processed. The FLPD began pouring water into the mouths of those still cable tied. After processing, government employees from all around the world were draped in blankets and led to a large clothes shop on the street at the back of the Atlantic Grand. All of the hostages were down to their underwear.

Ambulances began tending the hostages, trauma and flash-bang burns were common.

FBI Special Agents stood ready with clipboards. They took statements from all the hostages. After having had statements taken, they were formally released into the care of their respective governments.

CHAPTER FORTY THREE

There was a crackle of static in everyone's earpiece.

"The hotel is now secure. I repeat, the hotel is now secure," said Captain Hogan.

Stan, his troopers and Harry, made their way to the first floor and the California Great Hall.

Standing aside, a US Army Bomb Disposal team rushed past. Following behind them at a much slower pace was the technician who would diffuse the devices.

The technician moved slowly. He resembled a man walking on the moon in a dark green, seventy seven pound ballistic suit, thick panel covering the front half of his torso and vital organs, thick and heavy collar providing protection for his neck.

*

Stan finally got chance to shake Harry's hand in the California Great Hall. In fact Harry shook the hands of all the blades and Tommy and Rodney and most of the other operators as well. Everyone wanted to meet him. They all wanted their photograph taken with the lad who was quickly becoming a walking, talking, living legend. Harry wanted photographs too, but he knew he would have to black out the SF operator's eyes before he uploaded them to Facebook.

He spent the next hour talking through what he'd done in the hotel. Tommy took notes for reports. Harry mentioned the recon for Schlemmer. He told them how, with Kelsi's help, he had poisoned the terrorists. He told them about the fire extinguisher attack, zeroing the AK47 that would soon get jammed, checking out the fire exits and finding the anti-tank missiles. He spoke about the linen chute and his running fire-fight with the x-rays. The Molotov Cocktails he made and how he used them. He recalled rescuing Kelsi from the elevator shaft and throwing a terrorist out of a window. Apparently the fall-ing body narrowly missed a cop and had exploded all over the road when it landed. He told them how he lured Christian out by swapping clothes with a dead x-ray, killing Amanda with a diabetics pen and launching operation Snatch Kelsi Back. They all laughed when they heard what Harry said to Bothrops on the phone after he caught Pablo. That was it really, they knew the rest.

"Oh, there's a dead x-ray in a filing cabinet in the office," he said.

Stan took Harry to one side. He told him he could come down to Stirling Lines in a few months and meet the rest of the lads. They shook hands a second time and Harry made his way out of the Great Hall.

"Harry," Stan shouted after him, "don't forget, you're only as good as your last job."

He waved a huge thumbs up at Harry.

Getting recognition from the SAS was massive!

"I won't," Harry shouted back.

He left the California Great Hall very happy with what he had achieved.

US Army Bomb Disposal first deactivated the President's sui-cide vest. Their next job was to deactivate and remove the Clay-mores facing the front doors of the Atlantic Grand. Harry had said goodbye to his new mates from Delta Force, Seal Team Six and the SAS and intended on walking straight through the front doors and onto the Beach Boulevard.

The hotel lobby was awash with FBI Special Agents. They must have plenty to organise. No lesser important task was to find Bothrops Atrox, who had so far evaded capture. Stood behind the reception desk on the exact spot where he had strangled a terrorist, a Special Agent was on the phone. Harry didn't hear the whole conversation. Apparently someone had thrown a Mistress in the crusher and the thing had jammed. Surfer dude Mark Baxter would be back.

Harry hopped down the steps at corner one. Freedom beckoned. There was still one man he was yet to meet. After the 911 call dispatchers, he was the first person he had spoken to and the person he had spoken to the most. He made his way across the grass at the front of the hotel to Granada Street. Up ahead, he could see the FLPD mobile command truck. To his right an industrial jet washer started up. The workman was cleaning a large area of reddened pavement. To his left Tank Bolling was debriefing his SWAT team. He was the first to recognise Harry. Breaking up the meeting, he ran across the street to shake his hand.

"Harry, nice to finally meet you," he said.

After a few minutes of conversation, he led Harry to the command truck.

"Chief," Tank shouted, "I've got a young guy with me, who I believe you wanted to meet."

Chris Schlemmer bolted out of the door and ran down the steps. He had a smile on his face.

"Harry!" Chris announced.

Harry smiled back.

"How are you, dude?" Chris asked.

The chief and Harry hugged it out.

"I've been better to be honest. I've been clipped by a round from an AK, but all things considered, I'm not doing too badly, thanks," he said.

The pair burst out laughing.

"We'll get that fixed for you," Chris said, "I just wanted to say that we couldn't have done it without you. You did a truly fantastic job and the world is forever in your debt. Thank you."

"That's alright," Harry said with a shrug, "I wasn't up to much anyway."

Chris couldn't help but smile. *He liked Harry's sass.*

"One final question," Chris said. "You really learnt all your skills on that game, SAS: We Dare We Win?"

"That and a few books I read," Harry answered.

Chief Schlemmer showed Harry over to an ambulance in the streets surrounding the hotel. He took Harry's number and saved it in his smartphone under, 'The Gamer'.

"Hey, if you're ever in Florida again, give me a call," Chris said.

He handed Harry his business card.

The paramedics removed Harry's t-shirt and peeled away his self-applied wound covering. Harry winced as antiseptic was wiped around the wound again and a new, properly fitting bandage was applied. He was given a tetanus shot and the paramedic counted out pain killers for him. Harry saw his mum out of the corner of his eye. She was bolting towards him. Harry's dad followed close behind.

His mum hugged and kissed him like a new born baby. She finished her embarrassing display and his dad stepped forward.

"I should have done this at the airport," he said.

He wrapped his arms around his son and squeezed.

Harry was definitely flavour of the month, everyone wanted to speak to him. The next person was a doctor who specialised in post-traumatic stress disorder. Harry and the doctor, with his parents hanging off every word, spoke for half an hour. Harry told the doctor about everything he had seen and done, how he was feeling about it and any concerns or worries he had. He didn't have either. She asked if he was okay and how he felt having killed other human beings. Harry shrugged.

"They weren't humans," he said, "they were targets. I didn't have time to think. I pulled the trigger, they dropped, I moved on."

The doctor nodded.

She gave Harry's mum and dad a whole heap of paperwork and leaflets on PTSD. She told them the symptoms Harry might start to show. She would speak to some of her contacts in England and get Harry booked in for an appointment with them in a few weeks.

That evening Harry, his parents, Kelsi and Alison all enjoyed dinner together. He then spent yet another night in a hotel room with Kelsi. This time it was on their own terms and he wasn't bothered about leaving the light on.

Kelsi was as gorgeous as ever. He popped his cherry that night. A number of times.

She flew home to Biloxi the next day and Harry endured a whole day of talking to the FBI about what he had done in the Atlantic Grand. He was already bored of de-briefs.

CHAPTER FORTY FOUR

Harry's parents and Alison had originally planned a vacation road trip for him, driving from Fort Lauderdale, up the east coast to New York City. Harry had a different idea. They didn't flinch when he said that he wanted to drive to Mississippi to see Kelsi. Eight hours after setting off, they found themselves in the north Florida city of Tallahassee. The Grand Hotel Group didn't have a hotel there, but they paid for three sumptuous five star hotel rooms at an independent hotel.

The next day with his dad at the wheel and Harry sat up front next to him, the SUV rolled west and started to cover the three hundred miles to Biloxi. Harry's mum knew what her husband did for a job. Of course she did, she was his wife. Alison didn't know, she had only been his sister in-law for a short time. Even her ex-husband, his own brother, didn't know what career path John Fearn had taken. He glanced in the rear view mirror. Alison and Elizabeth were fast asleep in the back. Adamant Harry was now a member of the inner sanctum, John thought he should probably tell him about it.

The story he told Harry was one of espionage and surveillance. How he joined the Metropolitan Police service at eighteen. John was then seconded to SO13 and was involved in a number of high profile undercover cases. He'd impressed someone, because MI5 tapped him on the shoulder and asked him to join their ranks. He signed up to MI5-A4 as an undercover surveillance operator in the mid-nineties.

The IRA anti-terrorism work lightened after the Good Friday agreement was signed in 1998. The Security Service concentrated on rogue nations attempting to steal the United Kingdom's military technology. Then the world changed. The security world had been flipped on its head when only eleven days into September 2001, the World Trade centre was attacked. Extremist groups were top of the MI5 agenda. John told Harry how he worked his way through the ranks to become the section head of A4, then the director of A Branch. The next stop would be senior management of the Security Service.

"What's the name of the woman who works for MI5, the lady who was at the DW30?" Harry asked.

"Oh, you mean Jacinda?" his dad asked.

"Yeah, we had a chat in the gym. It was almost as if she knew you and you just called her by her first name. I could tell you worked together!" Harry whispered.

Harry's dad laughed.

"Yeah, of course we do," Harry's Dad chuckled, "she's my boss."

Harry looked at the road ahead and smiled. His dad was possibly the coolest dad on the planet.

"You'll meet her again anyway, we'll go for a beer at the Special Force's Club when we get back to London," his dad said.

Harry was amazed that such a thing existed.

"The what?" he asked.

"The Special Forces Club. It's not just special forces, it's for anyone who's a member of the inner sanctum. All the special forces. SAS. SBS. Delta Force and everyone in the spy game too. CIA. MI5. MI6. Mossad and any other security operator, but you'll have to leave your phone at home. Cameras aren't allowed," John said.

"How have you been able to keep your job a secret for so long?" Harry asked.

"Tradecraft," John answered.

As they had waited for a taxi to take Kelsi to the airport, Alison told her she could have as much time off as she needed.

She completely understood if she didn't want to come back to work at the Atlantic Grand. She could have a job in any other hotel in the chain, anywhere in the world. Kelsi told Alison she'd think about it. She had flown back to Mississippi to see her family. In the twenty four hours they had been apart, Harry and Kelsi had been sending messages to each constantly. Finally the Ford Expedition passed the last landmark Kelsi had described, before they needed to veer to the right and drive to her house.

The landmark was a strip mall that consisted of eight shops, a parking lot and standalone diner. Two of the outlets were clothes shops, one a woman's clothes shop, the other for both men and women, there was a pharmacy, a gun store, one sporting goods store, a stationery and electronics store, a giant bed and mattress superstore and a perfume outlet. Harry's eyes zeroed in on the penultimate store. He didn't know why, probably because he couldn't wait to get into his own bed and sleep on his own mattress.

He was enjoying being normal again, doing everyday things. He looked at people shopping, walking to their cars, driving trucks. People taking their dog for a walk and riding bicycles in local parks. He didn't want his mind to flit back to the hotel, but it did. The same thing had happened a few times recently. This time he was fairly certain he knew why. His mind just needed to go over it a little more.

The SUV swung onto Kelsi's street. Harry's dad turned the wheel and pulled onto the driveway of number twenty five. Kelsi's Mom's house.

She saw the hulking SUV pull up. The front door opened and Kelsi ran towards the her love. Harry wasn't hanging around either. His door was open and his feet hit the driveway before the wheels of the SUV stopped turning.

They met each other with open arms, hugged each other tightly. He lifted her free of the ground. Kelsi wrapped her legs around his waist as they kissed. Harry's mind should have been on Kelsi, but it wasn't. There were unknown forces working in his brain. The kiss didn't last as long as Kelsi hoped. He put her down.

"I need to borrow your phone, I know where he is!" exclaimed Harry.

"Who?" Kelsi asked.

"Yeah Harry, who?" said Alison.

She had climbed out of the Expedition and was making a path to embrace Kelsi's mother, who had come out front to the veranda.

"Bothrops. I know where Bothrops Atrox is. I need to use the phone, please?" asked Harry.

He couldn't wait to use Mrs Maguire's phone. He fumbled his smartphone out of his pocket. He knew the battery was low. He didn't have an in-car charger and he had forgotten to buy one. He pressed a button and the phone illuminated. Two percent battery.

"Bollocks," he said.

His heart was beating hard. He needed to get a message to the chief.

Kelsi's mom returned with the house phone. He pulled Chris Schlemmer's business card from his pocket and Harry tapped in his number.

The chief was in his backyard working on his boat, completing the job he had started on Wednesday.

He answered the call from an out of state number.

"I know where he is," said Harry.

"Is this you Harry?" Schlemmer asked.

"Yeah, I know where he is!" Harry repeated.

"You know where who is?" asked the chief.

"I know where Bothrops is," Harry said.

"Where do you think he is?" Schlemmer asked.

"Chris, I don't think. I KNOW WHERE HE IS!" he answered.

"Where is he then?" Schlemmer asked.

"In the hotel," Harry replied.

"That's impossible," Chris said. "The FBI have looked in every room and in every cupboard. He's not there. They're searching the storm drains as we speak, but given the time that has passed, he's probably out of the country by now."

"He's in the hotel," Harry urged, "I know he is."

"Why do you think he's in the hotel, Harry?" the chief asked.

"When I was leaving the hotel for the last time, there was someone on the phone at the reception desk. He was asking the crusher company to come to the hotel, because the crusher was jammed," he explained.

"What's the crusher?" Schlemmer asked.

"It the size of a shipping container and sits outside the loading bay. It crushes and compacts all the hotel's rubbish," replied Harry.

"What's the crusher got to do with where the Bothrops is?" Schlemmer asked.

"When I was leaving the hotel an FBI guy was on the phone to the crusher company. He was asking them to come out and fix the crusher, because someone had thrown a Mistress in there and the crusher got jammed, as in, it was broken. A Mistress obviously wasn't a person. I thought it might be some slang word for something a hotel uses, like a dressing table, or something a wife, or mistress might use to apply their makeup. I'm seventeen, I don't know everything. But I just realised the person wasn't saying mistress, they were saying mattress. Bothrops is hiding in a mattress," Harry urged.

"How do you know the crusher wasn't broken weeks ago?" Chris asked.

"Mark Baxter, he's the guy from the crusher company who came to give the thing its annual service, he handed me the report saying so. It was like new afterwards. I remember him well, he looked like a surfer in work boots," Harry said.

He hung up and passed the phone to Mrs Maguire. Harry looked around. Everyone was looking at him. The schoolboy who had just brought down the most wanted man in the world. No one stood in front of him was smiling more than Kelsi.

"You're smart," she said.

Harry shrugged and smirked.

"I'll take that," he said.

Her smile was beautiful. She bit her bottom lip and Harry knew the time was right. It was a question he had wanted to ask when he first met her, since they had stood on the roof at the end of their first shift together and drank a beer.

"How would you like to be my girlfriend?" he asked.

Kelsi's lips arced. Her face illuminated.

"Only if you'll be my boyfriend," she said.

Harry smiled.

"I can do that," he said.

Kelsi screeched and wrapped her arms around him.

"A trans-Atlantic girlfriend?" she asked.

She looked up at him. Big eyes and a wide smile.

"Nah," he said. "How do you fancy coming to England and working in the London Grand?"

Kelsi kissed him even harder. A kiss for lovers and an embrace that held dreams of the future.

"Will you come over in time for my birthday in September?" he asked.

"Definitely," she said.

They were lost in each other's eyes.

"I need the phone again," he said.

Harry selected the top number on the recent calls list. This time the chief answered on the second ring.

"Harry, what's up dude?" he asked.

"Don't get despondent when you find a hole in a mattress and Bothrops isn't there. That's his son's mattress. There will be two mattresses inside the crusher. I promise. I reckon you'll find both mattresses towards the top of the hotel," he said.

"Why?" Schlemmer asked.

"When people do something and don't get a result, they get sloppy. From the fourth floor until the seventeenth floor, the search teams won't find anything, but search the rooms on those floors just in case. The people searching will become lackadaisical. They won't do their jobs as efficiently as when they started. Make sure that whoever does the search uses thermal imaging cameras. You'll find him, but probably near the top of the hotel," Harry said.

He hung up.

Harry's Dad looked on in awe. His son was something else. The spy game. It wasn't just under his skin and in his blood. It was embedded his DNA.

"I'm so sorry, I haven't offered you a drink, what would you like?" asked Kelsi's Mom.

"Oh anything, a cold juice?" asked Alison.

Walking back to the house, Mrs Maguire stopped and turned to face her daughter.

"Kelsi, can you run down to the store and get me a bottle of juice, please? Sorry honey, I haven't wanted to go out for the last week," her mom asked.

"Sure mom," she replied "Harry, are you coming?"

"I was hoping I could use the toilet, I've been holding it for hours," he said.

"Okay," she smiled and kissed him on the lips, "I'll see you in a minute."

Mrs Maguire showed the four of them into her home and Harry where the bathroom was. Kelsi walked to the next block and the store.

If the driver of the car hadn't been in his late eighties and his car hadn't been twenty years old, then maybe it would have been alright. If the car had been serviced regularly, the mechanics would have noticed the wear on the bolts and they would have been changed. The driver of the car didn't know his steering was defective and was unaware of the problem The bolts sheered off the steering rack as he was making a turn. Kelsi was twenty feet from the store when the car involuntarily mounted the pavement. She didn't know about it until she was struck from behind.

Mrs Maguire had left the front door of her house open, ready for Kelsi's return, only the mesh fly screen filled the hole. Harry heard screams as he walked out of the bathroom. Immediately he knew something was wrong. His gut told him it was Kelsi. Sprinting out of the house and along the block, he made it to the corner and turned. The scene in front of him was one of utter devastation.

A car had been driven into a shopfront. A bystander was reaching into the car to turn the key and stop the engine. Glass was shattered and strewn on the floor. He couldn't see her. Where was Kelsi? Harry saw a group of shoppers, some standing, some kneeling. All looking down, one of them on his phone. Harry pushed past the crowd and looked down.

He got to the floor and cradled her face. Tears ran down his cheeks and he choked when he tried to speak. Her face was cut and grazed. She was still beautiful. He smiled the weakest of smiles and told her how much he loved her. Kelsi struggled to breathe, but managed to tell him the same. He lay next to her, stroked her hair. He spoke to her again. Told her to hang on, an ambulance was on its way. She was stronger than she ever knew, she needed to hang on, the ambulance would be here any minute. People didn't make it through what they had, only to be ran over and die in the street. Harry kissed her lips, looked into her eyes, told her that he had never loved anyone before, but he loved her. He smiled. He couldn't help it. She had induced it. She was beautiful. Kelsi managed to smile back between coughing. Harry kissed her again. He felt something wet on his lips. Running the back of his hand over his mouth, he saw blood. It wasn't his. Kelsi coughed and more blood came up. She coughed twice more. Her eyes closed. Harry could hear sirens, but he knew it would be too late.

"Say hello to your dad for me," he whispered in her ear.

Harry was unable to hold back the tears any longer.

It was 2am before Harry's family and Kelsi's Mom got back from the hospital. Harry didn't want to sleep. He didn't want to close his eyes. He knew he would see Kelsi in his dreams. He turned on the TV in living room and fell back on to the couch.

Mrs Maguire had evidently been watching NBC constantly since news of the siege broke. A special report flashed up. The ticker tape at the bottom of the screen read. 'Bothrops Atrox found hiding in mattress'.

For Harry, it was a hollow victory.

CHAPTER FORTY FIVE

Following the failed attack on the Drugs War Thirty summit, an almighty military force of eighty thousand troops from all the stakeholder countries of the DW30, flooded Colombia and disseminated Bothrops Atrox's organisation. Arresting hundreds of employees and destroying production facilities, it is estimated that the production capability of the now leaderless organisation was slashed by seventy percent, its export networks irreparably damaged.

*

Six months after the terrorist attack on the Atlantic Grand, Henry Bryce leant back in his leather office chair. He read the conclusion of a report on Bothrops' organisation. A ringing phone lifted his eyes from the paperwork. Answering, his secretary told him the motorcade of the President of the United States was five minutes away. He continued his read:

Through an extensive investigation carried out by the Central Intelligence Agency, Langley, Virginia and the Secret Intelligence Service (MI6), London, England, the following became clear:

- The Atlantic Grand hotel (Fort Lauderdale, Florida, USA), was host to the inaugural Drugs War Thirty summit (DW30). On the first day of the event, the hotel, aided by forces heavily imbedded in the hotel's operation, was besieged by a force of sixty armed men, led by Alejandro Diego Munoz (ADM, Bothrops Atrox, Barba Amarilla). Twelve

Secret Service Agents from the government of the United States were killed during the siege, four from the Diplomatic Protection Service of Great Britain, five from other attending governments.

- Operation Joint Venture, conducted by members of the special forces from eleven different stakeholder nations present at the summit, retook control of the Atlantic Grand. The hotel was handed to the FBI once the building was made secure. Three thorough searches of the building were conducted, one by special forces personnel during the assault itself and two by FBI Special Agents. ADM was not found. After information given to the Fort Lauderdale Chief of Police as to his whereabouts, a search was carried out using thermal imaging technology. He was found in the mattress of a bedroom on the nineteenth floor. ADM has been sent Guantanamo Bay detention camp in Cuba. A trial is yet to be scheduled, but he will serve a whole life prison sentence. The mattress had been specially made and contained room for two occupants. ADM was found alone. It is thought the unoccupied space in the mattress was for ADM's mistress and contact at the hotel, Marie Thouvenin. The lookalike mattress contained bedding, food and water, as well as lighting and twelve reading books. The hide also contained a waste storage system for bodily excretions. A second mattress of single occupancy was found on the eighteenth floor. This is thought to have been for occupation by his son, who was found bound and gagged in a store room on the nineteenth floor.

- It is the finding of this report that the two terrorists who committed suicide on the eighteenth floor were the escort party for ADM, who ensured he was securely placed in his hideaway. After escorting him to safety and realising they were not going to be able to escape themselves, they took their own lives.

- The ADM enterprise had pre-paid the families of each terrorist one million US Dollars. That sum is more than the average working wage of a Colombian for two lifetimes. The high price was paid as the terrorists who partook in the hostage taking, were in effect carrying out a suicide mission and had no real hope of survival.

- The two German mercenaries: Klaus Scholz and Christian Muller, were both former members of the German Police Force, Grenzschutgruppe9 (Border Protection Group9, GSG9). It is believed Christian looked towards Klaus as a father figure, he did not know his own father. Klaus saved his life while the pair where on a police operation in the German city of Leipzig. Klaus Scholz was suffering from an inoperable brain tumour and wanted to set his wife up financially in the result of his death. A larger seven figure sum was paid into each of the German's bank accounts three weeks before the hostage incident. The money has now been recovered.

- Government employees in the pay of the ADM enterprise from the stakeholder countries attending the Drugs War Thirty summit, leaked the summit's location and agenda to ADM. The likely outcome and war on drugs that would follow the summit concerned the enterprise to the extent that it thought it had to engage in a pre-emptive strike. This was to show the dominance of the ADM enterprise.

- It was the belief of ADM, following his attack at the Drugs War Thirty Summit and missile attack on the Wavecrest Royal (adjacent hotel), the eradication of politicians, leading figures in the military, special forces and intelligence communities, his organisation would be able to more easily manufacture and freely facilitate the distribution of cocaine globally.

- Through numerous shell corporations the ADM enterprise was able to buy into a New England based hedge fund. The hedge fund had recently purchased millions of square feet of warehousing and land for that purpose, primarily in North America and Europe.

- Senior employees of a European based international logistics freight forwarder who were on the payroll of the ADM enterprise, were to enable the distribution of narcotics to the newly acquired storage facilities. The logistics provider is currently under further investigation for its involvement in the Holocaust during World War II.

  It is widely known that two of the three original partners of the company were members of the Nazi Party, the third having been removed to Auschwitz Concentration Camp. The company was the haulier of choice for Jewish furniture (including priceless antiques and artwork whose location still remains unknown), which was transported from all over Europe back to Germany, to furnish homes of those who had had theirs bombed by the allies. It is the purpose of the fresh investigation to uncover what their involvement was in the Schutzstaffel (SS) and how far their involvement in the transportation of Jews to concentration camps extended.

- This investigation has uncovered members of sixty three governments on the payroll of the ADM enterprise. The employees recruited by ADM were heavily in debt and ranged from senior politicians to security chiefs. Everyone identified had been arrested.

- The sons of ADM: One was found bound, gagged and incarcerated in a store room in the hotel. The other was apprehended in a room external to the hotel, observing the FLPD and special forces. He, his brother and the two Colombian nationals aiding this secondary counter-surveillance operation, have been sent to Guantanamo Bay detention camp in Cuba. Trials are yet to be scheduled, but they will serve whole life prison sentences.

- Concerning the terrorist at the Atlantic Grand who posed as a hostage and got as far as to be evacuated into the car park, before being exposed: A request for extradition to stand trial in Colombia was made by the Colombian Government. This request has been denied. The terrorist has been sent to Guantanamo Bay detention camp. A trial is yet to be scheduled, but he will serve a whole life prison sentence.

- This report finds failings by the Drugs War Thirty Summit's organisers and recommends that private security companies are no longer used for events where a senior world leader, or leaders are present. Only military, or law enforcement agencies are to be utilised, regardless of cost.

Henry lifted his head from the report. He heard the buzzes of police sirens as the motorcade turned into Downing Street. The slamming of car doors sounded as the President's Secret Service detail exited their cars, before the leader of the free world was allowed to step onto the pavement.

It was evident the reign of the Munoz family as drug kingpins of the world was over. None of them would feature on the Forbes Rich List ever again. Henry rang his secretary and requested a pot of tea be made and two cups brought through once his guest had arrived.

He heard footfall outside in the corridor. There was a knock on his door.

"Come in," he said.

Henry got to his feet to greet the President of the United States of America.

The President pushed the door and stepped into his office.

"Hello Mrs President," said Henry, "such a shame to hear President Ace's mental health didn't recover. Is he still unresponsive?"

Printed in Great Britain
by Amazon